the Journey

the Journey

J K RODRIQUEZ

ISBN: Softcover 978-1-4990-9665-1
eBook 978-1-4990-9666-8

This is a work of fiction based on true events.
The names and characters have been changed.

Print information available on the last page.

Rev. date: 12/21/2020

To order additional copies of this book, contact:
Xlibris
UK TFN: 0800 0148620 (Toll Free inside the UK)
UK Local: 02036 956328 (+44 20 3695 6328 from outside the UK)
www.Xlibrispublishing.co.uk
Orders@Xlibrispublishing.co.uk
519491

Contents

The Journey

To Spring fourth

This book is dedicated

to

M, A, O, A, N, and A.

Thank you.

Acknowledgements

I would like to thank my Father who is in heaven for giving me the strength to write this story. Thank you, good Sir. To you be all the glory. I would also like to thank everyone who has believed in me and encouraged me and given me the support and resources to complete this sometimes very difficult and challenging work. Thank you.

Finally, I would like to thank M for going on this incredible journey with me and for enduring all that she did for me, with me and because of me. Thank you, thank you, and thank you.

And thank you to everyone who was there. I shall never forget you because You are family. I love you.

'Remembered through the eyes of a child
Retold through the memoirs of a woman'

'Spoken through the voice of a child'

Leaving Home

Out the gate, sharp right on the corner, I could hear my shiny new shoes smack, tap, tapping the wet, naked pavement beneath me. Quickened fingers fastened bag's buckle as I ran, long jump, jumping over the pedestrian in two as the green man flashes amber, back to red. Charged up Forester's Hill, as if in General Custer's first battalion, ready to meet death's enemy like the warrior ready for war. Was it all going to pan out like the defeat at Little Bighorn? Only time would tell.

Forward now, in direction, crushing autumn's evidence all spilled out across the ground like the guts of some vegetarian giant. I could hear the crunch, crunching of crispy rouges, mixed in with sunset auburns and burnt browns as if voicing their last rites as I crushed without mercy them under my feet; differing colors mixing without prejudice, without bias or discrimination.

Although my prison, this jungle concrete, was still not in sight – my heart beats loudly, pumping, pounding hard, on the inner cavity of my chest wall. A smoggy dampness sat in the air as if legally enthroned, birthing a discomfort, reminiscent of wet sand crunching under the sole of your shoe except in this instant it was on the roof of your mouth almost prohibiting the exchanging function of photosynthesis desperately required by man, although in this case, it was clearly making the most vital exchange – oxygen for carbon dioxide – difficult.

The jet-black railings stood their ground, dividing greens from greys, hard from soft, work from play, reappearing in continuous formation, snapshot from the corner of my eye.

As I reached the peak, I glanced quickly to the right, peering around the bend before placing right after left into the newly dressed-up road. I skipped and hopped over the freshly painted white lines as if to avoid making contact with them, but even if I had, so what? Nothing and no one could stop me now. I had come to a decision! I had made up my mind! Distant emotions pressed into me as I clicked my heels, but oh - so not Dorothy in the Land of Oz. Freedom had come to my house today, and I smiled. The shackles were finally being removed, today I was free.

I was now soon to experience some new-found liberty – of exactly what, I did not know, but I believed, and I knew that it had to be better than this. It just had to be. That was, what had been, for so many years; even those so short, appearing like a lifetime, which had presented itself rather like a ball and chain cleaving to my ankle ever tightening, ever squeezing what felt like the very life out of me... *It just had to be better than this,* I thought as I ran.

Faster and faster as if speed poured out of me, filling up my determined belief, as I made my way through the maze of beautifully decorated houses, on to the plain and down the street that led into the flats, under Bay 23, left at Bay 30, up at Port 27, along the gangway, only 100 yards to go now, and then the stairs, panting out loud, just eight flights to climb. We were not allowed to use the lift, you see, and after making contact more than once with Dad 's timber strip, *what you rookies call a 2' by 2',* I honestly think I somehow got the message.

Now at flight six, I could feel the rose water begin to drip, drip trickling down my spine into the small of my back. *I would learn later in life the beauty of the small of a woman's back.* Now with my brow shining, I pushed through the heavy-mesh reinforced glass door and continued running along the balcony, only four doors down to go now, tip, tap, tapping along to number 58 – that's me.

'*Did I make it*?' I breathed, questioning myself as I fixed myself up before knocking on the clean, slender, stainless steel letter box that stood in the middle of the light wooden framed door just below the large single glass pane that was mounted as its center piece. *Was that five minutes?* my mind questioned as I stood still. *Am I in time? Am I late?* Silence was so equivocal. I tap, tapped again, and waited. Just then it happened... Yes, the evidence of some larger-than-life form slowly moving down the hallway towards the front door and stopping. I could distinctly hear the persistent dragging of what I positively knew to be that old overgrown toenail connecting with the protective plastic whose only job in life was simply to cover and protect the brown carpet that lay still beneath it.

Eventually, the door opened its usual six inches, and I quickly slipped inside, not having the desire of wishing to be joined in with the door and seal as I had experienced so many times before, it quickly closed behind me. I bid good afternoon as usual, repeating myself several times like the resounding custom of a fainting echo. Shoes off neatly together under the stairs in Dad's home-made coat cupboard – he was good at making things like small tables upon which to study on, racks for hanging cups on, and plain old sticks to whip you with.

I went upstairs to wash up before my usual lunch of bread cut like doorsteps laden with Echo, cut like cheese, and half a tin cup of warm, milky tea. We were no longer allowed china, you see, I guess in case we broke it as had happened so many times before.

As I sat there and started to pick at the bread, I began to wonder, hold on ...Where was Odette? Suddenly, I realised that I had not seen her since I had left the school. I could feel myself becoming increasingly anxious – a knot of butterflies growing ever tighter, inside their chain linking and growing ever longer because we only had five minutes.

After a short while, Mordecka joined me. She positioned herself on a stool, leaving no part uncovered. She sat next to the door which remained wide open, as if indicating that she would eventually be making a run for it or something; fat chance I know. After a few minutes, she began to speak...

'I suppose you're wondering where that red thing is?' she asked my brother, who appeared not in the least bit interested in what she was saying. For all he knew, she could have been speaking French, double Dutch, or even German. She repeated the question again for what we both really knew was for my sole benefit. My heart began to sink. I could sense bad news a mile off, especially when it was coming from a *witch.*

I mean, all you Wicked Witches of the West, you ain't got nothing on this one, eat your heart out and your liver too. Fear wrestled me to my feet, but I quickly sat down again as exactly what she had done began to unfold.

Once she had made a full execution of this unwelcome news, which had been swimming around on the tip of her tongue for only God knows how long, she belched like a pig and retired back upstairs; even they trembled as she went.

I fed *bin* the remainder of my lunch. I loved bin; he never said no, never complained and his mouth was always wide open – every kid's best friend, I guess. After wiping up every sign of every crumb after me, I too went upstairs, eyes bursting with emotion, tightly clenching my sweaty youthful fists. Inside, I was screaming, without sound. I entered my room and closed the door quietly behind me.

From my bag, I took out a single plain piece of paper and permitted my pen to connect with it, goading her into relationship; not seeing through the tears… then it happened she danced across the paper, ink speaking as she moved. '*Dear Dad*,' her movement sang, and after many words, she ended, '*I love you, but… but I want to be with Odette. Love always from your daughter, Jacqueline.*'

Before I realised, I had completed a full page of A4. I placed a book across the page, exposing only some of the writing; I then left my room. There was no need for a final look around; I required no help to remember exactly what it was I was leaving behind. These pictures would forever be etched on the tabernacle of my mind. I went downstairs, put on my shoes, and left number 58 with one sole intention... never to return there again.

My pace to school was much slower than usual that afternoon – a plan in the making. Upon arriving back at my class, I immediately informed my tutor that, in fact, I had an appointment with the Head of Lower School and that I should not be late because this would displease him greatly. Well, I must have been so convincing because he invited me to go up about five minutes early. *Talk about getting your own way!* I sat outside with my knee shaking until I was called in.

'Come in, come in,' said the nicest voice that I had ever heard. 'Have a seat... sit down,' he said nervously. 'What can I do for you?' asked Mr. Wiltshire, Head of Lower School, as he didn't cease from his pottering around, trying his best to fix himself and freshen himself up and stuff. He was pear-shaped in appearance and had a welcoming countenance about him that was simple and kind. His hair was slowly turning silver and fine lines were beginning to appear on the upper regions of his face, yet it subtracted nothing from his gentle compassion. In attempting to answer his question, suddenly I found my tongue was stuck fast to the roof of my mouth, so no words could come out. Strange and different expressions began to appear on my face as I wrestled with myself in an attempt to speak; (*I say that because no one else was physically involved*).

He repeated the question again; I was now in a desperate position, attempting to release my tongue from pressing so tightly up against the roof of my mouth, using only my jaw for assistance. 'What *is* the matter...? Are you OK...? Is everything all right then?' He was speaking from behind the open door to his walk-in washroom.

Eventually, I spat them out. 'I- I- I'm leaving home Sir!' I finally blurted. He came to such a sudden halt with his dressing and fixing, like a train rushing into the station before coming to an emergency stop. 'Wh-Wh-What?' He fumbled with his words, now spluttering, and also stuttering. 'Wh-Wh-What do you mean?'

'I-I- I'm leaving home,' I repeated, my stutter still continuing.

'I- I- I d-d- don't understand,' he said, stuttering again.

He plonked himself down in front of his dark mahogany desk which was positioned opposite me. He opened his top right-hand drawer and removed a small, bottle with a dark label on and began to pour out the brown liquid into one of the small glasses lined up in front of him, asking if I needed a drink as he poured.

'No-no, thank you, sir,' I answered promptly. 'I am just leaving home,' I repeated.

'Wh-wh-why?' he asked. 'Wh-wh-what has happened?'

'I am just leaving home.'

'Oh,' he said. 'Just like that?' 'No explanation? No reason? Just woke up this morning and came to this rather drastic decision to... err... just leave home today?' he stated in-between gulping down the dark-brown liquid from out of his glass.

'Err ... well, no,' I answered promptly. 'I made up my mind about two weeks ago, and today I am doing it,' I affirmed.

'Oh, I see, and have you made any other interesting decisions, like where you will stay, for example?'

'Well, I err... I want to live with my sister,'

'Is she in this school?'

'Yes Sir, she is in Mrs. Huddersfield's year.'

'Ah yes, so she is a second year then?'

'Yes Sir,' I answered promptly.

'And her name is?'

'Odette Richardson.'

'OK, look, I will make some enquires and speak with Mrs. Huddersfield. You go into the hall and enjoy the show, and someone will come down and collect you before school's out,' he said kindly as he took the last swig of brown liquid that he had poured out from his little glass bottle, which appeared to do wonders for his stutter.

'Is that OK for you then?'

'Yes Sir.'

'You sure?'

'Yes Sir,' I replied again.

'Well, if you don't want to go home, no one can force you to,' he said warmly.

For the first time, ever, I walked with a bounce in my step. I slipped into the hall as the Year 5 students were in full swing with their rock concert, which they were performing for all years. I felt exhilarated. I sat with my classmates at the rear of the hall, and a huge smile began to map out its place across my face. 'Wow!' announced Billy, attempting to engage Sharon.

'What?' asked Sharon.

'Jacqueline is smiling,' replied Billy.

'And so?' said Janet, overhearing his remark now entering the conversation.

'Well, it's just that I've never seen Jacqueline smile before... That's all,' he said to himself and smiled. 'Keep it up. You've got a beautiful smile,' he added. And as for me, well, I just smiled.

As the afternoon ended and my classmates began to disperse in ones and twos, fear came knocking once more. Mr. Wiltshire had not got back to me. He had not come back for me. Fast filling with disappointment and all hope diminishing, I looked downwards, my eyes fixed on the floor. I began to play out different frightening scenarios in my mind's eye, each one ending in total despair. I subconsciously began to chew the odd-looking, water-filled ill positioned bumps upon the knuckles of both my hands.

My heart was pumping... off the scale now – hands all sweaty and wet, head thumping, and nausea on the bend. There were only five students left, and I had not been called! Just then, in that same moment amidst the swirl of fear injected thoughts, I heard my name being called as though it was echoing down a thousand corridors, only it was being called in a different voice than that of my teacher. I looked up only to see the school's porter who had come to escort me down to the main office *personally*.

There was a short exchange between him and my tutor, and a few seconds later I was permitted to go with him down to the main office. It would be there that my two and a half-hour wait was to commence. Too afraid to move, I just sat, and I sat, and I sat. My bum ached, but I sat. My legs ached, but I sat. In fact, I had never sat so much in my entire young life. In truth, I was all sat out, but too afraid to move so I just sat.

At approximately 5.30 p.m., they came out and said, 'OK, we have to go to your father's house now.' Fear ran across my face, freezing, my expression of hope gone sour, perhaps even resembling the after effects of having collided with a huge steamroller. My body started to shake and rattle, but this was *so* not rock and roll. It was just plain old trembling.

'It's OK,' they said, 'you don't have to stay. We just need your father to sign for you to go.'

'Then can I be with my sister?'

'Yes,' they answered.

'You promise?' I asked again, questioning them further in my own childlike voice, seeking affirmation of the confirmation. 'Yes,' they replied again.

We arrived at the flat, and the three of us went single file inside with them leading the way, but this was so not the *wedding march.* They continued into the living room, and the door closed firmly behind them. I remained standing in the passage as near to the front door as possible as if waiting for the red light to come on, indicating when to open the emergency exit on a Boeing 747, *parachute not intact. 'Oooooooooooooooooooooooooooooooooooh'*

Voice decibels raised and lowered as if to orchestrate in tensions as opposed to bars, but this was so not the Glenn Miller band. It was real life... my life, and time was tick-tock, tick-tock, ticking on by.

Another two hours' standing, and about now, I felt my bladder inform my brain that I needed to go to the bathroom. Imprisoned by fear, I just froze, not even moving a muscle, and then out of nowhere, my body began to do that dance you do – you know the one when you *really* want to go – yep, that's the one.

At that precise moment, courage stepped in and escorted me to the downstairs powder room; yes, the one that I had spent day after day cleaning, perfecting, shining, dusting, and re-dusting and re-shining and yet never having been permitted to use. Well, today was that day. I slipped into that powder room and pissed into *that* toilet. Yes, I pissed so hard that the first and the last both came together. *Man!* I was really all pissed out, and yes it felt *good*. I almost wished some had dripped on the '*oh* so very new- looking', unworn, untouched, virgin brown carpet – the one that I had for years got down on my hands and knees to clean, picking up the fluff from it with my eczema-ridden, wart-water-weeping, infested fingers.

Just as I stepped out, *she* came out, glaring at me as she drew nearer. I began to wonder if she knew what I had just done. With what I am sure was guilt written all over my face, I questioned myself - had she really heard the chain flush and the door close back ever so quietly? Or did she just see me on the damn toilet through two brick walls and a solid wooden staircase? She approached me, as if without moving her feet, in an alien like motion, her face elevated with disgust, her guise filled with antipathy. She escorted me into the meeting by the tip of my hand as if I was some dirty, stinking cloth she had just retrieved from blocking up the gutter. I went in and was invited to sit furthest from the door. Then dad asked me a question, which even to this day no longer remains within the memoirs of my mind and neither does the answer.

After more shouting, by what seemed like a congregation of raving ravens, then the raised voices suddenly became still. It was almost as if the night had dropped down a thick dark blanket covering everyone in the room holding us all in suspense. In that moment, you could have heard a pin drop.

In the moments that followed they started up again; their bickering and voice-overs were then dramatically interrupted by two little words, which then became three.

'I will!' ... 'I will sign,' she gleefully stated. All heads queued in her direction, as if ball following at Wimbledon, and with that, she picked up the papers from off the coffee table and simply signed me away like some faulty piece of furniture that was being returned *outside* the guarantee period.

With that done and all else said, *she* went upstairs and gathered up my belongings, all of which miraculously fit into a half crushed, small, brown box I never even knew we owned.

Not surprisingly, there were no clothes inside, just one white shirt with a missing button and a dirty, beat-up old doll with just one eye now remaining, wearing the most ghastly looking red nail varnish so disturbingly applied, which I understand was desperately resurrected out of a leaking red Bic biro pen: glue-ish like in appearance. It was the last intentional act of Odette before her silent departure. There was also a raggedy old teddy bear that had lost some of its fur during its travels, that came from *I don't know where*, but hey, no love lost there. I had certainly been here before.

She thrust the box at me, into me, and we walked along the hallway towards the front door. I pretended that I did not notice as I took charge of the box.

It was exactly fifteen paces to the front door, yet my mind's eye now paused on conjured thoughts of a primitive, distant oasis of what may lie behind it. Every intricate step forward appeared like fifteen back. I was desperately trying to keep in step with my rescuers, and this was indeed the longest walk I had ever made.

Finally, I was out of the door, and the sun was shining through the night. We continued down along the balcony towards the lift, and I tried very hard *not* to run.

Just when I thought I was safe, Dad called out my name once more. 'Jacqueline! Jacqueline!'. The three of us stopped dead in our tracks – still like tombstones. In my mind, I asked myself that dreaded question, *had he now changed his mind? Had he now decided that her signing was null and void and, in fact, not valid?* Fear came knocking once more, this time banging. *Had he now decided that, perhaps, I should not go?* My heart was pumping so loud it was deafening. My emotions were at Silverstone – Yes! On the tracks!

Was he now going to order me to stay? Suddenly, I needed the bathroom again, or maybe I needed that dark brown liquid from Mr. Wiltshire's little glass bottle. I wasn't sure *which,* confusion was rife from within. *Was he now going to demand that I stay? No! God, please! Had my internal celebrations been just a little too premature? Dear Lord, please save me now!* I breathed.

The gravel scrunched under our shoes like iron sharpening iron as we slowly turned to confront the reason for this hold-up of my exodus. We each exhaled in unison upon the gentle revelation that it was only my little brother who wanted me to wave and tell him goodbye. I opened the other eye and relaxed my shoulders down again. Little did I know that those two simple words were to be so final, in fact they were to be my last to him inside that decade and the last that I was to hear in return from his young, foolish lips until twenty-five years later. But, hey, today I was free, and it felt good.

We continued into the lift, pressing for its descent. Once inside, I knew I had overcome this fear, this excuse for a life, this reason for *not* living, and as we descended downwards, inside, I was ascending upwards. I had won *this* battle because *this was* 'leaving home'.

The Journey Begins

The door of the lift opened and for the first time I could smell the night. We walked diagonally across the large, open plan car park, which was almost empty. It was always practically empty. It was situated directly under the flats and I had seen its demise if not a hundred times in my dreams. Patiently, we waited for fumbling fingers to locate the right key from within the bulging bunch, the one that would unlock this beat-up old chariot, covered now in droplets of rain blown in by a north-easterly wind as the heavens began to open, as if in agreement to this act of tearing.

Clearly, this was not my first departure from home, and it certainly was not going to be my last either, albeit I did not know that then. However, it was indeed the last time that I would ever wake up at number '58', which had so poorly played out its part at being home, on and off and on again, over the last five of the past eleven years. And this I believed I was glad of. No more shouting, no more wrong accusations, no more beatings, on more being sworn at no more going to bed hungry and no more fights with my unruly selfish self-centered brother. Of this I was glad. And the very thought of what my life would be now, filled me with jubilation and anticipation.

However, not even in my wildest dreams could I have ever contemplated exactly what kind of ride this was going to be; certainly, it was not going to be a bed of roses, but I of course I did not know that then.

Addlestone Farm

My first experience of being away from home begins to play itself out in my mind's eye. It commences at the tender age of just six months. It was then that I was dramatically plucked from my mother's breast, *mid-drink no doubt*, after her sudden departure soon after the death of her own mother. I remember my frosty observation of that white, fluffy stuff above my head. Of course, I had no idea what it was back then, only that it was white and fluffy, I remember thinking if only I could just taste it then I would know what it was, and it would taste good. However, I learnt much later on in life that the white fluffy stuff was in fact the clouds in the sky. All along, I had been looking up at them whilst lying on my back in my Rolls Royce of a pram.

As I was still in the pram, the year must have been late 1965 or early 1966. It was bitterly cold, so it was certainly winter – anywhere from December to January, I guess. In any case, what was clear was that I had not turned one yet. I would find out many years later from reading various scraps of paper that we were in a place called the Nursery, or Addlestone Farm as it was commonly known back then, and we were accommodated there twice as the very same scraps of paper would reveal. This was the place of rigid regimes, meticulous methodology, and skillful organization; it was the beginning of institutionalism, only I didn't know it then.

During the lunchtimes, the farm always initiated the voluntary help of young local girls to cover the feeding frenzy, the burping, and the repetitive nappy-changing duties, which perhaps could have shared the comparison of a conveyor-type action. Sometimes, there could be as many as sixteen babies, all crying together, all needing attention all at the same time; once one started, it was very much like a chain reaction with the others not far behind. After a hearty luncheon of warm bottled milk, all the babies would be burped, changed, and put down to nap. There was a stark difference in the touch of the young girls who came to assist in comparison to that of the resident staff. They had a genuine love for the babies; they were always much kinder and gentler than many of the regular staff, particularly the older ones.

The young girls handled the babies with such tender loving care compared with the older women, who were harsh, rough, and often willfully reckless. The prams, once loaded with babies and tiny cover, were then all pushed out into the courtyard for their afternoon nap and to breathe in the crisp cool country air, which at times was perhaps a little too cool or rather too cold for comfort.

When the harsh winter came, the weather was unforgivingly cold, and with just one small cover I found it very difficult to keep warm or even to sleep. The normal practice at the farm was that once a baby could turn over whilst inside the pram, that baby would no longer be pushed outside after lunch, for fear that the pram would topple over baby and all; there was a lot of bounce in the Rolls Royce so once this discovery was made, the baby would then be put to sleep in the playroom upon a bed of warm cozy covers surrounded with soft cushions and, most of all, in the warm. I so wanted to be in the warm.

Lying there in my pram, I watched what I now know to be the sky, as it took itself through various shades of greys and whites before turning blue, bringing with every change a new season.

As more and more babies were learning to turn and therefore having to be brought inside, I knew that if I wanted to get in out of the cold, then I too had to make the turn. I had to make them see that I too could now turn over in my pram as well. They needed to see the pram shake and rattle but not roll. This was quite difficult as the baby could become entangled in the covers or even fall into a restricted position one where he or she was unable to breathe or even worse perhaps topple out altogether. Timing was everything. In getting ready to turn, I recognized the tone of the friendly young voice of one of the girls who frequently came to help. She had come out to check on the babies in the prams to ensure they were all asleep and OK. I knew this was my chance; it was my opportunity to demonstrate the fact that I too could turn over.

I desperately needed her to see my pram shake. 'Don't put the blue pram out!' she shouted. 'He can turn over.' So, the blue pram was then wheeled back inside, and the door quietly clicked, closed behind it. It was freezing that day, and I desperately wanted to be in the warm. I needed her to see that I too could turn over. '*Well, here goes*,' I thought as I managed to roll on to my side and then crash down on to my tummy, causing the pram to shake. Albeit no one came because no one saw. Unbeknown to me, they had all gone back inside. I thought if I can keep turning over, surely someone would see the pram rocking and come and get me.

It was my third attempt. I was pretty near to the edge of the pram; the pram could have toppled over if the weight was ill balanced or worst still baby could become entangled in the blanket. Thankfully, it was during my third turn that I was finally picked up out of the pram by the same young girl and held against something soft. That was the last time that I was put outside and left in the cold whilst at the farm, but the cold had already set into my bones.

Unfortunately, this was not the only downside to the nursery; there was also the sad sorry situation of bath time. It was here that there was an overzealous degree of deliberate and willful recklessness being applied to the children. Our little heads were held under the water perhaps just a little too long when hair washing was in process.

Our little teeth were brushed perhaps just a little too hard and yet not properly at all, and our skin was scrubbed just a little too aggressively with no cream or powder applied, just a 'ruff buff' incomplete towel dry. I always felt uncomfortable after bath time, my skin never fully dry, just damp and sometimes even still wet in places. I remember that there was one member of staff; I never saw her face or even the color of her hair neither the depth of her eyes. I could only identify her by the sternness of her voice and her deliberate noisy walk. I think her spirit was signaling that she did not really belong. She was very, very rough with the babies; and even burped them too hard plonking them down hard afterwards. *GOD, bless their little backs:* There were many more tears whenever she was on duty.

As I got older in months and was quickly weaned off the milk, I found that I could not eat most of the food provided by the nursery. To me it was all a mishmash of crazy colors, mainly reds and oranges all car crashed together. It was all so very unappealing and completely undistinguishable even in smell; hence, I hated mealtimes, especially the lunchtimes. Many of the children were force-fed; it was the worst time of day really. Those who could cry did, and those who cried the loudest were put down for a nap and given bananas and custard upon their return at the mercy of the young staff, always at the mercy of the young staff. I quickly realised I needed to up the ante on my crying skills. In any event, this certainly felt like a palatable compromise to me, and it was one which I went on to achieve day after day and month after month.

However, one fine day, they served sliced spam with mashed potatoes and salad cream for lunch. It was very plain, very simple, and very distinguishable. The colors were light pink and pale yellow – uncomplicated. Someone thought I should try it, so I did, and this was added to the list of things that I now found that I could eat along with soft boiled eggs, Rice Krispies, and toast. However, they could not make spam and mashed potatoes every day even with the salad cream. Therefore, on the days when the food looked unbearable, I just cried until I was put down for a nap, hoping to wake up to *something* and custard, usually bananas or a lovely fruit crumble and custard – emm yummy!

Clearly, this routine could not have gone on forever, but it was not until the introduction of bread and butter, jams, and fruits at mealtimes that this poor-eating pattern slowly began to evaporate. When ice cream was included, served usually at tea times, I would climb my way on to the bottom shelf of one of the trolleys that were promptly parked outside the dining rooms at 16:45 hours precisely each day and pull back the large white tablecloth which completely covered the trolley, draping over the sides and almost touching the floor.

Once I was underneath, I could not be seen, so I was free to work my way through the cakes, biscuits, desserts, and tuck into as much of the ice cream or the colorful layered trifle as I possibly could, usually until I felt physically sick. When my reward for punishment was bed, I was already stuffed to the brim, so I too was completely in favor of the idea. My behavior was for the most part consistent, at least until I could understand how upset the other children were at having no dessert with their tea, which in turn brought this repetitive bad behavior to a rather abrupt end.

Life was very simple at the farm as were our routines – mealtimes were always set, three times a day, on the hour, and bath dates with hair washing fixed, usually on the weekends, also on the hour; there were also mid-week baths. There was no spiritual input, so the only day we quickly came to identify the weekend with was Saturday. Primarily because this was the day that all the children had their hair washed. You also would have had it washed mid-week if it was matted or if there was some kind of food stuck in it. Staff would always say 'It's Saturday'.

A more interesting activity would occur once every two weeks, usually on a Wednesday. This was when we visited the big playhouse which was situated off-site. Our journey would involve a short walk out of the grounds and across a cattle-run, dirt road.

When we knew that the cattle were coming, we would sit on the bench at the rest stop and wait for them. It was a completely exhilarating experience to watch them pass. They were so noisy and smelly, and sometimes they would come up so close that you could almost touch them as they passed; it was thrilling. The farmer would speak a funny language to them, and the dogs would bark at them. They would *moo back*, and he would blow his whistle. I loved it. This was the highlight for me - once a fortnight.

On some days, we would wait and wait and wait, but the cattle would not show up. Those were my low days. It would leave me feeling so low and disappointed. It was almost as if there was some kind of transference of energy from them to me, so I needed to see them to pass me by. *The native Indian in me, I guess.* I can recall on one occasion, sitting at the rest stop, filled with excitement, and patiently waiting in desired anticipation for the ground to shake, the dust to rise, and the air to become filled with the scent of this large, strong, sometimes docile yet very obedient beast.

At every encounter, I felt the pull to reach out and connect with this fast moving, noisy beast. I had already made up my mind that the next time they went past, I was determined to reach out and touch one of them, just one.

On that occasion, we arrived at the rest stop in good time, we waited and waited and waited. Then I heard it ... the whistle of the farmer, the cry of the beast, and witnessed first-hand the dance of the grit on the dusty dirt road beneath us.

They were coming; yippee, I smiled. On this occasion, they came around the bend particularly fast, and there seemed to be a lot more of them too. Sally had already raised her position to standing on the seat beside me, but I was still sitting with my feet not yet able to touch the ground. My little legs swinging out in front of me before returning back under my seat as if swinging on a swing.

As they came closer, Sally shrieked for me to stand up beside her, "Get UP! Get UP!" she yelled, but I wanted to touch them; and not having anything to hold on to whilst standing, the chance was that I would probably be swept in and away with them as they passed. I stood for a moment as they came up, close and personal, but then sat down again quickly for fear of falling.

Sally shrieked for me to stand up again, "GET UP! GET UP!" she yelled at the top of her voice, but the desire to touch them far outweighed her apprehensive demands for me to rise back up to standing.

They came closer and closer; there must have been literally inches between us, and all 500 of them getting closer as they passed. I glanced up at Sally, who was not looking back at me, and outstretched my tiny hand as if gesturing to make contact with them as they passed, their prickly fur brushing against my knees. I felt myself sliding off the edge of the chair in their direction; the fur felt fabulous, so soft and strong when smoothed down, yet at the same time quite coarse and prickly when brushed the other way – then suddenly in the middle of my moment, as my bottom edged toward the end of my seat, a strong arm came down and swept me up into the air, with one almighty swoop - it was Sally...

We arrived earlier than usual at the playhouse that day and went inside. I will always remember the first time we entered; we could not believe our eyes; it was a toy heaven, a land of toys. You could dress up to be whosoever you wanted – cowboys, Indians, doctors, nurses, policemen, firemen, shop servers, Mummy, Daddy, and even baby. There were rocking horses, slides, tricycles, wheelbarrows, skates, dolls, Wendy houses, plates, cups, play food, cars, trains, building bricks, puzzles, and every possible toy a child could ever want or dream of. It was all there, and we could play with it. I think the first time Odette and I just sat there and stared at it all. We had to be coaxed into touching the toys. But once we got used to it, we were in our element, often forgetting time, never wanting to leave.

We would usually spend a good hour playing before having to return, always just in time for tea, and after being tucked up in bed, we would sleep so soundly after such an exertion of well-spent energy. I think I liked those days the best…

Getting A New Family

Another poignant occurrence at the farm was the decision which came down from above of the importance of family – suddenly we the children, it was decided, should all have our own families. We could visit these families every other week and the visit should take place on the weekends and we would stay over with these families from Saturday to Sunday.

Every child had their own family, and, strangely, siblings were not placed together. The family that was selected for me had a huge farm, and they bought me a lovely light tan puppy just like the Andrex Puppy, *as seen on TV.* He was so soft and beautiful. Every time he saw me, he would come running up to me in leaps and bounds; he would always jump up into my arms and start licking my face; it was as though he really knew me. I called him Benny and became very fond of him. However, our relationship was to be one that was very short lived, and the clock was ticking tick tock… tick tock...

The end came rather suddenly one hazy afternoon. Back then, so many farms had their lands backed on to one another, so the farm owners decided to identify their own land by drawing a boundary line of ownership erected out of spiked barbed wire. This was really awful stuff – incredibly sharp and very ugly to look at – but even worse than that was the fact that it could not be seen with the naked eye, in the warm, hazy sun, as it began its lazy descent, in the late afternoons. On that fateful day, I was out in the field with the farmhands, watching the baling of the hay and taking in the goldenness of the day.

I could see the green Land Rover in the distance, shimmering in the afternoon's rays. We were separated by the barbed wire, so I was unable to walk over and greet them as I usually would. After the vehicle slowed to a stop, the back door opened, and Benny, without hesitation, jumped out. Upon seeing me in the distance he immediately came bounding up towards me full steam ahead; he was so excited. I had no idea whether he would understand to stop upon reaching the barbed wire. He was running as fast as he could. As he got closer and closer and upon reaching the barbed wire, he jumped up into the air as if in an attempt to jump into my arms as he usually did when he saw me. However, this time, he landed spread eagle on to the barbed wire, becoming pinned in place by several of the prongs. Their razor-sharp teeth sunk deep into his fur, cutting right into his flesh. Benny let out such a loud screech and started to struggle, cutting himself further as the wire's teeth refused to let him go. I did not know what to do. I looked around for someone any one to help him... but there was no one there. I stood there helplessly. I looked up for the farmer; he was running as fast as he could. Benny began crying like a distressed little child and continued to wriggle, causing his little paws to sink deeper and deeper on to the spikes. I could not believe it; I didn't know what to do; I couldn't speak.

My eyes began to glaze over. I looked up again at my help – the Dad of the house. He was still running up towards us with the farmhands fast, following behind. It was as though he knew what had happened but could do nothing to stop it. He had been too far behind yet all the while screaming for Benny to stop, but Benny, overflowing with excitement abounding in pure joy, could not, would not stop, and probably could not even hear his name being called to stop so he did not stop.

When the farmer finally got to the fence, he gently attempted to unpin Benny, paw by paw, from off the barbed wire. Benny cried the entire way through it. But it was the spike sticking under his jaw that proved the trickiest. He was bleeding so badly and from so many places; he was crying so very loudly now, like a baby needing comfort. When they finally managed to unhook him, they wrapped him in the farmer's long green raincoat and carried him back to where he had parked. They laid him in the back of the Land Rover. I didn't go with them, I just stood there right where I was standing, paralyzed by what I had just witnessed; unable to move.

One of the farmhands went to get the vet. Benny cried continuously. The pain must have been immense. I could still hear him screaming even days after albeit in my head.

I think a part of me blamed myself that day because Benny always came running up to me, to greet me and always jumped up on to me. He would always want to lick my face; it was his way of saying hello to me. I believed everyone else blamed me too.

When the vet finally arrived, he examined Benny who was still whimpering in between crying out loud; after completing his examination, he looked up at the farmer and slowly shook his head from side to side before returning his eyes back to Benny. They thought I did not understand what was going on, but I did. They transported Benny to the vet's Land Rover, and he quietly drove away.

The farmer finished up what he could, and the afternoon very quickly turned to dusk. I watched him get into his green land rover and drive away, clearly, he had forgotten me. I had not moved from where I was standing. Unable to call out I just remained there. It was almost dark when he returned. I never saw Benny again. The image of his blood-stained coat stayed with me for years. When everything else was said, and done, Benny wasn't the only thing that was missing; suddenly, my voice was gone too. As time passed, they bought me another dog; it was a black Labrador puppy. He was so cute and cuddly, but he wasn't Benny, and we didn't bond. Perhaps, it was just me – he just wasn't Benny.

When the nursery eventually realised that I had stopped speaking, and learnt what had happened at the farm, it was quickly decided that I should not visit the family for a while. So, on the weekends, it was just me in the large house, all on my own. After a few weekends of being alone, it was decided that I could go with my sister and spend the weekend with her and her family, which I did, and everything seemed alright for a while.

One fine day, whilst I was outside, playing with another child, I heard the sound of screeching brakes – they belonged to that of a large saloon car. The street was the playground for the kids that lived on it back then so when visiting we simply joined in.

There were hardly any cars on the roads, and you were lucky if you saw even one parked in your street, and if you saw two, well, that was like good luck or something. We shared our imaginary playground, the street, with the house pets that ventured out of their owners' homes, who also lived in the street.

Upon seeing them, we would intuitively chase them, just to stroke them – mainly the cats, that is. It must have been a weekend towards the end of spring as the sky was whiter than grey. I had been playing with another child out on the pavement when a cat ran out into the road right before our very eyes causing the breaks on the oncoming car to scream to a halt and what I certainly thought was to be its last meow.

The collision appeared to have taken place at the offside of where another vehicle was parked. I ran over and bent down whilst remaining on the pavement to see if I could determine exactly what had happened, by peering under the stationary car. I could see nothing. I stood up and looked up only to see the Lord Jesus. '*Oh my gosh*!' I knew it was him don't ask me how, I just knew... He was standing on a huge white cloud with two men, one standing on either side of him, each one with huge, massive white wings sticking out behind them. My mouth just dropped wide open.

Jesus was wearing a white gown with a purple sash from shoulder to hip. His arms were open wide, as if ready to embrace me. As he came nearer, I could see what I now know are the nail marks on his hands. I was in awe as he descended, and when I thought he had landed, I bent down behind the car again to see if his feet had touched the ground. I could see nothing, so I stood back up again. I think I would have gone a bit nearer to say hello or something, as I looked up, I saw Jesus and the two men now ascending back up into the clouds. I stood there watching, mouth still open wide, until they had completely disappeared behind the sky. Once I could close my mouth, I ran back towards the direction of the house, shouting at the top of my lungs,

'Jesus is alive! Jesus is alive! I've just seen him! I've just seen him!' I was yelling this at the top of my lungs as I ran. Clearly my voice had returned...

'Oh, my Lord! The girl's gone raving mad,' said my sister's house mother. Odette then quickly came running up to me and shook me.

'What are you saying?' she asked.

'I... I saw Jesus,' I answered. 'He came out of the sky with two of his friends. The cat got knocked down, and Jesus came. It was Jesus I tell you,' I blurted it all out trying to get my words in order and my breath back simultaneously.

'Right!' said Odette. 'You never mention this again, or they will take you away. Do you hear, do you hear?' she demanded.

'Yes, Odette,' I replied in a soft-spoken voice.

She shook me again. 'Please, Jacqueline,' she affirmed, 'if they take you away from me, we may never see each other again, and then...' she paused, '... well, then, I couldn't bear it...'

They put children in the mental asylums for less than that in those days or so the rumors went.

'OK, Odette, I will not say anything about it ever again,' I promised faithfully. And I never did, not until thirty-one years later.

This sighting would remain with me buried deep within the contours of my heart silent within my subconscious until the winter of 2000 when I would triumphantly be reminded, and the clock was ticking tick-tock, tick-tock...

When we sat down to tea, late that afternoon, Odette's house mother asked me what had all the commotion been about earlier.

'Oh nothing,' I responded promptly.

'I thought you said you saw Jesus coming out of the sky or something?' she asked, smirking, trying not to laugh.

'Who, me?' I asked, trying to act surprised. 'Oh no, not me,' I answered, attempting to distance myself from the subject quite emphatically. 'The dog is under the table,' I said trying to change the subject. He wasn't allowed to be in the dining room when we were eating.

'Oh, she was just playing around,' Odette added for effect. 'You know, she's always making things up and stuff. She did not mean to upset anyone, and we are really sorry about that, Miss Betsey,' Odette continued.

Miss Betsey was an apple-shaped woman, who wore her washed-out blonde curls permanently in large rollers on the top of her head, held in place by a floral head scarf which matched the print on her apron. She was always busy with something or other and was always clothed in the same faded floral armor.

That night when we were safely tucked up in bed, Odette asked me again what had happened, and I explained it to her, this time in more detail.

'So, what were you doing right before you saw him?' she asked.

'We were just looking for the cat,' I said. 'I bent down to see where it had gone, and when I stood back up, I saw Jesus coming towards me. He had two friends with him, and they had really big silvery white wings on their backs.'

'They are his angels,' Odette confirmed, smiling.

'Why didn't he land? What does it mean?' I asked inquisitively.

'I don't know,' answered Odette.

'Maybe Jesus is coming for us soon,' I said. 'Perhaps it is a good sign.'

'Go to sleep now, Jacqueline,'

'OK, Odette, goodnight,'

'Goodnight,' said Odette.

The Visit

For those children who had their own families who visited them at the farm, visits were always religiously time-restricted and not encouraged at all, so they were few and far between. I never understood why then but would later come to learn that staff would not encourage the promotion of visits and you would not be wrong for thinking that perhaps they did not want their minute-by-minute, hour-by-hour, day by day, or week by week routines interrupted. What I called the conveyor belt of routines.

I remember quite vividly the details of my own visits. I had two in fact, from two very different ladies, completely unbeknown to me at the time as they were both being introduced as one and the same - My mother. Mother number one was softly spoken and very gentle in her manner so tender in her touch; perhaps a little shy even. It was as though this was all new to her. I don't recall ever seeing her before, but I knew I knew her, from where I knew not; but I knew she was a good person.

Both visits took place in the dining room; it was a large room, which always appeared to be darker than all the other rooms. I think its darkness was perhaps added to by the color of the walls, which were a dark emerald green and the curtains were burnt brown, which further contributed to the darkness. I can't ever remember a time when they were ever fully opened.

Sitting with the lady on the opposite side of the table was Dad and one member of staff, another stood behind me and to my left from where I was sitting, as if guarding the door. The great mahogany dining table lay between us, like a river it kept us apart. The entire set up was like that of some business meeting with them on one side and me on the other as if I was the one pitching; trying to sell something, myself perhaps.

It was all so very distant and all so very clinical – an environment where it was impossible to relax or talk or hug or even just be you. The other staff member who waited by the door would be the one to say, 'Come on now, time's up' because we only had five minutes. The lady stared and stared at me, it was as though she couldn't believe it was me; and then after the longest silence, she spoke to me, but I could not understand her words. Even today I cannot recall them. It was as though she spoke another language. Finally, she stretched out her hand across the table as if to stroke mine, but it was the table that kept us at arm's length, it was too vast; even so I could still sense her purity, her gentleness, her tenderness. In hindsight, looking back, it was really evident that she was a peaceful and loving person, angelic even. I felt as though she wanted to hold me close to her, but the big fat table lay between us, like some formidable abyss. I wanted what I sensed in her, and that was for her to hold me, to draw me close to her, and to hug me as she did when I was born, but I had no words to vocalise this.

'OK, time's up!' said the cold, motionless voice coming from the direction of the door behind me.

'Time's up!'

Just before the very end, she handed me a little doll. I took it without speaking and was told to leave the room. I left without hugging her. I was torn between wanting to run under the table and hug her leg and obeying the voice. I have no idea why I did what I did next but without any emotion I tore off the head, the legs, and the arms, and discarded it. Then I felt remorseful, sad even and hoped she would return and bring me back another one; I would look after it, I thought. I never ever saw her again.

Many years later, I came to realize that this lady was in fact my mother. It was the only memory I could capture and lock away deep within the contours of my heart. Just five minutes in that cold eerie room was all we were allowed. I have no memories of ever seeing her again after that day. *(This bit always makes me cry even now).* The next time I saw her, she wasn't moving, she wasn't breathing; she was standing still next to Dad in what seems like happier times gone by, their presence captured through the lens of a 45 mm still; black & white.

Dad loved photos he had so many, suitcases full even. I would be fifteen then, she must have been eighteen then, she was wearing furs in summer, so it was evident she was trying to hide something that sat out in front of her. She was pregnant with Odette, yet she looked so beautiful, so serene. It was shortly after this sighting that I, along with Odette, were informed by the SS that our mother had died. We did not believe it, not for a moment, and neither did we want to. She was apologising for giving us the news, but she didn't even have her facts straight neither had she even taken the time to get them straight ... but isn't that just typical of the SS? I mean how do you tell a child their mother is dead when you have no death certificate and in truth you don't really know?

There was one more occasion when I was taken back into the visiting room to see my mother. This time, I thought I was going to speak to her; this time, I was going to hug her and never let her go. I went into the room repeatedly reminding myself of what the task was at hand, I kept saying it over and over again in my mind and did not look up until she spoke. My head jolted upward as this was not the soft-spoken voice that had greeted me previously; it was a different voice, a strange voice, an unkind voice. Dad was still sitting next to her, which confused me more. I looked at him then back at her again, but it wasn't her. I began to cry; it wasn't my mother. She handed me a doll too, but I did not want it.

I could sense something dark in her, but clearly at the age of just three going to four, I could not explain it. I cried some more. Then I was asked to leave the room, which I did with a fuss. I did not like the feeling I had when I met this woman. I could sense the darkness in her; it was thick and stiff like black treacle. I would later come to learn that this woman was Mordecka; she would become Dad's second wife and the clock was ticking, tick - tock, - tick - tock.

She too gave me a doll, but this time in a fit of rage, I completely destroyed the doll, pulling off its arms and legs and attempting to rip out its hair and poke its eyes in.

Unbeknown to me back then was what I was sensing was the very spirit of the woman, and what I did know was that it was not good. Nevertheless, the events had already been set in motion, the matter had already been decided, which had never been within my control and the clock was ticking, tick – tock, tick – tock...

The Hunt for Father Christmas

As time pushed these unfortunate events further into the distance things eventually calmed back down, and as the year galloped on, Christmas was soon upon us. Perhaps one of my more joyful memories was the hunt for Father Christmas, and I can remember going on a hunt for the man himself; of course, not just anyone could join in the hunt!

First and foremost, you had to *really* disbelieve in the existence of Father Christmas, so you could *really* be surprised when we found him, and second, you had to believe that we would in fact find him. *A contradiction of sorts, I'm sure.*

Having met all the criteria, I joined in the hunt and I remember quite vividly walking down the huge, long corridors that seemed to go on forever. I remember becoming increasingly tired after some time and then being startled right back, to the peak of all alertness, at the sound of the cry from another child; he was yelling that he had found Father Christmas. However, when all the yelling was said and done, once we got up close and personal, there was no such evidence at all that this was indeed Father Christmas; there was no white beard and no red clothes and no black boots and no sack of presents. Therefore, alas, it was not him; it was a false alarm and so the journey continued. About now, I began to feel really, tired as we had been walking for what seemed like ages, and all I wanted to do was to turn back and join in the fun with all those who had remained behind, waiting patiently for the one and only, Mr. Father Christmas and his big bag of resents.

Just then, we entered another long corridor, and about halfway down, there was a room with its door wide open. There was a bed in the corner, to the right, upon which lay a body. *Could this be him?* I thought. Then another voice piped up,

'I hope this is him.' Inside, I really, hoped so too, for I had never walked so much in my entire short, little life, and the soles of my feet were really, aching now. The boldest children went over to the bed to see if this was indeed Mr. Santa. He was snoring quite loudly; but alas, it could not be determined. We decided to turn on the light, which involved the climbing up on top of the furniture in the room in order to flick the switch as none of us on our own were tall enough to reach it. There was a red hat and jacket on the back of the chair and a pair of big, black boots at the side of the bed.

I felt we had enough good evidence now, although this feeling was not unanimous amongst us. Just then, another child went over and gave an almighty tug at his beard, to which he roared, and we all ran out of the room together, becoming wedged in the doorway and toppling over each other in our bid to make a quick escape. Crying and screaming and banging into each other we ran all the way back down to the foyer overwhelmed with fright as we raced. We came rushing in where everyone else was waiting for the arrival of Santa and his big red sack full of exciting presents.

As we found our breath and recovered our composure, we camouflaged in with the other children. He surfaced before any questions of where we had been could be fired. We all cheered with the children who had remained and shouted Hooray! Hooray! Pretending, as if we had never departed. One by one, we took turns to go up and receive our presents from Santa; when it was my turn, he looked directly into my eyes and asked if I had been one of *those* to be counted. I did not answer. I only glared back in complete astonishment. He handed me my present, and I slid down from his knee, hot with guilt, and returned to the fold, trying my best to be invisible amongst them.

Going Home

It was not long after that our Dad returned to collect us from Addlestone Farm; only GOD knew his reasons. He arrived as the passenger of a dark-blue Ford saloon, from which he stepped out wearing a smart dark blue suit. From that moment, onwards he seemed to do no more than swoop us up into his mammoth arms along with our belongings on each occasion that we were to leave a place. I learnt much later that the driver was my uncle – Dad's half-brother. He would be the getaway driver each time we were to depart from the homes of the SS. However, we never returned to Addlestone Farm again.

All four of us piled into the humble one-room abode on the ground floor of this old Victorian house, which we would occupy with Dad and this woman, who at that time we were led to believe was our mother and whom we were told to call 'Mummy'. Little did I know that this was the very word which was to almost destroy me in later years to come, each time I would hear it. It was a word that I would eventually grow to hate but one which I would eventually learn to accept.

No Cats! No Dogs! No Irish! No Blacks!

In the 1960s, the sign for 'Rooms to Let' often read 'No cats, no dogs, no Irish, and no blacks'! However, after Dad left his marital home, we were quite lucky to find such a large, spacious room with just one upstairs neighbor who was Irish, and at no extra charge. We occupied this double spacious bedroom on the ground floor of the property, its windows looking out to the front of this old and very cold Victorian house situated on Burlington Street. Our curtains were always drawn, so no natural light was ever permitted to crowd out the darkness over spilling from the night.

We never saw the daylight unless we went outside, which was not very often. The main source of light was artificial. It was produced from just one bulb, which hung, without a shade, from the center of the room. Our only source of heat was from a paraffin heater which had a funny smell to it, and sometimes we used candles instead – that was usually when there was no electricity or when Dad was leaving us on our own, which was usually quite often but more so at night. He would always say, 'Don't get out of the bed unless you want to pee, and don't open the door or go to the window,' before leaving us on our own. I always felt afraid when I was left alone. I would shut my eyes really tight in an attempt to hurry myself to go to sleep, and I never got out of bed. I was just too afraid.

Our upstairs neighbor was a middle-aged Irish woman with shoulder length mousey hair and very pale skin. She was slim in build, of medium height and had a very strong accent. I remember the bitter arguments that she would engage in with Dad. They would go at it like two snarling, saliva-dribbling cross breeds for what seemed like hours and for reasons that were completely beyond my comprehension or intellect. One could almost be inclined to be convinced that their behavior was a normal practice, until one day, she threw a pail of urine down the stairs at him, which although narrowly missed him, the backsplash didn't. They never argued again after that. In fact, they never spoke again.

We had only an outside toilet as did most houses of that era, and it was normal for it to be shared by all the occupants in the house, so it was usual for families to have a metal pail with a lid, which would be emptied at the end of the day or once it became full or smelly.

There was no inside bath in this house either; however, we did have a tin bath, which Dad would half-fill before carrying it into our room and bathing us in it. After he had finished, he would then carry it back outside and empty it out in the backyard which we never saw either. We never went out the back; we were not allowed. Of course, the well-to-do people would have had the heavy roll-top baths stationed inside their homes – the sort that is much sought after today. It was only Dad who ever bathed and washed the two of us. I really enjoyed bath time, although it wasn't as frequent as I would have liked. I would always sleep exceedingly well after Dad had given me a bath; he would cream our skin and dress us in fresh pajamas... 'Emm'.

Whilst living in this room, we all shared the big double bed, which was positioned behind the door and pushed up tight against the wall. The wall was a safety net for Odette and me, so when we were sleeping on this side of the bed, we would not fall off the edge. There was always a pushing and shoving fight between the two of us to sleep next to Dad, of course; we both demanded the warmth and comfort of his body to keep us warm at night and the affection from that warmth to reaffirm his affection and love for us.

However, Dad was a bit of a night roller and slept rather soundly. He would frequently lift us up from off his chest, like sleeping puppies, and carefully place us gently down back next to the wall so that he did not crush us as he rolled during the night. However, if he did happen to roll over on top of us during the night, without realising, we were usually at the mercy of the angels to be rescued from suffocation.

Having already been prematurely plucked from my mother's breast, I would come to find great comfort in the sucking of Dad's nipples to soothe me off to sleep; sadly, this unorthodox nurture ended quite abruptly when, on one night, the nipple I had chosen to comfort myself on was not Dad's, but that of Mordecka, his girlfriend; it did appear rather larger than usual, and perhaps, I may have wondered just for a moment. Nevertheless, she was not so sympathetic or understanding, and in that moment, she picked me up by the scruff of my nightclothes and tossed me back in the direction of the wall, feeling the breath gone right out of me as I connected with it, now sliding down it, I did not know what had happened, but after a couple of these episodes, I soon got the message to stay far away from her, especially at night. I remember the feelings of fear for the first time and would often wake up in the night just to confirm who indeed I was actually sleeping next to.

This was perhaps the start of my anxiety, of course, unbeknown to me then. When we did have visitors, which was not very often, Mordecka would play the dutiful stepmom, speaking in sweet soft tones – you could have easily convinced yourself that it was in fact another mysterious language. Inevitably, she would show off, calling us to come to her, like good little puppies, and we remarkably would obey her, like good little puppies.

However, on one occasion, I refused, an insolence that she was not about to forget... at least, not in a hurry any way, and one that would certainly come back to bite me on the bum quite literally with a short sharp whack, Ow!

The night- time sleeping arrangements continued, as did her complaints of not having enough room, or covers, or being too hot, or too cold or whatever, right up until Dad could purchase our own two-fold-up, fold-down single beds.

They arrived by taxi with Dad, who almost succeeded in damaging the taxi in a rather aggressive attempt to remove the two larger than life boxes from out of the door that was not so obliging, therefore just catching the rim of the door as he pulled them through disturbing the rubber trim as he did.

After a brief exchange of sharp, loud, unfriendly words between Dad and the taxi driver, Dad paid the driver and carried the beds inside, with the two of us following close behind him.

It was there that he began to build the beds with total enthusiasm. They were all folded up with additional elements, which needed to be screwed on before the beds could be assembled. I remember that the mattresses were orange and brown with a whirly kind of pattern on them and the seams were brilliant white.

Dad, after he had finished building the beds and dressing them with some new sheets, blankets, and pillows, proudly invited us to pick one each and to come and sit on them and try them out. That night, we were going to sleep in our very own beds. I remember that it felt very cold and very lonely down there in our new beds that night, there was no one to snug up to no one to draw heat from, I felt I still needed human contact. Another downside of the fold up beds was that they took up a lot of the floor space and as we ran around the room our feet would often collide with the legs of the bed knocking out our baby toenails; followed by blood and tears.

However, it was not long before we were soon joined by her...really... yes really... big, fat Mordecka. When she became fed up with sharing with us, the complaints resumed, and we were eventually moved back up to the double bed with Dad. An arrangement which, in truth, I much preferred. In fact, I loved it. Dad was warm and cozy, and I had Dad's nipple to pacify me.

It was not long after we got the beds that we were on the move again. This time, we moved into a two-roomed apartment.

Two Rooms

I don't remember how we got there, but it did not take very long; therefore, I'm guessing that it could not have been too far away from the first house. In this house, we would share the kitchen and bathroom, which remarkably was inside the property, with the landlord and his family. Here we occupied two large bedrooms which meant Odette and I had our own room with our own single folding beds. Dad placed them on either side of a very large antique mahogany wardrobe, which stood in the center of the wall adjacent to the window with the door positioned at the end of the same wall. We had no living room in this house, and now being a little older, we were often left alone to find our own amusement.

We were now both walking and talking and both out of nappies, but our time spent there would be far from happy ever after or even happy at all. It was whilst we were here that Dad married and impregnated his live-in girlfriend – which came first, I don't know. Although we were not permitted to attend the ceremony, we could attend the after party, even if it was only for a moment. I loved the music that was played.

I remember the main living room belonging to the landlord was cleared of all furniture, except the glass cabinet which doubled as a bar, in expectation as if something was about to happen. He must have said dad could hold his reception there. I remember being told to wait and that Dad would return shortly. I remember that we were both dressed in our glad rags. Odette stood by the window, waiting in anticipation of his return, and I stood next to her, too small to see out of the window, so when I became bored of standing still, I would walk around the entire perimeter of the room until being told to stop by one of the adults in the room.

I also remember that there was very loud music being played, which eventually became more relaxing and soothed me off to sleep when the night-time came. I remember further the three large fruit cakes covered in the purest white icing. These were left in our room on top of a small wooden table. These came in handy as the intervals between Dad feeding us and the hunger pangs, which banged hard on the inside lining of our tummies, began to lengthen. I remember nibbling at the cake, innocently taking what began as mouse-like morsels to then determining which part I favored most, and just breaking off huge chunks, assuring myself that each large piece broken by hand was to be the last. *Did I really believe that my parents would not notice? What was I thinking?* When Mordecka saw the cake, she began to complain bitterly to the point of 'cry town', which even I, a child, found completely unconvincing; however, it was all just an act to get Dad's attention and perhaps more worrying, a larger portion of control over his already deeply wounded emotions.

Odette was never quite as hungry as I was, so I must have eaten quite a lot of it. Nevertheless, we both got told off, and we both received a good smacking. This was not the only trouble that I got into at that house.

It was not long before we began to realize the peculiar habits of the landlord, particularly on Sunday mornings to be precise. Every Sunday morning, he would, at about 6 a.m., begin to chop wood in the back garden, waking the entire household in the process... but, for which, I would get the blame and the beating and the bruises.

The chopping of the wood would echo up into the house, presenting itself as the equivalent noise to that of a continuous knocking sound. It woke everyone up and was completely irritating and very annoying to all but in particular my parents.

Given that Dad had parked our single beds on either side of the wooden wardrobe, which to some extent dominated the room, he convinced himself, beyond all reasonable doubt and of course with Mordecka's added input for extra effect, that the only reasonable explanation for this infuriating knocking sound was in fact *me.*

In his mind, this knocking sound was being orchestrated by me, knocking on the wardrobe, for which the punishment was a rather severe beating.

The chopping of wood continued, and the beatings followed, week in and week out. I had bruises on top of bruises, the surface of my skin was permanently red, it was as though the blood had moved up a level. It was not until perhaps after about the sixth week and the sixth beating that the landlord's wife, after finding me crying in the bathroom, decided to invite us all down to their table for dinner. She wanted us to share a meal with her and her husband; little did we know she had a motive.

At the time, I could not help but notice that our parents were very well behaved when in the company of other adults. And it was whilst sitting at this dinner table, after all the trivia of small talk and whilst the main contents of the meal were being chewed, swallowed, and enjoyed that the landlord's wife dropped her bombshell. Without so much as even a prompt, out of the blue she asked,

'Does my husband's early Sunday morning wood chopping disturb anyone else or is it just me?' Silence fell upon the table like a tablet of stone from the sky. Both Dad and Mordecka stopped munching on their food and stared at each other in total disbelief before returning their attention and focus back to the person who had delivered the question.

'Err No,' they answered simultaneously, in quiet, uncomfortable voices.

'Well, I can tell you it certainly annoys the hell out of me!' she said quite emphatically half laughing as if trying to retain the lightness of the atmosphere. Neither Mordecka nor Dad looked at me during the discovery of this 'sparkling' revelation and neither did either of them ever apologize for the false blame or the bitter beatings that had been dished out so quickly and so generously. 'Sunday is my only day off!' she exclaimed, taking another mouthful of her dessert. 'Who wants to be woken up at 6 a.m. on a Sunday morning? This is my only day off!' she affirmed eating with her mouth open and talking with her mouth full of something and custard.

It was with this statement that Mordecka cracked first.

'Well, yes I think it did wake me up a couple of times,' she admitted coyly, like a shy teenager being asked out on a date for the first time.

'Did you hear that, Edmond?' his wife asked.

'I'm really sorry about that,' the landlord said, repenting profusely. 'I just cut the wood for the fire on Sundays or make something out of the wood because there's just so much of it,' he confessed.

'Oh, I don't mind,' said Mordecka.

'Liar!' I thought.

'Well, perhaps maybe you could start a little later, though?" she continued.

'Certainly, what time do you get up?' he asked in his deep Bayesian accent.

'Well, after ten or eleven will be OK,' replied Mordecka laying on hers.

The landlord's wife was in total agreement, and I was relieved to learn first-hand that from that moment on, there was to be no more early morning knocking and no more beatings, at least not for the knocking sound anyway. We did go out to see all this wood that the landlord spoke of and he was right there was just so much of it.

It wasn't long before one thing ended and another commenced, and I soon learnt that this was the start of me being beaten for the acts and omissions of others on a regular basis. As I grew, I would soon come to accept that this was normal practice at least in his thinking or rather lack of it, which was indeed typical of a Caribbean upbringing.

Dad certainly brought with him all his suitcases stuffed to the brim with sad heartaches and angry disappointments from his own childhood into his first marriage, and now here where he had found himself right in the middle of his second with this strange woman, without even having gotten over his first, or even his own childhood for that matter. Not surprisingly, it was not too long before the cracks would begin to show again.

At one point, we hardly saw Dad; he appeared to go missing for days. It was during these times that we hardly ate, and his new wife, Mordecka, would tie us up, with her opaque-colored tights, to the bed or even together every day before she went out. She would be gone from dawn to dusk. Of course, it was no big deal; we knew how to remove the tights. It did not matter how tight she tied them either; we always managed to get out of them. They were stretchy and had a lot of give in them, and our ankles were small and thin. Odette realised quite quickly that if we turned our feet at a slight angle whilst she was tying us up, she was prohibited from making an impossibly tight knot. Therefore, we were able to untie ourselves once she had left and quickly get back in, once we heard the keys in the door.

It was always our Dad who would come to untie us. On one night, we unexpectedly heard the keys in the door much earlier than usual. We raced back to the bed to tie ourselves up again. It was Dad. We could sense the sadness drawn over him like a grey cloak of despair, and we could see the glazed-over look in his eyes as he began to untie us. He hugged us individually before returning to his room.

There were no arguments that night as Mordecka had gone out, and it was not until the next day before she decided to return. In the morning, we could hear them speaking at length. Dad was telling her that he would not accept her tying us up like this and leaving us, so she agreed not to repeat this action ever again, and she never did. She had something far more sinister up her sleeve. But for now, when she wanted to go out and leave us behind, she would just go. There was no 'I will see you later,' or 'I'm going out now,' and never did she say

'I love you'. The door would just click shut behind her; she always departed with her thick dark spirit intact. It followed her everywhere she went.

My worst experience whilst living at this property came when I had been drying the dishes in the kitchen, one morning after a late breakfast. I was with Odette, when suddenly Mordecka burst into the little kitchenette where we were and demanded to know exactly who was making all the noise and because it was me who was actually in the act of laughing at the time, of course Odette pointed the finger straight at me. I must have been about three going on four, at the time. I was led away by Mordecka like a lamb to the slaughter back to the bedroom she shared with Dad. Once there, she asked me to fetch her the hard-backed plastic slipper, which I did filled with enthusiasm, not realizing that her evil intentions were in fact to beat me senseless - simply for laughing.

'Didn't I tell you not to make any noise?' she demanded, but before I could answer, the slipper came crashing down with some considerable force, making contact with some part of my body. Unable to answer, she continued to beat me simultaneously with every word that she uttered from her mouth. I remember trying to run away from her, but she just stretched out her arm and pulled me back again, her fingernails catching my skin as she did. She held me by the arm and continued to strike me all over my body, as if she was having a fight with a kick boxer or something.

I remember screaming sore with pain, but it was of no significance; it was of no avail. She did not stop beating me until she was tired and out of breath; in hindsight, I guess it was like some kind of sadistic workout, with me as the punch bag. I could not understand why she was even hitting me to begin with, yet somewhere in the madness of it all, my eyes caught a glimpse of her face. It was twisted and contorted, almost deformed by rage, animal-looking even, and very frightening.

The only thing that was evident was an innate hatred, which I would have sworn ran 'riot' right through her veins; it was interesting that the beatings never took place in Dad's presence.

Once it finally came to an end with my last drop of energy, I clambered up off the floor on to the edge of the bed and collapsed. I sobbed, shuddering, and shaking like some lost, wet puppy, whimpering until almost asleep.

I remember being pulled up into the center of the bed by little warm hands and comforted. It was Odette, she pulled me up all the way on to her lap through her legs and hugged me, rubbing my back like a mother would. I closed my eyes and remembered nothing more, until I opened them to the pale white faces of Dukesbury House. I guess it must have been the syrup she was giving me...

Dukesbury House

I don't remember a single Christmas occurring whilst we were here, so it seemed certain that we arrived and departed in the same year, however, the poorly collated hand-written notes will say that we were here twice, but I cannot recall. We did have a summer holiday, though, so that meant there must have been a birthday too, yet I don't remember a cake or presents or anything.

During the summer holidays, I remember we visited a place called Margate. There was sun, sea, and sand everywhere. The latter two we had never seen before, neither tasted for that matter. The sea tasted salty and the sand gritty. Clearly, these were not experiences to be repeated, at least not intentionally any way.

One of the throws of the beach was that the older children would swing the younger children up into the air before allowing them to drop like rag dolls into the freezing cold salty water. If you couldn't swim, your first instinct was to drink your way back to shore, where upon arrival, you would be left in peace to regurgitate the salty water and perhaps even throw up whatever it was you had for lunch too. They also buried us alive in the sand with only our heads protruding, a pastime that I really did not like at all. Our holiday lasted exactly two weeks and included many, if not all of us, getting lost at least once.

Living at Dukesbury House was not all sun, sea, and sand, though, as the days soon began to reveal. The proprietor of the House was a Mrs. Manfred. She was a small woman of odd disposition with fast-fading hair, which appeared to go from mousey straight to white without even passing through silver or grey and it was thinning in every direction; I got to realize very quickly that something was strangely wrong with Mrs. Manfred.

I remember one occasion when I was in the sewing room. This was a large room with very high windows and even higher ceilings. The windows appeared to reach all the way up to the ceiling without stopping. They were adorned with burnt-orange curtains, which sort of matched the carpet, and they cascaded all the way down to meet it. There were chairs which didn't match as well as different odd-shaped cushions dotted around the room. Also, in the sewing room on this occasion was another lady, whose name I cannot recall; she never spoke, and we were not introduced at that moment. However, I do believe that she was Manfred's right-hand man. It was on this day that I made the fateful mistake of asking Mrs. Manfred for the sweets that Dad had brought for us a couple of days earlier on his last visit. I had been thinking about the sweets for some time now and how nice it would be to suck on the chocolate before chewing the caramel hidden inside. It was a packet of Rollo's.

At first, Mrs. Manfred just ignored my request, but when I repeated the question for the third time, she grabbed me by my clothes and started squeezing my thin arm, it was as if she was trying to stop my blood and at the same time pulling me on to her lap with one hand and after securing me in such a manner so that I could not move, she used the other hand to begin stabbing me repeatedly in the buttocks, using a very large and very sharp sewing needle.

'Ouch, that hurt,' I thought. After jabs three and four, I quickly realised this may not be stopping anytime soon. Now becoming fast, filled with fear, I wriggled and squirmed, unable to sound any kind of alarm and not sure exactly what was happening or why – only that it was extremely painful.

Eventually, I managed to wriggle my way out of her grip but not before receiving several more jabs to my rear end. I fell to the floor with a loud thud and just stared at her, not really believing what had just happened. She went to reach for me again, but I quickly scarpered away from her, moving backwards before scrambling to my feet and running out of the door, which had opened just at the right time to allow a staff to enter and for me to exit.

I learnt very quickly after this incident not to ask her for any of Dad's gifts ever again.

There was one more occasion though – when I threw up. Again, I made the mistake of telling Mrs. Manfred what had happened; in a short sharp action, she lunged out at me, grabbing hold of me, and dragged me all the way to the top of the long wide staircase by the scruff of my clothes and down the long hall. We went so fast that I could barely find my feet, they too barely touching the ground. We arrived at the toilet, and she pulled me inside the small cubicle, demanding that I show her the vomit.

Unsure of what this meant, I pointed to the toilet. She turned and looked into the toilet and then suddenly out of nowhere, Pow! She punched me, right in the stomach. I bowled over trying to regain my breath. When I could I returned to standing, then she repeated the question again. A second time I pointed to the toilet and again she punched me in exactly the same place, this time knocking all the wind right out of me and causing me to collapse in a heap on the floor.

At that point, she walked away, just leaving me there unattended. I lay there until Odette came up and found me. Dad had told Odette to look out for me; she would always come searching for me if she didn't see me in the usual places. It was at about this time that I realised that you do not speak to Mrs. Manfred. You do not smile at Mrs. Manfred. You do not inform her of anything – about sweets or sickness or anything; you stay out of her way. Clearly, the answer that she was looking for was 'no', but I didn't know it then. She ordered me to clean up the toilet and go to my room upon her departure; unable to move I just lay there. My face now pillowed by a mixture of saliva and bile.

When Odette came upstairs and found me crying, now kneeling, and trying to clean up the mess with toilet tissue that was really more like tracing paper, so it was quite difficult for the paper to absorb it. Holding back the tears, I tried to tell Odette of Mrs. Manfred's demands. Odette told me not to worry; she said she would clean up the mess. She tucked me into bed, and I cried myself to sleep, unable to understand what was going on or why, just simply unable to make any sense of it all. After a while, Odette came and gently woke me to see if I was OK. I did not tell her then either. I couldn't. I felt I wasn't able to speak to her about it not until we had a new girl who also vomited, and Odette was about to get Mrs. Manfred. 'No don't,' I told her.

'Why, what's wrong?'

So, then I explained what had happened to me. Odette was so angry, but we could not do anything about it. There was no phone to call anyone; no one came to see how we were, and Dad's visits were now too few and far between. Mrs. Manfred could hurt us and bad, and she was not afraid to do so, as she had already so confidently demonstrated with the pin stabbing incident in my bottom and the punches to my stomach. We cleaned up the vomit ourselves and went back downstairs. We told no one as it was difficult to know exactly whom to trust.

I remember, when chicken pox was going around, the methodology of the medical profession at that time was to quarantine the area, including the infected child. When it finally reached us, we were on lock-down in our room for four weeks, 24 hours a day; we took all our meals in our room, we played in our room and we even peed in our room too. I mean, in the bin, of course, if we were left too long because sometimes there was just no one available to escort us to the toilet, so it just made more sense, I guess.

Staff usually came first thing in the morning and last thing at night to escort us to the toilet. They would use the same opportunity to douse us with more calamine lotion and bring us up some food. It was the trips in-between that became so scarce until they ceased all together. It was then that the itching became unbearable. Eventually, we did manage to persuade them to leave us the lotion so that we could attend to each other's spots ourselves and cool the itching down. We told them, 'At least, we will not have to keep calling for you to come upstairs to dress us, as we can dress each other.' Incredibly, they agreed to our suggestion, so when the itching became too severe, we could administer the lotion to each other by ourselves, of course we caked ourselves in it, which was very funny.

Thank God, the spots did not last forever. After a maximum period of four weeks, it was all over, the spots were gone, and we were released from our captivity and once again permitted to mix in with the other children.

Monday mornings were 'unusually' interesting. Our breakfast time would be shrouded by the blood-curdling screams of Simon Walker. He was a bed-wetter. Mrs. Manfred's idea of dealing with the situation was to plonk Simon into a bath, half filled with freezing cold water and his sheets after him where he was ordered to wash them by hand.

Simon was just eight years old. The screams were enough to put anyone off their breakfast, more so if the turned milk had not already done the job; this sequence of events was repeated every Monday morning when Mrs. Manfred was on duty. Thankfully, the other staff members were not so brutal, except, of course, Mrs. McAlister, Mrs. Manfred's right-hand man, who was in fact a woman. She followed her instructions to the letter.

Eventually, it got to the point where each Monday morning we would find ourselves rooting for Simon, willing him not to have wet the bed from the pit of our stomachs, praying even that he would be dry. We would all hold our breath and wait, not even taking a morsel of food until we knew. Eventually, that day came, and we all cheered like crazy; it was a well-accepted ninth birthday present for Simon: he was dry.

During the winter months, we had a breakfast of stiff porridge made with water, adorned with a spoonful of golden syrup. We forced as much of this lumpy clay like, wallpaper paste down our throats as we could. Annoyingly, once, or twice a week the cook would get it wrong, serving black treacle instead of golden syrup. No one ever asked for more; on days like that you just went hungry.

As the seasons changed and the months became warmer, we ate things like cornflakes, sugar puffs, and Rice Krispies. However, there was a downside: they were usually complemented with the infusion of sour milk, which made breakfast time a bit of a nightmare. I soon learnt to spill it on the floor or all over the table, accidently on purpose of course and if there was any bread left, I would ask for toast, which was always adorned with thin scrapings of margarine posing as butter, which sat directly on the center of the bread and nowhere else. This would be washed down with a small cup of warm milky tea. It almost kept me until lunch.

Lunch was usually a roast dinner of some kind and included one of the following: chicken, beef, lamb, or pork with all the trimmings. Teatime could either be leftovers from dinner such as cold roast beef or some type of stew accompanied by sandwiches and fruits, usually apples, oranges, and bananas. Whenever it was one of the children's birthdays, we would have cakes and sweets as well, but that wasn't very often.

Dukesbury House was also home to many different types of pets. They were all kept in the animal room, which was in the new extension but was only accessible through its own external door. Every animal had its own cage, apart from the dog, a big floppy ginger retriever. He was a real sweetheart. Every Saturday afternoon, we would go into the animal room just for a few minutes to hold and stroke the animals before returning them to their respective cages. We also had a couple of tortoises, which although were afforded the liberty to roam freely around the garden during the day, were locked away safely at night – at least when we could find them that was.

Their lockable little wooden hut was placed at the end of the garden to keep out unwanted pests, such as Mr. Fox. However, there was one occasion when Mr. Tortoise disappeared for about three weeks. We were all very concerned, convinced in fact that he had been taken away by Mr. Fox, until suddenly, out of the blue, he reappeared again as if by magic. And finally, we had a couple of budgerigars, which although encaged were kept inside the house, in the playroom to be exact. They were never allowed outside the confines of this room, of course unbeknown to me at the time.

Our other animals included goldfish, rabbits, hamsters, and three kittens which we loved to bring into our den under the stairs, which was strewn with small scatter cushions, bits of old curtains, scraps of cut-off carpets, and a couple of blankets. Sometimes, we could have orange juice and biscuits too if nice helpers were on duty. We would snuggle up under there and listen to stories of old, told by the bigger girls that were supposed to make you jump if they didn't make you cry.

When we went out on excursions, we would always ensure that all the animals were securely put away in the animal room and that the door was securely locked.

It was late one Saturday afternoon when we returned home after an excursion to, I can't remember from where, but immediately as we entered the house, we were met by a strange noise that sounded like a crying baby. Without thinking, we spontaneously began to search for where the crying was coming from and what was causing it. When we reached the downstairs toilets, the crying appeared the loudest; we looked under the coats hanging on the pegs and inside the shoe boxes parked neatly underneath and even in the boxes which lay above, but nothing... Then Tina slowly opened the door of one of the cubicles and let out such a yell, I froze in my tracks; then the younger children were quickly ushered away, including me.

We were all shuffled into the TV room with the door closed behind us and ordered not to come out. We waited nervously for news. After a short while, Tina burst in with tears streaming down her face. In one hand, she was holding one of the kittens wrapped in a towel, and around the other was wrapped a makeshift bandage which made its way up her arm in an attempt to cover the rather deep scratches inflicted by the kitten as she had attempted to rescue it from out of the toilet.

Tina announced with a shaky voice that she would be taking the kitten to the vet in an attempt to save it; we all gasped in shock, horror even. The only person who had been at home all afternoon was Mrs. Manfred; it was remarkable that in all that time she did not hear the kitten crying – according to her that was.

After several hours, Tina returned to the house, sobbing uncontrollably without the kitten; it had to be put down, I had been here before. It had contracted pneumonia, and Tina had to have a tetanus shot. These bizarre kitten deaths continued until all three were dead. I remember Tina screaming and shouting hysterically after the death of each one. Clearly, the deaths had really distressed her. I mean, they were upsetting for all of us, but Tina was taking it the worst. It never dawned on me to make the connection back then, and I never understood why the deaths kept on happening. I guess three was quite excessive, even suspicious.

In later years, my sister would come to reveal that it was Mrs. Manfred who had deliberately and willfully murdered the little kittens by placing them down the toilet, and it was because they had been there in the cold water for so long that they all caught pneumonia. The heavy toilet seat and lids had also been deliberately closed, so they would be weighted down so there was no way out for the little mites. Veterinary medicine was very limited in the fifties and sixties, so when a pet took ill or was injured, if it could not be bandaged back together again the usual course of action was to have it put down. Tina's tears lasted for days. Every time she saw Mrs. Manfred, she would just start shouting at her, calling her a murderer amongst other things...

One of the many features of Dukesbury House was that it also boasted a very large rear garden, which was considerably underused, despite having balls, tricycles swings and a slide. At one end, slightly to the right of the boundary wall, was Mrs. Manfred's pride and joy – her rose garden. It was almost adjacent to the back door, where from the cloakroom window you had a pretty good view of it.

Matthew was another child also residing at Dukesbury House, he was about eight years old, and back then I must have been about four because the summer holidays had been and gone.

Occasionally, Matthew and I would play together in the garden and one particular game, which we loved to play was running through Mrs. Manfred's prized possession, armed with long sticks swinging them through the air from side to side slicing off the heads off all her beautiful, prized roses.

It would usually take two runs before we finally accomplished complete success. However, the thorns were no pushover; they gave as good as they got, in retaliation, they would reach out and stab back at us, scratching and clawing at us, all the way up and down our scrawny little arms and legs. My arms and legs were always bare because little girls were always dressed in very short dresses and very short socks. The irony was that we were always caught and punished by being made to miss supper, which always consisted of a packet of ready salted crisps, a cup of orange squash, and an apple or an orange; no love lost there then.

Occasionally, whilst in the rose garden, we would lie down amongst the shattered rose petals which had fallen to the ground. We would lie down, right next to each other, and Matthew would begin to caress me. He would place his scrawny little hands on my tummy, making gentle circle-like motions, which felt very soothing. He would make gentle patterns around my belly button. Then his hand would move down on to my upper thighs which tickled, before slipping them quite quickly and unexpectedly into my underpants, which I actually didn't like so much as it made me feel very uncomfortable and often hurt. Somehow, whilst lying there amongst the petals, I could just sense that we were being watched, but whenever I looked around, I could never actually see anyone standing at the open window, which had previously been closed.

Slicing the heads from off the roses wasn't my only sin or even my worst. One morning, for some bizarre reason, which to this day I still do not understand why, I walked into the playroom and walked right up to the cage in which sat the two-house budgies and opened it; and of course, they flew out. First into the playroom, where they just flew around and round and round before flying straight out of the open door, which led directly into the garden. Well, who on earth told me to do that? What on earth was I thinking? Who on earth possessed me? Just what was I thinking? I mean I had seen staff open the cage to clean it so many times, and the budgies would fly out and fly around the room for a while before flying back in.

On one occasion, staff had even asked Adrianna, another child also residing at the house, to open the cage on a Monday. Well, today was also a Monday, and I believed that I too could open the cage, and if they flew out, they would also fly back in again, just as I had seen them do on so many occasions before. I had no idea that the veranda doors were open or that they would eventually fly straight out or that birds raised in captivity don't usually come back. Well, they did not let me live it down for weeks. They went on and on and on about it every day, all day. Just about everyone put their two pence in. It was in this moment that I never wished so hard for the budgies to return and failing that, for me just to disappear altogether.

My stomach was in knots of turmoil, even my intestines must have been rubbing against each other. Of course, they never did and neither did I. However, at some point, I did see a pair; but of course, it was not them. At that time, although I was never physically punished, the emotional torture of being segregated from the other children and not being allowed to join in for excursions and days out combined with everyone constantly speaking about it was indeed perhaps far more excruciating, at least for a four-year-old. To me it felt as though this hostile climate would last forever; it felt very uncomfortable.

The final blow came one lunchtime, when someone said that captive birds cannot survive outside captivity; of course, this just made me feel even worse. I looked out through the long windows of the cold eerie dining room, my tear-filled eyes peering up at the sky, stopping at the roof of the church in the distance the spiral of which appeared to almost reach the sky, but it was upon the roof that so many birds would frequently perch. In the distance, they looked like moving black odd-shaped dots. I began wishing, willing, and even hoping that just one of these was one of the budgies. It really didn't matter, of course, because even if it was one of them, there was no way of capturing it, or even the bird returning ever again. Somehow, I managed to convince myself to believe in my heart that they would be taken care of and so life went on.

Another of our great past times was hide and seek. I loved this game. I remember on one occasion when I and another child hid in the walk-in food cupboard in the kitchen. Whilst waiting to be found, of course we looked around for anything we could get out scrawny little hands on to eat, – *children are always hungry you know.*

It was then that I noticed a glimpse of something shiny seated on the shelf, just above my eye level. Wow, I thought this must be some kind of wonderful, sweet. Quickly I unwrapped the shiny silver cube and popped the brown square sticky contents into my mouth closing my eyes in pure satisfaction expectant to meet delicious as my baby white teeth crushed down and my taste buds moved into action, rising to the challenge to capture and report back... Oh my goody gum drops. What on earth had I done? After two chews, this foreign object, which was now well and truly wedged between my teeth now brown and smeared completely all over my tongue; also, now brown I realized exactly what absolutely disgusting tasted like. I spat what I could out before finding a kitchen towel to scrape out the rest. 'Caught you,' shouted the seeker, 'ha, ha your it.' –

I guess you could call it calmer for slicing off the heads of the roses.,

On a brighter note, the good news was at least Dad did visit us, initially his visits had been every two weeks, but it wasn't long before this eventually trickled down to once every two months before stopping altogether, at least for a while anyway. We had not seen him for some time, during which Mrs. Manfred had decided that we needed a haircut, or rather a good hair hacking. They wanted to cut Odette's hair first; I would be made to sit and watch so that I would be more accepting of what was about to happen, without any fuss or fight when it was my turn. Our hair, at that time, had grown very long; it was right down our backs to our bums, and there was no one there who could manage it or rather who could be bothered to at least try to take care of it. It was usually ringed with rubber bands, but these would just become knotted in our long, thick hair, causing us to lose handfuls each time they were removed.

On a practical note, we just needed someone to brush it and to tie a pretty ribbon around it, as they did for the other children's hair, but no one did.

Staff had resorted to chasing Odette around the garden for ages that day. *If only Dad could have seen her faithfulness,* I thought. Eventually, after she tired, they caught her and dragged her back in kicking and screaming into the playroom. 'Nooooo! Noooo! Nooooo! Dad said you're not allowed to cut our hair!' she yelled. Alas, no one was listening because no one cared.

'Never mind,' Mrs. Manfred responded. 'Your Dad will be very happy with your new hair. In fact, he has said we should give it a little trim,' she stated so proudly, convincing only herself.

'Lies! Lies! All lies!' Odette screamed at the top of her voice. I watched without responding, without revealing any kind of emotion even.

After they had finished with Odette, it was my turn. I did not make as much fuss as Odette, if any at all, because according to Mrs. Manfred, Dad had given the OK. This statement seemed to resonate with me; perhaps, deep down, I wanted it too. I went to the chair, like a little lamb to the slaughter. And oh, dear Lord, did she hack at it and chop at it, as if she was cutting some overgrown, uncontrollable hedge or something, but not at all neatly.

Afterwards, they gathered up what remained, now all different lengths and scraped it back into the same rubber band again, which they knew full well would just become knotted and have to be ripped out when it was time to remove it. It really felt like they were just not bothered that this would in fact cause more pain or harm, and Mrs. Manfred was not the least bit concerned as evidenced by her complete lack of empathy. Never once did I ever see her spending time with anybody, myself included, never once could I even recall so much as one kind word and as for hugging... are you kidding...

It was not too long after the hair-cutting episode that Dad made a surprise visit. When he saw us, he shrieked in despair and cried aloud as if in undiluted distress, marked with anger. I had never heard Dad cry before; his hands covered his face. I was frightened. I did not know what was going to happen next. Dad started shouting at Mrs. Manfred as she walked past deliberately refusing to make eye contact with him. She hastened her pace taking her step up from her normal stride to a quickened step to a power walk to an actual run, eventually running into her office, like a bat out of hell. Dad was hot on her tail and Odette after him. But she got in too quick and locked the door behind her with the key, which she always kept around her neck.

Arriving at the door fast behind her he banged on it repeatedly with his fist, shouting through his tears as well as the locked door, 'What have you done? What have you done? If I ever get my hands on you, you'll see!' I simply waited for their return, sucking contently on one of the new sweets that Dad had just brought for us: a massive red lolly with a smiley face – 'emm' that tasted so good. 'What did I tell you?' Dad screamed. 'You said that you wouldn't cut their hair. You promised me!' he shouted. 'You promised me!' he continued. It seemed she had taken away more than just our hair. I guess dad was enlightened to the fact that he had no real control.

Later in life, I would come to learn that *a promise is but a comfort to a fool.* But a man or woman of honor is one who gives their word and keeps it.

Mrs. Manfred did not engage with Dad from behind her fortress; in fact, she completely ignored him. It was as if she would have us believe that in truth she was no longer in her office. However, we all knew that there was only one way in and one way out. Dad walked slowly back to where I was patiently waiting, scooping up Odette in his mammoth arms as he overtook her with his giant steps. 'How have you been?' he asked, sitting back down next to me with a raspberry croakiness in his soft broken voice.

'Good.' I replied nodding.

Odette climbed on to his lap; this time, he gave us all the sweets. We tried to eat as many as we could before he left, crunching right into them. We told him that usually she would take them away from us, and we would never see them again.

'What... Never?' he questioned. We nodded in confident affirmation still sucking on our sweets. All the while, she remained locked behind the office door. We knew full well that once Mrs. Manfred had loosened herself from behind the door, she would confiscate the remainder of whatever was left of the sweets. Once she got her thieving man like hands on them, we both knew that would be the end of them, and we would never see them again.

'So, are they treating you all good?' Dad questioned softly. I felt too afraid to tell him about the bum-stabbing incident, the blows to the stomach, or the abuse in the garden. So, we just answered, 'Yes, Daddy. Everything is fine.'

All you parents must realize that when your child says everything is 'fine', it's more than likely not. I have come to understand that 'fine' is a new word for 'no, it is not'.

As soon as we began to relax in his company it was time for him to go again; we never seemed to have much time with him before it was time for him to leave us again. He would be working that night and needed his rest, so his visit would be cut short from the usual visiting hour. We did not know when we would see him again as his visits had become further and further apart. But his departure did not wound me, and I did not miss him so much as to become so distressed about it. Before he left, he told us that he would return in exactly two weeks to collect us and that we should be packed and ready to leave.

'Really, Daddy?' We both asked together at the same time. I think we must have been really excited at the time. He repeated the statement to Mrs. Manfred, who was still locked in behind the office door.

'OK, Mr. Richardson,' came the old, squeaky voice in response.

'And don't cut their hair again! Don't cut it!' he ordered, shouting through the closed door, banging it with his fist as if making a manual full stop at the end of his sentence.

'Yes, Mr. Richardson. OK then,' came the horse response in a patronizing tone. With that, Dad hugged us both, pulling us in towards him and holding us close to his large chest with his strong arms. Then he kissed us both on our foreheads. His warm innocent hazel brown eyes glazed over with all the frustration and emotion of life, the water waiting for its moment to break forth like a dam, his cheeks damp from hidden tears already spilled, twice removed. There was something very gentle and sincere about him that day. His sweet affection was neither fake nor exaggerated and his vulnerability shone like a lamp in the darkness.

Dad was a very deliberate sort of man. He meant what he said and said what he meant. He was six feet plus tall with an athlete's physic, his hair cut like Elvis and he boasted an amazing permanent tan that caught every female eye. Dad always followed through with his word. It had really hurt him to see us go back and live with strange people again. He had himself been sent away from home as a child for reasons he could not understand and had been made to live with unkind people throughout his youth. Cutting our hair was the one thing he had asked them not to do, and they blatantly and deliberately went against his instructions and his wishes and cut it anyway; they cut it anyway, anyhow so recklessly, so carelessly. Dad was so hurt and let-down and very, very cross – another little piece of him was broken away that day, I guess. He was dealing with things that were clearly out of his control: the ramifications of divorce, separation and now a blended family.

Whilst residing at Dukesbury House, we began to attend Sunday school on a regular basis, and I don't know why but we all really loved it. We loved getting out of the house and enjoyed being out in the fresh air, even if it was just for the short walk there and back. We listened to Jesus stories and ate sweet biscuits, all washed down with diluted orange squash. Vaguely, I remember butting into a conversation once and demanded to know exactly who Jesus was. 'There is no such person,' I blurted out. It's interesting what a four-year-old will say just to get attention. Boy, was I going to find out!

When the fall came, it was decided that we should go to school. I was about four years and two months when I first went to school that autumn. The building was brand new; it was all very organic, but it was also very cold, my body always felt cold when I was there. I remember there were a lot of books, and I loved to turn the pages and take in the smell of the newness of them as well as the bright colorful pictures as they too told their own story, that is apart from the one that the words would also tell. At the end of the day, we would listen to a story told by the teacher, followed by a sing-song also led by the teacher. She would play her guitar and we would sit on the mat and listen, and unknown to me at the time, the music and the songs would minister to me on the inside. Sometimes, when it was too strong, tears would stream uncontrollably down my cheeks yet without sound. If she saw that I was crying, she would stop playing, yet I never wanted her to stop because the music made me feel better inside despite the tears that fell, it was as though her music was healing me. Eventually, I began to hide my face so she would not see my tears. I would become so relaxed that I would fall asleep in the makeshift perfect playhouse neatly parked in the corner of the classroom.

It was at this school that I learnt the song 'Kum ba yah my Lord, kum ba yah' and have carried it in my heart ever since: well, over forty-five years and counting. It would always release my tears no matter how much I fought not to cry. The words were so poignant that they made me feel as though they had real meaning, and that something spiritual was happening; particularly, where the words say, 'Someone is crying, my Lord'.

I think about these words when added to the Word that says, 'When we cry, the angels come and collect up all our tears into bottles and then bring them before our Father, who is in the highest heaven, and HE listens to the cry of each tear'. It seems to indicate that crying is an unknown language – one which only the Father can understand and translate.

It seems amazing – that tears are an unknown language I mean. I think I cannot recall ever hearing more beautiful words that truly display such compassion, such tenderness, such love. Perhaps, subconsciously I was thinking about my own mummy, her tender touch, the warmth of her breath, her loving embrace. Sometimes I do think about her and how she flew away like a frightened, broken bird before I could even draw her face with my finger tips and imprint it on the pages of my mind, where it would remain forever. I am at times angry with Dad for being so harsh with her, and then I'm angry with the church for being so brutal to him. But I do forgive them. I must. I have to.

The statement 'Violence only breeds violence' is no exaggeration. Whatever seeds you sow on the earth are also sown in the spirit and manifest in the flesh. So, whatever you sow, you shall surely reap. Therefore, if you give love, love is what you shall experience, love is what shall come back to you. If you give out violence, then violence is exactly what you shall experience, what will come back to you. Therefore, sow love, give love. For so freely have we received so freely we should give. Our debt to man, is to love each other.

The only memory I have of my mother is when she came to visit us at the nursery. I could sense her gentle spirit without even touching her, and when she reached out and handed me the doll, I wanted to touch her hand. I knew it would be soft and gentle I knew she would welcome me. The gentleness of her spirit evident in her heart reached out towards me. Speaking right into the depth of my own spirit, it was a pure unadulterated love that seemed to seep out of her. I knew intuitively that she would never push me away or try to hurt me. I knew that she would always be kind to me and that she would always permit me to cry upon her shoulder; without a single utterance of a spoken word I knew, I knew in my inner man, I knew in my spirit, I knew in my soul. Nevertheless, I was only permitted to remain in her presence for exactly five minutes. Clearly, it was by no means enough. As the deer pants for water, I needed her. I wanted to be there with her longer yet could not demand it. I needed to be there longer, but we were just not allowed.

In the years that followed, on our coming into maturity, I never asked Odette how it was for her; I don't know why. I'm sure she would have remembered more, being older and all.

Today, I do not know where she has flown to or whether she too has found her final resting place like that of her daughter before her, but she has gone, and I have never seen her since that day, and her face I remember not. I know that she did fight for us and even came back to see us after the great battle of their divorce was finalised, where it was revealed that she had lost... Mum had lost us; she had lost custody of us primarily because of the dark picture Dad's brother had painted of her as some common whore. The judge must have felt he was truly doing justice. Dad still... so fueled with rage, so growing with anger, and so overflowing with fierce unforgiveness, refused to even allow her the courtesy of any kind of access; she was prevented from seeing us, from kissing us goodbye even just once, for the last time. We never saw or heard from her ever again.

The child in me wants to cry out 'Goodbye mummy I love you.' Even now.

I cannot begin to tell you the degree of pain felt in never having had the opportunity to buy mum a Mother's Day card. I cannot begin to tell you the degree of pain felt in knowing there is no mum's shoulder upon which to cry on. I cannot begin to tell you the degree of pain felt in knowing that there is no mum with whom to pray with, best advice to all you ladies who think you know best – hold on to mum.

Back to Dad's Again

Dad returned as promised to remove us from Dukesbury House and take us home again. I'm not sure if it was exactly two weeks later, but I remember Mrs. Manfred fluttering around behind him, like some spooked chicken, all the while ensuring to keep her distance as she called out to ask him what he was doing and kept wanting to know whether he had permission to do what he was doing.

Of course, whilst reminiscing, I do wonder about all the good people we met along the way. I wonder where they all are now. Where are all those wonderful people who helped me, and showed me kindness? I wonder whether they are OK. I guess my thoughts about them would be in the form of a prayer and sound something like this:

'Dear Lord, please bless them and protect them. Bless their children and their grandchildren. Draw them close to you and bind them together forever deep in your love, deep in love with you. Thank you, Lord.'

Deep down, of course I do want to see them all again. I would love to see what they are all doing now. I would love to embrace them all and say thank you.

Remarkably, even at this young age, I now knew the difference between kindness and hostility, love and violence, tenderness, and harshness. The latter of each, both Dad and his new wife seemed to display in abundance.

During the period of the court case, Dad hid us at his friend's house, so no sooner had we arrived back home we were on the move again; his intention was to make absolutely sure our mother did not see us at all, not even for a moment, not even from a distance. Years later I would imagine her walking down the street looking through the front windows and knocking on different doors in search of us. I imagine her tears of frustration and collapsing on the ground at not finding us. I imagine the pain in her womb that carried us. We stayed there for about two weeks; I think. I remember that they had a really nice house. It was clean and tidy, but more than that, it was warm and peaceful, very quiet in fact. We were accepted by all and made to feel very comfortable. We never went hungry. They didn't beat their kids and hardly ever raised their voices, in fact there was no shouting at all. The hallway was covered in a thick burgundy carpet, it was very soft and I liked to walk on it bare foot.

For breakfast, I remember we would always have Rice Krispies, every morning. We ate them out of bowls that resembled little Viking ships, and unbeknown to us, they were in fact real little ships; they were the family ornaments, which in truth were really quite valuable. The bowls did not hold too much at a time, so we always had seconds. These little ships had real little oars that moved. Eating out of them made breakfast time much more enjoyable.

The youngest son was so sweet, he would give us their best silverware to eat with too; he really, honored our being there. He was so sweet. And yes, I do wonder where they all are now. We would always eat breakfast in our pajamas which was really, nice as soon as we got up in fact this became our daily routine every morning.

We would be so excited about breakfast. There was no waiting or hunger pangs, no drooling saliva, and no yellow vomit. His siblings, as well as their parents, were so very nice to us. There was nothing false or temporary about their kindness; it was really, genuine – heartfelt in fact. I felt their empathy for us; I had not experienced this before.

I knew I was safe here, and in my heart, I wished we could have stayed forever because to me even at the tender age of four I knew that this was the perfect home. Even though I loved Dad, I knew where I wanted to live, and it was right here with these lovely people and not with him. This was not because I didn't love him, but because I did.

When Dad eventually came to collect us, I remember asking him if we could stay with his English friends forever. His answer was an unequivocal and very resounding 'No!' It rang out in my ears like the bells of St Clements. However, I kept on and on and on, until about the fourth or fifth request, whilst on route back home, he shook me rather hard by the arm and became a tad more annoyed with me than he had been previously when he arrived. He warned me sternly not to mention them ever again. I began to cry. I think I cried all the way home. It was a very long walk back to Dad's house.

I obeyed him as far as not mentioning them again, although I could not help but feel a deep sense of sadness, a deep sense of loss. It was like something good had gone out of my life and I had no idea if it would ever return. I continued to think about them until the experience became no more than a distant oasis amongst the memoirs of my mind.

So now we were back at Dad's again, this time for perhaps three years. I don't remember exactly because birthdays were never marked or celebrated. There were no cakes or presents, and no one ever said, 'It's your birthday, happy birthday!' There was no happy birthday song. I had to rely on strangers to tell me my age, and the next time that I would be told my age would be at a place called Sandy Lodge.

Dad had a new place now. He had upgraded from the two rooms in the house of the landlord where we had all lived together. At this time, the political climate was that the Government had begun investing into the building of huge estates; that was flats on top of flats, flats opposite flats and flats beside flats. Every available space was to be built on with a block of flats or a tower of flats. They were grey, dull, and ugly, totally without character or beauty. It was a quick political response to dealing with the shortage of housing after the second world war. They were absolutely massive; you could literately walk across three blocks from one end to another without touching the ground.

Dad had a three up and two down with bathroom, extra loo, and a balcony. All three rooms were generous in size. We had no one above us, thankfully, but we did have neighbors below us and on both sides. The three short years would tick by until it was time for us to leave again. We would find out later the real truth, of our coming and going.

Christmas time was the same. For the three years that we spent at home Dad would buy a tree, and Mordecka would decorate it, but they never invited either of us to help or to take part. The closest I could get to taking part seemed to be walking past the tree as I entered the kitchen and came out again. Mordecka would place the presents underneath it, none of which were ever for Odette or me.

I remember one year there were three presents under the tree; none of them had any names on. Somehow, I became obsessed with believing that one, just one, was for me; I mean I so desperately wanted to believe it. Every day leading up to Christmas I would pick up the presents which were not named and say this one is for Odette this one is for me and the largest one is for our brother Bobby. By the time Christmas Day arrived, the presents were handed out. We sat there like lemons in foolish expectation. They were all for my brother. It was as though we did not exist. It was as though we weren't even there.

The following year, there were four presents under the tree. Mordecka's brother and his wife were spending Christmas with us that year. The good news was that we would not be beaten as long as our house guests remained. They had brought three presents with them– one for our brother, one for my sister, and one for me. However, both Mordecka and Dad had also brought a present each for our brother, so he now had three, and the two of us just had one each. When I opened mine, inside was a plastic knitting set, with hardly any wool included, I mean the entire length of the wool was almost the length of the needle, so it was practically impossible to knit anything; the packet read 'Made in China'. My brother received a great giant truck and a car and some other toy, I cannot remember what. Odette received a set of marbles. Clearly, not an ideal or well-thought-out present for a little girl, but at least it was better than the year before, when we both received – absolutely nothing. Being back at home was really quite awful; there was never anything good, and every Christmas and birthday was a pessimistic reminder of how much you were really valued really loved and just how awful it really was.

Mordecka had several brothers; some of whom had made the trip to England with her, and when she found out that one of her brothers was going to be alone during the Christmas period after the break-up of his own marriage, it was agreed that he would spend it with us. His name was Uncle Norman. He was tall, eccentric and had loads of big dark fluffy hair, which almost covered his entire face. He arrived the day before Christmas. When the door was opened, we found a pair of very long legs which went all the way up to meet a very large brown box that he was holding, and which completely covered his face and torso. He had a slight problem getting in through the door, but once he was in, out came an extremely large color TV. Excitement filled the air as he connected the wires and turned it on.

Uncle Norman wore his hair in an Afro and would allow us to touch it if we were good. It was so soft, just like marshmallows. When we asked him how he managed to keep it so soft, his answer was very brief. 'Daz.' Of course, we roared with laughter as we both knew that Daz was soap powder used for washing clothes. *However, I did try using it myself once or twice after leaving home.*

With Uncle Norman in the house, things would be much calmer. Dad would not raise his voice, and no one got beaten. Uncle Norman was very charismatic and exceptionally funny. 'Stand-up comedian' – no problem. Richard Prior and Eddie Murphy eat your heart out.

Along with the TV, inside the huge box were several very strong alcoholic drinks, which when Dad was not around, he would introduce us to. I found they always made my eyes water and took my breath away, and some even burnt the back of my throat. But Odette kept trying them one after the other. I was quite surprised that she never looked tipsy; albeit I was not too fond of this game: His company was great though, and it was nice to watch things in color on the big screen for a change.

One year, he brought a very large, very expensive bottle of champagne; it was beautiful. I certainly wanted more... I always felt he silently understood what we were really, going through despite not saying anything, and I always wished he could have stayed for ever. Life was just that bit more bearable, just that bit more breathable when he was around.

The last time we saw him, we begged him not to go. We held on to his trousers and dragged along behind him as he walked towards the front door as if wearing two large human boots. Upon approaching the door, he looked down at us and said, 'If I don't leave now, I will not be able to come back and visit you next year.' So, filled with an added slice of sadness, we released him and let him go.

After his departure, Bobby came running in asking whether I wanted any more champagne; well, of course I did, it was so delicious, like velvet on your tongue. He handed me the very large bottle and said I had to drink from it; it was very heavy. I placed the open rim of the extra-large very heavy dark green bottle on to my lips, opened my mouth wide, and knocked my head straight back aiming for the biggest gulp I had ever taken or could ever take. The thick liquid entered my mouth and hit the back of my throat, like a match to its box.

I swallowed hard coming up for a breath of air, but there was none to be had. It was in that moment that I realised that in fact it wasn't champagne, but it was something far more sinister, something far more ugly – it was washing up liquid.

'Oh no!' I thought. My evil little brother had mixed washing up liquid and a little water with the last drop of champagne that remained in the bottle. I went to tell him off, but only bubbles came pouring out of my mouth each time I attempted to speak. Both he and my sister were now laughing hysterically, as I continued speaking bubbles; *you could only imagine the scene.*

My throat felt as though it was on fire. I ran to the sink to wash out my mouth but to no avail, only more bubbles came pouring out, increasing in size; both Bobby and Odette fell about in complete hysterics of laughter. I started to cry; I was unable to contain the burning sensation in the back of my throat. My eyes were red sore and watering. It was only at this point that Odette began to realize the seriousness of my predicament and began to help me. She came up with the wonderful idea of placing my head under the bath tap and turning on the cold water fast with my mouth wide open under it. Our parents were upstairs in the room next door so we could not all plough into the bathroom together in case they became suspicious and a beating would certainly follow. In the end, I think she gave me some milk which helped reduce the burning sensation.

Can't Cook? Please Don't Try

When a man marries a woman, it is usually a bonus if she can cook and more so if she can cook well. Sadly, Dad's new wife did not behold many of the qualities or attributes that one might expect to find in a wife and mother. In fact, she could not cook to save her life. The one meal she honestly believed she could cook and cook rather well was the traditional Bayesian dish, 'Cornmeal' or 'Cook Coo' to you and me. It was a dish consisting of a clay-like yellow substance or '*muck*' for short adorned with okra, which resembled green slimy bogies. It would normally be served with any white over-cooked fish and in its entirety stunk to high heaven, closely resembling that of set vomit, which if thrown could definitely cause an injury or two.

Not really sure if this was the Caribbean take on fish and chips, but without the chips of course; just a lump of clay instead perhaps. However, I remember quite vividly – one evening, Dad began screaming at her. 'Is this the only dish you can cook?' he questioned, almost screaming in a very high-pitched tone. Indicating he had had enough.

'*Yes!* '*I* thought, '*you tell her!*' I tell you the truth; it was some crazy messed-up dish that certainly did not have a hope in hell of featuring in any cooking program ever, neither in any cookbook for that matter. In truth, all her cooking was the same – completely and utterly inedible, give you nightmares if you stared at it too long.

Back then, we took all our meals sitting at the long white freezer, facing the wall because, according to Mordecka, there was no room at the table for us.

Nevertheless, it was whilst sitting at this makeshift table that I learnt to scoop up my food, scrape it into my vest and tuck it into my knickers. I would disguise it by pulling my top down over it, walk upstairs to the bathroom, lock myself in, lift the lid, and flush it down the toilet. I would do this several times throughout the meal until all the food was gone. The last bit I would just topple into the bin and cover it with some other rubbish pulled up from the bottom of the bin. Taking the bin to the shoot was bin therapy. I would place the hand rapped parcels of food into the mouth of the shoot as if I was serving customers in a shop calling out the names of imaginary people and reminding them of their orders. 'here you are then Mrs. Thompson, two portions of baked Lasagna with extra Parmigiano Reggiano.' In my mind she would say

'thank you love.'

'Mrs. Wilson 2lbs of pigs trotters, just for you just as you like them'

Thanks, my lovely' she would reply. I would have these conversation until all the rubbish was gone.

I remember, on one occasion, she served up a plate of hard boiled white rice with a great big silver-colored fish, plonked on top of it with fins, tail, and eyes, still all intact. I could not believe it; I think I must have been about five at the time. I remember just staring down at the plate of food. I had never seen a real fish this close-up before. It stared up at me, and I looked down at it, eyeball to eyeball. It was all so daunting. *Perhaps a more pressing thought was that I had no idea of exactly how I was going to fit that fish into my knickers or even flush it down the toilet for that matter.*

Suddenly, my thoughts became distracted by a very loud, very heated conversation that Dad and Mordecka were having in the lounge. It had just turned into a shouting match, and they were going at it like cat and dog. It was as though someone had turned up the volume. I don't know what they were arguing about, when suddenly, Mordecka shouted out from the top of her voice, '… and by the way, I am not *ya all* mother! My name is Mordecka. *Ya all* mother left on the bus! But you can call me Aunty Mordecka.'

I could not really, comprehend exactly what her words meant or the far-reaching ramifications of them. It all sounded like gobbledygook to me. I mean I was just five years at the time.

We got down from our makeshift table, and Odette boldly scraped up all the food from both our plates into the bin and covered it with some other rubbish. She briefly tidied the kitchen, and I followed her upstairs, asking her repeatedly, as we went, to explain what had just happened, and what it all meant. After about the fifth request and her fifth response, she became rather annoyed. Still feeling very confused and puzzled, I left it at that. Eventually, she said, 'Look! She is not our mother! All right! Do you get it now?'

'Then who is our mother?' I asked, 'Where is she? What's her name?' My questions continued, 'who is that woman?'

In truth, Odette did not have all the answers or the patience. Clearly, she must have been experiencing her own kind of grief as well and in her own way. But in that moment, I probably never felt so displaced in my entire life as how I felt back then. 'She could never be my mother anyway!' I added angrily. 'She is too mean to be my mother!' Right there in that moment, in our hour of need, there was no one there to console us, not even a soft toy, no one to explain things properly, and no one to give us a hug and say, 'Don't worry about this. Everything is going to be all right, OK.' Dad didn't say a word. We just had to get through it the best way we knew how. The truth was we didn't and our friend as far-reaching as she was, would catch-up to us in time, and the clock was ticking…tick tock..tick..tock.

To look at, Mordecka was about 5', 11" tall, a very full woman in fact, she had massive thighs, a massive bum, and massive breasts. Her complexion was a permanent medium tan; perhaps one of the most noticeable things about her when she opened her mouth, was that she had a full set of perfect white teeth, but no hair. She would try to conceal this fact whenever she went out with what we later found out to be a wig set in the style of a Michael Jackson afro.

It was about this time that the beatings began to increase as did the segregation. If a glass broke, we got beaten. If my brother cried, we got beaten. I would blame Odette, and she would blame me and so on and on it went, and we would both get a beating. It was about this time too that it came to Dad's realization with Mordecka's help no doubt that someone was wetting the bed. When questioned, at approximately 2 am being the second hour of the day or rather the middle of the night whilst still half asleep, we both denied the accusations. Then came the bombardment of threats and I think I owned up just to keep the peace so we could all go back to sleep, whilst Dad was prepared to accept my confession Mordecka was *not* so easily convinced; intuitively she blamed Odette and well that was it. She would always blame Odette for everything.

I remember that Mordecka told Odette to make a makeshift mattress on the floor from the pages of the Daily Mail; it consisted of all the day's news; it was thrown down on top of a sheet of plastic spread out on the floor at the end of our bed right by the door to catch the draft. Odette was expected to sleep down there with no covers, no pants, and no pajama bottoms either. On one occasion, she was even made to sleep in the bathtub and on another sitting on the toilet all night. The worst thing was when she was made to sleep outside on the balcony. It was freezing out there. I mean we used to set jelly out there because it was that cold and in winter you could actually freeze things out there. I think she must have been about nine years old then; it was absolutely awful, and I felt so helpless. She had on no shoes, no pajama bottoms, and no knickers either. She would be wearing no more than a tiny little vest, a bit like a midriff, the kind you young girls wear in summer to show off your tummy's.

I would give her my blanket. In winter, it was the worst. I was always so cold that I would pull my slip of a nightdress down over my knees and try my best to keep warm with my knees pulled up to my chest and I would try hard to sleep, the thought of it all now still makes me cry; too afraid to pull the under sheet up around me just in case I got caught, we suffered in silence. But however, it was for me, I was sure it was a hundred times worse for Odette, who was standing outside half naked and bare foot on the freezing cold concrete balcony. I remember one night, which was particularly cold, Odette burst in from the balcony like a sudden wind and collapsed on the floor directly in front of the door. She was so cold that she could not even close the door behind her. Each night, as soon as Dad left for work, Mordecka would send her out there; I could feel myself screaming inside for someone, anyone, to help, to do something, anything. However, the thought of praying never crossed my mind.

One night, quite unexpectedly Dad returned home much earlier than usual. I mean his shift hadn't even fully started yet. He came straight upstairs, went into the bedroom, went over to the window, and looked outside. It was as if someone was leading him, directing him. It was as if he knew without even being told. He saw Odette standing there half naked, and at the top of his voice, he ordered her to come inside and told her never to go outside again, regardless of who said what! When he questioned Mordecka about what Odette was doing outside, she lied and said that she never told her to go outside, but the truth was that she most certainly did, and we all knew it. Dad really shouted at her over this incident. Clearly, she deserved it. I think I wanted them to break-up over this. Dad told Odette never to go outside on the balcony ever again, no matter who told her to. However, Mordecka's warped behavior did not stop there.

On another occasion, she did not give us anything to eat for two whole weeks. We hardly saw our Dad during that period; clearly, they must have been going through some more ups and downs. We were told not to venture downstairs under any circumstances. Obedient Odette faithfully kept this commandment like the good dutiful daughter. I, on the other hand, could not keep it up any longer. By the Sunday beginning the second week, the aroma of Sunday dinner was mouth-wateringly overwhelming. I crept downstairs in darkness and saw that a plate of food had been left on the stove. It started off with me believing that I would have just one mouthful, but it ended with me licking the plate so clean it required no washing.

When Dad did eventually return home, some fourteen days later, he came straight upstairs to our room to check on us. He asked us whether we had eaten to which I answered no. Odette was too weak to get out of the bed or to even answer him. He asked how long it had been since we had eaten. 'Two weeks,' I responded confidently. Somehow, it sounded far better than fourteen days. I had a bit more energy than Odette mainly because I had eaten someone's dinner two nights before – whose I don't know. I had tried my best to save some for Odette, but I could only manage five grains of rice and a shriveled-up tomato skin. I was so hungry that I just swallowed the food down whole without even chewing it. I couldn't stop myself. My taste buds were jumping around all over the place. Of course, the tomato skin and five rice grains were not going to revive Odette, *but I didn't know that then.*

Water Farm Primary

Before we started school, we were always allowed out to play on the estate which they had not yet finished building. We would often go out to play with the children of the families who began to fill up the same landing that we lived on. We were always in and out of each other's houses, which were almost maisonettes, meaning, two up and two down except these had four up and three down. As we popped in and out of our neighbor's houses we would have a share in their spoils, which often included chocolates and sweets as well as jam filled sandwiches; and whilst out playing we would ask complete strangers for money so that we could buy ice cream from the ice cream van when it came around. Strangely though, it was always middle-aged African men who responded generously to our requests. Our Dad never knew if he did, he would certainly kill us or so we thought.

One of our favorite games was hide-and-seek; this was living life in the fast lane for us preschool kids, until one day, I got stuck in the mud; this, however, was no ordinary mud, it was sinking mud, and Odette had to pull me out. It came right up, past my knees, it was really frightening. Lucky for me she was nearby to save me when I called out.

When we arrived home that day, our liberal Dad suddenly turned and said, 'That's it. You can't go out to play no-more.' I remember vaguely some talk of other children being injured in the sinking mud. So, that was it. From that moment, onwards, we just had to watch the other children play from our bedroom window. This torment lasted right up until the end. The other unsavory rule Dad made that day was that we were not allowed to use the lift either; apparently, somebody got stuck in that too... This time for hours and the caretaker was nowhere to be found; probably because he also had a real job on the side, as well as being the caretaker of the block, which no one ever really took too seriously in those days. Apparently, the fire brigade had to attend and rescue them. *How embarrassing!*

The night before the day we were to start school, we were both bathed, had our hair washed and plaited, and our clothes were ironed and neatly set out for the morning. Dad seemed really, proud. But before we retired to bed, Dad decided that he would give us some simple mental arithmetic and ask us to recall the letters of the alphabet. First, he asked Odette to count to a hundred and then past one hundred and then he asked her to say her alphabet forwards and then backwards and then he would randomly call out the number to which the letter of the alphabet related; and just like an obedient puppy retrieving the ball, she would call out the matching letters, and of course, she never made a mistake because at just six years old, she was brilliant. I was overwhelmed; I couldn't keep up. When Dad turned to me to repeat the process, I just burst into tears because I knew I certainly could not beat her nor match her.

On our first day at school, we were both placed in the reception class together. I was swept off my feet with all the toys to choose from. I spent most of my time in the playhouse, setting the table and sharing out pretend food and pouring out make-believe cups of tea in front of the dolls and the teddy bear, it was a busy life. In the afternoons when all the other children went off to learn their A, B, Cs on the mat in front of the teacher, I stayed and played in the playhouse. I felt too afraid and too intimidated to learn anything. I felt that I just could not do it after my ordeal with dad and so I didn't try.

I remember at the end of the day, we would always have a story on the mat, but I would always fall asleep inside the doll's cot in the playhouse. We had really nice teachers in our school back then. Our teacher was perfectly proportioned in stature. She was medium height and build. She had mousey hair which she wore with a fringe and shoulder length sides and back. She would always be in ankle blue jeans and a shirt, or a jumper if it was cold. Her name was Mrs. Emerson; she had a very kind aura about her, and I felt she really understood the needs of the children of families who had migrated to Britain. She seemed to hold a deep founded respect and understanding for those families who had given up the warmth of their homeland and answered the call to help in the re-building of the British economy. She never forced her authority over us, and she never told me to leave the playhouse, she had a lot of love and was always hugging the children me included, which I loved. They say that hugging is good medicine for the soul.

However, it wasn't long before there were three of us in the playhouse. I now had to learn to share with the other children. The feeling was uncomfortable. I remember one day I got so upset about something or other and started sobbing uncontrollably. My nice teacher picked me up and began hugging me; squeezing me right into her voluptuous breasts, and for whatever reason I knew not, then or now even till this day, I opened my mouth wide and closed it down hard, squeezing her big breast between my baby white milk teeth, even piercing through her sea green prickly jumper right into her skin.

At a guess, I would say that perhaps I was so stressed to the point of beyond frustration; things were just so stressful at home, and 99.9 per cent of the time, I was walking on eggshells even reminding myself of when to breathe. I was plagued with water bumps resembling ugly boil type balls which covered my tiny fingers, the skin from which I had eaten off from almost all my fingers at the knuckles. She pushed me away quickly, and I fell off from her lap and landed on the floor with a thud. I looked up into her sea blue eyes now glazed over. I guess I had blown any future chances of ever being in her warm embrace again.

Many days later, I overheard her telling another teacher, Mrs. Pickard to be exact, what had happened. Mrs. Pickard had short brown hair, cut exactly to her ear and she wore the sides flicked back over them. She was very well to do, always smartly dressed, always in a suit and she spoke as if she had a plum in her mouth. I felt absolutely awful. Mrs. Pickard answered and said, 'Well, you can't go around hugging *them*, now can you? You can't get too close to *them* either.' I felt so bad. I so wanted to make it right but did not know how to. I wanted to say sorry but did not know how.

Eventually, Christmas came, and we all had to bring something in to contribute to the Christmas party. Odette got Mrs. Emerson to write down for Dad the kind of things she wanted us to bring in, and he did not disappoint. He brought in the biggest crate of fairy cakes ever. They were all iced in the brilliant bright colors of Hermes and then the very next day he visited himself and brought in another crate. When we looked into the box, the colors were so vibrant. There were oranges and greens and pinks and blues and yellows. The sponge was so light and fluffy, he said he had made these personally. We were the talk of the school, and for one moment, just one moment, I felt so proud to be his daughter. Everybody was asking,

'Who brought in those cakes?'

'It was the Richardson girls,' our teacher said proudly, giving me a little one-armed hug. I was able to hug her back ever so gently and without biting her this time. I was really proud of myself that day.

The Missing Dinner Money

The new school year started with us being the laughing-stock of the class. After our hair, had almost grown back from the trauma suffered at the hands of the crazy Mrs. Manfred. Dad decided that it had not grown right so the night before school he shaved our heads completely. We could not believe it. We tried to keep our hats on for as long as we could but Mrs. Wilkey our new teacher wasn't having any of it. From the moment, we were told to remove our hats the class would roar with laughter. It didn't stop until Anna arrived who was also placed at our table.

Thankfully, Anna took the heat off for a while as she would not stop crying. I think she had never been separated from her mother before. Odette was then moved over to Mrs. Pickard's classroom, once the age difference was realised. The classrooms were still connected via the cloakrooms and the utilities area.

During our time at home, not only did we never receive Christmas and Birthday presents we never received any pocket money either, and it was always hard seeing the other children eating sweets and chewing gum all the time. We also wanted to eat sweets and chew gum. Noticeably, much of the gum chewed would find its way on to the ground or into the bin. Interestingly enough, upon closer inspection, we found that much of the bubble gum on the ground had not been properly chewed through, so we would frequently pick it up from the playground floor or take it out of the bin in the hope that it had landed on paper so that it would not have any grit on it, but in any event, we would still stretch it out under cold, running water and wash it, picking off any major grit or hair or other unsavory items of debris that could seriously interfere with the whole chewing experience, and then we would chew it, showing off by blowing huge bubbles. We did this for weeks until I realised that there were always spare coins on the teacher's desk, or so I thought.

Mrs. Wilkey was of medium height and build, perhaps more pear shaped than turnip shaped. She had mousey hair down to the shoulder, flicked over at the sides – it appeared to be the style of the 1970s. She spoke with a husky voice and always smelt of smoke. It was easy to arrive at the conclusion that she was disorganized as her desk was always in a mess, upon closer inspection I noticed that she had plenty of coins strewn all over it. They didn't seem to move or ever be put away. I began to believe that these coins did not belong to anyone because they were always there, so I thought that I could use them to purchase my own sweets and gum. I thought that I would get called to the teacher's desk by raising my hand and then pick up some of the odd coins at the same time before returning to my own table.

When I went up to her desk, I noticed that some of the coins had been put into little bags. And Mrs. Wilkey herself being quite scatty to the point where I was able to remove from her desk something like six bags of coins right in front of her face while she was seated at her desk. There were two bags each of five-pence coins, ten-pence coins, and fifty-pence coins. However, not being the brightest button in the room, I placed them all into a white plastic bag that held my plimsolls. I left the bag hanging up on the coat rack which was situated directly outside the side entrance to the classroom through which the children would enter and exit if they were going out or coming in after each play time.

I was about six years old at the time and had no idea of what the ramifications of my actions would be, or in fact that they even existed.

However, within approximately two minutes of returning to my table, I noticed that Mrs. Wilkey was trying to remain calm. Her voice was fading in and out of consciousness as she kept repeating the question of whether anyone had seen the bags of coins, which up to a moment ago were on her table. Oops, suddenly I felt that I had made a big boo-boo – *a mistake.*

When questioned, everyone was answering no, no, and no, they had not seen it. It was then that I realised that in fact I had made a big mistake; the coins were important. The teacher needed them. How was she going to get the coins back now? I really wanted to help Mrs. Wilkey but did not know what to do. Trying to remain calm, she began asking the children one by one whether they had seen the dinner money.

When Mrs. Wilkey finally got around to asking me whether I had seen the coins, I said absolutely nothing. Mrs. Wilkey then assembled the children in alphabetical order according to the positioning of their names in the register and ordered them one by one to retrieve their hats, coats, and bags from off the coat rack and then to line-up, in a straight line. Then all the children were frisked and searched like common criminals. My bag was the last to be taken down as my name was the last to be read from the register; there were no surnames past the letter R. I knew that the coins were in my bag. I could feel my heart beating faster and faster within the inner cavity of my chest wall.

I really, wanted to fix the situation, but just did not know what to do. I really, wanted to own up to it but fear held me back. I wanted to say, 'I'm sorry, it's me.' but did not know how to or even what to say or to whom. The one thing that was clear was that I was guilty. I walked over to the coat rack and took down only my coat and hat before returning to stand in line, completely ignoring the white plastic bag. Then the teacher from my sister's class, Mrs. Pickard asked, 'Isn't that your plastic bag, Jacqueline?' where did she come from I thought. Mrs. Pickard, I remembered from the previous year – she was a tall woman; this year her brown hair was cut very carefully around her face covering her ears; precision appeared to be everything. My breath was stuck in my throat, and I was unable to answer her.

'No, it's mine,' said another child moving forward to retrieve the bag. For a moment, I breathed what was to be a brief sigh of relief; someone else was going to pick up my bag and take ownership of it and I was not going to be in trouble for once. The other child was now going to get the blame.

'That's not your bag,' piped up Mrs. Wilkey.

'Oh, no,' I thought. The child stopped dead in his tracks and slowly removed his hand from off the white plastic bag, leaving it alone, still hanging there on the coat peg. He said nothing. Yes, in that moment, gripped by fear, I was about to let someone else take the blame for my own wrongdoing. *'How could I?'*

'That is Jacqueline's plimsoll bag,' said Mrs. Wilkey, quite sternly.

'That is your bag, isn't it?' she asked rather tersely, as if almost demanding confirmation.

'Yes, Miss,' I replied, almost whispering, in a soft-spoken voice, not wanting to be overheard and without realizing the full extent of what I had done or the far-reaching ramifications. I walked ever so slowly over to the rack, like a captured prisoner of war about to be shot at dawn. Then after picking up the white plastic bag from off the hook I re-joined the end of the line, my head hanging down low … in apparent shame.

Mrs. Wilkey began to search every coat pocket and peer into every bag with glee. She knew full well that what she was looking for was in *my* bag; in that moment, she reminded me of the busy bush badger, I had seen so many times on the wildlife programs, poking his nose in every den. *Dad always watched them back then.* I stood still, silently at the end of the line without moving. I was the last child to be searched. As she searched each child briefly, trying hard not to rush, looking up at me or in my direction in-between, peering in each child's bag and frisking their pockets, just like the Fantastic Mr. Fox?

As she neared the end of the line, her searching became less and less thorough. She could no longer contain herself from becoming overwhelmed with the excitement of knowing. She knew and I knew full well who had the dinner money. By the time, she got to the child next to me, she hardly frisked him at all and had to be reminded to look into the bag by the child holding it. 'Oh, yes dear,' she said, grinning like an overgrown Cheshire cat, turning towards me, her grin widening by the second; it was if she was going to eat me - *alive.*

Once she had finally arrived beside me, she let out such a sigh of relief, her eyes almost closing. It wasn't hard to guess that she must have heard the change jingle in the plastic bag as it was taken down from the coat rack. She did not look into the bag; neither did she search me. She simply summoned me over to her desk. As I walked across the classroom, I could hear the whispers,

'It's Jacqueline'.

'It's Jacqueline'.

'It's Jacqueline', racing around the classroom, like a train that could not be stopped.

Mrs. Wilkey told the class to sit down and be quiet; and to get on with some work. She then began to unload the bags of coins from out of the white plastic bag back onto her desk causing each one to make a distinctive clunk on to her desk as it made contact with it, which in turn caused the class to look up and see me standing there. *'How embarrassing'*

In 1971, lunch was just twelve pence per week which equated to sixty pence a month. In that moment, I felt ashamed, embarrassed, and humiliated. *'What on earth was I thinking?'* I thought. I had never wished so hard in all my young life that right then in that moment that the earth could have opened and just swallowed me up, I needed a Jonah in the whale moment right then. I had asked myself that question *'Why?'* so many times. *Why on this earth had I done this?* Even to this day, I still had no answer. My teacher also wanted the same question answered, but again, I could give no answer for I had none. Perhaps, I had watched too many 'Westerns', or perhaps I just wanted to buy some sweets like normal children did. OK, a lot of sweets. Only God knew.

In truth, it was never my intention to take all the bags of coins. I had no idea that this was the dinner money belonging to the entire class to pay for their lunches for the week or month. I only intended to take a few abandoned silver coins just to get some sweets. What had started out as a simple intention had now turned into a living nightmare, and of course, according to the teacher and the principal, I had committed the worst offence ever known to mankind, and of course, I was certainly made to feel it because things were about to get a whole lot worse.

The teacher began to count out the dinner money aloud. I was reminded of the nursery rhyme 'The king was in his counting house, counting out his money!' I had only seen it in 2D, but right now, I was living it live, in action. Just then, Mrs. Pickard, the other teacher, asked who else had been involved in this act, which by now was beginning to feel a bit like high treason, which was last committed in the United Kingdom in 1946 and certainly not by a child. She also began to attach my sister to the charge list.

'Tell me the truth!' she snapped. 'It was your sister, wasn't it? Wasn't it?' she hissed.

'Yes,' came my whimper of a response. From that moment on, I seemed to involve my sister in all my troubles, and together, we shared in all my punishments, with Odette always taking the brunt of the force with every beating, yet never complaining.

Then Mrs. Wilkey began to complain that another twenty pence was still missing, but I quickly pointed to where I had seen it roll under some muddled paperwork strewn over her desk.

'Oh,' she said, coming down from off her pretentious high, *not induced by amphetamines.* After finally confirming that all the money was present and accounted for, she then escorted me personally to the principal's office, and after admitting to the principal that Odette had also been involved, she too was summoned to the principal's office. Poor Odette – she had no idea of what had happened or why she was being summoned. We were just 6 and 7 years old.

I remember asking the same question repeatedly,

'Are you going to tell our Dad?' I asked anxiously.

'Are you going to tell our Dad?' We both asked again. Our questions fell on deaf ears as there was no forthcoming answer. I was more afraid of what he would do as opposed to what any teacher could ever do. It was only the school secretary who appeared to have any compassion for us in this situation. She asked whether our Dad would be very upset, to which we answered with a categorical 'Yes!' both nodding our heads in unison.

'Would he be upset to the point of being physical with you?' she enquired further. We looked at each other, knowing the full meaning of the word without even having heard it, before looking back at her and answering 'Yes,' in a whisper.

We spent four long days in the principal's office – seven hours each day, with no breaks, no refreshments, just our lunch which was taken in a small corner of the hall, all alone, after everyone else had eaten and gone. It was whatever had been left over, and it was always cold; my stomach felt cold as I swallowed. It was awful.

Every morning, as soon as the class register was taken, we were asked to go directly to the principal's office. It felt like a game of Monopoly: 'Do not pass go! Do not collect £200! Go straight to jail!' Only this time, in this situation, jail was the principal's office and there was no get-out-of-jail free card. The principal, from time to time, would march into the office and ask several questions to which she demanded immediate answers to explain our behavior. It probably could be compared to being in the army. Unfortunately, we had no answers, Odette had none because she was not actually involved and I had none because I was living in constant confusion, I never knew why I did half the things I did.

It was during her first visit that she demanded the clothes from off our backs. At first, we were unsure as to how to interpret this request or how even to respond to it. We just sat there frozen, not knowing how to respond.

'Take your clothes off now!' she snarled. We started to cry as we began to open the zips of our matching floral dresses. We began to remove the pretty matching floral-print dresses ever so slowly in the hope that she just might change her mind halfway through. But alas, how wrong could we have been, that certainly did not happen, and now we were both crying uncontrollably. Before the task was complete, she helped us to remove the last part of the dresses briskly and with some force; then she whisked them away with the same unpleasant breeze that had accompanied her when she came in. When she came in the second time, she demanded our shoes and socks, leaving us only wearing our pants and vest. It was very cold in her office. We would remain there all day, only being let out to use the toilet. In that instance and at the insistence of the secretary, we were handed back our clothes to use the toilet. No sooner had we returned we had to take them off again and hand them back to her. I remember feeling very cold and very tired just waiting and hanging around in the office all day, every day. In order to preoccupy myself I would play with the ornaments on her shelf.

On one occasion, she turned up completely out of the blue and unannounced, my hand shook and a few of the ornaments dropped to the floor and broke. I quickly scarpered back to the sofa unsure if a sudden whack across the shoulders would follow and started crying again; the principal gave me one of those '*I will kill you later*' looks and then left the room, the cold air following her. At the end of each day, our clothes were handed back to us to enable us to go home.

It was not long before we learnt that the principal had a reputation of making naughty little children stand outside her office, wearing nothing more than their vest and underpants. However, it was usually just the boys; I never saw any girls ever standing outside her office with or without clothes on.

The principal's methodology was simple – punishment through humiliation. I guess we should have been thankful that at least we were permitted to remain in her office throughout our punishment as warped as it was and for not having to stand in the hallway with all the naughty boys or in full view of all the passers-by.

Miss Du-prey was the unforgiving principal back then; I couldn't remember her face, as my eyes never went past the hem of her skirts. Until she came down to my level to ask me a question. It was then I noticed that her hair was short, brown in color with some Betty Boo-style curls at the front and sides. She was indeed a very fit woman, who was well built on every level and always wore a suit, mainly browns and burgundies; her shoes were raised up from off the ground by a 2.5-inch heel exactly, which were also usually brown in color, and they made a kind of knocking sound when she walked. Apparently, they helped shape her legs, which she kept covered in sheer seamed 10 denier Tivoli stockings, making them look longer and slender despite not actually having any shapely calf muscles in either leg.

It was at the start of the fifth day, and after some serious reflection – and perhaps more after a well-rehearsed apology, which was directed and edited by the secretary, who clearly felt even more compassion for us after getting to know us during those five days, which were indeed remembered as five of the longest days of my young life – we were finally permitted to apologize to the headmistress and do so rather profusely.

'We will never do anything like this ever again,' we promised, despite Odette not actually having done anything.

'I sincerely hope not!' she stomped without any compassion and even less forgiveness. It was then that we were permitted to return to our respective classes. She handed us back our clothes and gave us a couple of minutes to get dressed. She then marched us down the long corridor, like two little soldiers who had lost their company and with her shiny shoes knock, knock, knocking on the cold shiny floor as she went.

The door to the classroom swung open, and she stood in the doorway with an unmistakable countenance like that of Adolf Hitler, with each of us at either side, now transformed little puppies. She stared out at the class and waited patiently for their silent attention. Eventually, all conversations in transit ceased and all heads turned eastward to see who was about to enter the classroom; all eyes were on me, it was awful; I felt like I was on show or something but not because I had done anything good, quite the opposite in fact.

Of course, the principal did tell our Dad with dire results; and yes, we were beaten black and blue and back to black again. We both suffered raised welts on our arms and legs and bruises to our heads and shoulders and grazes to our backs, and we had bruises on top of bruises and we still had to continue to go to school like that – feeling very sore to the touch and in a lot of pain. Participation in games was nigh impossible. It was during that beating that Dad caught my finger with his elected tool of discipline, preventing me from being able to bend it from that day to this.

After some time, the swellings did go down, they always did; it was only the emotional scars that would remain from that day on. Whatever my condition after a good beating, it was always Odette who would be first on the scene to administer first aid – I would lie there lapping it up like a hungry little puppy – although she never allowed me to do the same for her. Odette always suffered in silence. She didn't just wear the multiple hats you would expect to find in a mother, a best friend, and a sister – she also applied first aid, pulled teeth, and made home-made bandages from toilet paper and old socks as well as sewed up any torn clothing.

However, the methodology for tooth extraction was quite a technical procedure, an operation in itself. First, she would unwind some cotton thread from off another garment; or if she could get into Mordecka's needlework box, she would pull plenty of cotton from off the reel. She would tie one end on to the door handle and the other end to my wobbly tooth. Then she would sit me down on the edge of the bed, and then - without a word of warning, she would slam the door shut as hard as she could, resulting in my tooth being ripped right out of my mouth, root, and all, in one short, sharp, sweep – ingenious! It was so quick and never really hurt, apart from the time when the door didn't slam shut, it simply bounced back open again whacking me right on the center of my forehead, knocking me over and right off the other side of the bed with feet up in the air. *You can just imagine the scene.* At least Odette found it funny: it was good to hear her laugh out loud.

Once back in the classroom, I was given the cold shoulder by everyone, including the class teacher. No friendships had actually been forged before this point, so no real love lost there then. This being the first class after reception no bonding had actually taken place yet either. Time spent at school up until that point had been no more than just acknowledging familiar faces and trying to comfort those who could not get over losing their mummies for seven hours a day Monday to Friday. Nevertheless, the icy treatment continued even for some time after that – until one-day Sally Featherstone, a thin girl from Ghana, who wore cotton wrapped around her hair, piped up and started talking in my defense in yet another debate that had commenced concerning my crazy actions.

All those participating were seated at the same table with me, and it included Tommy, Brian, and Anna, as well as Sally.

'It's not her fault you know,' said Sally, referring to me as if I was not at the table or even in the room for that matter.

'It's not her fault, she hasn't got any money,' she added sympathetically. 'I mean, what did you expect her to do?'

'Well, it's wrong,' said Tommy Lee, wearing a bad Leo Sayer hair day. 'She should have asked!' he affirmed, his curly fringe meeting his long lashes.

'Like she is really going to ask,' said Anna, in her strong Welsh accent now peppered with a London tone, also taking up my banner. 'I mean, what did you expect her to say? 'Oh, excuse me, can I borrow your dinner money please? I just need to buy some sweets, you know. Get real!' she blurted.

Anna was a slim girl with jet black hair, which she kept neatly pinned back, with one 1930s sweeping wave held in place by a plain gold plaited clip, which she wore to the right. She would always be in a cotton dress cut to just past her knees with white ankle socks and red buckle sandals. Before long, an argument ensued with me right in the middle of it.

'Look, look, you guys,' I interrupted timidly. 'Guys, guys, please, I'm really sorry, but can we please change the subject now?' I asked.

'I mean, she's only six!' Sally added.

'That's enough talking over there,' the teacher said in a raised penciled tone. Silence fell like a blanket; they all bowed their heads in unison and continued to work on their projects, which ironically were pig-shaped money boxes made from papier-mâché, which when dried would be painted and glazed over. A small incision would be made in the top for coins.

Remarkably, no one said another word, at least, not for the rest of the lesson anyway. The good news was that Sally, Anna, and me *all* became best friends; from this point on, we would sit together during lessons; we even moved our book drawers next to each other's, took lunch together, and spent every play time together.

This entire incident was one of the worst things that ever happened at Water Farm Primary. Perhaps that's why I remembered it so vividly. I was just six years old at the time, and Odette was seven. The good news was that I had made a best friend or two, and for the first time the school learnt the truth, that we were being violently abused at home.

It was not too long after that, the class teacher left the school. The class did not know why she left; we were not informed about it. Some said that she felt guilty that we had got beaten, and others said she was asked to leave because she was a bit scatty and kept losing the dinner money. Others said that she went to have a baby and start a family. Who knows? Who really cares anyway? She left and was replaced by a Mr. Malcolm. He was really thin and really tall. He had straight brown hair that covered his ears down each side from the center of his head, from where it was perfectly parted. The wave or quiff to the front curtained almost around his forehead, stopping timely at the top of the metal rim of his squared framed glasses. His hair was always greasy, and he always wore the same green polyester blazer over his green jumper and grey shirt, which he always wore with a tie and which he never seemed to remove even on the hottest of days. He had several gaps between his teeth, but these did nothing to subtract, or remove, or take away anything at all from his kindness, his compassion, or his understanding of those experiencing what could only be determined as a dysfunctional life.

On the day that he almost removed his polyester blazer, the class gasped in complete and utter shock which then nose-dived into a sigh as he did no more than to shuffle in it. I found that I got on rather well with Mr. Malcolm. To me, in my world, he was the only person who seemed to really understand me. He always allowed me to have a nap during story time at the end of the day.

The truth be known, I just could not help it really; whenever the class was quiet and the teacher was either talking or reading out loud in slow rhythmic decibels, I would fall into a daydream or simply nod off. His voice was very calming, and he read rather well too, paying attention to pace, rhythm, and tone. His methodology was to hug you when you were upset, and for a child who was not used to being hugged, who, in fact, had no other form of human contact, this could quite easily become addictive as it soon proved to be. And despite feeling very strange, it felt equally very nice and therefore left you feeling that you always wanted more. He wanted the best for his students – which was echoed through his actions he was always encouraging us to do better, to be better, and to reach higher. He was patient and kind and he would explain things several times in different ways until you got it. He was indeed one of my best teachers that I would ever meet.

Where are you now, Mr. Malcolm? I want to hug you back right now and say a big thank you to you; where are you now, Sir? You were there when it counted. Thank you, Sir.

Fight Club

I really enjoyed school especially the assemblies and the school dinners, I loved the songs such as 'Ten Thousand Men', 'Morning has Broken', 'Give Me Joy in My Heart Keep It Burning' and 'Sing Hosanna' – they gave me that feel good feeling, like something good was happening on the inside of me and something great was about to happen on the outside of me; nevertheless, I still had to go through phase one of everyone wanting to beat me up, mainly the boys; and it was always the same boy, come to think of it, with me standing my ground. I remember feeling that I just did not want to fight anymore.

I had begun to display terrible temper tantrums. Living with an aggressive father who could fly off the handle at a moment without notice, at any time, for any reason and who usually did, perhaps gave me the impetus to overprotect myself whenever I was outside of my natural environment, the 6x10 feet box room in which we spent most of our time. Anyone whom I could not manage, of course Odette would take them out for me. However, in this instance, she believed that I could take on Richard and win. He was a brown-skinned boy, very tall, and very lanky, and he wore a Jackson 5 Afro; clearly, he too was a fan.

Our first fight was to take place in the break time, but by the time the bell rang, we had not got past the pushing stage. *You know when the crowd encircles you and then it begins to push each of you from behind into each other, it's then you know it's on.* For many of them, this was the most exciting event in the calendar and certainly the most exciting event that they would experience all week. Some of the class instigators would usually arrange for the fight to continue on after school, as in this case. It would normally, commence around the corner from the school gates. The funny thing was that I did not even know Richard; he had done nothing to me, and I had certainly not done anything to him. I did not want to fight him, and I'm sure that he did not want to fight me. But kids being kids, they wanted some action; they were expecting a show.

Not every household owned a black and white back then; so, this was it, real life in color. They surrounded us and began to have their own deliberate debate about who should hit whom first. They told me to hit Richard. I said, 'No, I don't hit first.' Then they told Richard to hit me, but then they retracted the statement because they determined that a boy should not hit a girl first. Then Boris piped up, 'Oh sod this! We will be here all day.' And with that, he gave an almighty shove, so Richard and I collided hard, pushed back, and then started tearing chunks out of each other. Filled with adrenaline, and anxiety, I gave everything I had. He was covered in bloody scratches. I got him down until he cried out for me to get off him. One to me.

Following that, we had another two fights until it was settled who in fact was the toughest in our class; for me this meant I would not have to fight again. I held the title from our year all the way down to Year 1.

To this day, I have no idea where I got the energy or even the strength from. If Richard had not cried out when he did, I certainly was about to.

The fights continued with both girls and boys, and that is the part of primary school life that in truth I did not really care for much. I had enough violence and screaming and shouting at home to contend with, on a consistent basis. I did not want school to begin to mirror my home life too. I remember there was this one boy called Mustafa; he was also brown in skin color and had a really big head. We would call him egghead for fun. Mustafa was extremely aggravating; he really got on all our nerves, and one day, he decided to take me on in the classroom. This was unheard of; every child in the school knew the rules: no fighting in school, but oh no, not Mustafa – dumb arse!

We fought like two wild animals, crashing into tables knocking over chairs. We even rammed each other into the bookcase breaking shelves, knocking out books as we went whirling around as if in a mad uncontrollable storm. We completely deformed the rubbish bin; it was absolutely unrecognizable! Eventually, we were pulled apart by Jessie. Mustafa had cut my face and neck with his nails rather deeply. I was sent downstairs for first aid. However, my only fear at that time wasn't the punishment I may receive in school or even the prospect of what the principal was going to say, or do it was what *Dad* was going to say and do.

His methodology for fighting was, as long as you do more damage to your opponent than he does to you, fighting was justified. In that instance, he would not mind a few scratches. In truth, I hated it. However, if you came off worse than your opponent, then he would add to your humiliation of defeat by adding his own good old hiding on top of what you had just endured at school.

After a while, Mustafa left the school, and all the children were very, very happy. And then there was Boris. He was one rather small boy who just loved to fight; when I think about it, I think he loved that male contact – that male bonding feeling a little too much. He would often start with Lenny, a thin pale white boy with white yellow, cotton wool hair. Lenny was extremely funny. He dressed funny too and always had a story to tell, which was guaranteed to have you in stitches.

I remember that one day we were going around the class, talking about the happenings of our weekend. Lenny began to tell us of an excursion that he had embarked on with his mother and elder brother, who also attended our school; he was in Odette's year. They had begun their journey with the intention of visiting their Nan up North.

When they arrived at the station, they purchased their tickets as normal, went through the barriers as normal and then began the descent down the very long escalators which took you on to the platform at Kings Cross. I had never been on the underground or the escalators, so I had to build a mental picture of everything he was saying in my mind as he spoke.

At some point, during the descent, unbeknown to Lenny, his light cotton trousers had got caught up in the escalator. Apparently, the teeth of the escalator were set apart just a little too wide and as he reached the bottom and attempted to step off the escalator, his trousers remained firmly attached in-between its teeth. In that moment, an anxious tug of war ensued between Lenny and the escalator, his trousers the prize. In a nervous panic, he called out to his brother to assist him.

They worked together now, both pulling at the trousers. They tugged, and they pulled, they tugged, and they pulled; at this point, most of the class were in hysterics, some on the floor in laughter. In the end, it was the escalator that beheld the victory with one smooth action, ripping his trousers clean off his legs and bottom. Lenny was left standing in the station wearing no more than his T shirt and his thick rimmed Y front underpants. With that statement, the entire class erupted with an even louder roar of laughter. Although Lenny escaped unscathed from his ordeal, the downside was that it had cost him his trousers, to which his mother simply said, 'Oh, Lenny, stop being so silly.' In that moment Lenny almost got eaten alive by a real life escalator with real teeth and all his mother can say is 'oh Lenny stop being silly.'

However, upon realizing what had happened, they all had to return home in order for Lenny to put on another pair of trousers. The class, upon imagining the scene, were roaring with laughter; some children had even fallen off their chairs in stitches. From then on, Lenny had built up for himself a bit of a reputation for being a funny storyteller, but someone was jealous, and the clock was ticking…, tick …tock…, tick …tock.

School Dinners

Another good thing that school offered was excellent dinners. They were absolutely delicious. They ranged from roast chicken with gravy to roast lamb with mint sauce to roast beef, all served with their usual partner's roast pots and, sometimes even Yorkshire puds, yummy, and not forgetting, of course, yours truly, the usual suspects, which was always two veg: an unrecognizable combo of either carrots and cabbage, or carrots and peas, or greens and carrots – all half boiled to death, completely devoid of any normal coloring whatsoever.

On Fridays, we always had fish and chips, no matter what the weather, it was religiously served with green peas and finished with tartar sauce. It was always too much for me; I could never finish it. At Christmas, we always had roast chicken with stuffing, roast pots with all the trimmings, followed by mince pies and Christmas pudding with custard. Desserts gave new meaning to the word 'bliss'; they were absolutely heavenly. Every week, they rolled out chocolate cake and chocolate custard; a couple of days later, it would be jam-coated sponges, sprinkled with coconut and served with pink custard; another day, it would be treacle sponge or jam roly-poly also served with lumpy yellow custard, or sometimes we would have jelly and ice cream, or shortbread and ice cream. The list went on.

If you were smart, you could ask the cook to spoon you the custard from the bottom of the pot so as to avoid the lumps and the skin sitting on top. Not only did we always line up for seconds and sometimes even thirds, we would also sneak out of class and climb into the large dustbins parked outside the school in the bin house and continue eating the roast pots and anything else that was thrown away but not damaged.

Sally was in her element; she was simply obsessed by the roast potatoes. I mean, she loved them; once she had realised that even up to twenty minutes after lunch was over, they were still warm outside in the bin it was game on. We would actually climb into the bins to retrieve them. Until she ran off and left me in the bin with no one to help me out. *Thank God for gym class.*

School dinners spoke volumes – it was a new language, no matter what kind of day you were having, they always made it better. Whatever your home life was like or whatever it wasn't, school dinners were that Band-Aid that said, 'There, there, never mind'. It was the song that sang 'Every Little Thing Is Gonna Be All Right', apart from when Howard Cranberry came to sit at your table.

Howard was in our class and always had a runny nose. He would contently allow the mucus to run from his nose, making a positive beeline for his plate, dripping right into the contents of his dinner plate. Yuck! And if this wasn't enough, he would, as if nothing was wrong, just scoop it all up, and mix it all up together with his dinner and eat it: double yuck! It was absolutely disgusting and looked particularly distasteful too. It was enough to put anyone off shepherd's pie – *for life!*

On one occasion, Richard got so angry with him, he demanded he move away from our table immediately. Howard pleaded with him, saying he would not do it anymore, yet he still continued. I could not believe it. *Do you mean he was actually doing this on purpose?* I thought. I honestly thought he couldn't help it as we all did. Then Richard threatened to beat him up in the dinner hall in front of everyone. Well, self- inflicted embarrassment is certainly something you really don't want; it was then that Howard quite remarkably came to his senses and automatically stopped the ongoing episodes of allowing his nose to run into his food as well as sucking it up and swallowing it. We now knew that Howard was an actor; his actions had been calculated and deliberate with the sole purpose of making him the center of attention, a deliberate and willful attention seeker.

In truth, every lunchtime I hoped he would not sit at the same table as me, as did most of us; we just did not want to be put off our food. *Where are you now, Howard? I hope you're ok. However, in hindsight, looking back, I do wonder what his home life was like that he felt the need to behave in such a manner that got all of the attention, all of the time, but for all the wrong reasons.* In any event and on that day, Richard ordered him never to sit at our table ever again, and surprisingly Howard obeyed his request right up until Year 6, when he had finally stopped all that foolishness.

School, for the most part, did take some of the strain away from home life. It brought some normality with a pinch of peace and food that was edible and sometimes even quite delicious. *Bring back school dinners please.*

Our House

Dad, first arrived in the UK in 1963, by boat. The story of who paid his passage is at times conflicting depending on who is telling the story. His brother was a few years older than he was and had arrived first. He already had a job and accommodation, so he was able to receive dad. Sadly, one of the first things his brother taught him to do was to gamble. Dad would often place the odd bet on the horses, or he would play the pools; at times, yes, it's true he would win, and sometimes he would win quite big. But when you add it all up, I'm sure it was the bookies who, on more occasions than not, always had the better hand.

Dad would use his winnings to make large purchases on items such as the additional double bed, the three-piece orange sofa set, which on the contrary was plastic dressed up as leather, the orange blinds, the burnt orange carpet, and, of course, the chest freezer, which of course was not orange. The wallpaper was also some kind of disgusting orange color too. To this day, I do not know if the color orange held some kind of special allure for Dad, but for the most part, everything was usually some grizzly shade of orange, at least in the living room anyway.

When the freezer arrived, it was parked with its back up against the wall and from that moment on Mordecka wanted us to take all our meals sitting at it, facing the wall. In truth, I did not mind because sitting at the freezer, facing the wall, for me, this was far better than sitting at the small, rather intimate, round glass dining table with Dad on one side and her on the other, which for all intents and purposes only sought to increase my levels of nervousness and anxiety. He always had something to say about everything, and it made me so tense and very nervous all the time constantly wondering, was this the moment in which he was going to hit me. He would often hit me on the hand with a spoon or prick me in the hand with a fork because, according to him, I should use my right hand to hold my cup; it did not matter that I was born left-handed or that left-handed people are considered right brain dominant.

According to a study, the right brain controls creativity, emotion, and processes new information. Another truth was that my left hand was a lot stronger than my right, and when he told me that I was not allowed to pick up my cup with my left hand any more, I just cried as I knew I could not lift it with the right; it was just not strong enough. So, I just cried and stared at the hot cup of tea that I could not lift to drink.

Back then, we drank tea from baby-pink and baby-blue china mugs that were too big and too heavy even without the contents of a full cup of tea. Dad would also beat my hand whenever he caught me holding a pen in my left hand too. If my hands weren't bleeding and red raw from me biting the skin off my knuckles, they were inflamed and swollen and puffed up from being whacked repeatedly with the spoon, or the fork or the stick. My arms and hands were at times covered in defense wounds from me putting my hands up to protect my face from the slipper, the stick, the belt, or his hand. Nevertheless, it was usually out of sheer fear that we would always do as we were asked. Never challenging, never answering back.

Our food, if you could call it that, would always be just plonked down in front of us on top of the freezer. Sundays were not so bad though; we usually had rice and Congo peas with stewed chicken cooked by Dad, who actually could cook rather well. Unfortunately, the same could not be said of Mordecka. However, if Dad cooked, she would be quick to jump up to distribute the food and would deliberately always serve us either the neck of the chicken on which there was hardly any meat or the bum of the chicken on which housed absolutely no meat at all – *you know, the bits you usually throw away,* or if she fancied the bum, then one of us would be served the very tip of the chicken wing, which could be classified as virtual chicken, for the simple reason that it lacked any real identifiable meat on it at all.

We would fight like cat and dog over the neck because you could at least suck the juice from it and chew the bones; of course, it was Odette who always won. She would divide the meat as if caught from a cull. The chicken would be served on a bed of boiled rice mixed with Congo peas, the latter of which I just simply could not eat, complemented by a salad of beetroot, lettuce, cucumber, and tomatoes that I could.

It was not until ten years later that I would discover exactly what West Indian chicken tasted like and what it felt like to behold the breast of the chicken on your tongue and tear the flesh with my teeth and chew the meat in my mouth able to absorb all the flavors, the juices and the nutrients.

During the week, it would be Mordecka who would be on cooking duties or at least attempt to. It was not long before it became routine to scoop it off my plate and onto my vest roll it up in my vest, tuck it into my knickers and transport it upstairs. I would walk in to the bathroom, lock the door behind me, and flush it down the toilet where of course it definitely belonged. 'Good riddance!' I always thought as I watched the water whirl it away; this process would be repeated until all the food was gone. However, it was not all plain sailing…

During one of my excursions to the bathroom, I was wearing knickers that had one of the leg holes bigger than the other; in fact, it was very loose, perhaps because Odette had swung me around by them once too often. They were unable to support the weight of the food that was now rolled up inside the vest.

As I climbed the stairs in a hurry, the vest unraveled itself and the rice poured out through the leg of my knickers, spilling on to the carpet; I was now in a state of sheer panic with half the food for dumping in my knickers and the other half on the stairs. For one split moment, I did not know what to do or what to do first. All I could think of, was '*if Dad calls me now, I'm finished.*' I composed myself and tried to scrape up as much of the rice and gravy as I possibly could from off the carpet; however, the more I did, the more the rice slid out and down my leg; it appeared a never-ending cycle. Then, just as I had feared.

'Jacqueline!' Dad shouted at the top of his voice.

'*Shit!*' I whispered to myself, now running to the bathroom to offload.

'Yes, Daddy,' I replied promptly, knocking before entering Dad's room, ready to address his request or rather the issues of the day; my hand was full of grease from the food, but he didn't notice that: thank Goodness.

On another occasion, Dad summoned me whilst I was in mid-transit of a dumping exercise.

'Jacqueline!' he shouted. I remember my heart moved from its usual resting position to that of a racing horse bolting out of the stocks at Aintree, picking up speed on the first bend, each beat harder than the previous one. I could feel the intensity like a fast drum beating within my chest. Acknowledging his call, I stood at the door of the living room and announced my presence with a subtle.

'Yes, Daddy'. He did not seem to notice that I had not moved fully into the room but stood still at the door approximately one-foot way from the opening and perhaps twelve feet away from where he was sitting. Had he called me to move a step nearer? I was sure he was going to see the large lump of Cuc Coo and fish stuffed down the front of my pants or, even worse, smell it.

'What are you standing up there for?' he yelled. I moved in a little closer, trying not to tremble, even shaking too much could cause it to start slipping down my leg particularly if I was wearing the wrong knickers.

'Take this to the kitchen,' he said, gesturing at the cup and plate set down before him. I froze for a minute, and then he took his eyes off me and fixed them back on the TV show he was watching on the box. I guess like most parents with time on their hands, he was on his way to becoming an addict. He was engrossed with a soap called *Coronation Street.*

The show had started almost ten years earlier and was about the lives of ordinary people who lived and worked on the same street. In truth, it was not much different to real life back then or even today. Like a snail, I began to move slowly in his direction to collect the plate and cup, I was so close with just a few steps to go, when my little shit brother, four years my junior, whipped up the plate and cup, tipping all the crumbs and leftovers on to the stiff woolen carpet, and began running around the room holding them above his head like a lunatic, giving me more work to do so I now had to sweep up his mess *as well as* empty my knickers. Bobby was a thin, scrawny, and very annoying little child. He was very agile and had hair like Dad, very soft, Indian like.

In that moment as he began to run around the room, swinging the plate and cup through the air until Dad interjected, snapping at him coarsely, demanding that he hand me the crockery immediately! He instantly obeyed promptly handing me the plate and cup. Dad then ordered me to sweep up the crumbs and tidy up the place. As I walked slowly back to the kitchen, all the while trying to keep my legs together to prevent any more food from leaving my knickers prematurely, I could feel the oil from the food now begin to trickle down my inner thigh. All the while I was contemplating whether I had enough time to run upstairs, dump my load down the toilet, and be back sweeping up the crumbs before Dad had time to notice and scream my name out loud again. I decided to take a chance, which meant that I had to run and run quickly in to the bathroom and back again. I placed the crockery in the kitchen, and with all speed proceeded to the stairs, but as soon as I placed my foot on the bottom step, Dad called out my name once more.

'Jacqueline!' he yelled. 'Jacqueline!'

'No! no!' I whispered under my breath. I now knew that I did not have enough time to run up to the bathroom and dump my load and with Bobby hard on my heels, like some stoned lost puppy, I turned and went into the downstairs toilet, the one that I was strictly forbidden to enter unless I was cleaning it, or cleaning it and, oh yes, or cleaning it some more, which was more often than not.

I tried to distract my brother by giving him some random obsolete chore to go and do, but he wasn't buying it. Then without a word, I raised the seat cover, raised up my top and emptied my load into the toilet and flushed the chain. I then closed back the lid right in front of him. He didn't say a word. I washed the grease off my hands, dried them on my T-shirt, and closed the door quietly all the while in full view of Bobby, who, after bearing witness to what must have seemed like a really bizarre affair, was now speechless mouth still ajar.

He had never witnessed anyone throwing food down the toilet before and neither had he seen a yellow-stained white vest. Realizing that he could now blackmail me at a whim, I tucked in my yellow-stained, now wet, vest back into my knickers, lowered my T-shirt over it, and proceeded to the kitchen. I picked up the dustpan and brush on my way back to the living room to sweep up the crumbs, which were now annoying Dad as they held their position on the carpet which clearly spoke volumes at least to him anyway.

In short, that was what home life was primarily all about. As I looked up, I noticed my brother's sister, my half-sister, building a collage of pictures made from her very own feces using the radiator as her canvass. Upon my return, I decided to sit as far away from all of the action as I possibly could, not wanting to be dragged in.

Once Dad had finally noticed exactly what it was, she was happily playing with, he screamed for Odette to help him clean it up. In fact, it felt like that was the sole purpose of our existence at home, not to be encouraged, not to be inspired, not to be praised, not to be thanked not even to be loved but to just continue cleaning the four up, three down, ensuring that it was always spotlessly clean and tidy, and of course, not forgetting to wake up in the middle of the night to take my brother to the bathroom as well.

It was during one of these midnight trips that I noticed the china books placed on the dresser; imprinted on one was the prayer, 'the LORD is my Shepherd' on the other 'Amazing Grace'. I would read up to the word 'wretch' and would read no more. I could not understand why something that seemed so special would have such a horrible word in it. The word wretch was Mordecka's nick- name of choice for both Odette and me but mainly Odette.

Reading that left me feeling very confused and always unable to read any further. All this as well as being served up inedible food day after day and not forgetting to take the blame and the beatings for even the smallest of things including those I had not done, except on Sundays of course when the food was not so bad.

After sweeping up the living room, I went back to the kitchen, washed up the plates and cups, wiped the sides and the table and swept the floor before returning to the bathroom to wash out the turmeric from the fibers of my vest. I found that the best way to remove turmeric or curry powder from my clothes was to use a little water, little soap, and a lot of saliva before washing as usual.

Our general routine, once we returned from school, was to change out of our uniform, have a wash using a badly chipped metal basin, clean up the flat, have our dinner, which usually ended up in the bin – thank God for school dinners back then – and clean up the kitchen, before going straight to bed: this was the conveyor belt of our lives, it never changed it never altered. I remember I would get down on my hands and knees to pick up the white speckles of fluff from off the carpets every single day spent in that flat and sometimes three or four times a day.

The hallway carpet was brown, so it revealed every last speck of white fluff, which to me seemed to shine out like diamonds. When I had finished cleaning the bathrooms, the taps were so shiny that they easily resembled those belonging to the bathroom of some five-star hotel, if not better. And you could even see your reflection in them including the white Armitage Shanks sink.

On one occasion, Mordecka made me clean the downstairs toilet five times before she was satisfied. No one could dispute the fact that it looked brand new; it was so clean you could eat your dinner off it.

Home life was very much characterized by chores, shouting, beatings, and going hungry, all of which caused immense stress.

Ever y weekend, from Friday through to Sunday, I would wash approximately twenty-four Terry's nappies belonging at that time to my brother and then rinse them thoroughly before trying to ring them out with my bare hands. It was so hard to get rid of bright yellow baby poo from 100 per cent cotton that was normally so white, but I had no intention of using my saliva to assist me on this occasion.

Being as small as I was, I had to half lean over the bath to wash them because I was too small to kneel in front of the bath. My back felt as though it was breaking, and my hands were red sore from the friction created by the rubbing action, and they stung from the detergents, which seeped into my already open wounds and caused my hands to become really itchy. Sometimes, my water bumps on my fingers would leak or burst. I felt like this was it; this was the last straw. Physically, I just could not take it anymore – my hands stung, my back ached, and my knees were sore. My tears of frustration became lost in the soapy water as they marched down my face and jumped off my chin to their premature death by drowning in the baby bath water below.

My brother was in nappies until he was about eighteen months, and when his younger sister came along, I simply repeated the process all over again. Then, one day out of the blue as if by some miracle, Dad came into the bathroom and said that he would take over now. I could not believe my ears. '*Was I hearing right?*' It was a miracle, an absolute miracle. By that single action and those few words, my tears of frustration were simply wiped away, at least for that moment, regarding the nappies, I mean. Albeit we still had to wash our own socks and pants every day once we returned home from school. Usually Odette washed mine because of the broken skin on my hands. It was impossible for me to wash my socks clean enough so to save me from a beating she would do it.

I also had to wash the bath out every time Dad had a bath, which I absolutely hated. I hated the sight of the grey scum which clung around the sides of the bath like some big, dark-speckled necklace of scum. I hated wiping the sponge through the scum, which would also become a dirty grey from having made contact with the scum, I always wanted to throw it away afterwards, it was no longer fit to be a bath sponge.

On one occasion, I remember Mordecka had what could only be determined as a brainwave and felt we should wash all our own clothes and even wanted us to wash our own blankets and sheets too. '*Yeeeeh crazy woman.*' On that day, she burst in the bathroom, bringing more and more items in with her each time she entered and dumped them on the floor or in the bath.

We had one blanket, one sheet, two pillows, and two pillowcases. I felt it was really too much for me, I think. I was about six years old at this time. Thank God, we only had one blanket and one sheet. I just looked at it and cried. '*how on earth could I wash something so big?*' I could not even get my hands around this double blanket to wring out the water from it.

Just at that point Odette came in and saw me crying and told me to go back to our room. I obeyed her instructions immediately without question. All of this was occurring around the same time that Mordecka suspected that Dad was having an affair, and she wasn't wrong. He would frequently use our bed for his sins, which was also a double.

At that time, our room was adjacent to theirs. Both rooms were connected via a secret passage through the wardrobe; we would often use it with our siblings, if playing hide-and-seek once our parents had gone out of course. Dad would always leave our sheets soaking wet, usually down one side of the bed after he had fulfilled his lustful encounter with his then mistress whose name also was Jacqueline, ironically.

We had devised our own system for sleeping in our bed, and Dad had just messed everything up including our bed. Odette had her side of the bed nearest to the window, and I had mine nearest to the door, which, of course, had been purposely assigned to me by Odette because she was the boss of our bed, the boss of our room and the boss of me. However, this came to a sudden and abrupt change after Dad had messed in her side of the bed. She then informed me quite emphatically that I now had to sleep on her side of the bed right in the middle of the mess. It was, without doubt, absolutely awful; as far as experiences go, this had to be the worst. I think it was perhaps worse than actually being beaten because at least the bruises would eventually heal and disappear, although it's no secret that the emotional trauma can inevitably last a life time, however, I felt completely degraded.

I would attempt to sleep as close to Odette as I possibly could, but I would be repeatedly thumped right back over to where my side of the bed was determined to be, landing me right in the middle of it again; *'yuk!'*

Tired of being punched, I would then seek to lie at the very edge of the bed; it was really a balancing act at which I failed miserably time after time. At some point during the night, I would fall either into the puddle of bodily fluids or on to the floor with a thump.

When I did fall into the mess, my nightclothes would become soiled wet and smelly, and it would permeate on to my skin. It was disgusting - I hated it. I would have to get up in the dark and find a dry vest, pants, and if possible, a nightdress. Eventually, I learnt to cover the mess with something dry, such as old clothes or even my towel and then just use the tip of that when getting dry. I would fold my towel in half and place it over the mess just so that I had a dry area upon which to sleep on; I slept much better then. I guess the upside was that it gave me a good training ground from which to become a practical thinker. However, Dad was not the shrewdest adulterer in town, and it wasn't long before Mordecka suspected he was up to no good.

One day, she came home early, shouting at the top of her voice, promising to boil the kettle and pour it all over Dad's new mistress... '*if only she could find her...*' Then she did actually boil the kettle and stood at the front door, shouting at the top of her voice for all and sundry to hear that she was going to pour boiling water over Dad's new mistress; if you didn't know her, you would have sworn she was nuts... I'm kidding, if you knew her, the way we knew her, then you too would know that in fact she was nuts.

At one point, they both stood at the front door with her making all the threats she could think of, including the one that she was leaving. This, to my mind, sounded like the best threat so far. '*Yes'!* I thought, '*yes, please leave. We can take care of Dad, and I'm sure Odette can take care of Bobby.* I mean, wasn't she already taking care of him anyway?' Odette would often skip school to look after Bobby, and when Corina came along, she would simply repeat the process. However, sadly, Mordecka did not leave, but we did, the room that was, and Dad carried on with his lustful affair with his mistress but thankfully no longer in our room or on our bed. However, on a spiritual note he had changed the course of our history and the clock was ticking. . .tick. . .tock...tick. . .tock.

We soon learnt that everything Dad did before Mordecka's eyes was wrong to her, and she would always inevitably take it out on us – hence the beatings without cause, the midnight raids, the blankets in the bath and, on a few occasions, all our dirty clothes too, and this was on top of cleaning the flat in its entirety.

There was no hand cream to soothe our hands from the washing detergents or the soreness of the friction caused by the rubbing of the clothes and there was no comfort conditioner for our clothes. Life at home was pretty grim, predominately one never-ending chore of hard labor. Deep down, I really wanted everything to be OK.

I just wanted Mordecka to like us, and if possible to accept us. In fact, we did go through a period when it appeared that Mordecka was sort of nice to us, at least we thought she was being sincere in volunteering to wash and style our hair. The plan was that she would wash it and dry it and then style it using the hot comb, the operative word being the word *hot*, and then make twists with it until we had a whole head full of twists. We were both very excited. She had never groomed our hair before. She was very good at plaiting and making different styles, as it happened.

When I saw the sunshine washing-up liquid on the side of the bath, I did wonder why it was upstairs. I mean it belonged in the kitchen – '*didn't it?*' We had Jif to clean the bath with – so why was it up here I thought; I was baffled as to why she would have the washing up liquid upstairs; I mean it wasn't shampoo – '*was it?*'. When it was my turn to lean over the bath, I tried to keep one eye on the washing up liquid and the other on the bucket, and true to form, she poured it into my hair and began to wash my hair with it just like it was shampoo. Even Dad commented if it was possible to do that.

'It's all the same,' she answered in her broken English. I was not sure if I could feel any more degraded than what I already felt in that moment. It took forever to get the soap suds out of my hair. I counted at least five, five-liter bucket loads of water being poured over my head and that was just the first wash; then Dad came in to take over. In truth, I much preferred Mordecka to rinse my hair than Dad, because at least her rinsing intervals were predictable, which allowed me to gasp for breath and breathe again at the right time in-between the bucket loads of water that were being gushed out over my head. However, the same could not be said with Dad. I was completely unable to catch his rhythm so ended up swallowing more water in futile attempts of trying to catch my breath between rinses and the tops of my t-shirts would also become wet.

Hair washing very quickly became an ordeal in which I had to convince myself repeatedly that my parents were not - killing me softly. I remember once standing up to catch my breath before receiving a short sharp thud to the back, which quickly brought me back down again to the bent-over-the-bath position. After the hair washing was over, she dried it, sectioned it, greased it, then prepared to straighten it with the hot comb, and then finish by twisting small sections, and it would look really nice, even if I do say so myself.

The hot comb was, in short, a piece of iron with a handle at one end and teeth protruding out at the other. In fact, it was an iron comb, hence its name *'hot comb'*. It was this instrument that would be placed on the gas stove until it turned blue, blue hot in fact – that's the next step past red hot, and it was this which was the tool of choice for Caribbean people to use back then in the fifties and sixties to straighten their hair, long before the invention of hair relaxers, tongs, and GHDs. You had to be very careful though and apply a lot of Blue Magic hair grease.

This was the super-thick, super-blue, super-sticky hair grease that was used to protect the hair and the scalp before applying the hot comb to it. I guess we were fools to think that this was a sign of love, affection, or even friendship. This was her opportunity to torture us, ironically with our own consent, using the blue hot, hot comb as her weapon of choice, deliberately and repeatedly burning our heads and our ears with every stroke, regardless of how still we sat. I think this was her ultimate display of undiluted hatred, and she appeared to be enjoying every minute of it. I never knew how it affected Odette because we never spoke about it; But for me it was a living nightmare from start to finish.

I would be seated between her huge overbearing, bulging thighs with my little head just about popping up above them, not really sure if perhaps it was these that were going to smother me to death or the hot comb that was going to burn me to death. She would usually have me seated on top of a couple of cushions, which was, in fact, far better and more comfortable than sitting on the hard, bare cold concrete floor that Odette had to endure, which was usually sprinkled with prickly crumbs knocked off the table from the last meal had before the event by my rebellious brother.

Your legs would usually be the first to cramp up for having to sit just a little over an hour in the same position without moving. She would have to position herself so that she was close enough to reach the handle of the comb emerging from the stove without having to get up. She would pat the comb into a towel, causing it to smoke profusely, and then she would blow the smoke away before placing it into our heads as close to the roots as possible and holding it there. '*Ouch!*' I told myself trying desperately hard not to flinch during the process.

'Keep still!' she said. Now, I thought I would hold my breath and clench all the muscles in my body from the moment she began to blow the comb until the moment she began to pass the comb through my long hair, keeping completely still. My hands were sweating, the areas behind my knees were sweating, and my entire body was rigid with tension.

Finally, she would bring the ordeal to a close by producing a completely beautiful head of long, elegant twists. In truth, it felt like what she really wanted to do was to burn our heads and our ears as many times as she could in one hour as well as dislocate as many of the vertebrae in our necks with sudden jolts to our hair as though she was in a tug of war or something. The entire process was always a palm-sweating, jaw-tightening, leg-cramping, bum- aching hell of an ordeal. She would make out that we were moving even if we weren't and hit us in the head regardless and with the hot comb, which was made from cast iron, and if we tried to rub our head, she would whack our fingers as well also with the hot comb. *Ouch! Ouch! And double Ouch!*

The hot comb was a very heavy piece of equipment. It was the price of vanity during the fifties and sixties and was still top of every girls must have beauty list in the seventies, at least until perming took off in the early 1980s. Every time I sat on the floor in front of her, between her fat legs, it felt like I did so with my life in the balance, never knowing how many burns and how many whacks I would escape with, despite making myself as rigid as a piece of wood to not give her an excuse to hit me or to burn me.

I could feel the palms of my clenched fists filling up with water and even my underarms were desperately perspiring. Having Mordecka do your hair was indeed far worse than having the hairdresser from hell do it. They might get the color wrong or cut it too short or lopsided or perhaps even over-process it; whatever they did, it would grow back, and it was never going to be that bad. Mordecka, on the other hand, was out to maim and scar you, any which way she could; having *her* do your hair was clearly opening yourself up to grievous bodily harm by consent and at the very least, actual bodily harm for which there was no recourse; *at least none we knew of.*

I think the blinding thing was when she said, 'Don't let anyone touch your hair because they just want to destroy it.' I thought that was rather rich coming from her, to say the least. I mean, one hour of sitting between her legs and you were lucky if you weren't scarred for life, mentally as well as physically. I mean, what on earth was she trying to do back then?

When she realised that we had improved dramatically at sitting still, her warped kindness dressed up as hair offers soon ceased. Thank God for that!

We were probably about half way through the 1971/72 academic year, still at ages six and seven when we were being shipped off to a different place again, another home, another town, another people. She was pregnant - again. We were getting to know the signs by now.

On the day of our departure the SS just turned up at our house unannounced and unexpected. We were both called down to the front room to what appeared to be a room full of unknown white faces. We came in and sat on the floor like two good Labradors one either side of dad's chair. We were asked whether we were happy. I almost cracked. We instantly looked up at Dad before looking at each other and then, looking quite wide eyed, back at the person who had asked the question. Of course, I wanted to tell them 'No!'

but I could not open my mouth to answer, so I just looked down at the floor, hoping, praying even that they could hear the still quiet voice that was speaking deep from within the pit of me, hoping that they could read my mind, I was sure the writing was on the wall.

Then we were asked whether we would like to visit a new house with new children and new people. Well of course we did. We looked at each other and then looked at Dad before reverting our eyes to the person who had asked the question. We sat in silence not moving. I wished he could have read my mind '*well yes of course we did*,' I mean I certainly did. I don't remember answering, so I'm guessing I must have just nodded my head in agreement. We were always worried about what Dad would do and say. So, we always erred on the side of caution and learnt never to express our true emotions. In a flash, we seemed to be packed up and going out the door again. We were handed our coats as we went and told that we could continue at the same school - which was always good news.

So off we went. No clothes, no bags, and no toys. I felt a little apprehensive to say the least, yet a part of me just didn't care anymore; I was so glad to be leaving home.

New Home: Sandy Lodge

We were driven to a place called Sandy Lodge. It was a lodge situated slap bang on the middle of Muswell Hill, in North London. It was run by a Dr Sootu and his wife, Mrs. Sootu. They had two sons who also lived with them, Tim, and Arron. They all resided together in a little granny flat built on to the west wing of the lodge, and we occasionally visited them there, which was nice.

The Sootus were originally from West Germany, but now resided in the UK. Life had been good to them, and they wanted to give something back I believe.

Dr Sootu was a professor or something, he had all the letters after his name. He was very tall, easily exceeding six feet when standing. His hair was already white and most of what had been on top had already made its departure. He wore the thickest seeing glasses I had ever seen and was always properly dressed in trousers, shirt, and tie, and covered by an over jumper if not a blazer.

Mrs. Sootu was about half his size when standing, and her hair was silver and flooded with curls which seemed to glisten in the light. She had a good figure with curves, the kind you would expect from a mother and a wife and she always dressed rather fashionably too. She usually kept herself busy with something or other. Her boys were almost as tall as their Dad they were very gentle and very kind. We liked the Sootus for one reason and one reason only – they were opposed to violence. Dr Sootu was particularly repulsed by violence, and more so against women. He would not allow any of the boys to ever raise their hands against the girls, let alone hit the girls, which, of course, was music to my ears. He would always shout at the top of his voice 'N-N-No fighting in my house, please!' He had a pure stutter, which we always took the 'Mickey' out of, *behind his back of course.*

Another important fact about Sandy Lodge, was that the staff members were not permitted to hit the children either, and so it just got better; I felt as though I could relax here. I remember one incident, though, when Odette had been playing with one of the Sootu children and ran into their flat with one of their son's hot on her heels and by mistake she blurted out, 'He hit me! He hit me!'

Well, that was certainly a mistake. Dr Sootu jumped up and, without even a word, slapped his son across his face; it was so hard that it caused his son's face to jolt, exerting a spray of saliva which filled the air in tiny bubbles, as if in slow motion, but this was so not Rocky Balboa. His son ran to his room, shrouded in embarrassment, and shut the door quietly behind him. I tried to make an excuse to see him by telling him I wanted to return his toy to him.

In truth, I just wanted to make sure he was OK. He was so polite; he opened the door and allowed me in. I could see his face was still red on one side. I did not know where to look, yet I could not help but look at him. I wanted to stroke him, But I was standing too far away. I desperately wanted to stay to try and make it better, but I was out of my depth. I did not know what to say or what to do. Then from out of the awkward silence he made his excuses. I handed him the small toy; as he stretched over to receive it, I looked into his eyes and just for a second they caught mine, I could see that they were thickly glazed over. I felt awful that my sister could have done such a careless thing that day. If I had known to hug him I would certainly have done so, being that it is a medicine *and all.* I was sure he was crying after I left. Out of his bedroom, I backtracked to the flat door and re-entered the main part of the house again.

At some point, surely, Odette had to admit that he hadn't actually hit her, that they were just playing, which had turned into a chase, and he was chasing her, hard on her heals because she had taken something belonging to him, a toy of some kind. Odette went into the garden and sat in Miss Daisy. I followed her but did not join her. Clearly, she was very upset too, and knowing her as I did, I knew when to leave her alone.

We still attended the same school whilst at the lodge, and any free time was spent playing with all the toys, usually on the weekends. I would use the different-colored bricks to build a house. I was always building a house. As I got to understand how the bricks worked I managed to incorporate a seat and table into the build. Subconsciously I pined for a home a real home, however, in my mind, this was that home, the perfect house. As I got to the end of the build, I would always end up fighting with Jude, another child, similar in age to myself, because one of us always had too many bricks, and of course our home-made homes would always get smashed to pieces in the process.

Mrs. Sootu would enter the playroom and just stand at the door, sometimes she would call out in her strong German accent,

'You both ok then?', we would then simply abandon our building projects and go on to do something completely different as if the housing projects had never existed. But when we got it right and learnt to share, we would lie down in our self-built houses the party wall running between us; and when we were good Mrs. Sootu would allow us to use an old bed spread for the roof.

It was here, at the lodge that I learnt to play chess and became the undefeated champion even as young as seven. No-one could beat me. We also had a large garden at the lodge with enough bushes and hedges to play hide-and-seek in; it was to my mind a mini forest which secretly led all the way up to Alley Pally, or Alexandra Palace as it is actually known.

We even had a tree house, which we were constantly building and reconstructing, and renovating, and refurbishing. We furnished it with odd bits of non-matching carpet, small chairs, and a small table. Mrs. Sootu was indeed our faithful encourager. She was always the first to give us bits of old carpets, cut-off material for curtains, odd bits of furniture, and of course a tablecloth. Sometimes, we could even have juice and biscuits up there. It was all really quite therapeutic. Only perhaps we didn't know it then.

Also, in the garden was an old car. Apart from driving Miss Daisy, we would take turns to set her on fire *(talk about love hate relationships)*. Then we would all join forces to put out the flames. It was a real team-bonding exercise, which we all thoroughly enjoyed, until one day the fire got so big that we could not put it out, so we had to call the real fire brigade – *what a total embarrassment that was.* Then Daisy had to be towed away because she was so severely burnt out and spoilt the look of the garden, *or so they said.* We thought the Sootus were great, and we appreciated and respected their methodology and philosophy around child rearing. We trusted their judgement implicitly.

Our bedroom was up on the first floor, which we shared with two other girls – one was a teenager who had already lost her virginity at, apparently, well - a very young age. I would later find out how. The other was around our age or just younger.

At night, the teenager, who was not more than thirteen or fourteen, would go downstairs and as bold as brass open the front door and bring into the house two of her male school chums. She would bring them upstairs into our room and into her bed. It was there that she would have sex with them. - (*At the time of course, I did not know it was sex ... I just knew it was something strictly forbidden and that really scared me).*

My bed was right next to hers, and her friends would take it in turns to sit on the edge of my bed whilst the other was making out with her. One night, one of her friends accidently sat on my legs and it woke me up. He was then threatening to get into bed with me whilst she was in bed with his friend, if she didn't hurry up. I was so terrified, too frightened to even breathe. I had no idea of what was going to happen next. I was only six years old at this time. I think in my heart I was willing for someone any one to come in.

He stood up and gestured with his clothes; I held my breath, not even flinching a muscle; I had had good practice of that. *No wonder I always won musical statues at the school Christmas parties.* But this wasn't musical statues; it was real life, my life; there were no prizes to be given out here, only fear and the unknown. But the worst was yet to come. She then had to push off the one that she was in bed with and started making out with the other one, just to control the situation. I was so scared that I kept wishing someone, anyone, would come in, but no one did. I managed to turn onto my side and coil myself into a ball and remain like that until they left.

Her behavior went on night after night, unnoticed. I think I must have prayed for her to get caught. I was so glad and relieved when they set a honey trap for her and caught her in the act with the boys downstairs in the foyer, just as they came in the front door. The boys were immediately removed from off the premises, and the next day, she was packed up and shipped out without so much as even a goodbye or a thank you very much. I felt relieved and was now able to relax, at least for a while anyway.

Every year at the lodge, all the children were routinely checked for spots, rickets, head lice, and malnutrition. We were weighed, measured, poked, and prodded. The examination lasted approximately 20 minutes. I really wanted it to last longer, it was the most attention I had ever received in my young life up until that point. I remember that the doctor had very soft hands, it was quite evident that he had never done a hard day's work in his life; he was very gentle, and his touch was very tender. However, this was the only acceptable physical contact. I had overheard the doctor say to Mrs. Sootu,

'Yes, they are fine, but they are a little undernourished. Feed them up a bit, would you?' This transpired to extra meat and potatoes at mealtimes, extra toast at breakfast, and seconds if we wished and extra fruit at super. This was great as my relationship with food was also beginning to improve quite considerably since arriving.

We both celebrated a birthday each whilst at the lodge; however, I still did not know how old I was because my parents had never afforded me the privilege of acknowledging a birthday, and I had lost count since our time at Dukesbury House, so many moons ago, where, unbeknown to me at the time, I had turned four. I was too embarrassed to let on to anyone, so I thought I would wait until the cake arrived and then quickly count the candles as the cake made its journey over to the table so I could determine how old I was as I was sure that the question would eventually be asked. Unfortunately, when it arrived, it would have an extra candle on it, because back then, you always blew out an extra candle for luck, only this time they had lit them altogether.

'So how old are you then?' asked John Candy, a rather large and bothersome child also staying at the lodge. The truth was I had no idea how old I was. Up until then I had never had a birthday celebration before. So, from ages one to seven, I had no idea on what day or in what month I was born or how old I was. I looked across at the cake, in the hope that I would quickly be able to count all the candles before it arrived at the table. Truth be known it was still too far away to see all the candles to count, so I pretended that I did not hear him. Then he repeated the question again, only louder.

'So how old are you then Jacqueline?'

'Err...' Now thinking on my feet, I still couldn't see, so I quickly dropped a piece of cutlery as another detour and hovered about down on the floor whilst the cake made its way towards me and then coming up, I quickly counted the candles. 'Err, eight!' I blurted out at a quick guess.

'What?' questioned John. 'Wasn't your sister eight on her birthday just last week?' I looked down in shame. 'And aren't you a year younger?' he prodded further.

'Err... Yes, that's right!' I answered before distancing myself again from him and his probing questions.

'ha ha, ha ha Jacqueline doesn't know how old she is, Jacqueline doesn't know how old she is!' he blurted. All heads began to queue in my direction.

'*Well who made you detective constable?*' I thought to myself. I remember this birthday particularly well, but for all the wrong reasons. And it was about to go from bad to worse in just one afternoon.

One of the gifts I received was a new shiny fifty pence piece. I was so excited; it was the first time I had ever received any money in my entire young life, and it was mine, all mine. It felt completely exhilarating, I was on cloud nine. I placed it in my new purse and put my new purse into my new bag, both of which I had also received as birthday presents.

I couldn't remember ever having received a present on my birthday before, but if this was how it felt, it felt great. I was on top of the world, clothed in pure elation. I began to imagine all the things I could buy at our local sweet shop that we sometimes visited on a Saturday after lunch; it was situated just at the bottom of the hill. Now I had a reason to go, I felt really chuffed.

In my mind a list appeared to go on and on of all the lovely sweets I could buy. It was decided we were going to visit the sweet shop at the bottom of the hill just before tea; I could not wait. I was filled to the brim with pure excitement, it was seeping out of me; I now had a bounce in my step. I continued walking around the house so proudly showing off my new bag, inside of which my new purse housed my new shiny fifty pence piece. I had attained a new position in life, and I wanted everyone to know about it. I walked the length and breadth of the lodge telling all and sundry as I waited for the moment when we would go down to the sweet shop.

One of the people I told was Leban Abyion. He was one of the older children staying at the lodge. He had been doing some ironing in the laundry room at the time. He was very distant and always quiet; his countenance was almost as dark as his complexion; there was something really odd about him that made me feel really uncomfortable when in his presence, but I didn't know what. He had not been at my tea party, and so he asked to see my shiny new fifty-pence piece. Full of pride I opened my new bag, took out my new purse, and showed him the new shiny fifty-pence piece. He then asked whether I had somewhere safe to keep it.

'Of course,' I answered.

'Well, I think you should put it in a *really* safe place,' he said.

'Like where?' I asked, beginning to doubt myself.

'Like under your pillow or in your drawer,' he said. 'No one would ever think about looking for it there,' he added.

Filled with innocent belief, I followed his advice and ran upstairs to my bedroom and placed my new purse with my new shiny fifty-pence piece under my pillow and went back downstairs. When the time came to go to the shop, I ran upstairs to collect my purse and placed it in my bag with the confident assurance that my money was safe inside. I ran downstairs to meet Sandy and all those who were going with us to the sweet shop. We all walked down the hill to the shop together. I had a real bounce in my step; I was so happy I was humming to myself.

Once inside, we all looked around at all the sweets; it was like sweetie heaven. Today, I could afford any sweet I liked, I thought. Filled with static elation, we all had a good look around before beginning to select our sweets. We kept changing our minds until we were then hurried by the young impatient shop assistant. I chose some chewy cigarettes, which were four for half a penny, some Black Jacks and Fruit Salads, which were also four for half a penny, and two packets of posher wrapped Trebor mints, one green and one white. I had never tried Trebor mints before, and I was really excited about experiencing this new taste on my tongue. I had noticed them always seated in the same position next to the till.

They were so beautifully wrapped in matching polythene plastic – one white, the other green; they looked so very smart next to each other. Full of pride, I placed my selection of goodies on the counter. The cashier added up the total on one of those old-fashioned tills, which screeched *ker-ching* every time you pulled the lever for the total. The total bill came to thirty-seven pence exactly, giving me, thirteen pence change for the following week.

'That's thirty-seven pence please,' requested the cashier. I reached into my new bag, took out my new purse, pulled back the zip and slipped my fingers inside to take out the shiny new fifty pence. Not feeling the fifty pence piece straight away I moved my fingers up and down the lining of the purse, expecting that, in any moment, we would unite, expecting that in any moment my fingers would make contact with that shiny slender silver coin. But I couldn't feel a thing. I tried again and again but – nothing. Trying to remain calm, I nervously pulled the purse towards me and began to search frantically looking into it and turning it inside out. Alas! Nothing was inside; it was completely empty. The money had gone. I could not believe it; my heart started to race. I emptied the purse and the bag on to the counter, but there was nothing. Nothing was inside. Both were completely empty. I turned to Sandy, my eyes glazed over, trying hard to remain composed and said,

'My money is gone! My fifty pence has gone!' Someone has stolen my fifty pence!'

'So, do you want these sweets or not?' asked the cashier completely devoid of any compassion or understanding. My pride turned into total embarrassment, shame, and humiliation.

'No!' came my choked response. 'My money is gone!' I shrieked, now losing my composure completely. 'Someone has stolen my money!' I repeated hysterically. My eyes began to well up with tears. Sandy made no response. The other children made their purchases, and we left the shop in silence. Silent tears began, once more, to find their way down my cheeks, diving off the edge of my chin, mixing in with the dust before meeting their demise and splattering onto my party top.

'Someone has stolen my money!' I began to cry and cry and cry; I cried inside. I cried out loud. I sobbed and sobbed for the entire journey home.

When we returned to the house, I ran upstairs and pulled back the bed sheets and removed the pillow from off my bed in search of my shiny new fifty pence piece. I even looked under the bed, in my bedside cupboard drawer, and even in my wardrobe. I was sobbing uncontrollably now, and nasal mucus had begun to mix in with my tears and dribble, as it slid down the rest of my face.

As I sat on my bed, now stripped, amongst all the chaos of out turned drawers and strewn clothes and possessions across the room I thought about all the people who knew where I had placed the money. It was then that I remembered my conversation with Leban.

I remembered that it was Leban and Leban alone who had advised me where to hide the money, and I had told no one else as per his instruction. Convinced by my evidence I went to find him. He was still in the laundry room, finishing off his ironing. Upon seeing him I instantly accused him.

'You stole my money!' I said. He remained remarkably cool; he did not utter a word; not a single word. I continued to accuse him, raising my voice with every accusation, screaming at times. Still Leban refused to answer; he was cooler than a cucumber. Then quite dramatically I demanded my money back; still there was no response. As he tried to leave the laundry room, I latched on to one of his trouser legs, and he dragged me along behind him as he went, not even trying to push me off and still without saying a word.

He just kept on walking with me attached to his leg, dragging me along as he walked across the cold, stone-tiled floors. About now, I was screaming the words, 'Give me back my money! You stole it! Give me back my money! You stole it!' I was now beginning to draw attention to myself with some of the children beginning to gather around. Eventually Bill came and pulled me off him. He took me away to calm me down. I was sobbing uncontrollably again, but Bill did not give up in trying to calm me down. He took me back to my room sat me down on the bed and tried to talk to me.

I think the tears were for all the years of not ever having had any birthday presents or Christmas presents or anything of my own, and the one time that I did, it was snatched right away from me: stolen. Bill said that if I did not stop crying, I would have to remain in my room alone because I was upsetting *all* the other children.

'*Oh, gee thanks Bill,*' I thought. His words cut me like a knife. Staff always said this. And it was beginning to really grate on me, because right now in this moment there was nothing wrong with the other children – they hadn't had their birthday money stolen, and there was nothing wrong with crying.

The Help never truly understood the emotion of tears or the language they spoke, so whenever it happened, they never knew what to say or what to do; consequently, they would always say stop crying and eventually walk away from you as if you were a leper or something, as if crying was contagious. *I mean can you really catch crying.* None of them had the patience to just sit and wait with you or the compassion to just silently cry with you too.

Sometimes, it is just better to allow the child to cry or even to cry with them or just give them a hug or a word of comfort.

I calmed down a bit following his threat to leave me in the room alone because I did not want to stay in the room by myself. I had not done anything wrong, and yet it felt like I was the one being punished. Bill asked whether I had seen Leban take the money.

'No.' I gestured, slowly shaking my head from side to side.

'Did you see Leban near your room?'

'No,' came my repeated gesture.

'Well, how can you accuse him then?' asked Bill.

'Because he was the one who told me to put the money under my pillow, and I did,' came my faint response.

'That may well be the case,' said Bill, 'but unless you saw him take it, you cannot accuse him! Do you understand?'

'Yes,' I answered after a long pause. This was a hard lesson I learnt that day and an even harder pill to swallow; nevertheless, it was learnt. I wiped away my tears and went back downstairs for tea.

For tea we usually ate things like baked beans on toast, served with bacon or sausages, or eggs or tomatoes also on toast all with extra bread, and sometimes there was even fish and chips served with green sweet peas. Bread and butter were king of the table at every meal, and there were plenty of spreads to choose from too, followed by an assortment of fresh fruits all washed down with milky tea with two and a half sugars.

It's amazing what behaviors and patterns founded in childhood will follow you into adult life, and what characteristics will follow you too. The one thing I really hated about supper-time was that the boys would always put their unwanted, previously fingered or licked or dropped-on-the- floor food on your plate, after distracting your attention away from the table, usually behind you or under the table, leaving you to unwittingly eat their left overs or leave your own because you were unable to tell the difference – which was also very annoying, particularly so if you had been enjoying what you were eating. Then they would all burst out laughing. You never knew whether they had licked it or even if it had actually fallen on the floor or what; but if you ate it the joke was on you and the laughing would commence.

One of the things I liked most about Sandy Lodge were the long days out. I found that I loved travelling, the motion of the vehicle moving, the sun and breeze in my face. I usually fell asleep and would wake up just as we would arrive. We would, from time to time, visit a place we self-named '*The rocks*'. It was truly an amazing place; the trees appeared to kiss the sky good morning. They were so tall, and the sky was always happy to see us, boasting a beautiful blue, and we seemed to be so high up that I felt as though I could do anything, I could be anyone, I felt so elated up there. We would take our time to climb these massive beauties, sometimes becoming stuck or lost, yet always making it back, just in the nick of time, just before our departure back home again.

I felt a great sense of freedom here and a great sense of 'I can achieve everything'. A couple of times on the journey there, we even drove through a rainbow, and I made a wish. A couple of times I got stuck up on a high rock unable to find my way back down but of course in the end I always did.

On Saturday morning's we would make the short journey up to the top of the hill to the picture house where we would enjoy films like *Black Beauty*, *Lassie*, Enid Marple and *Zorro*. In those days, we would have a break between films and the ice cream ladies would bring you refreshments right to your seats, but you did feel as though you wanted to stretch your legs. My favorite was the fabulous Fab ice lolly, it was made up of ⅓ strawberry ice, ⅓ vanilla cream, ⅓ covered in chocolate with the first third sprinkled with 100s & 1000s – absolutely delicious, and all held in place by the strawberry ice which ran up through the center of the lolly. Of course, this was all before being introduced to the banana lolly which soon took first place at being my favorite; nevertheless, I really looked forward to this treat each time we visited the cinema.

Whilst at the lodge, we would also experience the second holiday in our young life; this time, it was to Pontins Holiday Camp. We would not be accompanied by the Sootus as they were headed back to Germany with their children for their own private family holiday, which they did every year; this meant they had to get extra cover because we were a couple of staff short. There seemed to be a real problem in trying to allocate enough staff for the trip, and for a moment, the holiday was almost off. However, in the 11th hour and 59th minute, up the drive came an odd-looking man, dressed all in black, we weren't sure if he was a priest or something.

Apparently, *this* was Mr. Mondi! they had used an agency in the end; I don't remember which one. We were to find out later that some of Mr. Mondi's interests were as dark as his clothing. He was in fact as perverse as he appeared strange. No sooner had the Sootus left did he turn into Mr. Jekyll.

To this day, I remember his name and his antics as though it was this morning. I mean, how could I forget? He was from Pakistan and spoke with a deep Pakistani accent. We were soon to find out that Mr. Mondi was a psychotic child abuser, who enjoyed abusing children, but no one knew it back then; I mean, why would they? But when they did, no one did anything anyway, and no one said a word – it felt like no one could hear what we were saying, it felt like no one cared... apart from Sandy that is.

No sooner had the Sootus left, did he jump into action, attacking the children for nothing, for no reason, and at every opportunity.

He would twist the children's arms up behind their backs and slap them around the head and face, whilst he had their thin little limbs painfully pinned behind them high up on their backs. He would twist our arms around and round behind our backs, just one twist short of snapping them out of their sockets, and whilst holding them tight with one hand, he would then bend our legs up behind our backs, pulling them towards our heads with the other. Then whilst holding our legs and arms pinned behind our backs, he would slap us around the head and face repeatedly, making us recite absolute rubbish. The more you screamed the more slaps you got. The more you wriggled, the tighter he would twist your arms. If you screamed for anyone to help or screamed for anyone to call the police, he would threaten to kill you and them.

I remember that Sunday morning as if it was the Sunday just gone by. I just happened to walk into the front room, happy as Larry, singing to myself as I always did. I must have reached almost the center of the room when I realized something was wrong, very wrong. I turned my head over my left shoulder only to witness Mr. Mondi in the middle of torturing Jude.

Mr. Mondi appeared to be thoroughly enjoying himself whilst Jude was screaming out in absolute agony. I had no idea how long Jude had been in that position or how long this treatment had been going on for. But Mr. Mondi was laughing as hard as Jude was screaming for anyone to get him help. Upon realizing I was there; he began shouting at me to get help.

'Call the police!' he screamed. 'Call the police!' he screamed again. 'Do anything! Hel-elp!' he continued screaming at the top of his voice. For a moment, I just froze, not being able to move or speak. As my senses returned to me, I turned ninety degrees, realizing I had walked too far into the room to be able to move back out with just one step or a jump. I looked over at the big wide door and the big brass door handle and then glanced over at Mr. Mondi who was seated in the center of the sofa, which had its back up against the same wall where the door was positioned at the end.

I looked at Jude lying next to him, the top of his torso half bent over Mr. Mondi's left knee. Everything appeared to be happening in slow motion and for a moment, I did not know what to do or which way to run. Then, in an act of pure panic, suddenly I began to run, and run as fast as my little legs could carry me in the direction of the door. Alas! My judgement was wrong; it was the wrong call. Just as I extended out my scrawny little arm in front of me, my fingers almost just kissing the large round brass handle, ready to draw it into the palm of my hand and swing open the large lazy heavy door, Mr. Mondi, in full motion, slid down the sofa as quick as a lizard's tongue, releasing one hand from off of Jude and in one sharp swift swoop reached over and grabbed me. 'Noooooooooooo.' I screamed, everything appearing in slow motion.

Clearly, Jude seized this moment and made his eager escape – in the same second, he was gone. He had wriggled so hard that Mr. Mondi could no longer hold him and reach for me simultaneously. As Jude made his escape, Mr. Mondi pulled me in towards him, and now with two hands free, he began to twist my arms up behind my back, pulled my legs up behind my back to my head, and began to hold me in the same position in which he had held Jude, now slapping my face with his free hand. Without looking back, Jude busted out of the garden doors still screaming and shouting out in anger as he went. Like a man on fire. Apparently, the only thing Jude had been doing was switching the channels to see what was on the TV when Mr. Mondi came in and just grabbed him. This was what Jude did every Sunday morning after breakfast.

Now I was the one screaming at the top of my voice.

'Help me! Anyone!, Help me! Someone, anyone, please help meeeee!' I screamed as I struggled. 'Please let me go,' I screamed and screamed. I could not understand why no one was coming to my aid. *Why was no one coming to help me?*

Just then, Jack and big Jude came into the room. Grasping quite quickly that something was not right, Jack managed to run back out of the room, but big Jude had stopped dead in his tracks, perhaps four feet or so away from the garden doors and eight feet away from the living room door. Mr. Mondi threatened big Jude with the same treatment if he intervened. He asked him if he thought he could make it out of the doors before he got to him. With a short run and one jump, Jude also managed to burst through the garden doors.

'Jude, please, please help me!' I pleaded. 'Please get help!' I screamed. I could no longer see Jude now; he had disappeared from my sight completely. The torture continued as did the screaming. Then the front room door was opened just ajar; someone was standing at the door watching, and it then closed back to resting on the latch but not fully closed. Mr. Mondi turned to look. Suddenly, the door was made to swing open wide, and I screamed my hardest for all and sundry to hear. Mr. Mondi got up to close the door, during which I realised that his grip had slackened.

I began to struggle, but alas, I was not quick enough. With one mighty step, his long body followed his long legs, and he closed the door by the handle with one hand whilst still retaining his grip upon me with the other. I continued screaming with dribble now running out from my mouth; he began to smudge it over my cheeks and face and continued slapping me around my face. Just then, the door opened again and closed to just resting on the latch. Then as he got up, still holding my wrists behind my back, the door swung open, almost whacking him in the face; as his body jolted his grip loosened, I wriggled as hard as I possibly could, adding high-pitched screams into the mix but to no avail as his grip still tightened even more, and again, he began slapping me across the face until I stopped screaming. Just then the door swung open again. This time little voices cried out, 'The police are coming. The police are coming to get you!' I took full advantage of his apprehension and lack of concentration which permitted his intensified grip to slacken again just slightly, and this time I wriggled like it was about to go out of fashion. Without screaming, all my energy was focused on wriggling out of his hands, and this time I did it. I wriggled free as my body fell on to the floor. I quickly scrambled through his legs on my hands and knees, stood up on my feet, and just ran. I did not look back to see whether I was being chased by Mr. Mondi. I just ran out through the garden doors and out into the garden. I ran till I was all out of breath and completely out of sight, deep into the bushes that spread out over the rear and to the side of the garden.

Eventually, I slowed to a fast-paced walk, picking up a thrasher with which to whip the leaves from off the hedge rows. My pace eventually slowed to a walk as I calmed right down. It was in this moment, I think, I knew true hate, and that day, it had entered my heart in abundance. That day, I hated Mr. Mondi with a pure, undiluted hatred; if I could have wished him dead, I would have. If I could have wished him to be hurt, I would have. If I could have paid someone, anyone, all my pocket money to hurt him, I would have. However, I wasn't sure exactly how much *hurt* twelve pence was capable of instilling in those days.

In short, I wanted him out! I wanted him to leave the lodge immediately! Mr. Mondi was undeniably a very evil man. It was not long before I found myself back at the house; still sobbing, I went inside to look for another member of staff to report the awful truth of what had just happened. I went to the office first, but it was locked, and no one answered from inside the room after I had banged on the door several times, so my guess was that no one was there. Then I went across to the kitchen and pantry, but there was no one there either. Lastly, I went into the art and crafts room and found Bill, our driver, good old Bill indulging in a game of pool with one of the older boys. 'How long have you been here?' I demanded to know. Bill did not even look up from his game. 'Did you hear me?' I screamed at him. 'Did you hear me screaming at the top of my voice?' I demanded to know. 'Why didn't you help me?' I screamed at him and started sobbing again. He just stared at me without answering. I screamed at him again and again, but he did not answer me; He did not even say one word. No sorry no empathy no nothing. When I heard of his premature death seven years later I didn't even blink. I had no words, no comment, no nothing. He had every opportunity to be a voice for the voiceless but instead he did nothing and said nothing, and children suffered at his nothing.

With that, I went outside, picked up several rocks, and began to throw them, smashing every window in the entire house. I also began to let off every fire extinguisher and every fire alarm. Staff members began to run around in a panic like loose headless chickens; they did not know if there really was a fire or not. Ten minutes later, the fire engines stormed up the drive. I ran out into the bushes again; I felt almost satisfied, almost justified, but not quite... I remained in the bushes and watched the commotion unfold like a real-life movie; of course, it was, only it was my movie, the movie of my life.

On the inside, it felt like something had snapped and snapped in the atmosphere too, for that day, I also had become just like Dad. Unbeknown to me then, I had become filled with rage – pure, undiluted rage. From that day forward, this was the new me; my new motto was simply this: every time Mr. Mondi decided to attack me, I would smash every window and let off every fire alarm and open as many fire extinguishers as I possibly could.

Once it became apparent, that he was physically and brutally abusing all of us, we all agreed that if ever he touched any of us again, we would all smash all the windows and release all the fire alarms and then run to hide out in the garden. We would leave it to the staff to do all the explaining to whomsoever they wanted and whenever they wanted. The staff members soon became frightened; they were running out of money, paying for all the glass. And the fire brigade was threatening to charge if they came back out again to reset the alarms and check the extinguishers.

Worrying whispers were rife amongst staff, who for the most part had no idea of what they should do to keep control of the children, but none of them, not one of them, was listening to the children about our complaints against Mr. Mondi, until one day, Sandy, a young hippy worker, caught him in action mocking one of the children and then stood up to Mr. Mondi and told him not to touch any of us again or she would report him to the authorities. However, at every opportunity he got, he would savor the moment, particularly on Sandy's off days or when he thought she was not around, and when he couldn't physically touch any of us, he would jeer at us and mime the threat of an attack, in an attempt to intimidate us when staff members were not looking.

Subconsciously, we knew that our strength lay in numbers, and we had to stay together. Sandy began to take us up to her private dwelling, just to get us out of the house and away from Mr. Mondi, whom she now realised could not be trusted with any of the children; I wondered if it was in that moment that she also realised that Mr. Mondi was a sick, twisted, and completely deranged man, but she was helpless to do anything about it other than to keep us with her because no one was listening to her. We liked going out with Sandy, we felt safe with her.

The first time we visited her home, which wasn't far, just up the hill, we noticed a great big blue tent set up in the garden. It looked like a bouncy castle. One by one we all took turns to dive on to it before realizing that, in fact, the base was very hard, as the surface it was sitting on was grass covered mud, which had become rock hard with all the hot weather we had been having. It was then that she told us it was a tent.

Sandy had a beautiful black upright Bechstein in her very small front room, which seemed to take up a large part of it, and she afforded us all the patience to teach us all a little tune called the 'Melody'. Sadly, we could not continue to keep going to Sandy's home. I think she got told off by other staff members or something. I can still remember the tune, which I have carried in my heart even to this day and passed it on to my own daughters. *Thank you, Sandy, where are you now? We miss you Sandy.*

The Holiday

Eventually, the day arrived for our journey to begin and we were on our way to Pontins Holiday Camp. It was a bit like Butlins, only better.

All the girls shared a chalet together which made perfect sense of course and the boys did the same. There were about eight of us in total. In our chalet, we had two rooms each with two sets of bunk beds, so the sofa beds also had to be pulled out at nighttime. During the day, we would go over to the main hall for breakfast and dinner. Lunch was usually sandwiches or pizza, and we could make light things to eat in the chalet, such as warm beans or soups or have a bowl of cereal with tea, coffee, and biscuits all on tap. Throughout the days, we would enjoy all the activities such as the rides and the pool, and in the evening, there was the disco.

On our first day at the pool, I accidently shoved my sister, causing her to fall into the water. As she came up covered in water, which sort of clung to her like a transparent masque, we all burst out laughing; unfortunately, she could not see the funny side of it. '*Well, who fi tell me to do dat?*' I thought painfully in my limited imitation of a Bayesian accent. Emerging from the pool, dripping wet, fully dressed, I witnessed the contorted expression on her face, which was far from friendly. I knew she was not about to let me forget it either. She chased me all over the pool area, up the stairs, down the slides, and along the sides of both pools, vowing to get me; I knew once she did, it was not going to be nice; I knew intuitively she would hurt me. She was very good at hurting me, and I was afraid of her anger, and she knew it.

The last time she hurt me bad was when we were lying down in our bed at home. It was night-time, and it was time to go to sleep. However, Odette felt that I was taking too much of the blanket which was perhaps a little more suited for a large single bed as opposed to a regular double. In short, it was too small to cover the bed and could never be tucked under at the sides even without two bodies under it. Each time I turned over, the blanket came off her, perhaps more so because she was always parked right up against the very edge of the bed for some unknown reason. After our usual tug of war with the blanket, which neither of us ever won, she invited me to come over and lie next to her, I couldn't believe it, did she really love me after all? I thought. I loved being close to her and I guess I needed a bit of a hug, so in complete naivety, I did. As I lay there, on my back, completely relaxed and just about to doze off, I could not believe what was about to happen next, I could not have imagined not for one moment what she was going to do to me. Suddenly my body had literally jolted up wards into the V shape position.

Clearly, this must have looked funny at a glance, but on a more serious note, I was now fighting - just to breathe. My sister had, with all her might, elbowed me, as hard as she possibly could, in the stomach, completely knocking the wind right out of me. I mean, all of it, every last drop of it. I lay there just desperately trying to breathe, legs still in the air. When she realised I was in trouble, she turned on the light to see what she had done, but she then had to turn it back off again quickly in case Dad or Mordecka found out. I think neither of us could have coped with an almighty beating at that moment, simply for having the light on after lights out, *that would have definitely been the end of me.*

Odette tried to pick me up into her arms but had to put me back down again as my squirms for breath got louder. I could not see the worry in her face or the tears in her eyes because we were in complete darkness; however, somehow, I could sense her anxiety and genuine concern for my disposition. I think this was the first true experience we both had of her untamed strength. She then tried to hold my face and blow on me. In truth, she did not know what to do and neither did I. None of her attempts were making it any easier for me to breathe. I continued to fight for snippets of breath, rolling from side to side in complete agony; she was telling me to breathe.

'Come on, breathe!' she panicked. 'Breathe.' Then she began crying, whispering that she was sorry. She begged me to be OK. Slowly breath began to come back into my body, and I began to receive more breath with every small inhale. Eventually, I began to breathe normally again but was now left with a particularly sore abdomen. I think we both silently cried ourselves to sleep that night. We woke up the next morning, still in each other's embrace. I wish we could have stayed like that for ever really. In my sister's embrace.

As my mind returned to the present, I found myself still at Pontins Holiday Camp, with her hot on my heels, still chasing me around the poolside; I was becoming tired from being chased, so I stopped allowing her to catch me in the shallow water. I quickly jumped in, my mind eliminating the possibility of having to be thrown in. When she did eventually catch up to me, she jumped in the pool after me still fully clothed and began to hold my head under the water for such a long time that I did not know whether I should struggle free from her grip or start drinking the water, just to get oxygen.

I did feel that the length of time she held me under was a little unfair, considering that I had given myself up. I began drinking the water. I was running out of breath. I struggled to push my head up from out of the pool, but I could not. When she did finally release me, I didn't bother to go to the pool again for the rest of the holiday, for the fear that she wasn't finished with me yet was still a daunting thought hovering in the back of my mind. Still I had learnt another useful lesson that day, which I remember even till now. *'Do not ever play a prank on your elder sister by pushing her in the pool ever again.'*

Every evening after tea, we would go to the disco and have a dance for an hour or so, and on Fridays, we would all stay up and watch the late-night movie in our chalet until one by one we all fell asleep. On our first Friday film night, *King Kong* was the movie, it was in black and white. As the movie unfolded, I could not believe my eyes. This was exactly like the big monkey that had been chasing me in my dreams in the years gone by. I remembered the dreams that I had whilst at Dukesbury House. It was a reoccurring dream that I had experienced night after night. In the dream, I was being chased by a huge monkey, almost the size of a double- story house, and it was identical to the big monkey in the movie we were watching - King Kong; it could have been his brother, I guess. I would jump over white picket fences which mapped out the boundary lines running out neatly in front of formally aligned, pretty houses, encompassing beautifully cut lawns, rolled out from the base of the houses, however, there were no white picket fences in the movie neither neatly cut lawns. I never understood the dreams even up to this day and never felt able to share them with anyone, not even my sister.

These dreams had started whilst I was at Dukesbury House. *Perhaps even more so after the Jesus incident.* kids back then, were too quick to mock you and the tags and labels from all the banter were just too hard to shake off. Every dream ended at the same point with me running into the last house in the row, which was my own house, also complete with neatly kept green lawns and white picket fences. I would run inside, slamming the door hard behind me just in the nick of time. He never ever got me and neither did he ever get into the house. Once inside, I knew I was safe, I would run upstairs, jump into bed, and pull the covers up over my head trying to be still and trying to hold my breath.

I suffered these dreams from the moment I arrived at Dukesbury House right up until I started Sunday school. At which point they just stopped as suddenly as they had begun. I had no idea of what it all meant even until today. However, in the actual film, I did find it quite distressing particularly when it got to the part where King Kong fell from the tower and was killed. I too cried then.

As for Mr. Mondi, well, he spent the entire holiday in his room like a good doggy; I mean, we did not see him at all for the entire two weeks that we were there, which for us was pure bliss as far as we were all concerned.

On day fourteen of the holiday, we were all packed up and ready to return to the lodge. We had enjoyed our holiday, and now we were particularly eager to see the Sootus and inform them of the warped and twisted behavior of Mr. Mondi. We could not wait. Upon their return, they called the staff members to the office one by one. They paid them their salaries and asked how things had been. We were shocked to see that not one of the staffs was prepared to tell on Mr. Mondi. Then suddenly big Jude, one of the older children, forced his way into the office and blurted it out – all that had been happening whilst the Sootus had been away. Sandy was then recalled back into the office, who completely corroborated his story, whilst all the other children stood outside the office and started shouting out what kind of sordid things he had been up to. Mr. Mondi was eventually called in to answer the allegations laid against him. We all stood outside, chanting, 'Child abuser! Brutalizer! Maniac! Madman!'

Thank God, the Sootus believed us, and not only did they expel him on the spot, but they did so without paying him his full wages. 'Ha! Ha! Ha!' All of us jeered at him as he walked down the drive. Approximately halfway down the drive, true to form, he picked up some stones and began throwing them at us but each one missed. Seeing what was happening Mrs. Sootu came running out and chased him off the property with a very large brush used to sweep outside, cursing him as she went. We all laughed and jeered at him some more. The further he got, the louder we all jeered, and it was in that same moment, that we were justified. But the emotional scars of our ordeal would lie dormant for many years to come, just waiting to be triggered so that it too could raise its ugly head.

As the summer came to an end, we went berry picking in the long drive that led all the way up to Alley Pally. There used to be so many berries at the bottom of the drive and it was lovely to make the long walk uphill to the top, picking and eating them as we went. Alley Pally was our nickname for Alexandra Palace; it was our little part of the countryside slap bang in the city, it was our secret garden which we were fortunate enough to have right on our back-door step.

That year, we picked so many berries, mainly blackberries; they were so big and fat and plump and juicy. Sometimes, the juice would burst right into your face, run down your chin, and splat on to your T-shirt and your fingers and tongue would color deep purple in evidence; it was lovely. We ate all the strawberries and raspberries as we went because there were not that many of them, but they were just so sweet and juicy. The blackberries appeared in abundance, I mean they were everywhere, however, we had nothing to carry them back in. In that moment, I remembered that I use to load food I didn't want into my vest when I was at home, so now what's to say I couldn't do the same only keep it, so I pulled out my vest and began to load them on to it, then everyone else upon seeing what I was doing also began to follow my lead; it must have been an odd-looking picture as we all whipped out our vests or T shirts and began loading black berries in to them.

Perhaps even as far back as then I was indeed a practical forward thinker in the making. Sandy soon found a discarded plastic bag slowly blowing in the breeze; it had become trapped between some branches. We all poured our blackberries into it, until it was almost half filled and quite heavy. When we arrived back at the house, we blended blackberries with milk for shakes. We baked blackberries in pastry for tarts and turnovers, we boiled blackberries in pots for jams and jellies, and we whisked blackberries with cream sugar and egg whites to make mouse, after which we were all thoroughly black berried out. We put our feet up in front of the TV. 'This is great,' I sighed. It was great, and I loved it.

As the summer made a Bee line for autumn and the autumn season came to an end, in came the fireworks, sparklers, and bonfires. I remember the papers the following day, they were filled with stories of all the children who had been injured by fireworks or who had been burnt from being too close to the fire or a firework. I remember feeling very fearful of the words that were being read out and feeling very traumatized by all the pictures. I guess it was from that day forward, I would always associate fireworks and bonfire night as being a dreadful thing. I never wanted to be a partaker in this type of festivity, that had been for years shrouded in tragedy. The emotional anxiety felt every year at this time has remained with me even to this day – well over forty years now.

Winter quickly followed autumn, which was accompanied by the white stuff. That winter was great; school closed unexpectedly so we spent most of our time at Alley Pally, sliding down the snow-covered hills on toboggans, throwing snowballs, and rolling around in the white stuff; it was pure bliss. We did not have a single care in the world at that moment, and for that season, life was good, and I was normal even if it was only for one day. Our screams of joy bounced back at us from off the trees and tickled our ears and we laughed out loud wholeheartedly. It was all so much fun; each afternoon, we returned home, soaking wet and freezing cold and yet full of contented merriment.

At every teatime, we would relive the fun and laughter experienced throughout the day all over again and laugh out loud once more. Can I have some more please? Albeit the statement 'All good things must come to an end' was never far behind us and could not have come at a worse time.

Disappointment and sadness were fast approaching, as was Christmas. Dad, who had remained blissfully absent all year, now without even so much as a letter or phone call, had turned up, just like that. No indication, no notice, no nothing. His brother in tow, in his usual position behind the wheel. He had come to collect us and take us back home again. 'What!' I thought... I could not bloody believe it. Uncle Matthew still had his dark-blue car, which he never got out of. He would just wait in the driveway like the getaway driver of some big heist, engine running and horn occasionally honking, except that it was us that they had come for. We were the prize. For the first time, I felt angry with Dad, disappointed even. '*How dare he turn up out of the blue and spoil our fun?'* I mean, he had not visited us all year, and now suddenly he turns up out of I don't know where as usual, expecting us to just drop everything and to leave with him – not a single phone call all year, not a card or even a letter. No notice, no warning, or anything, but just like that, he turned up to take us home.

Well, for the second time, I did not actually want to go with him. I did not want to leave. I had experienced true laughter, pure joy, and blissful happiness, and if this was 'as good as it gets', I wanted to take it – or rather keep it right here right now. I wanted to stay with the Sootus, and I wanted to tell him so right to his face, but I was too afraid to say 'No! We don't want to go!' I knew if we didn't go with him, one thing we could both be certain of was a good old-fashioned Caribbean beating, right there in front of Mrs. Sootus and we both knew it only too well. I was standing on about the fourth step of the center staircase which was wider than the average and curled upward in almost a spiral, when he appeared at the door just like that! But this was *so* not Tommy Cooper, no, it was real life: my life!

The staircase led up to all the dorms, separating off to the left and right after about the twelfth step. It was situated in the middle of an overzealous hallway. Up the stairs the first branch off to the left was the front door of the Sootus' apartment, continuing up and to the right brought you all the way up to the children's dormitories and if you continued up you came to the staff members' sleeping quarters. I began to climb the staircase in sheer disbelief of what was unfolding, and my eyes were already welling up. Mrs. Sootu, upon realizing our anxiety, tried her best to salvage the situation by trying to persuade him to allow us to stay.

'At least just for Christmas,' she said. However, he wasn't having any of it. And to add to the confusion, Uncle Matthew who had by now, perhaps been waiting for approximately ten minutes for all of us to come out, had become quite irritated and was now trying to hurry Dad by honking his horn intermittently, and Dad, in turn, was trying to hurry us as the spirit of anxiety took a hold of him, now looking for its third victim. As the third hand kissed the 59th second in each minute, we were sure that this was the second he was going to start screaming for us to hurry up. We were just unsure in which minute it would commence.

We collected our things, hastily holding them with our bare hands, before making it known that we were ready to depart, standing in formation like good little soldiers and taking our place in the '*500*'. Leaving so many things behind, including our clothes.

Mrs. Sootu ran into the office like an Olympic athlete, to get the rest of our Christmas presents out and was still stuffing extra items into the boot of the car, as the doors on this dark blue Ford saloon slammed shut with such ferocity and the wheels began to kiss the dust goodbye, as they rolled slowly down the driveway, before picking up momentum and speeding out on to the busy hill and out of sight. We made our way back to the farm, vis-à-vis the concrete jungle, filled with a deep melancholy.

Back at the Farm

The next morning, I felt utterly sick and very depressed all over again to wake up and find myself back in Dad's house – to be at this home again.

I looked out of the window only to see the extent of this grey, cold, and very hard concrete jungle staring right back at me. Completely immersed in my thoughts, my mind quickly returned to earth by the creaking of doors opening and closing in the small hallway immediately on the other side of our bedroom door. I turned around just in time to see the handle of our own bedroom door move slowly downward. I began to walk towards the door as it opened to greet my visitor. It was Dad. He came in and sat down next to me on the edge of the bottom of the bed. I felt slightly uncomfortable, not knowing what was going to happen next: was I in trouble already or what? Suddenly, he placed his arm across my shoulder and forced me to lie down backwards. I was so frightened my body became completely rigid, and my heart was beating so fast I was almost waiting to exhale. We were both lying there with our feet and legs hanging off the edge of the bed, *at least mine were*. I had no idea of what was going to happen next. *Was I in trouble? Was I about to be on the receiving end of more unwelcome news?* The not knowing filled me with a fearful awkwardness. Then out of the silence Dad spoke.

'You know I love you, don't you?'

'Yes, Daddy,' came my start-stop whisper in response, which I completely struggled to get out. I hadn't spoken up until that point, so my mouth was quite dry from the night before and my words were cloaked in fear.

'I want you to know that I will never allow ya all to go away again,' he said, choking on his words as he delivered his lines. 'OK!' he added almost succeeding in his attempt to tickle me. Only this was not a joyful day for me, and this was not good news. In fact, for me it was the worst news of my life. I wanted to cry and cry and cry and then just cry all over again. I mean it felt like I had just been handed down a sentence from hell. Mordecka no longer had to keep telling me I was going to prison; I was already there. *You don't have to be in prison to be in a prison.* I wondered whether somehow, he thought that brief speech was supposed to make everything all right. Because I just wanted to return immediately, I wanted to remain with the Sootus, I wanted to go back; but after my last experience of telling him my feelings, I did not have the guts or the courage to tell him of my desires; so, to that effect, my response was also a very choked, 'Yes, Daddy.' My mouth still completely dry. These very words would, just three years later, become a curse in the battle for freedom, my freedom. But I didn't know it then and the clock was ticking, tick tock, tick tock, tick tock.

I had, during the episodes of our retreats, become fully aware that different environments triggered different emotions, and I began to despise being back at home again. I wanted to leave Dad's life right away but did not know how to or even what to do to make it happen. After Dad, had finished his short speech, which I am sure he meant sincerely, he went off to repeat it to Odette. I don't know how she felt about it or whether she even believed him as it was something we never discussed. Nevertheless, this was the first time I had ever heard the words 'I love you' spoken from his lips and that meant a lot. I carried them forever in my heart from that day to this and I believed them; on the journey that was ahead of me they would keep me going, they would keep me strong, they would keep me alive.

As the days turned into weeks and the weeks turned into months the honeymoon period came to a marked end, it was not long before the beatings and the shouting started all over again, along with the trips to the loo to flush away the sloppy slops, or rather Mordecka's pathetic model for food. In just a matter of a few short months, Mordecka had succeeded in throwing away all my toys, leaving not even one behind, but of course, her own children had loads of toys. I now had to use my imagination for creative play and stimulation.

I found some abandoned batteries lying around the house and an unclaimed notebook. The batteries became my toys, my little people, from that moment on, right up until the end. I would tear out the empty pages of this unused notebook, gently cutting away at the pages, using just my fingers as scissors. I would make an array of things, including clothes to dress them in and weapons for them to fight with. At one point, I became so creative that I even surprised myself, making them tiny cups, cutlery, and plates with food on. I even managed to make them a car and all from paper; of course, they were too heavy to ride in it. Before long, I had made so many accessories for the batteries, which almost filled one-quarter of an empty plastic bag in which I kept them all safe. I would hide them deep under the bed where I knew Dad would not look.

Another well-known game I would play with my brother was ships and sharks. In this game, the bed was our ship and the carpet was the sea, being big and blue it was very fitting, and all the marine life that dwelt therein was in our imagination. We took turns killing sharks in the sea; sometimes we would have to wrestle with them, so a pillow would be thrown in for effect. Then we would cook and eat all the fish that we had caught. Another game we would play was a driving game. The edge of the bed was our car, and we had a square steering wheel attached to a three-legged stool, which doubled as a table. Dad had made a table using the legs of a broken stool. He made the top out of spare wood left over from making the coatroom.

Once the table top had become loose from bad handling, in particular, my brother throwing it around in temper on countless occasions, it doubled nicely as the steering wheel for our imaginary car because you could turn it a full 360 degrees, as long as you didn't mind a square steering wheel, or the occasional splinters that went with it.

When we really felt creative, we would allow our brother to slide down the stairs in his baby bath, which also doubled as a car only without wheels. This was a game that was thoroughly enjoyed by all until after that fateful encounter where he had leaned too far forward on the descent and had actually toppled out of the bath, whilst travelling at full speed down the stairs. Upon reaching the bottom with a loud bang, his head had become lodged rather firmly under the pipes to the central heating system, which lay like broccoli, horizontally across the wall adjacent to the bottom of the stairs. My God, did he cry, and oh my God, did we scarper when we heard Dad get up and come out of his room, shouting at the top of his voice. For us, this had to be another of those 'Put the blame on Bobby' incidents.

As Dad came to the top of the stairs, still shouting, we gradually emerged from the living room, one by one, trying to act completely shocked and dismayed at the scene and innocently questioning Bobby as to what had happened and whether he was alright. Everyone was speaking all together, so Dad could not understand what my brother was saying or that he was in fact selling us down the river – little shit!

Thankfully, Dad didn't realize either that both Odette and I were just pretending to have been in the living room the entire time of the calamity. In the end, he just said, 'All ya just go and watch the TV, ya hear!'

'Yes, Daddy, Yes, Daddy,' came our confident, good little girl responses. He called out to Odette and instructed her to turn on the TV. *Sesame Street* was the number one hit children's program back in the 1970s, at least for us anyway as we were all big fans of the show. We all loved it, and it was just about time for the show to start. My brother was still mumbling and murmuring about his ordeal, but as our Dad had already gone back to bed, it was only himself who was listening.

We tried to make the best of school holidays and the weekends spent at home, but for the most part, they were usually so boring that we could not wait to get back to school. I cannot recall us ever missing a single day due to illness; however, Odette missed more than enough through having to look after Bobby first and then Corina second; Dad and Mordecka never brought in outside help to care for their children, just us, but mainly Odette. However, every time Mordecka would get pregnant it was us that were always sent away only permitted to return after the child was born.

Back in the early 1970s, in-between having three children for Dad, Mordecka was studying midwifery, and she was no pushover. I think she saw herself as a bit of a detective. I mean, she was always carrying out dawn raids on our room, except it wasn't dawn. It was usually about one or two in the morning, and to make matters worse, her raids were always carried out on a school night. She would make as much noise as possible, banging and knocking, and tipping things over, and pulling things out, and dropping things on the floor.

The crash-bash wallop usually always woke us up, but we would never let on that we had woken up; otherwise, she would have you up and out of bed to carry out some bizarre chore at that crazy hour. She would always leave our room in a mess and the lights on so we would have to get up to turn it off. Her little sidekick, our brother, was always in tow. As we got older, we began to recognize the signs. Clearly, Dad had upset her again over some little thing or other, and she had arrived in her usual fashion to tell us all about it in her typical manner of storytelling, delivered in true form of her tipping things over and banging things regardless of the time of night, or the fact that we were actually asleep, or even that we had school the next day. Between that and the knocking and banging, it was like some warped, messed-up, crazy version of Morse code.

In truth, we were just not that bothered. Her complaints would always take a U-turn and go on to unwarranted attacks against our mother, who, according to Mordecka, left on the bus, because she was a prostitute, wearing a red coat, and that's what prostitutes do. They leave on the bus, wearing red coats, and we were just like our mother. We were prostitutes, and we would end up in the prison, but we didn't have any red coats. We were just seven and eight years of age, we were not prostitutes, and being in this house with her was already like living in some kind of prison: You don't have to be in a prison to be in prison. On one occasion, during a random dawn raid occurring at about the stroke of midnight, she decided to give to my brother a rather large sewing needle, not a knitting needle, a sewing needle, it was very sharp at one end because that was the end that was used to pierce the item of clothing that you might be sewing.

In any event, he, in turn, thought it would be a jolly good idea to poke us in the head with it whilst we were pretending to be asleep. He started with Odette first. He slid his scrawny little hand under the headboard of the bed, for which there was rather a large gap, perhaps created by all the jumping we had done on to it over the years first from the head board and then later from the window ledge, he was reaching for one of us. As he did, I saw a glimmer of something shiny in his hand. I tried to warn Odette that something was in his hand, but she could not hear me or understand me as I was trying to warn her without moving or talking.

When I saw, what was coming next, I moved as far away from the headboard as I could down to the middle of the bed and watched as his scrawny little destructive hand shoot under the headboard as quick as a lizard's tongue. Unfortunately, it was Odette, who was lying nearest to the edge of the bed, and who had nowhere to move to. Our little brother then pushed his scrawny little arm back under the headboard and lunged the needle right into Odette's ear with which she let out such a loud yell. 'Ouch!' she shouted in a loud voice.

'*Shit!*' I thought, '*now we are really gonna get it.*' Mordecka stopped dead in her tracks; even she was frightened. It just goes to show that a bully will continue to be a bully until the day they are challenged pulled up and confronted.

Bobby quickly pulled his hand back out from under the headboard. Mordecka had never heard us raise our voices before. 'He just poked me with something!' shouted Odette in a very loud voice. With this, Mordecka immediately looked down to where Odette was now sitting then she looked over at Bobby, saw the needle in his hand, and remarkably told him not to do that again, completely failing to remove it from his hand, and of course, he did do it again. And of course, Odette complained again, this time raising her voice even louder, and Mordecka knocked the needle out of his hand and instructed him to leave our bedroom, which he did. Odette's ear was now bleeding.

However, Mordecka offered no sympathy, no concern, and no first aid. She simply left the room, turning out the light as she went this time. Odette had to attend to her ear by herself and in the dark. From then on, when they entered our room, we would both move down right into the middle of the bed pulling up the covers right over our heads so Bobby couldn't interfere with us whilst we were in bed. And if he dared place his little scrawny hand back under the headboard and under the covers, he would be pinched quite hard or have his hand jolted and twisted very hard so that he could quickly get it out from under our covers; at least by me anyway.

Whenever Mordecka was bored or restless, she would often wait for our Dad to go off to work and then burst into our room and beat us up for no good or apparent reason or start ransacking our room. She would make up stories that we were talking too loudly, or laughing, or making a noise of some kind, which according to mankind probably hadn't yet even been invented, but in any event, it was disturbing her.

Mordecka's conversations would always deviate dramatically, switching to ranting raves on the topic of our mother and it was always the same old story. Perhaps, she was the one who was really traumatized by the fact that our mother had left and that was why she felt the dramatized need to keep bringing it up all the time. It did not really make much sense to me back then, but I think Odette was very hurt by the things that she said. Nevertheless, Odette never spoke about her feelings and neither did either of us ever attempt to defend our mother's reputation by answering her back; she was bigger and stronger than us then, but it wouldn't always be that way.

One night, Mordecka burst into our room at approximately 20.20 hours, *that's 8.20 p.m. to you and me.* She was demanding to know who had washed up that evening. Of course, it was Odette. It was always Odette if it wasn't Dad and it wasn't her and it certainly wasn't me and never Bobby so of course it was Odette. It was Odette who also usually was the one to answer first any questions that were fired at us too. So, Odette answered, admitting that it was she who had in fact washed up. But Mordecka already knew it was Odette who had washed up because I never did big wash ups, and Dad was not at home.

'Well, the dishes smell fresh!' she moaned, stomping back across the short hallway to her own room like some spoilt, overweight, overgrown teenager. So, Odette got up, got dressed, went downstairs, and began to wash up all the cups, glasses, dishes, pots, plates, bowls, and cutlery again.

We lived in a household where when our parents cooked, they would never wash up as they went, so by the end of the day, you were guaranteed that almost every plate, dish, cutlery, cup, pot, and glass in the kitchen would be piled up high on the sideboard like a mountain from pot crockery kingdom, crying out to be washed.

It was just after nine when she returned to our bedroom and climbed into bed. And it was about two minutes after that when Mordecka marched back in, still complaining that the dishes smelled 'fresh', a Caribbean term for unclean or not clean enough. Odette got back up, got dressed, went back downstairs for a second time, and washed up every plate, dish, cutlery, cup, pot, bowl, and glass that she had already just washed up. She returned just after 10 p.m., and two minutes later, so did Mordecka. According to her, she was still not satisfied. So, Odette got up again, got dressed, and went downstairs to wash and rinse them all again for a third time. Odette returned at something past 11 p.m., and, true to form, Mordecka was not far behind repeating her previous demand that the dishes were still not clean, so Odette had to return, yet again, back to the kitchen and wash them all up. This was now the fourth time that she had got dressed and went downstairs to repeat the process. It was now about 12.20hrs in the morning. We had to get up for school in less than seven hours. We should have been asleep by 21: 00hrs at the latest. With what little understanding I had and with even less understanding of spiritual things, I just said, 'Dear God, please do not let Odette have to go downstairs to wash the dishes again, please let Mordecka find no fault with the dishes. Please God, thank you.'

When Odette returned, her body was freezing cold. She had been standing down there on the cold floor in just her light summer clothes, wearing no slippers; the central heating was off, and Mordecka had deliberately left the kitchen window wide open, perhaps in the demented hope that Odette would catch a cold or something. When she got into bed, she would not permit me to warm her up. We had just one blanket on our bed that could not be tucked in on any side as it was ridiculously too small for the bed, and with two of us in the bed, unless we slept right next to each other, it was inevitable that one of us was going to fall out from under the covers and wake up prematurely from the cold. I think I just gave her the entire blanket that night, but she still shared it with me. *Odette is my dearest beloved sister, and I have always loved her, and I always will.*

Walls have ears

Sometimes at night I would hear the raised muffled voices of Mordecka and Dad not in agreement. I found that if I placed my ear to the wall I could hear more clearly. Mordecka would be telling Dad that they could no longer afford to keep the both of us anymore; of course, this did wonders for my anxiety. Another night I would hear her telling Dad that she wanted to go to America but that they could not afford for both of us to go with them;

she made him agree that one of us would not go but I couldn't hear who it was, that was to stay. I didn't tell Odette but the knowing made me feel even more anxious.

Usually when doing chores in the kitchen Odette would always be the one to wash up, unless Dad did it, and I would be the one responsible for drying up and putting away. Whenever we were working together, we would always find something to laugh about whilst doing the washing-up together, so much so that a breakage or two would usually occur. Instantly, we would become fast filled with fear and instinctively we would begin to blame each other all the way up to the reporting of the incident before Dad, whose rather perverse approach was if we were both blaming each other, then we were both to blame, and therefore we should both be punished, and that punishment should be a good old-fashioned Caribbean beating, ouch! His beatings would usually last approximately twenty to thirty minutes, during which we would jump around the room, crying, and peeing in our pants.

Usually, once we had cleaned up after the evening meal, it was normal practice for us to go into Dad's bedroom, to watch TV until bedtime. There was always some sort of film on – either a John Wayne western or a Sissy Spencer shoot-out or an Alfred Hitchcock thriller, post-war film noir, such as The *Third Man,* which was spy film. The types of series we would watch would inevitably be *Star Trek*, starring William Shatner, which I could never see the point of, or the *Streets of San Francisco* with Michael Douglas in his glory days as a young actor.

As a child, I hated looking at the large ugly bulbous, badly reset nose of his much older partner. And then there was *Starsky & Hutch*, whom every young girl enjoyed watching – never mind the story line. Albeit, after a severe beating, we usually went straight to our room, and on this occasion, we went straight to bed with welts rising and purple bruises firmly seated on top of purple bruises now covering our arms and thighs. With tears in our eyes and still arguing over who was to blame, we eventually got into bed and fell asleep. At this point, it seemed apparent that if honesty was to be rewarded with violence, then clearly what was the point? Sometimes, I thought Dad beat us just for the sake of beating us, to get out his own frustrations. I mean, why he couldn't take up squash or something I don't know. However, what we did learn from that point onwards was, if anything else ever got broken, it went straight to the bottom of the bin, and our parents were none the wiser. Occasionally, you would hear them asking each other whether they had seen this or that, and if you were in the kitchen that was your cue to exit. but from that moment on we never reported any further breakages to them ever again and so that was one less thing to get beaten for. '*Clever thinking,*' I thought. But something was forming deep down, right down inside the pit of us; something was taking root and at the right time it would bring forth its fruit. Sadly, joy and any kind of laughter was always short-lived in our house as scarce as it was.

I remember one occasion when I was walking back from the kitchen, returning upstairs through the living room, the same way that I had passed to the kitchen and had passed Dad who was in the front room watching Saturday afternoon sports with Dickie Davies on commentary when he just happened to look over at me as I was about to go out of the room. Unfortunately, for me he noticed the two very small holes in my jumper next to the buttonholes from approximately 10-15 feet away. As I placed my hand on the door handle and began to pull it downward to open the door and make my exit, he called out to me. 'Jacqueline!' I stopped dead in my tracks turning slowly to face him. I looked straight at him, but his eyes were firmly back on the telly. Then for a single moment, he locked his eyes on me and asked me what was wrong with my jumper.

'Nothing,' came my timid response in a baby-bear like voice.

'What?' he demanded, almost screaming back at me in a humongous Daddy bear like voice.

'Nothing,' came my apprehensive response in a high pitched almost mummy-bear like voice.

'Come here!' he screeched in his even bigger Daddy-bear like voice. I began my snail-like pace in his direction.

'Come here!' he shouted in his even louder grand Daddy-bear voice.

Suddenly I needed the loo again. I began wishing if only I could disappear, right now, in this moment... Inevitably, I arrived right in front of him. But I don't remember my legs moving to get there.

'I asked you, what is wrong with your shirt?' he screamed.

'Nothing,' came my whimper of a response.

POW! Came the thump which connected to my shoulder.

'Ow!' came my screech of a response when met by the element of surprise.

'What's wrong with your shirt?' came his repeated now heated question.

'I I don't know,' came my tearful response.

'Look at it! Look at it!' came his orders. I turned my neck to look at it almost crossed eyed. POW! – Again, came the next strike, bringing me down to the floor with a thud.

'Get up! Get up!' came the hysterical screaming order. I began to think that perhaps he thought he was in the ring, but with whom, I knew not.

'Dad, this is me.' I thought. Had he not realised it was me? I slowly began to climb back up to standing.

'Well!' came the observation. POW! Came the next hit.

'You stand there and tell me what is wrong with your shirt?' he screamed.

I looked down at my jumper as if I didn't know what it was, he wanted me to witness, as if I was expecting to be suddenly surprised or something. 'Err...it...it…it…has...err…a very small hole in it,' I replied, full of tears.

'It has a very small hole in it,' he said in a little funny voice as if to mimic me.

Except he was not joking, not this time. Today I was in trouble, big trouble, and there was no lie on earth that was going to help me, and no one to come to my aid and no one to put the blame on or share this beating with me.

'It's ripped!' he screamed. 'It's ripped!' he repeated like some crazy incensed person who had just lost the plot. Then like a foreign person from distant lands, he began to speak faster and faster, each word accompanied by a contact blow to my person, causing me to fall from the spot upon which I had been ordered to stand on.

'Did you see the hole when you put the jumper on this morning?' he screamed violently.

Too afraid of what his response would be to a 'yes' answer, 'No!' came the uncertain sheepish response in the form of an even quieter whisper. Of course, I was lying.

'What?' he screamed.

'N-n-no, Daddy,' came my answer, another lie, this time accompanied with the return of my stammer.

I was crying and sobbing and saying that I was sorry and telling him that I would never do it again and peeing in my pants all in the same moment. But my *'I'm sorry, Daddy'* and pleas for mercy all fell on deaf ears as he continued to strike me and hit me and smack me and thump me.

'What did I tell you?' he screamed.

'Never...' I tried to speak.

POW! Came another blow. 'How dare you walk around with ripped clothes on?' he shouted at the top of his voice. POW! Again, another whack.

'I'm sorry,' I sobbed. 'I'm sorry.'

'When you have a hole in your clothes, what should you do? 'he ranted.

Up until this point my responses were mainly 'Yes, Daddy', 'I'm sorry, Daddy', and 'I won't do it again, Daddy.' And 'I beg you please stop, Daddy.'

Every word spoken was said in the same sad, fearful, tearful tempo. I did not know what the right answer was, so I said everything, hoping to hit the jackpot, but alas, I missed.

'You damn well sew it up!' he screamed.

'Yes, Daddy,' came my response trying to sound positive. That's the right answer I thought. Sew it up. Completely distressed and shaking like a leaf in the wind, I could see that Dad was almost out of breath, and this was a good sign. *'It would all be over soon,'* I thought. Delivering a beating was for him, a bit like having an upper-body workout, I guess. And just as I thought we were finishing and just as I began to believe it was all over, enter

Mordecka. *'Crap no,'* I thought. She came down and just stuck her big nose in with comments like 'Look at her!', and 'Just look at her!', and 'She is not even crying', and 'Not even a tear in sight', and 'Look at her, those are just crocodile tears', and 'What a good actress she is!'

The beating then started all over again. This time it continued for a further twenty minutes because now Mordecka was on the scene, and she did what she did best, which was to wind Dad up just like an alarm clock, then let him go. She just loved seeing us getting a good beating. I remember on one occasion an argument ensued between them because she was going on and on and on about Odette wetting the bed. 'Well, what do you want me to do?' he shouted. 'Beat her to death?' She was silent as if she did not have a response; then after a few moments, she piped up, 'well, now you're talking, now you're talking.' I had no more emotion to cry and no more energy for sound. He beat me without me speaking a single word – no more pleading, no more cries for mercy and no more, I'm sorry. After this second beating came to an end, I was dismissed from Dad's sight and slowly left the room.

I began my ascent back upstairs. I had to climb the stairs one at a time. I tried holding on to the banister for support, but it was very difficult, crying as I went. I was in so much pain, the bruises had already taken up their usual places on the different parts of my body. It took longer to make it up the stairs; upon reaching the top I could barely pull down the door handle in order to open the door to our bedroom as my hands were so swollen and numb from being caught up in the mayhem of trying to protect my face and head. I could barely move my hands. Looking for some kind of empathy from Odette, I asked her whether she had heard anything whilst I was downstairs, she answered with a bewildered 'No... !' and with such absolute certainty, which, in turn, made me angry because I wanted her to have heard that I had just got beaten again, and for nothing. I wanted her to hug me and tell me it was all gonna be OK like she usually did. But she didn't hear a thing, she had been playing and laughing and joking with Corina.

I couldn't talk, so I took my flannel off the heater, went to the bathroom, to wipe the tracks of my pee from off my inner thighs. I could barely move my hands as I tried to rinse out the flannel; they were so swollen red and purple in color. They looked like the hands of an overweight child I could barely bend my fingers. Upon returning to our room I placed the flannel back on the radiator. I put on clean knickers, climbed into our bed, and cried myself silently to sleep.

The truth was I knew that there had been a hole in my jumper, but I was too afraid to ask for a sewing needle and cotton to stitch it back up; in truth, the thought never even entered my head, and, as such, things like all rips and tears and holes or missing buttons, they were all simply ignored, up until that day that was. I had worn that jumper twenty times, if I had worn it once and up until that point, Dad had never noticed any hole in it before and if he did there had never been an issue with it. Living at home often felt like the goal post was never set in stone and had a tendency to keep moving all over the pitch: at times, it was difficult to keep up.

How I wished we had gone with our mother. How I wished I had stayed at Sandy Lodge. How I wished that we didn't live here anymore. Surely anything had to be better than this. Sometimes at night, I would look up at the starry sky and wish with all my might to be somewhere else, to be somewhere better. I wished that we could have a holiday every year forever, I wished for a great big doll of my own that I could take care of, something to take care of. And I think somewhere deep in the pit of me I wished for someone to love me for me. Sometimes the night would be full of stars, and whenever I saw one that even remotely looked as though it was twinkling, I would make out that it was a falling star and make a wish. I didn't care if in truth it was really a helicopter or even some light aircraft with its flashing identification light. It was my beacon of hope, and on it, so I wished. Whenever I had time, I would look up at the sky and will myself out of this place. Little did I know that the clock was ticking, and that day was soon about to arrive, tick tock, tick tock.

Bringing home, the shopping

I think I must have been about nine, when Dad decided that I was old enough to do more. What he had in his mind was that I could now take part in the monthly shopping expedition. He wanted me, little me, to carry all the bags of shopping back from the shops in the main shopping area, approximately three miles south from the farm.

On the point of walking Dad was a bit of a natural walker; he walked everywhere that he could, and he would usually walk for miles and usually with us in tow, which I absolutely detested. If you walked too far ahead of him, suddenly he would turn left or right without any warning, and you would be left in a panic, trying to find which road he had just turned in to; and if you walked too far behind him, he would do the same and again you would be left to run and catch up. If ever you were out walking with him, you had better be paying attention as well as keeping one eye out for dog shit. That would be another beating, and your shoes would be thrown in the bin: then you would be back to wearing your old ones again, the toe squeezers. After two episodes of this, I realised that if I just washed them, no one was none the wiser.

Perhaps out of fear that I might lose something, Dad decided he would accompany me back to about the halfway point at Mount Pleasant Road, expecting me, without doubt, to make it back to the farm with all the bags intact and on my own. It was at that point that he would simultaneously hand to me 4 or 5 and sometimes 6 sturdy plastic bags, each one containing approximately eight or nine cans. This equated to roughly about one month's supply of processed foods, which included Heinz baked beans (x8 large cans), Heinz spaghetti (x8 large cans), tinned pilchards (x6 large cans, one size only), tinned sardines (x10 packs, one size only), Princes corned beef (x5 large tins), Nestlé carnation milk (x8 large cans), Nestlé condensed milk (× 8 large cans, one size only), Nestlé Milo drink (x1 large tin), and Nescafé coffee (x1 large jar). It was only Dad who drank coffee in our house; everybody else drank tea and sometimes Milo, but not in the same sitting of course. I think the coffee must have helped him to keep awake during the midnight hours whilst working the night shift at the bakery. In any event, it was my job to get the cans and the coffee from the crossroads at Mount Pleasant Road to the fourth floor on Stapleford. The distance was probably just under a mile but felt more like twenty-five. When we arrived at the *'you're on your own'* point, he would say, 'OK, you know the way from here, don't you?'

'Yes, Daddy,' I would painfully whisper back.

'Well, off you go then,' he would say, as though he was releasing a little boat on to the water to be carried off by the breeze on some lovely sunny day. I divided the bags as equally as I could between my two little hands and began to walk in the direction of the flats. I could feel my back and my belly strain together as I attempted to lift these bags, they were so heavy. Tears of sheer frustration filled my eyes and began to slowly slide down my cheeks. I cried, I strained, I spluttered, I struggled, and I swore, I took two steps forward then had to put the bags down. I absolutely hated every minute of it. It was nothing short of sheer torture for me. I could do no more than to muster up the strength to move me and the bags just two steps at a time before having to crash them back down to the ground again. I wanted to walk away and just leave them there on the side of the road; if only I could make up a convincing enough story that my parents would fall for. I just wanted to throw the cans away, but I knew I couldn't.

I wanted to run away, but I couldn't. Where would I go, and to whom I knew not. I knew no-one who could help me. After composing myself once more, again, I strained to pick the bags back up and take another two steps before crashing the bags back down to the floor again. I repeated this process until I arrived back at the flats.

The good news was from Wilson Road the street level adjoined the flats at the first floor, so I was able to use a tenants door mat to slide the bags down the corridor giving me some relief from carrying them. We were not allowed to use the lift, so I then had to drag the bags up the four flights of stairs from the first floor and along the landing up to our door. Only God knew how long it took me to get home that day, at a guess I think the entire trip must have taken me about two hours... Upon my arrival, I rung the bell with my hands set in a claw- like position, the undersides were a sort of pink turning red in color, with the underside now raised up and stiffened, set like clay from the relentless weight of the cans pulling down the bag handles, pressing deep into my skin. They appeared to be hell-bent on warping and twisting my skin almost as if in rebellious retaliation to being carried. I waited patiently for someone, anyone to open the door. I could hear Mordecka calling out to Bobby, ordering him to open the door straight away. I thought if he messes me about today of all days, I was gonna kick his scrawny little arse all over that flat and beat him good and proper, and I certainly was not going to hesitate or be deterred from his threats of telling Dad; if we collided that day, I would make sure he never forgot that it was I who was his older sister. Lucky for him, he came straight away and opened the door and immediately moved out of my way. I walked quickly into the kitchen and with my last squirt of energy, swung the bags up and onto the top of the freezer bringing them down with a crash.

Dad and Odette had taken the bus to wherever it was that they had travelled to that day and had taken it back again too. They came back just five minutes after me. The tins had to be counted before being put away to be sure I had not lost one. After separating my hands from the carrier bags, which were all stretched out and at the point of ripping.

I stacked up the cans on the side and went upstairs to the bathroom where I washed the salt tracks from off my face; the remaining evidence that I had been crying. I tried to soothe my hands under the cold running water, in an attempt to see if the skin would return to normal. But they remained as a reminder to me for a short while after.

Afterwards I went to my room and cried silent tears of sheer frustration. I lay down on the bed completely exhausted and attempted to rest. My brother began as usual to annoy me by opening and closing the door continuously and making his voice heard. That day, in that moment, I just had to ignore him; my body needed to recover, and I needed to rest.

Red Dishes

In our house, when it came to washing-up, drying up, and putting away the dishes, Odette and I were always the usual suspects. When it came to picking up the fluff and any white particles from off the carpet, we were the only suspects, and when it came to wiping and shining and buffing and sparkling, and making clean every little thing, we were still the usual suspects.

On this bright, sunny morning, the sun's rays were pouring in through the kitchen window; it was as if a fleet of angels had pulled up and parked right outside our house. The sunlight flooded in like a river running through it. The day was so beautiful that it invoked a real sense of feel good to it. We were doing the washing-up, and for some reason in that moment, just in that moment, we were happy.

It was only Odette and I in the kitchen at the time. Our brother was upstairs, out of sight, out of mind and out of our way, and Mordecka was entertaining a guest in the front room, *probably another Jehovah's Witness*; they tended to visit us a lot back then. We were singing and fooling around as we washed and dried the dishes trying our best not to make too much noise. As I got to drying up the knives, I began to reminisce about one of the films that we had seen so frequently at the Coronet on Saturday mornings called *Zorro*.

We had regularly attended the picture house when we were at the Lodge. Goading Odette into joining in, we began our sword fight, taking turns to use the sharpest knife. 'En gard!' I shouted, waving my knife at my sister, who responded by dropping her pots back into the soapy water and picking up the meat knife to block my swing.

'En gard!' came her robotic response. The knives connected in the air with a '*ker-ching*' and continued to sing the same tune on each quick succession of swings as they made contact. Then, at my insistence, we swapped knives. She, with the bread knife now and me with the steak knife; unbeknown to either of us, Dad had just very recently sharpened the bread knife; it was therefore the sharpest of the t wo and the most dangerous.

'En gard!' I shouted, swinging my knife quickly through the air. *This is great,* I thought. *It's just like a real sword fight.*

'En gard,' she responded, moving into each swing with her body weight behind it for extra effect. Our knives connected on every strike; this was real fighting, I thought. We were both pushing each other, increasing our strength with every swing. Then suddenly without warning or indication, my knife slipped out from my hand, causing her knife to continue moving through the air, making contact with my neck as it split the air slicing me open from ear to throat as gravity forced her arm downward and back in to the resting position.

Quickly, my neck began to bleed out, but I had not even noticed; I didn't feel a thing. Her face changed to a look of horror as she saw the blood. She put her knife down quickly and began to start washing the dishes again, causing me to worry now. Still I had not noticed the blood.

'What is it?' I asked, sensing her tension.

'Oh my God, you're bleeding,' she said. 'Dad is going to kill me.'

'What?' I looked down to witness a supply of blood fast spilling out of me, like water from a flowing tap that could not be turned off. I looked dazed and appeared paralyzed not knowing what to do next.

'Quick, come here.' She pulled me over to her as she attempted to apply pressure to the wound using dirty tea towels and dishcloths; that was all we had. The washing-up water turned red, the tea towels turned red, the dishcloths turned red, and even the white plates became a glazed over red. Then thinking quickly, she took lots of toilet paper and applied it to my neck, applying a lot of pressure to it. We had to stop the bleeding, or we were both gonna be dead; beaten black and blue. Eventually, the bleeding slowed, and we began to hatch a water-tight account of what had happened and who was involved and who was to blame – our brother: of course. We were just going to place the entire blame squarely upon his shoulders. Whatever was to come of this, he could certainly bear it. We knew he was a safe bet as the chances were one hundred to one that he wouldn't get into any trouble.

'Right! That's what I'm gonna say,' I confirmed.

'OK. Run it by me one more time,' she said. 'Just to make sure you have it.' I rehearsed the lie again and again to make sure I had it down to a T. Just then, Bobby came into the kitchen, and we started to play with him, coaxing him to a sword fight, which he was really falling for. In so doing, the wound began to bleed out again. This time so much blood came out that even all the dishes were red again and had to be rewashed as did the tea towels and the cloths. Odette beckoned me to go into the living room and tell Mordecka; she was still with the Jehovah's Witness, so the chances were she would not really be listening to a thing I was saying.

I knocked on the door and waited for an answer before entering, but there was none. Feeling the heat, I knocked again. Still there was no answer. I knocked again for the third time, this time in quick succession and went in. Upon finding myself a quarter of the way in and with both Mordecka and her guest now looking in my direction, I immediately started speaking, delivering the cock-and-bull story of how I was drying up, and Bobby came in and started swinging the knife around, and it just caught me, scratching me on the left side of my neck. '... but it's not bleeding now though and I'm OK,' I added. Before I had even finished speaking, they both had already looked away and continued with their own conversation.

After I had delivered my speech, without a speech writer, Mordecka did not even move a muscle. She did not stand up, she did not come over to me or call me to come nearer to her, she did not even inspect the wound, given that she was a nurse and all, and neither did she look back across the room at me whilst I continued speaking. It was as though I did not even exist. It was as though I wasn't even there. I stood there for a while to see whether any response was forthcoming, however small. But after completing my speech, it was really time to go, as she just simply carried on talking to her guest as if there had never been an interruption at all.

It must have been in the late afternoon of the following day or the day after that she spoke in my earshot now contesting the very lie that I had testified to earlier, regarding the blame for the incident. Still, despite being a nurse, there was no first aid offered and no advice given. She did not even check the wound. I was so fortunate to have Odette as a sister back then, as she would always nurse all my wounds as well as change my bandages on a daily basis, which ironically were always made from toilet paper; Thank God for Andrex. We seemed to have it in abundance back then and the rolls were really, really thick and seemed to last all week, even for a family of five.

She provided me with clothes to wear that hid the scar. Lucky for both of us, my wound did not go septic or get infected. I think the angels were really with us that day, I think they must have stuck me back together again. However, my brother was still slightly in shock and not quite sure what had actually happened that day; his confusion was added to by the fact that he did not get into trouble either. Today my scar still stands as a gentle reminder despite having shrunk considerably.

No Friend of Ours

When you first meet new people, you do what I call 'try them' or 'test drive them'. You begin by subconsciously looking for things or facts which you share or have in common to bond you together or make you closer than those with whom you have nothing in common with. Familiar identifiable facts could be anything from a name in common; for example, she had the same name as your cousin twice removed or he has a birthday in the same month as your Dad or you grew up in the same town or went to the same school or church even whenever, wherever, and so on and so forth. And when the new neighbors moved in next door, we did exactly that; we tried out the children.

However, they were nothing like the children of the family who had just moved out. In fact, they were the complete opposite. The old family was warm and generous, and the new family was cold and tight. There was a strange feeling when we entered their house, but we were perhaps too young to be able to psychoanalyze the children, the home, or even the situation. However, being the friendly pair that we were, we simply extended our friendship to them.

Their daughter's name was Yasmin; the family was from West Africa. I found her name as emphatic as her demeanors. However, the awful truth to her character did not begin emerging until after Dad had placed us under house arrest, for no apparent reason which, in truth, was the basis of most of his bizarre decisions relating to discipline. Our absence was taken as a snub against her personally. What she failed to realize was that this was a sanction against us and had nothing at all to do with her personally. Clearly, bad vibes started to go down at school, and Odette, therefore, determined that Yasmin would not be a member within her *inner circle.* Perhaps this rather harsh action incensed Yasmin to the very core and to the point where she took it upon herself to pick up a paint brush dripping in blue paint and with it wrote on the second-floor wall in the south stairwell such monstrosities about Odette and the biggest hunk in the school – Damien De Cruz. Of course, we hardly ever used the south stairwell, so we never got to see the septic, poorly written, misspelt lies spread across the wall. Nevertheless, at that time, we were still unfamiliar with all the friends of our parents or their associates, and even to this day, we would be unable to identify any, if still living in, near, or around the farm. And it was one of these, what I call nosey, gossiping acquaintances, who had brought to the attention of Mordecka, of all people, this gruesome find. Of course, Mordecka was in her element, and according to her, she now had a legal and wholly legitimate reason to kick-off non-stop, cursing and swearing and carrying on within our ear shot, wherein she was clearly in her safe place and in her element no doubt. And oh, boy, did she kick-off for all of five hours of non-stop bitching and swearing and carrying on. I was absolutely sure there was not a neighbor on our landing who didn't know the sad sorry sagas of our delinquent crazy messed up household.

The day had started off quite calmly. We got up, went to school, had a lovely lunch, of roast beef, roast pots plus two veg *of course*, each half boiled to death, followed by pink sponge with pink custard topped with coconut sprinkles. We finished our lessons, returned home, got washed, tidied up, and sat in our room until we were summoned to Dad's bedroom at around 6 p.m.

The TV was switched off, which was usually a bad sign. We were ordered to sit on the floor and wait, which we did, like good little puppies.

Then without any warning or notice or reason, she began slagging off our mother again.

'Oh really, what again?' I thought. Of course, she was in her element as she began shouting.

'Ya all just like ya all mother. She was a prostitute. She left on the bus, and she was wearing a red coat!' We still had no idea what the reason was for her current kick-off. After that, she began to threaten to take us to the doctor to get some pill or other, for what I did not know, but I guessed that this was the pill that made all children good. It all sounded like another language to me back then, but that was the only thing that I could make out. It all sounded so double Dutch. Then Dad interjected, saying, 'She is only nine, you know. That's not possible... is it... is that even possible?' he asked.

'You crazy?' Mordecka asserted. 'Of course, it's possible.'

Then Dad said, 'Well, she,' (referring to me) 'is only eight, and that's definitely not possible.'

Mordecka answered, saying, 'Maybe. I'm not sure about eight, but definitely nine. You should take her to the GP and get the bloody pill.'

She was shouting at times, screaming at others '... If not, you're gonna look after it. I'm not looking after nothing; I got mine!' she screamed, just one decibel away from complete hysteria; her voice now becoming husky from all the screaming and shouting. All I could make out was that Damien was a bad person. He had done something terrible to Odette and something further about pills and the GP.

I remember saying, 'God, please just give me the pills. If these pills will make me a better person, if these pills will make Mordecka like us, and if they will make us good so we will never get into trouble again. If they will make us good, then please give us the pills. Please God.' We were sent to our room at about 11 p.m. I was exhausted just from trying to make sense of it all; we had to get up at 7 a.m. for school the next day. *What madness! Still, thank God we didn't get a beating.*

Portable Cabins – Makeshift Classrooms

It was 1973, the charts were still pouring out a mixture of folk, soul, and rock and roll over the air waves and some might have even argued that it was the Jackson 5 vs the Osmond's.

Our school had just received an injection of money to build an extension for it to cater for more children now flooding on to the farm. Whilst the work was in progress, some of the classes were to be housed in the two new portable cabins. I was glad that our class had been chosen to be one of the two selected. To me, it was kind of cozy and more intimate and we could at times make a lot of noise that did not disturb the rest of the school. We had our own cloakroom area, which was separate from the actual class, and doubled up into a multifunctional room able to host the weekly bundles where physical contact was made between the sexes and or where the occasional fight would take place.

There was one fight that none of us would ever forget – at least not those who were there. It was the usual time after lunch when we would slowly begin to make our way back to our portable cabin for the afternoon lessons. We were all busy chatting and some of us were standing around in the cloakroom, also chatting, when Boris entered mumbling under his breath something or other about Lenny. I liked Lenny; he was naturally very, very funny; you know the type that made you laugh out loud without trying. *(Michael McIntyre, please move over.)*

Lenny had an older brother also in the school, in the same year as Odette, in fact. They lived with just their mother, a single parent, who was also barely coping. Lenny had very pale skin, almost-emerald eyes, and white cotton wool hair. He was very thin and tall in stature; he could usually be found in the same clothes – washed-out green khaki pants and a light-colored T-shirt which had faded in the wash. This was his uniform day after day, yet he never smelled, and no one ever commented. I think I felt some sort of compassion for him or something but could not understand it and never really knew why. Boris, on the other hand, was very much smaller than Lenny. He had curly black hair, the kind of curls we women would without thought pay hundreds of pounds to secure, and he had beautiful speckle-free, milky, coffee-colored skin. He too had had an older sibling, a sister, Urnah, also at the school, who at some earlier stage had taken possession of Mordecka's diamond necklace, handed to her by Odette of course, who had instructed Urnah to hide it as if from some heist or something. In this case, the 'safe' from whence it came was Mordecka's black handbag, and the 'bank' was the top of her wardrobe.

The necklace had been kept in the tummy of her doll and at some point, had become broken into two or three pieces, and this was how it was returned to us in two or three pieces as we found when we went to collect it.

The punishment given was to spend the entire night standing in the bathroom, this was after having spent the entire day outside attempting to find the jewelry, and after not having any supper, and being whacked back to consciousness by Mordecka and her metal basin every time I fell asleep or I had accidently fallen on the floor, probably because I had fallen asleep whilst standing up. And, yes, I had school the next day too.

I mean, I did not even know that my sister had taken the damn necklace, or that she had given it to Urnah, or that it was broken in two or three pieces, or even that Urnah had placed it inside her doll. *I knew nothing! Every time our parents went out, she would start searching in Mordecka's things. Odette appeared to have an epiphany with her jewelry. She would put it on and then look out the window as if showing it off to the world. Of course, Mordecka would arrive back unannounced and Odette would have no time to return it; upon hearing the key go through the door it must have been a bit like Olly and Hardy on fast play forward as we ran around bumping into one another trying to put everything back and take our positions before our parents came in. Unfortunately, Odette didn't make it to put everything back on this occasion, so the diamond necklace was given to Urnah and the onyx earring was held in the center of the bed under the mattress until spotted by Dad during one of his spring-cleaning expeditions. And* this was how we became acquainted with their family.

The Fight

There were two portable cabins that were delivered to our school and Years 4 and 5 rotated their way through each one before ending up in the completed new building just in time for Year 6. We were in Year 5 now, and it was our second year in the portable cabins. The new build was within our sights and we could not wait to get into it.

When Boris entered the portal cabin he was mumbling, murmuring, and complaining all under his breath. He continued stomping around in the coat area before disappearing under the coats yet keeping a watchful eye through an exhausted buttonhole that had lost its shape on some old worn-out coat belonging to one of the 31 inside. It was almost like some evil third eye for, whom I can only presume was, Lenny.

When Lenny entered the coat area, he was as happy as Larry, sharing his idea of humor as he interacted with us. As he moved over to the back of the coat area, the arm of one of the coats moved up, and we all gasped with surprise. With that, Lenny turned around, and out jumped Boris upwards into the air before crashing down on to Lenny, like some wild black panther descending on its prey. He slid down Lenny like a snake slithering down a tree trunk and they held on to each other before pushing outward and separating.

Pushing only. This was usually associated with 'stage one' of the fight. It did go on rather longer than usual until Lenny broke the rhythm with an almighty thump to the side of Boris' face. Secretly, I did want Lenny to win, as Boris was, in my estimation, such a *little shit.* He was the one who had, not so many moons before, caused both me and Richard to fight like cat and dog, and this happened on so many occasions.

We would fight each other for absolutely nothing, perhaps because he had to satisfy some sick, sadistic, desire; deep within the fabric of his unbalanced mind as to who was the toughest, all the time. Now, Boris was punching back, taking it up to level 3 and completely skipping level 2. Lenny followed suit, now stepping it up to level 4. He was also punching even harder, about a level 4.2. Then suddenly, like some wild possessed cat, Boris stepped backward, we thought it was all over, then he jumped up on to Lenny, pushing him backwards down on to the floor with a crash.

We watched as they rolled around as if glued together on top of the coats and bags that fell with them. Lenny was pulling Boris's jumper up and over his head, punching him simultaneously in the head and face; And of course, it was hurting Boris, who was now becoming more and more angry. He began swearing with saliva frothing out from his mouth.

'Fff! Fff! Fff'! I think he was trying to say, 'Oh shit' or something. Next, Lenny wrapped one leg around Boris's neck, and without hesitation or warning, Boris bit into Lenny's leg. Bearing the pain, Lenny then wrapped the other leg around Boris's neck and began to ever so slowly *squeeeeeeeze.* It must have felt like a clamp. Tighter and tighter and tighter. Lenny was quite deliberately reducing Boris's intake of oxygen. Boris's head was in a complete headlock and Lenny began to *squeeeeeze* even tighter. Boris now had to release his mouth from off Lenny's leg, in order to acquire the correct amount of oxygen he required, if he was at all interested in continuing his existence on this earth, and perhaps, more importantly, staying in the fight. At this point, Lenny appeared to be winning by a clear leg ahead or so we thought. *Was Boris now about to give in? we questioned.*

It was clear that Lenny had the upper hand or rather the upper leg, and it looked as if there was no conceivable way that Boris could get out of this position or come back on top. Our eyes were locked down on the pair of them as we followed them, entwined together across the floor. It was at this point that Lenny was lying on his back with Boris's head firmly between his thighs. *Clearly not the ideal position for two heterosexual males, but in this situation, it could not be helped.* Boris was sort of lying sideways to Lenny's leg. A small non-paying audience had now gathered in what available space was left in the coatroom. Boris then said that he couldn't breathe, but Lenny was not letting up; he was making his grip still tighter and tighter and tighter. Then in a fuel filled, crazy frenzy, Boris started struggling like a mad cow; he must have mustered up all the strength he could to move his position. Then, suddenly, from nowhere, Lenny let out an almighty shriek. Our eyes poised as if to say 'What!' Then it came, 'Arrh! Arrh! My balls!' he screamed. 'He has got my balls!'

'What?' we all asked simultaneously.

'He's got my balls! Get him off my balls!' Lenny cried out again. I could not see any balls and wondered exactly what balls he was referring to. I began to look around the floor for his balls, looking under the coats and bags, all the while thinking to myself that I was sure, that I had not seen Lenny playing with any balls today and wondering whether this was what the fight was all about some balls?

'His nuts... you know... his willy,' explained Richard, interrupting my thoughts. Well, blow me down and call me Daisy! I had never heard of the male genitalia being referred to in this manner before. This was certainly a new concept to me. And I won't tell you what my brother's is called.

We all took turns to bend over the pair. Of those who did bear witness, we could certainly testify with absolute certainty that Boris absolutely had Lenny's balls in his mouth. Boris's jaw was in lockdown, like a set of sharp piercing iron gates, relentlessly holding on to Lenny's balls without even so much as a millimeter of mercy. We could not pull Boris off Lenny because Lenny's balls were going with him, as they were stuck to Lenny. *Ouch!* Plan B please – we could not hit, punch, or kick Boris because his jaw would just get tighter and tighter and tighter. Plan C – we told them that the teacher was coming... but nothing, not a flinch. We did not know what to do, so we all started shouting at Boris, believing that our raised voices would cause him to let go of Lenny's balls. But it was all to no avail! Boris was not giving an inch, or rather a centimeter. I told Richard to tell Boris that he would beat him up personally if he did not get off, thinking we could scare him into submission. (*Richard was the second toughest in the class.*) Alas! That did not work either. Just then, without word or warning, a tall lanky Richard walked over to the pair, leant over Boris, and pressed quite firmly just behind his left ear lobe. With that, Boris's jaw dropped down open, and Lenny pulled his trousers, including his willy out from Boris's mouth and pushed him off him. He scrambled to his feet and ran to the loo like a bat out of hell, to check his willy.

I had no idea of what the fight had even been about. But Boris was always getting in the thick of it with someone. I'm sure we can all understand that alpha male, male bravado, male macho contact and all that, but this was taking it a step too far by anyone's standards.

We had all enjoyed a glorious dinner that day. It was Wednesday, so we would have probably indulged ourselves in a plate of roasted chicken, roasted potatoes, wet with gravy, and two veg, of course all half boiled to death, followed by warm chocolate sponge and chocolate custard. So, on that note, there was completely no need for it. But it wasn't over yet, not by a long shot. When Lenny emerged from the bathroom, we all asked him if 'it' was OK. Oddly, he only answered Richard, informing him that he had just grazed the skin a little. Well, that was it. The war was on – Boris was going to get some serious licks from Lenny, and he would have to endure some hefty punches too.

At first, we all stood in the way, preventing Boris any mode of escape so Lenny could get the better of him, and Boris was taking his medicine like a good little boy. However, he was saved by the bell as we saw our class teacher emerge from the staffroom and begin to walk casually across the courtyard in the direction of the portable cabin. Most of us went back in to sit down as she climbed up the few steps before entering the coat area immediately preceding the classroom.

When she saw, Boris rolling around on top of the coats and bags that were still strewn across the floor from the fight, she sternly ordered him to pick them up, every one of them, and then to tidy up the coat area. Clearly, she had no idea that Boris had been punched in to that position on to the floor. Nevertheless, this request made Boris quite angry, and he began throwing all the coats everywhere; the coatroom very much resembled the aftermath of a tornado. In the end, Boris was physically removed from the classroom by the caretaker; one of his other ad hoc duties, I guess.

He then escorted Boris directly outside the principal's office, where he spent the remainder of the afternoon, wearing only his vest and his y-fronts under pants for all and sundry to see. Everybody else, on the other hand, spent their afternoon enjoying our regular weekly history lesson followed by a long cool drink of milk, which we always had at the end of the day. It was absolutely delicious, thank you, Labour.

Teacher's Grace

I never got close to my teachers, particularly after the reception class incident. I guess I had always been rather a withdrawn and a very quiet child in the company of strangers which included my teachers.

Our teacher in year five was a middle-aged woman named Mrs. Radcliff. She was of slender build; she wore nice conservative clothes and had one of those new curly perms. There was a gentle warmth in her face that I could not explain. It was just nice to be standing next to her; she had such a peaceful aura. However, one day, on my way back from the principal's office, where I had been given a letter to take home to Dad. I stepped into the girls' toilet on route, opened the letter, attempted to quickly read it, but after concluding that I couldn't make any real sense of it and believing everything to be a complaint, I tore it to pieces and flushed it down the toilet.

Upon re-entering the portable cabin, my class teacher asked me to remain behind after the lesson. Convinced that she had seen me with the letter, I believed that she was going to interrogate me as to its whereabouts. As the afternoon came to an end, I hoped she might have forgotten her request. As the class began to disperse, I thought I could just fall in behind the children and leave the classroom without her realizing. So as the class emptied, I joined the line, hoping that she might not notice me attempting to leave. 'Jacqueline,' she said softly. 'Do you want to wait by my desk for me?' she asked politely.

'Damn, I'm busted,' I thought. I began plotting nervously about what I could say that would in fact make any sense. As all the children began to leave the classroom and our eyes met in acknowledgement even from across the room, she pointed to her desk, indicating for me to wait there. I moved slowly in that direction and waited nervously by it. I began making up stories in my mind about what had happened to the letter.

After the last person had left, she pulled the doors closed. As she came towards me, I looked down and started mumbling my version of events, but she wasn't even looking at me. To my surprise and total amazement, she bent down and pulled out from under her desk a huge bag, I mean it was really big and from it unveiled a great big baby doll. I mean, it was massive, it was just like a real baby, and she handed it to me. 'Do you like it?' she asked. I just stared in disbelief, shock even, not really knowing what to say or how to say it. I was barely able to even nod my head in acceptance, I had no voice, and then she handed me an extra-large coloring book, and with it, twenty-four multi-colored, superior quality, felt-tip pens.

This was all so huge – her generosity, her kindness, her compassion, it was all too much, knocking the wind right out of me... I had no words. *How did she know? Why was she doing this? Had she heard my hearts cry?* Completely unsure of how to respond or react, I just stared almost transfixed but for a moment. I mean, this was the kind of thing a girl like me could only ever get close to in a dream or a magazine – the latter being extremely scarce.

I could not believe my eyes. *Was my life now turning around for good before me?* She asked me not to tell the class that she had given them to me in case it caused problems. *I was the queen of secrets so no problem on that front.* She never did explain why she had given me these things or why she felt that I needed them.

In truth, I had gone so long without toys that I no longer cared for them anymore. Nevertheless, I did manage to get them home undetected, but as soon as Odette saw them, she confiscated them from me, saying they were hers now. She completed most of the coloring book and painted the doll's nails with that horrid glue-like ink, which had seeped out from a broken, red, Bic, biro pen. My brother completed the remainder of her scary transformation, by poking in one of her eyes, making it more of a horror doll from the *Chucky* family or some other scary movie as opposed to a loveable baby doll; the kind you would think of taking to bed with you to comfort you in the night time hour. In truth, I never really got to play with it. However, it was this doll that was to accompany me in my final exit; and the clock was ticking, tick-tock tick tock. But for here, right now let me say thank you, Mrs. Radcliff, where are you now Miss?

The Easter of 1974

The Easter holidays were exactly three weeks, after which we would return to school. We were about halfway through the first week. We got up as usual, got washed, tidied our room, and had a breakfast of bread cut like doorsteps to be washed down with milky tea. We tidied up the kitchen and returned to our room. Odette would always spend her time reading or drawing and seemed content in that world which she had created for herself. She was excellent at drawing, and she even drew my picture once.

I had given some thought to the remarks Mordecka had made during one of her ranting speeches that we never spoke to her. I took it upon myself to go boldly into her room and speak to her about anything just to have some communication with her. We must have chatted away for about two hours when she asked me to instruct Odette to carry out some task or other. I returned to our bedroom to deliver the message to Odette; however, Odette was not there. Believing she must have gone downstairs, I then went to the kitchen to speak to her there, but she was not there either. I looked in the back room, and she was not there. I checked the lounge and the toilet, and there was still no sign of her. Finally, I checked the upstairs bathroom before having to report back to Mordecka that Odette was not in the house. Suddenly I felt fearful again. I did not know what to do. I thought about pretending that I had given her the news. I stood outside her room squeezing my hands, in a whirlwind of options all untrue and mixed in with anxiety; she called me to her. I knocked once before re-entering to deliver my findings to her. Mordecka looked at me and I stared right back at her trying my best not to make eye contact which was a sign of insolence according to Caribbean's. She sent me back again to go and repeat exactly what I had just done, which was to look for Odette again in every room in the house. From the front door, right back up to our bedroom.

Upon entering our room, a second time I noticed that Odette had left the window open a small measure. I went to the window, opened it, and after hesitating, wondered if what I was about to see was a jump gone wrong. My thinking was one of escape not one of suicide, *little did I know*. I quickly popped my head out of the window eyes shut tight expecting to see the worst: expecting to see her flat as a pancake on the patio floor four stories below. I opened them quickly. Thank GOD, to my pleasant surprise she was not there. I then started to feel nervous. Suddenly, I knew intuitively how Mordecka would be thinking in her mind, she would instinctively jump to the conclusion that I had willfully and deliberately plotted with Odette to purposely keep her busy, deep in conversation, so that Odette could make her escape. Suddenly, I began to feel sick to my stomach and very anxious. However, what I could not determine was whether I was going to get another beating or not, because of it. It appeared that either way, I was the loser, so I thought it best to break the news to her just as I had found it and allow her to make her own assumptions. I desperately hoped that I would miss another beating. I had no idea of how long Odette had been out of the house or where she had gone or even why. I returned to my parents' room and very nervously knocked on the door again. I stood outside all the while wondering what to do. I came to the conclusion that it was better to face the music. After a long while, Mordecka answered and invited me back in. I broke the news to her that Odette was not in the house. She stared at me with such an expressionless look it was chillingly. I had never seen such a look before. I think she was wondering what Dad would say. I mean if your child runs away from home clearly there is something wrong in the home.

He had not returned home from working the night shift yet. He always worked late on a Friday and would sometimes go to the bookies straight after. My guess was that he was in the betting shop again, under the spell of trying to 'get rich quick'. I think Mordecka's main concern was whether she would be in trouble. Eventually, she prized herself up from off the chair upon which she had been sitting and began to look for Odette. She searched the whole flat, even on the balcony where she had on so many occasions made her sleep; but had to conclude also that Odette was not in the flat. She then decided to wait for Dad to return home from work before taking any further action.

When Dad returned home, Mordecka broke the news to him. After a while, he called me in for questioning and asked about her movements, in particular, whether she had said anything prior to her disappearance. I had only a limited response for him, which was an unequivocal *no.* And I could do no more than to take him through the steps of our usual routine, which I could have performed blindfolded even to this day. It felt empty and lonely without Odette, but life still went on.

It must have been approximately two weeks later when Odette returned home. She was distant, silent, and strangely sad. When I tried to question her reasons for her sudden and rather abrupt departure, her responses were all very limited, but what she did say very clearly and very finally was that she had had enough. I did not know if, at that time, I fully understood the meaning of those words spoken so softly. In truth, I could not blame her; even white folks treated their animals better than how she was treated.

Children have a deep sense of justice even from a very young age, and if there is a time in a child's life where they are unable to speak out against the shame and injustices that are present and active in their own lives, they will, at some stage, begin to act them out, which in this case is exactly what she did.

It must have been approximately 14 days before her sudden disappearance that Dad had beaten her quite severely. The reason was that my brother had placed a blue, Bic, biro pen in my parents' laundry, which was on route to the launderette. Odette was in charge. Clearly, the end result was that it ruined most, if not all, of their clothes. And of course, the blame was laid squarely upon Odette's shoulders; according to the mad methodology of the would-be-Mafioso, Mordecka, since it was Odette who took the clothes to the laundry and since Odette placed the clothes into the washing machine, it followed that the onus was upon Odette to have checked the load before placing it into the machine.

To that effect, Mordecka goaded Dad quite seriously, spurring him on until he conceded and delivered a good old Caribbean beating with all the warped energy of a mad frenzied crowd watching live wrestling from the front row. At the end of the day, Mordecka wasn't satisfied unless someone was getting a good arse licking, kicking, being sworn at, shouted at, screamed at, or humiliated, and that someone was always eight times out of ten Odette.

The beatings were dished out like awards and on a regular basis. They were an ordeal in themselves. However, if I had to choose between receiving a beating from my parents or 10 rounds in the ring with Mick McManus, I think good old Mick would win hands down every time. Ironically, Dad loved the 'wrestling' even to this day. I have no idea whether the two were interlinked in any way.

It was stomach-wrenching, intestine twisting, bloody blue murder awful having to listen to her cries of apologies, her pleas for mercy, and her promises of never letting it happen again, all of which simply fell on deaf ears. Even I was angry at my brother for that one. I mean, if he wasn't putting the loo roll down the toilet, then it was your toothbrush he was cleaning it with; if he wasn't pulling your hair out, then he was taking your things or just messing them up; and if he wasn't doing any of these, then, of course, he was probably drowning his tonsils in tomato ketchup or better than all the above - fallen fast asleep, a deep sleep, in fact.

I felt quite justified when one fine day, he, after taking my bracelet without my permission, and after stretching it out so that it could no longer be recognized as a bracelet and poking it into the live plug socket, located low down by the door to the right as you entered our room, he literally got blown right across to the other side of the room and smacked into the wall before sliding down it. After crashing to the floor, he still got a good slapping from Dad. *Yes*, I thought, *'serves you right, you little rat.'* But the beatings we were receiving were clearly taking their toll on the both of us. The welts and bruises were taking longer and longer to disappear, and the back of my head felt dented after repeated attempts of trying to move quickly out of the path of Dad's huge hand as it came at speed, swooping through the air with the direct intention of making contact with my face. As Dad, would come towards me, shouting, and screaming, like a great giant out from the trees in a children's story book. The slightest hand gesture would always cause me to flinch, and in so doing, I would repeatedly bash the back of my head on the wall if I was standing too close to it behind me.

On one occasion, Odette's head actually made a dent in the kitchen wall, and then she got beaten for that too. I became so tense and so nervous I was completely unable to relax at all; it was frightening if not nerve-racking living at home. All the time we were walking on eggshells. If you needed any kind of medical attention neither of us mentioned it.

I think we both could have benefited from braces but as far as our parents were concerned, we just had to forget it. I remember I would go to bed at night holding my front teeth pressing them down as they were beginning to protrude further and further forward than was necessary. When the talk started at school about big lips and big noses, I had a challenging time trying to press down my teeth, hold my nose and hold my lips in all at the same time. This bizarre bedtime behavior ended abruptly upon the arrival of my wisdom teeth. I then spent my nighttime rolling around in bed in utter pain trying to press them back down again.

Getting Caught

I guess there is a time in every child's life when, at some stage, they will have to prove themselves, particularly to their peers, whether over possessions, strength, wealth, or intellect. Well, that day could not have arrived any sooner for me when my peers had noticed that I was always the one who never had any sweets for sharing. Rumors quickly began to circulate that I was poor, and my parents could not afford to give me any pocket money. In fact, the rumors were not so far from the truth. Indeed, they were all true.

There were two incidents that I can still remember: both included Dad being brought before the court because he could not afford to pay his taxes, and on the second occasion, it was so serious that even Mordecka, Odette, and Bobby attended the court with him, in case things went really bad, *I guess.*

I was left home alone, with the usual view from the window as my only solace. I hated being left alone as it brought an uncertain eerie discomfort to me that I was just not able to contend with, nor understand. I stood on the little ledge that protruded out from the balcony door so that I could stare up and out from the window; I stood there on the ledge and stared out until the day was almost gone and only the dusk remained. Just as I was about to step down, I heard the key turn in the lock – assurance was restored. Thank

God, all of them had returned. Odette revealed later that Dad had got off because someone had paid his taxes for him. 'Oh,' I responded, not really understanding the ramifications of it all but just feeling very relieved that they had all returned home safely.

Back in the classroom I felt that I could not allow them to believe for a moment that I was poor or for the mocking to start to circulate. We were halfway through Year 6 now at Water Farm Primary, and we had finally taken our place in the new building, which was indeed rather nice. Our class was upstairs now, as the new build had two levels, which gave the building more character I guess. I assured my peers quite emphatically that I was not poor and that I would return the next day with goodies for all of them to prove it. Clearly, I had no idea as to how I was going to fulfil this promise, but I knew that my reputation was on the line if I could not.

The next day, I literally stumbled across a few pence in the street and went directly to the fruit and veg man, on my way back to school after lunch. We were back on home lunches again; so, the Conservatives were in Number 10, and free lunches were now back off the menu.

I asked the greengrocer for as many apples as three pence could buy, a request to which he responded with just two apples. I reluctantly pleaded for a third, to which he firmly resisted and warned me rather sternly not to ask him again or to return to his shop for that matter. His staff stopped dead in their tracks to witness the bizarreness of what was unfolding before them.

'Now get out of here!' he shouted. I scarpered out of the shop and ran back down to the school as fast as my little legs could carry me.

Upon my arrival, back in the classroom, Sally once again began speaking out about my shortfall, at which point I pulled out the brown paper bag that I had been holding in my coat pocket; I distributed the apples with a satisfied contentment. Unfortunately, Sally was not happy with the apples. '*oh no.*' They were not sweets, so apples did not count. The next day, I had to pull sweets out of the bag or else. The following day, on my way back to school, just before the end of the lunch hour, I visited my own local convenience store – the same one my parents would send me to if they had forgotten anything or run out of anything in-between the big shop.

That day I was wearing my faded crimson jacket, with the ripped-out pockets – it had been passed down to me from Odette. The ripped-out pockets were purpose made secret compartments in which to store more sweets in. Unfortunately, I had no access to the sweets as they were right next to the till, which was always manned.

As I hovered, hesitating, walking up and down the aisles, and thinking what to do next, time was simply running out. I had to start making my way back to school, or else I was going to be late and then I was definitely going to be in trouble. As I walked past the milk-and-dairy counter for the fifth time, I noticed the yogurts. They were packaged in fancy containers. *Maybe they might like to have a pot of yogurt instead? I thought and so I* began to stuff as many as I could into my pockets in absolute oblivion that I was being watched by the proprietor on CCTV. On the contrary, his request for me to accompany him into his very small office came as a complete surprise. He now had in his possession two of the five yogurts pots, which he placed on the table in front of me. I began to cry.

'Please don't tell Dad,' I sobbed. He was silent in his response just staring at me, as if watching a show. I went on and on, begging him, pleading with him, and telling him how sorry I was and promising him that I would never do it again.

'Where do you live?' he snapped.

'Over there,' I replied, pointing south.

'Which block?' he snarled.

'Stapleford, Sir,' I replied promptly in a mouse-like voice. 'Please, Sir!' I pleaded again. 'I will give you all the yogurts.' And with that, I pulled out the other two, concealed in the inner lining of my jacket. His eyebrow raised as I placed the yogurts on the table.

'What school do you go to?' he demanded sharply assembling the yogurts in a straight line on the table.

'Water Farm Primary, Sir,' I answered quickly. 'Please don't tell Dad,' I begged again. 'You can tell the school all you like, but just please don't tell Dad.'

'Strict, is he?' asked the manager, looking as though he understood the fear associated with physical discipline. I affirmed the answer by nodding my head in quick repeated succession.

'Emmmm,' he thought aloud for a moment, and after a short pause, he said, 'Right!' 'I'm gonna let you go this time, but you're banned from this shop. Do you hear?' he said, raising his voice with every word. 'Banned!'

'Err, yes, Sir!' I answered. 'Yes, Sir! I'm so sorry, Sir. I will never do it again,' I said.

'Oh, I know you won't,' he said, 'because you're banned! Do you hear, "banned"? Now get out of here!' he yelled.

I left the store in such a hurry that you would have thought that I was running the hundred-meter sprint. I ran all the way back to the school, without stopping, as fast as I could, wiping the tears from off my face as I went; I was late.

At that moment, I felt as though I completely despised and hated my friends.

'Why did Sally always have to be on my case?' I thought. Nevertheless, the bonds which had once held us so firmly together were now slowly becoming undone, or were they?

Upon my arrival, back to school, although they did appear to notice that I had arrived empty handed, none of them made any mention of the fact and neither did any of them harass me further. The afternoon passed by quickly, and as soon as class was out, I scarpered – not hanging around for a moment. I did not see or speak to a single person. I went straight home without seeing or chatting to any of my inner circle.

That afternoon, no sooner had I arrived home, got washed, changed, picked up the fluff from off the brown carpet, cleaned the bathroom, sinks and toilets and completed all other ad hoc chores, I recoiled to learn that I was only being sent back to the very same shop which only hours earlier I had been ejected from and forever banned. Mordecka was now sending me out to buy some Bisto gravy powder. 'Could this day get any worse?' I asked myself. *Today, I can confess that it is actually good stuff* – the gravy that is. I could not believe it. I walked slowly over to the store, wondering whether I would be let in and wondering how I would explain it all to my parents if I had to return home without it, the Bisto gravy, that is. I also thought about asking a stranger to make the purchase for me, but on thinking again, I thought that perhaps this was not such a good idea after all. I mean what if they were to run off with the money or something? Mordecka would have a field day and a good beating was most certainly going to follow. She had given me a one-pound note, so she was clearly expecting change. If I returned home without both components, there would certainly be trouble. It was all too much. I stood outside the shop, looking in through the window. If only I could reach the Bisto without having to go in, I thought.

Then suddenly I remembered that Linda, my school chum, lived just upstairs. Eagerly I clambered up the six flights of stairs with fresh enthusiasm. Unfortunately, I could not remember the actual door number or the floor on which Linda lived. I tried to recall the landing by trying to remember what it was that I had seen, directly in front of the last step. I closed my eyes and tried to remember. It was plant pots; in my mind's eye I could see plant pots. I ran up the stairs only to find that there were now plant pots on every landing. I became distressed and disheartened. I just couldn't remember.

In a final attempt, I stood in front of what I believed was Linda's door, with a willing belief and just a glimmer of hope, that she might be in and would agree to make the purchase for me. I knocked on the door with some desperation using the letter box knocker and then waited. There was no answer. I knocked again: *rat tat tat tat*. This time a little louder. Not waiting for a response, I called Linda's name through the letter box.

'Linda! Linda!' There was still no answer. I went down to the floor below and repeated my actions again: *rat tat tat tat* 'Linda! Linda!' – again, there was no answer. I continued to repeat the same process on every floor before finding myself back on the first floor again, adjacent to the shop.

My spirit slumped to an all-time low, as I walked slowly back down to the shop. I stood outside the door of the shop again, only this time I began to cry; I cried rather loudly, still too afraid to go in, my mind now fanning out turbulent scenarios of how this was all going to end... in more tears no doubt and bruises too. Just then, from out of nowhere, came a rather well-dressed gentleman, who seemed to usher me into the store with him as he entered. Perhaps he thought that I had been unable to open the door, which was rather heavy.

Then quite bizarrely I actually began acting as though we were together, wherever he went, I followed entering the same aisles as him, stopping in front of the same food products as he did, and each time he noticed me, he simply smiled kindly, and in that moment, I wished he could have just swept me up and taken me away with him into his life; I was sure his life was better than mine; it just had to be.

As we passed the gravy aisle, I held out my arm, latching on to the Bisto gravy as we breezed past. I even queued up ever so closely behind him, at the checkout and I pushed the Bisto ever so closely next to his items.

'You together?' asked the cashier in her Northern accent as she scanned the last item belonging to the man. I quickly looked in the other direction to avoid making any eye contact with the cashier whom I clearly recognized from my earlier visit that day.

'Certainly not!' The man answered looking down at me, almost in abhorrence at the idea that we should be together. Once he had finished, he packed up his things into a plastic carrier and immediately left the shop, his long coat hem following behind him. Now it was my turn. The cashier slowly scanned my single item, one packet of Bisto gravy.

'Is that all you have?' she asked. I nodded repetitively, still refusing to make eye contact with her. Now it was my turn to pay; my heart was in my mouth. I daren't even breathe a breath as I crunched closed my eyes at the same time handing the cashier the money. I was completely full of nerves, wondering whether in what moment I would, in fact, be recognized. With that thought in mind, I began having visions of being physically picked up and literally thrown out of the shop without the gravy and in front of everyone – *how embarrassing!* Thank God, they didn't recognize me. I completed my transaction and left the shop, breathing a sigh of relief as I came out. I ran all the way home as dusk had already fallen and it was getting darker by the minute. When I arrived back, I was pleasantly surprised to see that the long duration of my absence had gone completely unnoticed, or if they had, they certainly made no comment of it. Thank God for that too.

Burnt Crispy Fingers

The following day, my thoughts returned to torment me. *What am I going to do?* I thought. *I couldn't turn up empty handed yet again...and I could not return to the shop either.* After wrestling with my thoughts in the depths of my mind, I eventually decided to take some change from Dad's pocket, believing that he would never notice... *How wrong could I be?*

That day, after I had finished my lunch of bread cut as thick as doorsteps, spread thickly with margarine, cut like cheese posing as butter, and milky tea, which resembled slightly tanned milk and served out of my old, chipped, tin cup I brushed my teeth and was ready to return to school. I called out to Dad to tell him that I was leaving now but heard no response. Believing him to be asleep, I slipped my arm into his home-made coatroom, placed my hand deep inside his coat pocket and retrieved a ten-pence piece. *Lucky me,* I thought – this should get them off my back. I left the flat, closing the door ever so quietly behind me.

On the way to school, I stopped off at the sweet shop and brought an assortment of chews and jellies for my peers. They lapped up the sweets like wild wolves to raw meat. Respect was finally restored, or so I believed. At the end of the last lesson, they placed their orders for the following day. Foolishly I did not object. I couldn't, but I did feel very uneasy about the whole thing.

In truth, up until that point, it had been a relatively easy mission pulling change from Dad's pocket. I was completely convinced that Dad would not miss a few pennies from amongst his bulging change-filled pockets. I repeated the same act the following day and the day after that; however, on the fourth day, there was no change in his pockets. I searched frantically my fingers probing around in the dark, but there were only about three pence in his overcoat. In my desperation, I took it. I visited the shop as I had done the day before and brought what few sweets I could.

When I returned home at the end of the day, I was very surprised to see Mordecka downstairs. It was as though she had been expecting me... or rather, waiting for me. I mean, I had raised my hand to knock on the letter box, but the door just opened as if by itself, and Mordecka drifted off into the kitchen like a Tardis out of Dr Who, as if beckoning me to follow after her. Then to clarify the point she ordered me to come straight into the kitchen. No one could have imagined what was about to unfold. I began to feel very nervous and even more uncomfortable; my stomach began to churn as if attempting to soften butter and turn it into cream but not the kind you put on your face. I stood there, waiting for someone to say something…, anything.

Mordecka and Dad began having a conversation about me as if I was not in the room, which didn't really seem that bad, up until the moment when he got *so* psyched up, that he began firing questions at me, right out of the blue, as if firing bullets from an AK- 47; suddenly, I was in the conversation. He was questioning me without pausing and without even giving me a chance to answer. I could not think straight or quick enough. Suddenly, I wanted to go to the loo. Then it happened. Dad asked me to pass him Mordecka's hard backed slipper.

'Oh, Noooooooooo,' I thought. *'Why is it that Caribbean parents always allow their children to handle the mode of weaponry that they intended to use in their children's demise?'* I began to cry as I took my time, searching for the slipper under the stairs before being ordered out by Dad's very loud, authoritative

voice. 'Come 'ere!' he shouted. 'What did you take from the cupboard?' he demanded to know. I was crying before he had even begun.

'I... I'm...' Before I could finish answering, the beating had commenced. At some point, the slipper must have caught my ear as it was now bleeding. The blood was dripping on to my shirt, but the beating was not affected; he continued without concern or even an ounce of empathy. He was screaming and shouting in his highest ever voice, and Mordecka was on the commentary as if at Aintree. This was what she did best, of course.

Whenever he spoke with such intensity, I found him completely incoherent, which, in turn, caused him to hit me longer and harder and with every word. 'What – whack –did – whack – I - whack – tell - whack -you -whack?' Mordecka was still commentating, and Dad had to raise his voice above hers just to be heard. Just then, Odette walked in and by mistake entered the kitchen to say good afternoon. She had no idea what she had walked into.

'And I bet it was that red thing that put her up to it, wasn't it? Wasn't it?' Mordecka demanded, staring straight at me for an answer. At this point, I would have admitted to stealing the crown jewels, anything, because I was just unable to physically and emotionally take any more.

Dad screamed at Odette to go and get changed for what we both knew was going to be a serious bloody beating. After what seemed like forever was over, Dad then turned on the gas cooker. I had no idea as to why he had turned it on as nothing was cooking. '*Was he now going to multitask and beat me as he cooked?*' I thought. No one could have imagined what was about to happen next. At that moment, he dragged me towards where he was standing, grabbed my hand, and began pulling it forward towards the flames. In one flash of an awful moment, I suddenly knew what was going to happen next.

'Noooooooooo, Daddy!' I screamed. 'Noooooooooo, Daddy! I promise I'll be good,' I pleaded. Pee now began to trickle down my leg again. A frenzied struggle ensued between me and dad but came to a sudden halt with a short sharp blow to my shoulder.

'You see any tears?' Mordecka piped up, questioning Dad as if she was the military; he did not answer. He was completely transfixed on what he was about to do next. His actions were like that of a young scientist heating the Bunsen burner before commencing the experiment, adjusting the flame to just the right color. 'I don't see any,' she added. Then he forced my fingers open; it was then that I realised he was completely crazy, and the level that I feared him the most had just increased to off the scale.

He held my fingers over the flames until he had burnt each one under the dancing blue and orange flames. I believed he was going to burn my fingers right off. I screamed and struggled frantically albeit without success. He stood there burning each finger one by one. I continued to wriggle and struggle in an undiluted attempt to break loose from his giant grip, but, alas, it was all to no avail; I just could not break free. I don't remember how many times I wet myself before the beating and burning finally stopped. But it was at that moment when I was standing there shaking and sobbing with salted tear tracks ingrained down my face and pee tracks ingrained down my inner thighs, that I realised he really had lost the plot.

Just then, Odette returned from having got out of her uniform in order to receive her portion of the beating for a crime she had had no part in and had no knowledge of. She went so humbly into the path of the raging lion, like an innocent lamb to the slaughter. She went so quietly without even a single word of protest to receive her portion of what would be inevitably a disturbing and sadistic beating for something she knew nothing about and had no part in. I felt absolutely awful so helpless. What could I do? I could take no more. There were no words. My heart blead for her. I mean she had just returned from school and had only stepped one foot into the kitchen to say good afternoon and explain her lateness when Mordecka turned on her, dragging her hook, line, and sinker right into the thick of it.

'I bet it was she who put her up to it, wasn't it? Wasn't it?' she demanded. At this point, it was clear I would have said *yes* to anything – anything to stop the beating, anything to stop the burning.

'Yes! Yes!' came my response in a whisper of a cry.

'Yes, who?' she demanded.

'Yes, Aunty Mordecka,' came my reply. Odette looked at me, and I looked at her, still shaking traumatically and crying like some whimpering, broken, and bleeding animal lost in the rain. Then Dad suddenly grabbed Odette and started to beat her. He shouted for me to go upstairs.

The screams started as I went. I could hardly move. I had to take one step at a time leading with the same leg before reaching the top. I tried to wash my hands thinking the burning sensation would stop and the evidence would all be washed away from my nails and fingers; of course, it did not. I had raised welts on top of raised welts on both my arms and legs and bruises up and down my back, across my shoulders and a bloody ear.

The top of my hands looked as though they belonged to a fat person, whose lymph glands had just given up the ghost, or even someone suffering from an acute allergic reaction; however, in my case the cause was a beating. Most of my fingernails had melted away from the heat, and my fingerprints had been completely removed by the flames. When the screaming had finally stopped and Odette was released, she too came upstairs. She did not speak until she happened to see that my eyes were still glazed over. It was then that she asked if I was OK. Her compassion made me cry again.

I could see that this moment had marked a turning point in our already-strained relationship. I could see that Odette's attitude towards me had changed. I could not blame her really. From that day, something more had been broken away in her too, but I did not really understand it all back then. I was so deeply sorry but was completely unable to tell her, that her sharing in my beating, had saved me as I could not mentally, physically, or emotionally endure any more. When I held out my hands and Odette realised that Dad had burned my fingers, she felt absolute compassion for me and began to cry for me. We hugged each other that night, crying in each other's embrace. We went to bed, hugging each other and fell asleep in each other's arms. The next day, she tried as far as possible to cut off what she could of my burnt fingernails in an attempt to hide the warped and twisted blackness from my peers.

I knew that if my friends saw it, I would probably be made the laughingstock of the entire class and perhaps the whole school. This was a risk I just could not afford to take; more so after the madness of Year 1; I asked her if she could still smell the burning. 'Just a little,' she replied. I was unable to eat, brush my teeth, or wash myself properly as my fingers caused me so much pain when they touched anything at all.

At school, I found that I could not even write properly if at all. I mean just holding the pen caused me so much pain. I tried as much as possible to write with my left hand, which was really quite ironic, given that I was actually born lefthanded before being forced by Dad to use only my right.

Throughout the day, I could not stop bursting into tears, as it was all just too much. I could not even hold a book or turn its pages in order to read it. I had to keep going to the toilet to wash away my tears of sadness and cool my fingers under the cold tap in an attempt to soothe the pain. My fingers felt as though they were still on fire.

I kept wishing and hoping that it would all just go away.

Each time I went to the toilet, I was followed by Sally and Anna. Once the afternoon arrived, you knew it was almost the end of the day. I had managed to keep my terrible secret from them up until that point. But now, they were having no more of my secrets and lies, and they both demanded to know exactly what was going on. Why I kept on going to the bathroom? Why I kept washing my face? Why were my sleeves pulled down over my hands and fingers? I could no longer keep up the pretense of pleasantries. In the end, I caved in and told them my horrible truth.

Sally cried for me on the spot, which in turn made me cry even more, followed by Anna, who cried very loudly, indeed, to the point where we began to fear that our teacher would hear her and come in, placing us all in detention, which would have resulted in another beating for me as it meant I would be late home. I had no idea of what my teacher would do, as nice as she was, so upon that basis and for that reason she could not know my secret: it was all so embarrassing anyway.

Eventually, my wounds healed, and things returned to as normal as they possibly could. I continued to excel in sports, which I loved, such as rounder's and running, and was even made captain of the netball team. I could play every position on the court, but would usually be found playing the center position. Our team won every game both home and away.

Four Blue Notes

We were in the new building now, which came complete with its own first-aid room, and this was like a little bedroom where you could go if you needed to have a power nap. Up until that point, I had never been to the Water Farm's first-aid room before, and after rave reviews from Sally, we all had to try it. There was already a child lying down on the bed when it was my turn to visit, so I had to sit on the chair, which seemed rather boring. After a while, I decided to go back to class and just before leaving, I happened to look down, as I was about to push myself up from off the chair and in so doing, I saw something that grabbed my attention. It was a shiny crispy blue note. It stared up at me from inside the opened bag parked right under my chair. As I looked down it was as though it was beckoning me to touch it.

We stared at each other. It must have been approximately five minutes before I reached down in one swooping movement and snatched it from its position; holding it firmly in my hand as I drew my hand back up it felt thick. Without looking I stuffed it into my sock and left the room just as the first aider came back in to check on us. Once out of the room I immediately went into the toilet to investigate exactly what I had taken, I realised that there were four blue notes, each one as shiny and as crisp as the other. I had never seen so much money before in my entire life. Upon seeing that this was really too much I immediately went straight back to the first aid room to return it, but the room was now permanently manned by the first aider who had taken to pacing the doorway. *'How am I going to put the money back?' I thought.* I did not know what to do or how to put the money back, so throughout the day, I kept checking for an opening in order to try to put the notes back. By the time I did finally manage to get back into the room, it was almost the end of the day and the bag had already gone. I thought about leaving the money under the cabinet in the room but was put off this thought when I realised that perhaps no one would find it there. I decided to bring the notes home with me and thought that the best thing to do, was to try and spend the money, as fast as I could, in order to get rid of it. I decided to hide the blue notes under the carpet, in our bedroom.

There was a section about the size of half a square foot that had been cut out by Mordecka under the bed. (Your guess is as good as mine as to why.) I pushed the money down as far as I could under the carpet. The next day, just before leaving for school, I took one of the blue notes, thinking that I would get my school friends some sweets. I tried to spend as much of it as I could in one go, but it was exceedingly difficult to spend so much money on sweets, because sweets were so cheap, and the pound was so strong. I mean you got so much for your money back then; '*this is going to take forever,*' I thought.

By the third day, my teacher had noticed that I and my group of friends had a lot of sweets; the word was out in the staff room about the missing money, so she began to question us one by one.

Unbeknown to me all the teachers knew about the missing money and had been briefed to be vigilant for any unusual or suspicious behavior. Then it was my turn; I was called in and questioned by my own class teacher. My heart was racing. In a gentle voice my teacher said, 'Listen, Jacqueline, we all make mistakes, love, every last one of us. We all take the cookies out of the cookie jar without asking.'

In that moment, my mind ran over our cookie jar at home... We didn't have one... in my mind's eye I could only see an empty cookie jar. She continued, '...but the only thing that is worse than a thief is a liar. Is there anything you want to tell me?'

I looked up with fear in my eyes and shook my head in the negative. I was so afraid that I just did not know what to do. I desperately wanted to tell her the truth, just so I could be relieved of this heavy burden that I was now carrying, but I was being held captive by the chains of fear dominating my mind and felt that I just could not. The questioning went on for about three days. On the third day, my teacher said,

'Are you worried about your Dad, Jacqueline?'

'Yes,' came my quiet response.

'Jacqueline, I promise you. Nothing is going to happen to you.'

'You don't know Dad,' I said.

'I promise you that he is not going to hit you.'

'He will.'

'Is there something you want to tell me?' she asked again.

I nodded in the affirmative.

'I'm sorry,' I said. 'I didn't mean to take the money. I thought it was just one pound. I didn't think one pound would matter,' now becoming quite distressed about it all.

'I know, I know honey,' she said. 'It's OK. It's OK.'

I began to cry and sob, but Jessie hugged me any way, she was so patient and so sympathetic until I stopped. Jessie was such an understanding teacher and such a compassionate person. Looking back, she really was one in a million.

'where are all the notes now?' she asked ever so tenderly.

'under the carpet in my bedroom,' I answered in a whisper.

'how many do you have left?'

'three notes and some change.'

'the first-aider claimed there were five.'

'no, there were only four,' I affirmed.

'OK, OK. I believe you,' Jessie said. 'Even adults tell lies and cheat sometimes.'

The school decided to take us home with back up from the SS, the principal, and Jessie all in tow to try and explain to Dad what had happened.

I knew it was a bad idea from the start; I could not understand what they thought they were going to achieve from this little episode. They all arrived at the flat together. Dad was watching something on TV when they went in and walked right up to him. I went straight upstairs. After they left, I was beaten with the belt this time. Dad was even more angry that anyone could think they could stop him from bringing up his kids the way he believed was right or the way he wanted to.

Bobby had conveniently found the belt, which I thought I had buried deep, in the back of the cupboard under the stairs, so many moons ago. I had hidden it there just a few months before the last beating when I got my fingers burned and was ordered to get Mordecka's hard back slipper. Odette got beaten that day too, despite having nothing at all to do with any of it.

As the warmer months came upon us, it became increasingly difficult to hide our welts and bruises, and Odette's teacher, after seeing Odette's welts on her very thin arms during a games lesson, marched us both back up to Dad's with Jessie and the SS in an attempt to order him not to hit us again; it was quite comical really.

'Or what?' he snapped back at them, refusing to rise from his chair to greet them.

'Or, Mr. Richardson, yo-yo, you will get yourself in to a lot of trouble,' she snapped back, half stuttering. 'And you could find that the girls will be removed from your care,' she added, finding her confidence. He just laughed in their faces. They told him again that he was not allowed to hit us anymore, and if he did, he would be in trouble, big trouble, and they would return with the police.

This was his final warning. His laughter turned to a grainy grin when he heard the word 'police' mentioned, but in truth, he did not know anything else. He did not know any other way of disciplining his children because this was how he had been taught; by the church, his mother, his elder brother, and even by his guardians, who always wrongly accused him of picking and eating the mangoes from the mango tree in their garden and then beating him for it regardless.

After his own experiences, it seemed apparent that violence was very much ingrained into his mind. A mindset created by all those who had authority or responsibility over his care, from his earliest memoirs, all of whom had abused their positions and their titles. It was all that Dad had in his cupboard of experience, on life, concerning his ideology on discipline and parenting. It was now his nature. When he opened the doors of his cupboards on life, perhaps, all he saw on the upper shelf were belts, sticks, and slippers and on the shelf, below, shouting and swearing in abundance. To be perfectly honest, I really didn't care anymore. I just wanted out. I just wanted to leave. I had had enough.

Roberta Flack's 'The first time Ever I Saw Your Face' played on the radio. The song seemed to be connecting to something inside me, weaving something deep in the very depth of me. It was really quite haunting.

I believe the SS came a further two times to visit us. The second time, they asked Dad whether he would give permission for us to go on a camping trip. Dad said he did not know and that it was up to us. He told the SS that they could ask us if they wanted. He called us down to answer their questions. Of course, there was nothing we were ever going to say against Dad, whether in or out of his presence because clearly, we would pay the price later once they had left and we both knew it. Then they asked us whether we would like to go on a week's camping trip. Well, of course we did! A free getaway from our parents! This was the equivalent to a free get out of jail card on the monopoly board! Well, that was certainly music to my ears.

The trip was to take place in exactly one week from that day – that being a Tuesday. The lady from the SS promised faithfully that she would return the following Tuesday to take us on this camping trip. She told us we would have all kinds of fun. We would take part in boating, climbing, swimming, pony riding, and sitting around the campfire listening to stories and eating barbecued sausages. I could not wait. Every time I thought about the fun I was going to have; I was filled with excitement and such elation that a smile became permanently etched over my face. However, Odette did not allow herself to get sucked in with the same degree of excitement. I couldn't understand why. I began to imagine it. *Roll on,* I thought...

The Invisible Trip

I began to count the days down from seven to one. I put all the clothes that I would take with me to one side and was careful not to wear them. I made sure that no-one came too close to the bag so as to crush them or crease them, and we kept out of our parents' way so that there was no reason whatsoever for them to change their mind.

When Tuesday finally arrived, I was so excited I could not contain myself. We waited in controlled anticipation, trying not to let the excitement bubble over, trying not to cry out for joy.

My plastic bag was packed, every item inside folded neatly, and it was precisely parked by the bedroom door, ready to go; even my toothbrush was wrapped in toilet tissue; my makeshift toothbrush holder. However, the hours of the morning ticked tocked on by, only to reveal that in fact there was no lady coming to pick us up. The hours belonging to the afternoon did the same, which was repeated by the evening.

As my excitement whittled down to plain old disappointment, it was not long before anguish, hurt, and upset all began to rush in; and day soon became night. I tried to convince myself that perhaps I had got the day wrong and that, in fact, perhaps, she did not mean Tuesday, but she meant Wednesday. As Wednesday came and went, I convinced myself that it was Thursday, then Friday, and then Saturday. '*Yes, it was definitely Saturday,*' I *thought because this was the most likely day of the week a trip should start on,* I thought. By the time Tuesday came around again, I began to start wringing my hands in hopeless disappointment, as if wringing out the washing. My stomach was churning itself into unknown knots, yet to be discovered by sailors, as my emotions began to display themselves once more down my cheeks, leaving white tracks, as if they were the new paint of pain.

The days eventually turned into weeks, but there was still no sign of her – no letter, no message no nothing. *'What a let-down! How could an adult do that to a ten- year-old child?'* I asked myself. I would come to learn later that 'letting kids down' was what the SS did, and they did it so well. They were the masters of disappointment. We never saw or heard from her ever again. It was as though she had never really existed.

In that moment, I remember willing so hard with every grain of my being and with every molecule of my existence - just to leave home. I wanted out. I had had enough. I continued wringing out my hands again, this time in unison with my stomach turning over. My heart overflowed with thick, black disappointment, like soot gathering in an unclean chimney. Little did I know the clock was ticking, tick - tock, tick - tock.

Message to all you parents out there, *'don't let them go, move town to a quieter place if you have to, change job; but just don't let them go.'*

If we as parents don't care, can't be bothered to care then we can't expect anyone else to and you open up doors of unjust and unfair treatment for them; so please don't let them go.

Back to School

Once we returned to school after Spring Break, we realised that our teacher had somehow learnt of what had happened to us during the holiday period. She was riled to the point of actually using angry words, particularly those beginning with the letter 'f' and 'b'. Well, it was true to say that the SS were notorious for making promises that they did not keep, would not keep, or just could not be bothered to keep.

When Jessie heard the news, she immediately arranged a trip to Brighton for us within two weeks. Sally, my best mate, was to come too, but then she dropped out at the last minute, because her parents would not allow her to travel out of London, – *strange but true*. We had the time of our lives on this trip; she even made us the biggest and the bestest packed lunch any child had ever seen and, in that moment, just for a moment, life was bliss, and it was good again. But it only lasted for as long as we were with Jessie, it was just for that moment. With Jessie, life really was heaven on earth. I never wanted it to end. It was like going round and round on the merry go round without stopping and with a warm friendly breeze in your hair, yes it made me smile.

We splashed each other in the small waves and got our trousers all wet and got sand in between our toes. We enjoyed eating real ice cream. We were so full of fun, food, and joy. I was so high on life I thought I was going to burst with happiness – but it was just for a moment. And this, well this was the moment I wanted to be captured by - forever.

On the journey, back, we were all completely silent. It was as though I blinked, and here we were, back in the car, going home again. The only thing on my mind was when? When could we do it all over again? I thought about asking the question for almost the entire journey home. Unable to contain myself a moment longer, I had to get it out, I had to ask that question; and then, suddenly, without any intro or build-up, I blurted it out.

'When can we do this again?' I was full of anxiety, as I directed my question straight at Jessie.

'Soon,' she replied, 'soon.'

'How long is soon?' I enquired further.

'Err... two weeks,'

'Really?'

'Yes, don't worry. I will not let you down,' she affirmed. At least, we were going to see Jessie the following day at school and that was a great comfort. Secretly, the more I got to know her, the more I just wanted to be around her, the more I wanted to stay in her presence and the more I wanted to live with her. I knew I was safe with Jessie and John.

The following day at school I was smiling, as I reminisced about the day before, each time I looked at Jessie I was reminded of all the fun and the laughter. I knew something none of the other children knew and it made life a little easier, a little more bearable, a little more livable. I could not translate into words of how my life made me feel but these excursions made it just that bit easier.

Two weeks later, she had kept her word to the letter. On this trip, we were travelling to Clay Hill. A Place out of the city. We ran through the woods, swung on the trees, fell in the nettles, and got all muddy in the puddles; and at the prescribed moment, we all sat down to enjoy another wonderful picnic. I tried foods that I had never seen before and threw my head back as though I had not a care in the world and laughed out loud again; and my laughter sounded good; it was like a medicine you could not buy. We joked and played with each other. Yes, it was OK to laugh and laugh out loud. It was great.

We had such fun. I did not want it to end. We got to know her daughter, Sissy, a bit better too. She was not her real daughter; she was her sister's child. Her sister could not take care of her, so Jessie stepped up to the challenge. Jessie was truly an extraordinary woman; I felt truly special just to know her.

On the way, back, in the car, I repeated the same question. 'When can we do this again?' It was like medicine for my soul, good medicine.

'Two weeks,'

'Really?'

'Really,' she answered.

I knew now if Jessie said two weeks, then it really was two weeks. Jessie was a woman of her word. A woman of principal.

Our next trip was to Epping Forest. It was out of London and I fell asleep on the way there. Upon our arrival we ran through the verges, kicking up the leaves into the air as we ran. I loved the sound of the crisp, crunch, crunching leaves under the soles of my shoes; it was exhilarating. We shouted at the top of our voices, and our voices echoed right back at us. We were free to be over the top, with no one to tell us off, no one to complain about us, and no one to burst in and beat us up. It really was heaven on earth – truly it was. Was this what they meant when they talked about 'the abundant-filled life'? Because it was great; life was great again. At least, for a moment – that moment – it was OK to forget who I was or where I had come from.

After running wild and screaming like crazy, we all came together to enjoy another wonderful picnic. After lunch, Jessie took us up to see our deputy head, Mr. Kyle- Arthur. He was a round man of over-weight stockiness. Every part of him resembling the O in OXO. He was losing his hair on top but had managed to retain the color as best he could, a sort of washed out ginger with silver on the rise. He was very surprised to see us all standing there at the door.

Mr. Kyle Arthur lived in a lovely house on a quiet little road that was off a road that was off a road that was off another road. I was astounded by the amount of beautiful, polished wood in his house. He appeared to have an element of it in every room. I had never seen such a beautiful bespoke wooden staircase which went up through the middle of what was two large connecting rooms he used for his lounge. It made me feel a deep sense of peace, all the wood I mean.

We asked if we could have a look at the stairs and we climbed them all the way to the top. Ours had always been covered with carpet, so I never knew what was underneath; however, I was sure it was nowhere near as wonderful or as beautiful as Mr. Kyle-Arthur's. His was truly magnificent; I loved the look of it and the feel of it, even the smell of it. I kept touching it and stroking it and even placed my face on it.

Mr. Kyle-Arthur felt nervous that we were there in his house and eventually his nerves began to get the better of him. He kept asking Jessie whether it was OK for us to be there. She tried her best to reassure him, but in the end, after he had given us a glass of Pepsi each..., we left. I think we visited him once more on our days out together and then never again. I think his words made Jessie feel uncomfortable.

On the journey home, in the back of Jessie's car, the bubbles fizzed and popped in my nose. It was perfect. We rarely ever had fizz at home, if at all really.

When we got back, it was late again. Jessie came up with us to apologize to Dad for bringing us back so late. He did not answer her, he did not even blink an eye lid at her, he just walked away, leaving her and us standing at the door. She gave us a big two-armed hug, one in each arm, which was really nice. I did not want her to let go; I hugged her back with all of me, with every fiber of my being. I think Odette did the same too. I could not remember the last time I ever had one of those, *from anyone*. Looking down at our faces and reading us as though we were two open pages of the same book, both opened at the same page, she promised to return and take us out again soon. I wanted to ask how long *soon* was, but didn't as I was afraid Dad might hear. It was so important for me to know. It gave me a reason to keep on hoping and to keep on holding on.

As we went inside, our happy countenance was quickly exchanged for one of sadness and despair. The cloak of depression birthing was once again returned to my shoulders. We were very tired, so we went straight to bed without speaking, without smiling, without reminiscing.

It did not take me long to realize that Jessie was incredibly good for my well-being, my sanity, and my peace of mind. Every act of her kindness succeeded in sewing up just one more of my gaping wounds, which were torn deep down inside my soul. I wanted to live with her; she was safe to be with. Whenever we had been with her, I did not have a single worry. All my anxiety would dissipate; my stomach would stop knotting up like a sailor's rope and subconsciously I would stop wringing out my hands. My mind and my spirit were in unison and at peace, whenever I was in her company.

Jessie did not just take us out on weekends; her kindness, her generosity, and her compassion extended to the classroom too. She made it possible for us to take part in all school trips and excursions as it became more and more apparent that Dad was never going to allow us to go on any. His mindset was evident by the continuous non-existence of a packed lunch or signed permission slip.

As far as Jessie was concerned, attending trips was very important for a child's normal academic, emotional, and creative development as well as their mental and emotional growth; therefore, in her opinion, every child should attend, and, according to her, every last one of her children would attend, and that included me.

When the day finally came for me to hand in my consent form for the geography trip, I told Jessie that Dad had refused permission for me to go. Jessie asked me whether things were really difficult at home. I just nodded in confirmation. In that moment, I became so overwhelmed, caused by all the pent-up emotion and unexpressed anxiety that had been steadily building up since we left Sandy Lodge.

'Well, look,' she said, caringly, 'just get your Dad to sign the consent form, and I will do the rest.' I raced back home to ask Dad to sign the form. I did not have much time before the children would leave. I arrived there out of breath from running the entire journey without stopping.

Dad was asleep in his room as per usual, after a hard night's work at the bakery. Odette was also at home that day, looking after our brother. I knocked quietly on his door and waited, but there was no answer. I knocked again, a little harder this time, and again I waited. Then came the dreaded response.

'Yea, what?' he questioned from behind the door without getting up to open it. I began to try to explain what it was I wanted, but speaking from my position behind the door, was in truth very difficult. I was stuttering now about the trip, unable to get my words out in a consistent flow, another idiosyncrasy of my disposition. However, it did not matter as his answer was the same as it had been previously, and the time before that, and the time before that – an unequivocal no! My heart sank even lower. I went into our bedroom, sat down, and began to cry pure tears of sheer frustration.

Just then, I heard the bedroom door open; I got up, wiped my face, and prepared to return to school. I met my sister in the hallway, who gestured for me to go back into the bedroom and to wait for her there. Odette finished in the bathroom and met me in the bedroom.

'What is it?' she asked.

Eyes welling up I showed her the form.

'Do you just need Daddy to sign it?' she asked.

'Yes,' I answered. She took the form and went back into Dad's room and told him that the form had to be signed whether I was or was not to go on the trip.

Time stands still for no man, but for me, it really seemed to be flying. I had to get back to school, or I was going to miss the coach and the trip altogether.

Dad searched for a pen, which Odette intuitively had ready in her hand. He told her to sign the form and allow him to sleep. Odette signed the form on the '*I give consent*' line.

'Thanks, Odette,' I said, leaning over to hug her. I really had to run now – down the stairs, out the door, along the balcony, down the eight flights of stairs, jumping before reaching the bottom on each flight. Out of the flats, across the quiet road, along the hard pavement paths adjacent to the grassy green square areas. Through the underpass of the high-rise flats, across another road, and down along the pavement towards the main entrance of the school.

As I approached the gates, the children were already coming out in their pairs and had already begun to board the coach.

'Wait for me!' screamed my inner man, as I held the piece of paper out in front of me, holding on tightly and waving it in the air as I increased my running speed.

'Jessie! Jessie!' I screamed at the top of my voice, running at full speed up the long road, waving the signed paper out in front of me, only coming to a halt after crashing into Jessie head-on as she turned to see who was screaming out her name.

'Cor, you've got powerful lungs!' she exclaimed. 'Well done. You made it! Your partner is Lesley Lytham.' She said as she checked her list, 'find her and join the queue,' she added.

'OK,' I said, panting, all out of breath now. We were taking the coach to the river and then taking a river boat up and down the River Thames so that we could record what we could see on the banks; it was an important part of our geography block. I was glad to be present and be a part of the experience.

It was freezing cold on-board the boat, more so because I had no jacket; I did not have the time to collect it from the classroom before boarding the coach. The water sprays delivered up from the side of the boat wet my T-shirt, making me feel even colder. The temperature was much cooler on the river as opposed to up on land, and I felt very cold.

Jessie's idea was that we would have lunch on the boat and then we would spend about thirty minutes or so recording our findings before returning back to the coach and then driving back to school. I was so cold that I began to shiver uncontrollably. I kept thinking about boarding the coach again. It was much warmer in there. Jessie noticed my predicament and gave me her own cardigan to wear, which helped a little, as the shivering became intermittent, however upon noticing me she then gave me her jacket as well.

When it was time for lunch, I reminded Jessie that I had none. She was always so calm, she took everything in her stride, and her no-worry response was,

'Hold on, back in a minute.' Then she said, 'Right! Listen up, everyone. Has anyone got too many sandwiches or any sandwiches they don't really want or don't really like?' Hands went up all over the boat; there were so many offers of food that I was spoilt for choice. However, I decided against the jam and cheese, which although common amongst youngsters, never tasted right to me, so I opted for the Spam, – it had saved my life before, so there seemed to be no reason why it could not do it again now. Before long, I had too many sandwiches, a packet of crisps, and a drink. Jessie had done exceedingly well.

'Thank you, Jessie,' I said. *Well done, miss,* I thought contently as I tucked into the sandwiches which also helped with the warming-up process.

The trip was an immense success; I had an enjoyable time. Apart from being cold and wet, more importantly I had been able to contribute to the geography block with an excellent-graded piece of work.

Jessie continued to take us out every other weekend. I just used to count the day's in-between excursions. I could not really get enough of that funny, fuzzy feeling from all the places she took us to or from just being out with her. I trusted Jessie implicitly and loved being in her company. I really felt that she cared for us. I mean, you could not really miss the fact that she cared. Albeit I never revealed my feelings to her. I do not know why, or to anyone else for that matter; about how I really felt, deep down inside about things.

Disappearing from Home

The next school trip was at the end of the year. It was a four day retreat. This trip was one of the best things that the school had to offer the Year 6 pupils. Every effort was afforded to ensure that all the children went and had an enjoyable time. Many of them had never been out of London before or even off the estate for that matter. The cost was £78, which today would perhaps be more like £780.00, but Jessie had my back financially as well as socially – thank God for Jessie.

However, my dilemma was not the money, Jessie had that sorted, it was not the food, the school had that sorted, it was not the clothes, I had that sorted; it was the permission, without which, exactly how was I going to escape? Knowing Dad as I did, I knew he was not going to give permission for me to go. *So how on earth was I going to pull this off? How was I going to disappear for five days and four nights without being noticed, without being detected, or without being called by Dad or even Mordecka for that matter, and what about my brother? Surely, he would notice.*

The trip itinerary sounded too good to be true and too good to be missed. We would be staying in a hostel, taking part in activities such as abseiling, rock climbing, tree walking, indoor and outdoor swimming, canoeing, cycling, and walking. We were going to sit around the campfire, cooking sausages and telling stories late into the night. The one single thing that was certain was my intention to go. I desperately wanted to go even at the cost of a beating. The price in my eyes was definitely worth it.

Returning home, the afternoon before the morning of our departure, I somehow found the courage to speak to Dad, at least so I thought, and to ask him for his permission. I got as far as the living room, knocked on the door, waited, and then backed down before walking away. At one point during the evening, he called me and began talking to me nicely. I was not sure if he knew what I was about to ask him before our conversation was abruptly interrupted, and I was given an instruction to do something else. I left the lounge, carried out my chores, returned to our room, and delegated verbal instructions to my sister as to what she should do and say in my absence to give the impression that I was still present, when, in fact, I was not.

'If Dad calls me, make excuses for me, OK? Pretend like I'm in the toilet,' I said.

'How many times can I do that?' she asked irritably.

'Just think of something please,' I pleaded.

'I'm not going to get into trouble for you!' she stated quite emphatically.

'OK, OK,' I replied as I walked around the room and began to stuff items of clothing into a white plastic carrier bag.

'Hey... that's mine', she said pulling a white top from the bag.

'Well, just eat my meals then,' I said. 'Or throw them in the bin. Say goodbye twice, when you go to school and say good evening twice when you return,' I insisted. I had our usual habits marked down to a T. In hindsight, looking back, I do not know where I got the courage. I guess it really is inside you when you need it most.

The following day I left for school, carrier bags intact, knowing full well that I would not be returning that afternoon; or for the four whole days that followed and nights too.

Jessie gave me a rucksack in which to place my things in.

'I thought you might need this,' she said handing it to me. She had also brought me a packed lunch. As the coach pulled off, I tried to forget my life and put my cares behind me. These were some of the best days of my young life, that I would carry in my heart forever.

I listened contently to the stories of other children's lives and tried to imagine even a glimpse of this remote normality as part of my own. We laughed at each other's jokes, talking into the small hours before rising again with the morning as the day broke, to start a new day all over again; and embrace another adventure.

The trees were so tall in this place, their leaves were so lush, and the grass was so green. The sun shone, and the weather was warm, accompanied by a cool breeze throughout our entire stay. It was just so great, and we had nice food too. I did not want it to end; for those five days, I forgot who I was and which family I had come from or where I was going back to. I heard the sound of laughter, my laughter, and it sounded good. Throughout those five days, I just let my inhibitions go.

On the last night, I realised that once we got back to school, there would not be much time before the end of term. I was really concerned as to whether we would still be able to see Jessie, as she had been such a formidable character, and had filled such a huge void, at this vulnerable time in our young lives. For the most part, Jessie was our very own incredibly special fairy godmother, our guardian angel even.

On the journey home, my mind began to flicker on to fragmented scenarios of how Dad was going to respond to me once I had returned home. And my eyes filled up once more like great wells as I wondered whether Dad had indeed noticed that I was missing... and had been, for the past five days! *Had my sister even bothered to cover for me?* Her charity towards me was, at times, as unpredictable as the weather. Well, that was a whole other topic. *Was this an open opportunity for her to pay me back for all the unwarranted beatings she had endured on my behalf over the years?*

Upon returning home, Dad said absolutely nothing. He made no references, no utterances, and no comments to my absence at all. It was as though he had not even noticed that I had been missing. I asked Odette whether he had called me?

'Once!' she answered diffidently.

'So, what did you say? What did you do?' I asked, anxiously as if dipping my toe in hot water.

'Oh, I just made up some excuse or other,' she answered, ever so casually, not really giving anything away.

After following our usual routine of cleaning up, tidying up, and having to dispose of yet another disappointing dinner, we brushed our teeth and got ready for bed; we hugged affectionately and drifted off to sleep, with me retelling the entire goings-on and all the funny stories I had heard on the trip.

The next day, quite surprisingly, Dad began to call my name for every little thing; it was as if it was now payback for being absent. However, it was a small price to pay for all the fun, joy, and peace that I had just experienced over the past five days; in considering this, I responded without complaint.

Our excursions with Jessie had become an important event for me. They had really got me through the last year of having to endure life at home. The trips continued right up until I left Water Farm Primary School that summer and joined Odette at Darlington Bassett Grammar School that autumn of the same year; just one year behind her.

Moving on Up: The Big School

Darlington Bassett Grammar School was the secondary school Odette had selected exactly two years before, and I was now expected to follow in her footsteps, which I did. My uniform was Odette's old hand-me-down from the year before, – nothing new there then. I received all her hand-me-downs, but it was not much because we did not have much. The contents of my entire wardrobe were held up on no more than five hangers.

I remember, on one occasion, Dad had brought Odette a lovely pair of new sandals from Clarks. We were both still at the farm at the time. They were bright ruby red with shiny silver buckles on each side. They were lovely, and she was trying to hide her elated approval of them. He called me in as he finished fastening the last shiny buckle, and, in doing so whilst still on his knees and from that position, he handed me her old ones with the curled-up strap ends and the scuffed toes. My heart sank.

The trouble was that my feet were not that far behind hers. Odette had worn these old sandals until her toes were ready to burst through. She had been in pain for a long time before she could pluck up the courage to tell Dad that they were hurting her feet. So, Dad gave them to me, believing that they would fit me, and I would get even more wear out of them for a while. However, as soon as I put them on, my feet were hurting too. Burning in fact. I had to wear them with my toes crunched up. It was a long time before I too could pluck up the courage to tell Dad that they were also too small for me and thus my toes really suffered. *Toe surgeon anyone?*

In the 1970s, you usually got the school of your choice. The lottery back then was which one of your peers you would also get to share your new class with.

Our school spelt Education. With E symbolizing the highest academic class, then there were three groups under each letter in all core subjects, such as Math's, English, and Science right down to A. If you were in T-N, then clearly you needed help and a lot of it. I, like my sister, was in D, and I was in the middle set for Math's and English. However, she was in the top set for both subjects. I was in the same class as Lesley Lytham, who had come up with me from Water Farm Primary. We had also been in the same class back then too. We shared the same workstation, and we got on relatively well although I did not really know her that well. I would still meet my friends from the farm, Sally and Anna, in the break times or at lunch. Well, that was until I met a new girl, Flavia Featherstone, and my old chums took up smoking. It was something I was just not prepared to get myself involved with, as I knew exactly what Dad's response would be, if ever he was to smell even so much as a whiff of it on my clothes. And I was as certain as day was light and night was not that he would probably kill me; And so, it was a subtle goodbye from me to my old farm yard chums.

Flavia was also in my class, she sat at the front and on one occasion we just happened to be paired up to work together on a history and geography session, for which we were both marked with an 'A' for our efforts, and it was based upon this realization that we decided to work together on all our subjects. We even decided that we would sit together in form class.

It was not difficult for me to swap with Flavia's classroom partner or for her to swap with me to sit with Lesley, so we did. Our class was, purely by coincidence, grouped according to the origins of its inhabitants. So, we had the Turkish quarter near the door; the Jamaican quarter far right and to the rear; the English quarter front, right, and center; and the very loud Cypriot quarter far left and to the rear. Now the Turks and the Cypriots were always in some heavy deliberate debate on some issue of life. If they were not discussing clothing labels, it was food, culture, or even music. It all sounded the same to me. Their debates were always passionate, and at times even hilarious; apart from when they got us all a detention. No one was laughing then.

Our school was perhaps just a little over a mile from where we lived, and that was probably OK for the most part. I mean, it was an interesting and scenic walk until Dad determined *out of the blue* that we had to get out of the class, out of the building, through the gates, which were sometimes locked, up the hill, down the other side and along some very long roads, under the flats, across t wo car parks, up eight flights of stairs, and along our balcony and in through our front door in just five minutes.

In hindsight, I am not at all sure who was more insane, him for suggesting it, or me for actually trying it. I mean the school was at the bottom of Wood Green or rather Turnpike Lane amongst the backstreets somewhere, and we lived in the heart of Tottenham near Wilson Road, a small portion of which could be seen from the front walk way on the balcony. In any event, the pure notion of it just added to my stress levels, skin conditions, and stomach complaints.

I do remember that on one day, in early autumn, I came out to meet the gates locked and shut up tight. What shock, what horror! The anxiety I was now feeling was ten times worse than that experienced from watching *Nightmare on Elm Street and so* was the ending going to be if I did not find a way out and get home immediately. Panic drew itself all over my face as my eyes met with the giant padlock held fast, securing the giant black gates, and holding them locked in place. They themselves seemed to go onwards and upwards forever, almost reaching the sky. Their black cast-iron spikes conjoined at the top in perfect harmony as if holding hands, but this was not *ring – a – ring – a - roses.* The usual opening was being held tightly shut together by some mammoth monster chain.

A small congregation of children had now gathered at the gates where a self-elected spokesman (*one of the children*) was giving out instructions to some of the other children to go and find the caretaker. They were sent out in twos and threes to check out all his usual haunts. Our school caretaker, it appeared, had perfected the very art of taking his time in doing all things and that included getting to the required location once he was found, even if it was an emergency. Some of the remaining children, also waiting to leave, began to shake the gates in irritation. It did not matter how much they shook them though because that padlock was not coming off, not for love nor for money and certainly not without the key.

I could feel time slip, slip, slipping by, and my heart began to beat faster and faster. Impatience mounted as the brave took action and began to climb the gates like animals seeking a higher advantage over their prey, making themselves ready to pounce. Without a second thought, I too had joined them. The gates now began to sway with our weight as we went upwards upon it. As each child reached the top, one by one they descended with one jump down on to the hard pavement on the other side. Then it was my turn, and as I bent my knees down, to make the jump, unbeknown to me, one of the spokes had quietly slipped itself up under my skirt. Totally oblivious as to what was about to unfold, I jumped, eyes shut tight, to make my rapid descent down onto the other side. It was now, in that same moment, that the caretaker finally arrived, with me now in mid-air, and it was his wish for everyone to dismount the gate before he opened it. I was still in mid-air, about to start my rapid descent, when suddenly my flight came to an abrupt and rather sudden halt, as I was now pinned to the gate, held in place by one of the spokes which was now protruding right through the seam in my skirt. Now completely puzzled, the caretaker contemplated upon his options… Should he open the gate whilst I was still attached, or should he open the middle gates on the other side of the building? As he scratched his head and pondered on what was, for him a rather difficult decision. I was still hanging almost upside down as if stuck in a parachute that had got lodged in a tree. I was lowered a bit more as my skirt ripped further from the force of my weight being drawn down to the ground by the law of gravity which was now seeking to bring me even closer to the cold, hard, unsympathetic pavement below. A child who was speaking began to engage in conversation with me whilst I was still half upside down. As the blood rushed to my head, I felt slightly dazed or intoxicated, not sure which. As the caretaker placed the giant key into the giant lock and began to turn it, the last piece of my skirt ripped open, and I fell to the ground with a smack. In a flash, I got up, brushed myself off, and began to run home, as fast as my little legs could carry me.

'*Were my five minutes up? Was I late? Would Dad be up? Would he notice? Oh, my God, he's going to kill me, I thought all at once. My skirt was clearly ripped, that will definitely be death times two*,' I thought.

Well, I guess luck was on my side – my waist being as thin as it was, meant that the skirt could easily be turned around, so as I went in, the split was to the rear, and as I walked past Dad, I could pull it back round to the front. I was quite good at it, and Dad never even noticed.

Upon my return to school, all my friends made a fuss of me. One sewed my skirt, another did my hair, one brought in snacks and sweets and another told funny stories. They were all great; this was family. My family. And life seemed bearable again, but just for a moment, because of them: thank you guys. Where are you all now?? *I wanna say thank you to you guys.*

The Bully Police: No Bullies Allowed

At every school, there is always someone who will hold them self out to be the bully of the school or '*the school bully*' as perhaps the phrase is better known. But at this school, I quickly built myself a reputation for one who stood up against injustice – of course, there was a lot of bullying back then, no different from today really. However, I was determined to stand up to the bullies; there was one occasion when two girls had their dinner money taken by two other girls who clearly fancied themselves as a pair of *ladettes* and were trying to build a reputation for themselves as a pair of bullies.

Once I had learnt what had happened, I became so incensed that I began to roam the playground, like a hungry lioness looking for food, in search of them, and my friends were not far behind. Just then, somebody called out.

'That's them! That's them! Over there, at 12 o clock.' They were moving across the center of the playground almost like celestial beings, as the sun's rays appeared to be piercing right through them, like glistening sand. There they were, so full of themselves, laughing between themselves, probably at their own pathetic achievements, which to date no doubt included robbing their latest victims. But it was all about to come to an embarrassing end now that *we* had spotted them. It was all about to come tumbling down like a pack of cards around them. I increased my pace to catch up to them, and upon so doing, I came right up close and personal, right into their personal air space. I was now standing face to face, nose to nose, and eyeball to eyeball with the more bolshie one.

'What?' she said, filled with the same self-gratifying arrogance, that she had probably displayed, when she took the lead role in taking the dinner money from off the girls. I asked them with a rather bold and somewhat impatient authority, which one had taken the dinner money. They both looked at each other in an unqualified disbelief before looking back at me as if to say, 'Are you for real?'

Then one perked up and said, 'What's it to you?'

Ignoring both their questions, I repeated the question 'Have you got their dinner money?'

'*No!*' came the cheeky cock-eyed response. I then turned to the victims and asked them which one of the bullies had taken the money. They both answered, at the same time. But before they could answer the bullies piped up. 'We both did,' they said. 'And we shared it,' they added gloating.

'Well, you have exactly five seconds to return it. Five, four...' I said aloud as I began counting down loudly and rather boldly.

'But we haven't got it now!' the bolshie one said.

'Three... two... one.' And I began to take off my blazer and roll up my shirt sleeves, arranging my arms into the folding position with fists up. Then Sally quickly piped up. 'Listen, whosoever has got it, just give it back now quickly. Once she gets going, we cannot stop her!' she pleaded, with saliva flying everywhere as she spoke. By this time, a small crowd had begun gathering behind us, as the rumors of a possible punch-up flew around the playground like a river run through it. It appeared as tough children came out of the woodwork from all directions to see what all the commotion was all about.

A crowd had now formed, and a circle had encompassed us; I witnessed firsthand the expressions of these self-confessed ladettes turn from pouted arrogance and pride into fear and remorse. They had not got a single morsel of moral support, not one person was on their side. Slowly, they began to take out their money, making out as if they did not really have that much;

of course, I simply snatched the blazers off them and shook them both upside down.

The girls remained completely still, not even flinching a muscle as the change poured out on to the ground like little jingling bells.

Meanwhile, all the other children watching helped in giving the dinner money back to the girls who had been the victims of bullying. They received back more than just their dinner money that day, which was a sort of compensation for them, I guess. Then we warned the bullies sternly never to take anyone else's dinner money ever again or they would be deeply sorry. Fortunately for us, no teachers came out to inspect what could have easily been interpreted as an affray for which we would all have been in serious trouble. I vaguely remember the caretaker just beginning to arrive in the 11th hour and 59th minute, but it was all over. The crowd had already dispersed, and the pupils were in the process of making their way back to their respective blocks for the rest of the morning's lessons. That day, Flavia and I had carved out a reputation as the protectors; it felt rather exhilarating, using my energy to stand up for justice and become a restorer of the breach. Surprisingly, at the end of that break time, we all made it back to class *just in the nick of time.*

Losing Odette

Life continued very much the same at school until one fine day Odette disappeared without any word or warning or anything. I mean, I had no idea. I did not even see it coming. We must have been no more than three weeks into the term, when *bang!* Just like that, she was gone. Girl gone.

Mordecka had kept that plan very well hidden. Neither of my parents had said a single thing. No indicators, no hints, no nothing; we didn't even get to say goodbye to each other. It felt like someone had cut me open and ripped out a piece of my heart. I needed to keep on keeping on; a part of me needed to survive but it was really hard. If asked to stick a pin somewhere in a timeline it would have to be in that moment. It was from then on that my life began to deteriorate; something was wrong, very wrong and something inside was dying, like a plant without water, a flower without sunshine.

I wanted to lie down and not rise with the sun ever again, albeit my longing for Odette far out-weighed any harm due, but it was going to get a lot worse, and the clock was ticking…tick…tock…tick …tock.

In school, my concentration began to go skew-whiff. I was daydreaming big time. Before I knew it, I was being escorted, or rather frog marched before my head of year. I was told to wait outside her office because, quite innocently, whilst within the confines of the safety of a daydream, during double chemistry of course, I had subconsciously and quite accidently colored in the picture of a test tube, with a black Bic biro pen in a brand-new science textbook... '*Oh poo.*' Once I had returned to the land of the living, I could not believe it... Of course, my subject teacher had seen me do it; there was no use in lying.

He moved around the room slowly, from desk to desk, like some giant cobra, wearing a white coat, not able to contain himself, until he got to mine. I had been here before, so no love lost there then... 'Did you do this?' he asked in a slithering voice, his tongue protruding in and out from his mouth as he spoke, like the serpent. My eyes fell to the page.

'Don't even think about lying,' he asserted.

'Yes, sir,' came my mouse-like response without excuse or reason. For me, right then, in that moment, things clearly could not have got any worse.

'Right, class dismissed!' He announced. 'You, on the other hand, can stay there and accompany me to Mrs. Peppermouth's office.' he sniggered incredibly pleased with himself, in his well-spoken, well to do voice, which incidentally never changed in tone.

I looked at him wondering whether he was joking because his voice was so unconvincing, yet his face wasn't. It was this small detail that often caused confusion. He didn't need Botox. All his expressions were exactly the same, all of the time, plain and unmovable.

I said nothing. I was all out of begging and pleading for mercy. I thought I would just take this one on the chin. He took his time in tidying his desk and packing up his bag ever so neatly before escorting me to the office of our head of year. Before that moment, I had never actually met the woman. Thank God for small mercies because from the moment, I got in there, until the moment I left, the screaming and shouting did not stop. Of course, she reminded me of my cue of when to come in and say, 'Yes Miss and No Miss,' – she had to... I was completely lost; no sooner had she started no sooner had I simply switched off again. I sincerely hoped I would never have the misfortune of ever having to meet her again; she was an absolutely horrid woman: a car wreck of a teacher! But little did I know ... and the clock was ticking ... tick… tock., tick… tock.

Leaving Home

Every two weeks on a Thursday afternoon, Odette and I were in the same block for our lessons, and our classrooms were next door to each other. I waited hesitantly in the hallway near her class nervously hoping that she would turn up. She didn't. I returned to my class cold and dejected. I would now have to wait another two weeks before the opportunity arose again to try and see her. Two weeks later and again, I waited in the hallway, my class had gone in, but she did not arrive. Again, I returned to my class sad and disappointed. Another two weeks would pass, and I would wait again like a lover for his love. Then, just as I was about to give up and leave, I saw her. She was late. I quickly ran up to her and threw my arms around her. She was distant and cold.

'I'm leaving home.'

'No, please don't,' she said, staring at me deeply.

'I am,' I gestured as I walked back to my class. The teacher had come out and was now summoning me in.

It was awful returning home alone each day and going to bed alone. I felt so alone. I had no one to talk to, no one to hug me, no one to help me with the issues of life. The grief was absolutely unbearable.

Two weeks later, I too *had* left home. So, all the threats of Mrs. Peppermouth saying,

'I'll tell your Dad, and I'll get him down to the school' and 'you'll be in trouble' – all fell to the ground and evaporated just like melted snowflakes. Thankfully!

And so, I thought that was the end of her. Not quite, as I would later find out; and the clock was ticking, tick… tock…, tick… tock.

Catching up with Odette

Holding on steadfastly to that one thing – which was predestined to take me to my new life, and the thought of being reunited with Odette, I was filled with elation.

We drove for what seemed like never-ending hours, escorted purely by the night's lights that snaked in allurement, leading us on our journey, guiding us on our way. The streetlamps were positioned in some kind of symbolic orderly co-ordination in a futile attempt to light up the night, albeit without any real success. There were reds and oranges alternating in arrangement like precious stones reflecting the sunsets once gone by.

I cannot quite explain the feeling of freedom, but it felt good – damn good. It was like the intoxicating smell of a sweet rose first opened, like bare feet running on the morning's new dew, during unofficial spring; or like naked toes teasing the tide of summer on sandy beaches, or like running wild through crispy, crunchy leaves in autumn's Labor of love, or like exasperating thrills captured on the snow-covered hills fast descending in old toboggans. Yes, it felt good I tell you. The buzz in my nostrils was like the bubbles of good champagne popping in my nose. And the lights now appearing in parallel formation as if beckoning me, luring me into the abyss that awaited me as we travelled on.

We drove for what seemed like hours, yet the night had not moved. The blackness retained its same eternal depth, even our surroundings appeared the same. It was as though we were on some sort of merry-go-round. From one angle it was as though we were standing still at the same place from where we had first left off from – only the Earth was moving.

Eventually, we pulled off the busy road into a quiet street and then after a few moments, we pulled into a pebble-filled driveway, which appeared to replicate the sound of clapping hands as the wheels of the car rolled over them, before coming to a crunchy halt. I stared up in amazement. The house was the biggest I had ever seen looking up to see the whole of it. It was bright in color and stood detached in its position yet not alone on this quiet street. It was set gently back from the road. I think you would most certainly have called it a mansion. It went all the way up to the sky and was as wide as a football pitch if not wider, or so it seemed. The sash windows were as big as extra-large table tennis tables. This was Sanquingay Park.

The tiny stones appeared to scream out as we crunched them under our shoes whilst walking up to the enormous solid wooden door, which had been painted over in white.

It opened wide like the mouth of some giant fish and beckoned us in, quite mysteriously in fact, as there was no one standing on the other side of it. *Perhaps, it had been opened all along,* I thought. It was as if the house itself had been expecting us, but this was not nightmare on Elm Street, that was yet to come, and the clock was ticking. Tick…tock…, tick…tock.

With half a witty smile emerging ever so subtly, I followed my party inside, wondering all the while what gay excitement lay ahead of me, but above all, I was bursting to see Odette. I could not wait to wrap my arms around her and sink into her motherly embrace one more time.

The Arrival

Once we were all inside, I was disappointed to learn that there was simply more hanging around to endure, whilst the person with the authority was tracked down to sign more paperwork; but I tried not to show it. As we waited, I could not help but notice the high elaborate paneled walls and doors; and the stone tiled floors, but as glamorous as it was, there was an eerie coldness that filled the air. It was one that I simply could not put my finger on; it kept me constantly on edge throughout the duration of my stay. Eventually, all the paperwork was finally completed, and then they made the exchange. '*The girl for the goods,*' I thought. *Except there were no goods... the girl was the goods.*

Each party had their own batch of paper photocopies ready to be signed and filed away until some 20 something years into the future when it would be demanded by a court. The door slammed shut tightly behind them as they left. A chilling coldness filled the air almost completely consuming the extremely large hallway; the harshness of it appeared capable of freezing, in an instant, the coolest of dripping water into an icicle. I shuddered in my shoes.

This creepiness was enough to raise the thickest of hair, on the back of any brazen neck. It brought a shudder to my person, the atmosphere was indeed filled with a particular unrest, but from that day until the day of our departure I never set eyes on my rescuers again, not once during that season.

That was it; they had taken me as far as they were permitted in my journey. It was as though, from that moment on, they too had become no more than a figment of my imagination, or were they? I would often question myself in the years that followed. *What had really happened back then? And why now was I scarcely whispering to myself about it?*

After the pretense of petite introductions and that pathetic handshake you do, you know, the one where you are barely touching because one or both of you do not really want to touch, well, after that was all over, I was shown to my room. I would be sharing this with up to four other girls. The good news was at least I was with my sister, so I was happy about that and did not really mind the others so much. I took my shoe box of simple possessions and put them away. I had nothing else to unpack. I placed the empty box neatly under my bed, almost in alignment with the joining line that connected the two large pieces of cold organic vinyl flooring upon which all the furniture in the room sat.

'It can't go there!' said a stern voice from out of the covers. Fearfully startled, I quickly spun around to see who it was that was speaking. I had not noticed anyone else in the room when I had entered. As I looked around the room, I could not see anyone, for they were cleverly concealed under a simple covering of sheets and blankets spread over a bed, parked over in the darkest corner of the room.

'OK then,' I replied out loud, not wanting to step on anyone's toes; at least not on my first day or rather night as the case was. I moved the box to an empty drawer located at the bottom in the robin chest, which stood in the middle of the room between the two sets of bunk beds. I quietly squeezed the box into the drawer and closed it back ever so gently before vacating the room, in cautioned silence.

It was lights out at 10 p.m., here in this place. There were no ifs, no buts, and no maybes about it: just lights out at Ten. The rules were never questioned, everyone just simply obeyed them.

Don Padwick was the manager – the man in charge. He was described as being small in height, with short, dark, curly hair which was always extremely greasy. He was exceptionally clean shaven yet stunk to high heaven of cheap aftershave, on top of cheap aftershave – I think you call it old aftershave. His origins were either from Cyprus or Turkey. But we never heard his mother tongue, so we were not able to know for certain. Rumor had it that Don liked little boys, particularly blond-haired little boys with blue eyes. Oddly, he had a rather large picture of a little boy with blond hair and blue eyes mounted on the wall positioned directly above his desk, which simply gave weight to the rumors that were definitely unsettling. And there were even more disturbing rumors of Mr. Padwick actually interfering with little boys. As scary as this information was, I never actually saw him throughout my entire stay, and neither did I see or meet any of his alleged victims. I am not sure why, but in some strange way, it all appeared to ring true as I would eventually come to find out exactly five years on, and the clock was ticking. Tick tock, tick tock.

After a simple supper of cheese sandwiches and a cup of tea followed by a quick tour of the building, it was time for bed. It had been one heck of a journey getting here, and I, for one, was certainly not about to object to lights out this night. We brushed our teeth, had our showers, and sunk down deep into our beds. I was not used to so much bedding. For the first time in years, I felt warm, yet I was still unable to uncurl down or stretch out from the fetal position. I had become habitually locked into sleeping with my knees pressed up tight against my chest, in what was always a futile attempt of trying to keep myself warm, it was now so difficult to unravel them or even to stretch them out.

After a brief chat with the mystery voice emanating from the darkened corner, who explained all the dos and don'ts so eloquently and in such a detailed way, she now wanted to know who I was, who I was attached to and where I had come from and how long I would be staying. After what seemed like 20 questions, we all went to sleep.

It must have been about 3 a.m. when, suddenly, we were all abruptly awoken by the banging of doors and the sound of fast running feet. There were sudden bursts of loud shouts and contagious laughter. We were all quite perturbed, to say the least, not really knowing whether to get up and join in or lay still like broccoli and be silent. Whilst pondering the thought of what to do, the voice of wisdom spoke again from over there in the far corner, shrouded in darkness.

'Be quiet and do not answer!' it was more like an order than a suggestion or general advice. We simply responded in fearful obedience.

'OK,' we whispered back. The door was secured, and we all went quietly back to sleep.

The very next morning, we were to witness first-hand the damage that had been caused by the sheer reckless behavior of the night before. The ladies in long blue overalls picked up the pieces, scrubbed off the marks and removed all the evidence of broken parts as they usually did from the night before.

Oddly, we ate breakfast standing up, which we had prepared ourselves, before going off to school, which was strange. We had to take a bus from the stop by the clock tower in Crouch End, thankfully Odette knew the way. Some of the children packed cheese sandwiches with no drink, others packed drinks and no sandwiches, and still others packed nothing. There seemed to be no guidance and no direction. It all felt... well... very empty really, as if there was indirectly some voice guiding us in this area; but in truth it was as if we were really all alone.

Upon our return to the house, it was the same weird feeling which accompanied me, whilst no one questioned things; it was as though this was the new normal. But there was no sense of community, no sense of unity, and no coming together. People, young and old, ate at separate times, and everybody did pretty much their own thing. There was a serious lack of structure, order, and a total void of all emotion. It was truly a wonder of just how on earth anything worked in this place, or did it? Perhaps, everything somehow just fell into place at the very last minute, which would be quite miraculous, or was it all just simply hanging by a string?

I found an old record player and some records of different genres. It was not long before I began to lose myself in the music and I began to choreograph movement through dance. Sometimes, the boys would come in and watch; they would laugh and joke and make fun of me, but it did not deter me. I did not care. Each day, just before bedtime, I would slip away into the music room where I could lose myself in the music, and just dance and dance and dance.

Approximately two weeks into my stay, we had some new arrivals. They were two young girls, around the same age as us who were also sisters. They were placed in our room to share with us. Probably the thinking behind it was that two sets of sisters should get along; and in fact, we did. It was always exciting when a new face came to stay. We would always stay up late into the night, talking about our journey to date, of why and how we came to find ourselves here and get to know each other a little better. Each midnight chat was followed by a midnight raid on the larder. *Now this was the real fun.*

After all that talking, you could be very hungry and thirsty you know. We would creep down to the kitchen in the dead of night and make sandwiches of either sandwich spread or marmite, which would be washed down with loads of orange squash. We would creep back upstairs and continue chatting and then would come the serious question.

'So, what are you doing here then?' I asked without contemplating that for some this could be perhaps a rather deeply personal question. They seemed quite happy to have anything wrong, I thought. As it transpired, it was another case of abuse, but not the type of abuse that we were familiar with.

'Well, what happened exactly?' I asked in complete naivety of exactly what abuses were out there, totally oblivious as to how bad the answer could possibly be. I was not sure I even understood the meaning of that word back then.

'Well, you see,' she said, pausing.

'Yes,' I said, chewing my last mouthful of my sandwich spread filled sandwich.

'Well my uncle, see,' she continued.

'Yes,' I said.

'Well... he took me... see and he –' she continued.

'Yes, I said again.

'Well... well, he... he put... you know,' she said, kind of smirking. Well no I did not actually.

'Know what? I said in complete innocence. 'I don't understand,' I added, now even more puzzled; but half expecting her to say something funny.

Looking back now, I can see that even at 11, I was still very green. So, then she showed me… I thought she was going to absolutely suffocate me... with her mouth. I screwed up my eyes tight shut and held my breath until her clammy hands released my face from their hold. Utterly shocked from that moment, I became very wary of her and did not want to be left alone with her, not even for a moment. I was terrified. I had never experienced anything like this in my entire young life.

Then there was Siena. She was another girl staying at the house. Her eyes were always permanently glazed over. It was as if she was about to cry, but never did. She was extremely thin and always on her own. I thought I would ask her what her story was. I was not prepared for what was to unfold. It was as though I was in a real-life horror movie, and the horror of her tale was to follow me even right up until this day. She was an only child of Southern Irish descent. After the sudden departure of her dad, her mother had taken in a live-in lover who would return drunk every night and come – in her room and abuse her night after night. I could hardly breathe from what I was hearing. Impatiently I asked what her mother did?

'What did she say?' 'Did you tell her?' I asked all at once. Her answer was simple

'I don't know.'

'What do you mean? So how did you get here then?'

'My teacher called the people.'

'Oh,' I said filling in the blanks remembering my own exodus.

'So, what did your mum say when you left?'

'Nothing, I didn't see her.'

'So, don't you miss her?'

'I don't know.' Her answer as bleak as it was, seemed to speak volumes. I knew it all without her having to say another word.

As quietly as she had arrived was as quietly as she disappeared and without a trace. No good bye, no forwarding address, no nothing. I was too afraid to ask where she had gone, or if she would return.

Chores for Cash

I could not believe my ears when at the end of my second week I was instructed to carry out chores. I thought it was some kind of joke. I just stared back at the instructor without any expression, not really knowing exactly how much seriousness to attach to the instruction. Then the instruction was given again.

'Your job is to sweep the leaves from the backyard,' repeated the voice. I turned to look to see exactly where the backyard was.

'You have got to be kidding me,' my brain said to my mind as I turned away in total disgust.

'You have to sweep outside,' repeated the voice for a third time.

'Err, no!' came my rather deliberate emphatic response.

'Well, you have to,' said the voice, trumpeting up the sound of authority.

'Well, I'm not going to!' I said with all concrete certainty.

'Well, you won't get any pocket money then.'

'What pocket money? What is pocket money?' I had completely

forgotten those days whilst at Sandy Lodge. I guess they were really too few and far between.

'Well, everyone here gets pocket money every week.' 'usually on a Saturday, after they have done their chores.'

'How much is the pocket money?' I asked inquisitively.

'How old are you?'

'11.'

'35 pence.'

'Keep it!' I replied assertively, and without a second thought on the matter. After five years of cleaning up, polishing, washing, sweeping and more cleaning up the house for Mordecka, Dad, and the children they shared between them, I had no intention of ever carrying out another chore as long as I lived. As far as I was concerned, I was on a permanent cleaning vacation, or so I thought... We were all expected to undertake chores at the house. It was rather big, huge in fact; unfortunately, I just could not get my head around this one request, so therefore I declined to participate, and to the amazement of everyone, apparently, no one had ever said no before, at least, not a child anyway.

Our lifestyle and routine here at Sanquingay Park continued in the same manner for exactly three and a half weeks to the day, yet it seemed much longer. Then without a word, without any kind of notice or warning, it happened. It was whilst we were on our way to school, I remember it as though it was yesterday. We had just got to the fruit & veg man we always knocked his apples off as we turned the corner.

On this particular day, a large white car appeared out of nowhere, it slowed to the pace at which we were walking. The window came down. We were told to get in. Just Odette and me. We looked at each other and upon recognizing the driver we obeyed the command.

We were picked up and whisked off to somewhere else *just like that!* Oh, but this was *so* not Henry Cooper. It was nothing short of espionage and kidnap. *Up, up, and away*, I thought. Again, we were on the move, to another home, another town, and another people: New people. But this place of intention was certainly no bed of roses and it did not sit well on the categories of *homes* as we were soon about to find out. It felt like an even longer drive to Potters Bar, when in truth it was not that far, well in fact we were travelling just a little further north than that.

The roads were long, steep, and silent, with not even a house in sight. As we pulled out on to the suburbs it became apparent that they were all very well concealed, hidden in fact, behind the neatly cut hedgerows, and beautiful sculpted bushes. Others were hidden behind very large trees that seemed to curtain the entrance of every long drive. From what I could make out some were eighty, ninety, even a hundred feet long. Even the walkways and pathways were left unclaimed by pedestrians. I am guessing that everyone had a car as the roads went on forever. They too were quiet and bare.

The scenery was filled with many vast open spaces boasting many shades of green and all kinds of trees, hedges, and shrubbery. This time, however, we were on the road to Perdition, but neither of us knew it yet.

The Second Arrival (Number 10)

After a long-drawn-out drive, completely devoid of any clear ending in sight, it was so sudden when the large white car, in which we had been travelling, abruptly swung sharp right into what appeared to be a long, abandoned, driveway. It was cleverly concealed by a hidden entrance of overgrown brambles and bushes. A broken sign read *'No Trespassers'*. It all felt very eerie and even more uncomfortable. As we drove up the long drive, it eventually revealed a 'larger than life' almighty estate at the end of it, like the type you see in scary movies.

It was surrounded by grounds that beheld no visible boundaries. We arrived at that place, and it was as though it just appeared out of the ground, standing bold, arrogant, and deliberate. It was indeed an ugly-looking place. Perhaps even a little uncomfortable, I mean there was nothing cosy about it. Unbeknown to us, it was a place where children's screams frequented the hallways and their blood cleaved to the cracks around the doorposts and had been left to dry between the open joints that divided the linoleum floors.

It was a place where children were locked up alone without reason and in darkness. It was a place where the blue lady was said to walk the long corridors and stand immoveable on landings, floating up staircases on every level, at every full moon, as soon as the clock struck 03.00hrs. And she would curse anyone she found in her path.

It was a place where adults beat children and children beat children until they wanted to die and die again. It was a place where no one paid attention to your screams where you had no dreams and no hope. This was a place where your only savior was the ambulance man; that was, if only they could get to you in time.

Those who could run, did, but were usually caught a short while later. Their shoes were removed, and they were sat on until the screams died out and they struggled no more. This was a place where it was hoped that you would finally be forgotten and speak no more. This was Grimshaw Hall.

Little did I know that my blood would also join the blood that already lay in the cracks of the linoleum; And the clock was ticking, tick tock… tick tock…tick tock…tick tock.

Hell, on Earth is Real

We stood in what I would have called the ballroom hallway, completely naïve and totally oblivious as to what lay ahead. It was four times the square footage of a luxury one-bed pad in the New Docklands, for which you would certainly pay more than £660,000. The high-paneled ceilings were elegantly decorated with tasteful Georgian covings, which clearly would not have been an added feature in any modern-day pad... They simply went on forever, and they were certainly eye catching, if not breathtakingly beautiful. The beaded surround trim was in brilliant white laying transfixed against an emerald-green backdrop. It was a powerful combination of sophistication dancing on opulence. This beauty was added to by the paisley etching which was carved out in gold stitching on the velvet facing, which was completed to an eye-catching finish.

The floor directly in front of the large entrance door, spread throughout the reception area was a superior high quality parquet paneling. Polished to a high mahogany mirror finish, capped by shin high old oak skirting board immaculately finished in high gloss. You could still smell the faint scent of fresh expensive polish which lingered in the foyer from the morning cleaning teams.

The window boxes were also finished in a high white gloss, dust free, but without cushions, wide enough to sit on or even hide on once the heavy lead weighted, brown, velvet, curtains were permitted to be closed. It was all very 17th Century French Madonna, I believe.

The front entrance doors were as wide as four people and as solid as a tree. They were all finished in oak varnish and dressed in brass that was kept so shiny, by another silent invisible team.

There was a long brown unworn sofa, which sat opposite the open fire, which was never lit. Surprisingly the sofa was big enough to hide in, as I would later find out. The reception area was so enormous that it could have passed as a TV room, except there was no TV, just an old radiogram from the 1930s. It was brown in color and was adorned with just two large dials on the face of it: one for volume, the other for channel selection. It was well positioned in the center of the coffee table. I had no idea whether it actually worked, but it did give a semi homely feel to the presented arrangement, whatever homely was, that is. Eventually I too realised that we were still waiting to be attended to; we waited and waited for someone, anyone really, who had any manners to notice us and to meet and greet us, to welcome us even; but perhaps that was asking for just a little too much. Wishful desires but clearly not highly abnormal, given the circumstances, one might have thought.

After a while, we found Flannigan, or rather, he found us. His knuckles where red and his sleeves were scuffed up to his elbows. The lace on his right trainer was open, and he was perspiring mildly from his brow; oddly, I noticed that there was a small piece from his front tooth missing, whilst I wasn't sure whether the loss had occurred in that moment it was difficult to say when it might have happened, but it was hard not to wonder. His cotton wool colored hair although thinning on top was all disheveled, and he had one side of his shirt that was not completely tucked in to match the other. For one who was in charge of children, it was difficult not to wonder what on earth he had been doing and what had taken him so long.

Quickly we were ushered over to a massively grand room, which we later learned was the office of Mr. Frank whom we did not meet on this occasion. We were not invited to sit down. However, I would later discover that he too hated children – the extent of which would come at a cost that would haunt me for most of my years ahead.

They did that paper-exchange thing again, and Flannigan began to try to explain where or what he had been doing. No one really paid him much attention though, – at least not until we were abruptly interrupted by one of the older children, who blurted out, 'Reese has escaped again.' Clearly, we all felt unsettled by the news but were put at ease with some lame, low, nonsense excuse of how or why any child with no better prospects would even want to escape from a place like this. With that at the forefront of one's mind, you could not actually help wondering exactly what kind of a place this was. Somehow, I knew that I did not like the feeling that was beginning to permeate the air, it was like a bad odor that not even expensive air freshener could cover over or even dilute.

I felt, intuitively that I did not like this place. It was indeed a God forsaken place, perhaps, even forgotten and, certainly by the SS – in any event, we were destined to soon find out. The wind of no peace was rampantly present and demanded to be fueled continuously whatever the cost. I followed Odette everywhere, including the bathroom, which rather annoyed her somewhat.

In the lounge, I sat right up close next to her and would have sat in the same chair as her if she had let me. This too annoyed her quite immensely. She had looked after us all for far too long, and now she wanted to escape this life. She wanted to take up the title of her age.

After tea, they announced that I would go down to the lower quarters and reside there, because I was a year younger than her. '*Noooooooooo*,' I thought. My eyes glazed over, ready to drop huge tears of discontent. Honestly, I could not bear it. I could not bear my sister to be out of my sight, not even for a moment. I knew this was truly a horrid place. I could feel it, I could just sense the evil, and it most certainly was haunted, but not with ghosts covered with white sheets, oh no. I know this because I waited up for them on more than one occasion.

Our rescuers had just left us, abandoned us even, and now we were on our own once more. But this time it was different. I did not like the feeling, I did not like the people, and I did not even like the children. They were all crazy in my book. Only God knew how long we would have to stay in this forsaken place; it was indeed hell on earth as I was soon about to find out.

After tea, I was reminded again that I had to go down to B group. Of course, I did not want that. After Odette's reassurances that her strong hand of protection could without fail reach all the way down to B section, and batter anyone who upset her little sister, I hesitantly and reluctantly repositioned myself down in B section. Almost immediately, the trouble began. Children wanted to flex their muscles and affirm their ground, ready to carve out their boundaries once more and in blood if they had to. Adults threw children around like rag dolls, affirming their dominance revealing their unquestionable authority.

Our first night was one of non-stop storytelling, speaking right into the early hours of the morning. It was just as dawn began to break that we would go downstairs without using any lights and raid the larder. We made cheese and pickle and sandwich spread sandwiches. Then out of nowhere Sarah began shouting at the top of her voice, for no apparent reason and then just like she turned on all the kitchen lights. '*Crazy bitch.*' We could have got caught at any moment, now we all had to scarper back across the hall and up the stairs, in complete darkness, as fast as our little legs could carry us, leaving a big mess behind in the kitchen. We all jumped into our respective beds, my heart still pounding as I lay there with the sheets pulled up right over my head. Of course, the next day Sarah told on us, which was even more baffling. And so, the craziness continued. But as long as Odette was there, no one really troubled me, and I went with the flow and, for the most part, I did feel pretty safe.

Our mornings were filled with arts, crafts, and board games. We would, if we felt like it, help with the set-up of mid-morning snack and set the tables for lunch and dinner throughout the day. If we wanted to, our help would extend further than just setting the tables. We could if we wanted to get involved in the opening of large packets and giant tins or peel the kilos of potatoes that were on route to the lunchtime table; mashed, boiled or roasted. We had some funny contraption into which you would place the potatoes at one end and turn the handle in the middle, and the potatoes were supposed to move along through the center of the chamber and somehow arrive at the other end, completely peeled, but like the cook, it really wasn't very good.

Cook was hardly cut out to be a chef; she was round in dimension, she wore one of those old-fashioned aprons with a matching head apron under which all her frizzy ginger hair could not fit, it stuck out from one side as if to be giving confusing directions. Once the potatoes came out you still had to finish them off by hand in order to arrive at that perfectly peeled potato. Sometimes I would try and add extra seasoning when cook was not looking; unfortunately, there is only so much you can do with white ground pepper and table salt. Albeit my time in the kitchen became dramatically reduced, but not without first making my thoughts clear.

The upside of living here was that on the weekends we could go horse riding or swimming, as well as non-stop TV from sun up to sundown; it was as though it was never actually turned off. Perhaps the most unusual thing was that there was no school – not even a day of it. Apparently, not that long ago, some of the longer-attending children had abused the taxi service and had bunked off school for a total period not exceeding a full six months, to which no one was none the wiser and the bill stood at £300, which in today's money is probably about £3,000. Personally, I had never seen so much money and was unable to imagine what it could even look like or what the color of it would be.

It was further revealed that they had instructed the taxicab driver to drop them off anywhere and everywhere except their school of intent and the damn idiot fool obliged them; *can you believe it?* And it took six months for the sorry saga to even be detected and thus the unrepentant story went. The consequence of this rather disgraceful act was that there was no more school for those who remained or for those who would follow. *Was this even legal?* – I mean, I actually enjoyed school at least what I had experienced of it up until then. I mean it had always been a lifeline for me for so many years, the last six in fact.

It was a place of escapism, where I could just daydream the day away in peace of better times of a life gone by. It was where I knew I was safe, where I would not be beaten or thrown or have my head banged on the wall, or endure defense wounds on top of defense wounds, where I would not be called names by my teachers; it was the place where I could stomach the cuisine. But that was that – no more school.

Funny how you never know how much you miss something, until it's gone, – *even* school. Funny thing that! Without school, there was no routine, no direction and no sense of real structure and there was clearly only so many arts and crafts and TV, one could stomach before being bored to tears. My brain needed more stimulation than just games and making stuff.

I remember on one of my discovery walkabouts I heard a noise coming from the downstairs girls' toilet. As I approached and pushed the door ajar, I saw my sister standing there with two other girls; there was a strange smell in the room that I had not experienced before. On the floor were some cleaning bottles all with the tops off. I looked at Odette then lowered my eyes to look at the bottles then I looked back at Odette, she was staring right at me but did not say a word.

Before I could say anything a member of staff came bouncing in and pushed me out of the way, and then out of the door. He shut the door in my face. I could hear him shouting at the girls as I walked away. I never spoke to Odette about what she was doing that day or about what I saw, not that day or in that season.

Later I would come to understand, that the pain, which is felt so deep inside must be oppressed, because it cannot be trusted and in many cases the method of control selected is by the affliction of self-harm sometimes called abuse.

I would later come to find out these things personally in my own life; and the clock was ticking, tick, tock...tick, tock.

The Nightmare Begins

It was one fine day, just before the commencement of the Christmas season, when out of the blue, we received a telephone call. It was Jessie. She had finally found us. '*Thank GOD!*' I thought. At last, a sane person – good old Jessie.

'How did you find us?' I asked, smiling slowly down the phone. I knew then that it was Jessie who was indeed our fairy godmother, – our earthly guardian angel.

'Well, you know me – a bit of this, a bit of that, and Bob's your uncle...I have my ways,' she laughed.

After moving here, I thought we would never see her again. We had not seen or heard from her in weeks, which seemed like months. For a moment, I began reminiscing on the days out we spent together. I loved our trips to the beach, Clay Hill and Epping Forest. I always felt so safe with Jessie I was at peace knowing that she would never harm us, no matter how many times we messed up no matter how many mistakes we made. She always allowed us time to grow and that included learning by making mistakes too.

With Jessie, making a mistake wasn't a crisis it was an opportunity to rethink and start again. Jessie was indeed a very clever woman. Secretly, I had always wanted us to live with her and John; but I never revealed it.

'How are you?' she smiled.

'Don't ask,' I responded. I was not really sure of exactly how much I should actually enlighten her with at this stage, and not wanting to scare her off completely, I simply did not answer. The line went quiet at my end as my eyes filled up again.

'Guess what?' she exclaimed excitedly trying to pick me back up. At this point, I really did not want to guess. I just needed some really good news like *I'm taking you out of there today! or We are coming for you at dawn, dynamite, and all, and we are gonna bust you out of there!* Any one of those sentences would have sufficed for me right then in that moment.

'Just tell me,' I answered without emotion or expression, trying my best not to hope, yet quietly driving my mind back to reality and struggling to sound enthusiastic.

'Well, how would you guys like to come and spend the Christmas hols with us this year?'

'Was this her idea of a joke?' I thought silently. *'Did she really just say what I thought she just said?'* The line was faint. *'I mean exactly who did she think she was – Houdini or someone?'*

'Re-really?' I stuttered; I went all weak at the knees, and my head started to spin. I began hesitating not wanting to get my hopes up.

'Yep, you bet ya!' her voice now louder.'

'That would be great', I thought. But I was absolutely convinced that Mr. Frank was not going to allow it even if he had to personally wedge himself between the solid oak door and the door frame, with Super Glue 3, to prevent us from going, if he had to. He was just too mean to be asked.

'Ye-yes. Oh, oh, OK,' I answered delivering my words carefully..

'OK then, I will come back to you. Let me sort it out,' she said.

'OK then,' I responded trying my best to remain positive.

As the phone tone went out, I began to allow myself to hope and hope again. Every time I thought about it, I said, *'Please, please let it happen. Please don't let anything happen to prevent Jessie from coming and taking us for the holidays.'*

However, in that window of waiting, yes, you guessed it, something terrible did happen – but at least it did not start off that way. But it would scar me for life.

It was a Saturday, exactly three weeks before Christmas. Strangely all the girls ended up outside in the courtyard for some reason or other cannot remember why. There were six of us in total.

'Let's go into town,' said Sarah.

'That's too far!' asserted Sophie.

'Where is the nearest shop?' asked Odette.

'Just ten minutes up the road,' answered Sarah.

'In town,' said Sophie.

'OK, let's go to the shop,' blurted out Sally.

'But we have no money!' said Sophie.

'Let's ask people for money,' suggested Marley.

'I know let's sing carols all the way to the shop and see how much money we can raise,' said Sarah.

'Yes!' We all jumped up in agreement. We sung 'Away in a Manger', 'Silent Night', 'Good King Wenceslas', 'Oh When the Saints Come Marching In' and 'Jingle Bells' all the way. We must have sounded like a choir of angels that day because the tips just kept on coming. Those who had no coins gave us warm buttered scones and rich fruit bread; juice and milk were also in heavy supply. As we continued knocking doors in the direction of the shops some of the girls went on ahead with me and Marley lagging behind. When we eventually caught up to them, we realised that they were inside a house; I asked what was going on, but no one was answering me. I called out for Odette as I stood in the doorway. I noticed that the house was very dim, and it was apparent that the owner was not there. I felt afraid and begged them to leave, finally they did but no one would shut the front door. I had a very unsettling feeling, so I walked back up the dirt drive to close the front door and place the key back under the plant pot.

Surprisingly, once we had totaled up all our coins, we had raised a grand total of five pounds and 75 pence; *almost the national rate per hour in modern times for an unskilled worker aged 18-20. I*n that moment life was amazing.

We walked skipped and ran the last few hundred meters to the shop, each discussing with excitement what sweets we would buy.

As we stood outside, the older girls shared out the money with everyone and with the odd change that was left over, we all agreed that it should be shared between the older girls, Odette included. We young ones did not mind. We had never seen so many sweets before. We must have had 2-3 bags of the white paper bags each, and each bag containing all our favorite sweets. I had strawberry and lemon bonbons, Black Jacks, and Fruit Salads, chewy cigarettes, one bag each of jellybeans, jelly babies, humbugs, hard-boiled lemons, and hard-boiled Liquorice – all with chewy centers. I loved chewy centers.

There were some joking verbal exchanges on the slow walk back to the estate. However, the laughter soon came to a sudden halt at the prospect that somehow, we would have to hide these sweets. We instinctively knew no one would ever believe, that we had raised the funds ourselves through carol singing and made an honest purchase of the sweets. Fortunately for us, Odette had a large carrier on her person, which she pulled out from under her poncho; *strange but true. A*s we arrived at the gate to the long bendy driveway which stopped at the large front door, we all placed our bags of sweets into Odette's carrier bag, she then hid the bag under her poncho, and we slipped back inside.

No sooner had we arrived back, we were all instantly summoned to Mr. Frank 's office for an in-depth and rather intense grilling. Questioning did not really feature; it was more a case of deliberate accusations being deliberately fired as if from a loaded pistol!

Meanwhile, our rooms were in the throes of being willfully and deliberately *ransacked*, with all our belongings being strewn across the floors in all of the bedrooms. The sweets were eventually found and slammed on to Mr. Frank 's desk.

'I'm asking you for the last time, – where did you get these sweets from?'

It was now nine o'clock in the evening. We had missed our tea, of course, and now we had missed supper too. Odette and I were silent; somehow, we had learnt there was no point in arguing with or even answering our old friends – *hysteria and crazy*. We had certainly, been here before. But the other girls began to cry as he threatened to call the police and have them '*rot in jail!*' – I believe his exact words were. And yes, he did call the police.

The police came around in their blue and white-panda police car, only identified by the flashing blue light as it came screaming up the long drive in pitch blackness. The siren wailing like some frantic mother who had just been given the awful news that she had lost her children. They jumped out from the car quite quickly as they expected to come face to face with some great emergency: *Some real life emergency.*

When the police came in and heard the saga, though disappointed, they agreed that as it was now rather late, and given the fact that the shop had already closed for the night, it would be best if we all went to the shop in the morning all together to conclude whether the sweets had in fact been stolen.

I remember that we ate nothing that night, and we could not swallow at breakfast either. A somber mood filled the grand hall as we anticipated the return of the boys in blue. My stomach did summersault after summersault until that hour when they arrived once more. They entered but for a moment, and as they departed, so did the six of us. They bundled us into the rear of the police car and off we went back to the corner shop. Some sat on laps, one sat on the floor.

On that day, I found the police to be very civilized, likable even, in their elected procedure and in the manner of how they would handle the situation, so after the last person was served, they politely closed the shop in order that they could question the cashier further. It was the same cashier who had served us the previous evening, and they questioned her at length. She confirmed that she clearly remembered us from the day before partly because we could not make up our minds and secondly because there were so many of us and she also confirmed without doubt that we had in fact purchased all the sweets in the carrier bag. *Great*, I thought, *let's go as I headed towards the door*. However, her word alone was not enough for the police. I stopped still in my tracks as if being physically held. Apparently, they now required conclusive, corroborated evidence. '*What does that mean?*' I thought apprehensively.

'Did you happen to have a copy of the till receipt, madam?' the fat constable asked in his rather deep and heavy voice.

'Why, of course, sir,' answered the lady.

'*I loved her already*.' She opened the till, pressed a couple of buttons, and the till performed this act, where it just spewed out almost a complete roll of typed-over paper. She quickly scrolled down to the date and time that we had made our transaction. It was the afternoon of the day before, at approximately 15.17 hours, and hey! Bingo! There was the till receipt that could not lie. There was our conclusive, corroborated, documented, and non-contestable evidence.

'Yes!' we all shouted, filled with elation as our innocence was firmly established.

This case was proved conclusively, beyond all reasonable doubt, with the completely corroborated and undisputed documented evidence that we had not stolen the sweets. I could picture us all on our way back to Grimshaw Hall, as grisly as that thought was. They had to let us go now. I was convinced of it, we all were, or so we thought. Nevertheless, when the news reached back to Mr. Frank, he was red with fury. He was not having any of it and completely refused to accept the truth as fact. We could hear him screaming down the phone at the police and he ordered that the police arrest us in any event, and he demanded that they find something, anything and arrest us for that. He did not care what, just so long as they kept us there until such time as we confessed up to something, anything. To which, they obliged. *Is that even legal?* We could not believe it. We were innocent. We had committed no crime. We had not done anything wrong. Yet each morning, after breakfast, we were picked up by the boys in blue and carted off to the local police station with the intention being that, sooner or later, we would break and confess to something, anything.

In hindsight, looking back, I cannot believe that the police actually carried out his insane instructions, but they did.

On day one of our arrival at the station, which was a little after 10 am., the interrogation would begin almost straight away, and then every 45-50 minutes thereafter. Each interrogation period would last approximately 15 minutes, non-stop.

'Right,' said the officer in his most abrupt voice. 'Where did you get the sweets from?' he demanded to know! There was never an appropriate adult present, and we were never asked if we wanted a lawyer or if we wanted to phone a friend and they never informed the SS. *Is that right, is that even legal?*

'From the sweet shop next door,' we answered together in unison. (ironically, the police station was right next door to the shop but set further back from the road.)

'Did you steal the sweets?' demanded the officer.

'No, we did not! We paid for the sweets just like the lady told you we did,' we all answered, again in unison. This line of questioning went on and on hour after hour and day after day after day.

Throughout the week, we would arrive at the station each morning between 9.30 am and 10 am and we would be returned to Grimshaw Hall between 4.30 pm and 5 pm, just in time for tea. I think it was on the second day that they decided to separate us into different rooms. Whilst in their care we believed that we were all being treated the same. This myth quickly evaporated on day three when, upon my return to the interrogation room after asking to go to the toilet, I remember looking around for the others. It wasn't long before I found Martha and Marley, and sisters Sarah and

Sophie, all in one room, enjoying their time, coloring, and making pictures at the hospitality of the police, but as for Odette and myself, we were placed in separate rooms and were left to simply sit and look at the four walls. We had no colors for coloring, no paper upon which to color, no glue for sticking, and no scissors for cutting out.

'What was wrong with us?' I thought. *'Why didn't we have the same as the others?'* By the fourth day, the situation became completely unbearable. I was bored beyond belief and could take no more. I remember asking the young rookie officer if we could make something up just so that we could leave.

'No,' he snapped. 'It has to be true,' he snarled. He too was now becoming quite irritable, short tempered, and somewhat lethargic. It was in that moment that it came to my mind that Sarah had asked me to steal a pair of tights for her. I told her that I would not. But then, Sarah began to threaten me with a good beating from bigger than life itself, Shirley. She was much larger than any of the other children, in every direction, she was taller as well as broader and was not afraid to use her weight, height or her width to get you to do whatever she wanted. Her reputation certainly exceeded her, and she took no prisoners, she just beat them to pulp as I would later discover personally. If she had had a CV, her core skills would have certainly included intimidation, bullying, and actual physical violence. Her stance on beating up those younger and smaller than her was perhaps 100 per cent. I am not sure why I decided to pass this information on to the young police rookie, but I did. I guess I just wanted to get out of there. Four days was more than enough for me. How was I to know that this information was to be twisted and re-sculpted and misrepresented and then used to destroy my name for a lifetime?

'But, in hindsight, looking back, I would come to understand that it was here, from this point that an altar was erected. I would come to learn that it was I who was of the weaker disposition than my counterparts when it came to giving in, when it came to confessing up to things that I had not actually done. I would in the years that followed, come to find out and all to my own detriment that you simply

cannot own up to things that you did not do, and then expect them to disappear; there are far reaching ramifications as I would later come to find out.'

Surprisingly, this young rookie took the information to his sergeant, who in turn informed Mr. Frank, who slammed, 'Book 'em! Book 'em!' with what was, for him, I expect great lip-licking satisfaction.

However, no tights were ever found. I do not recall what happened next, but I do remember that we were eventually all permitted to return to Grimshaw Hall. The police finally decided to transport us by car after a long debate as to whether they should permit us to walk back or not. Again, we all bundled into the back of the little pale blue and white Ford Panda. Of course, it was no supper for us again that day. We were now the low-lifers, the unacceptable, the unclean, – shunned by all. Yet what was completely annoying about the whole sweets' saga was that they were handed back to Mr. Frank. The police had said that the shop keeper was adamant that they were not stolen, they had the receipt to prove it and therefore could not take them back. So, they were held at Grimshaw Hall and then later used as giveaway prizes, for the winners of the in- house bingo, during the New Year indoor games. *'Can you bloody believe it?'*

As time passed, the incident died down, and we were no longer the talk of the town or rather the estate, and eventually that long-awaited day came for Jessie to arrive and collect us for the Christmas break. I never did ask her what it was that drove her to start looking for us. I could not bear the painful thought of piecing together what kindness and compassion really looked like, – enough tears already. I mean we had already left the primary school in which she worked. I had left that summer, and Odette the summer before so there was no reason for her to continue to care. Truth be known, Jessie really was our guardian angel, at least, to us anyway, but we did not know it back then. I was so glad that she had searched for us and found us. *'I guess there really is a GOD.'*

When that morning arrived, I remember feeling so tense, so pent up. I felt that my stomach was filled to the brim with butterflies; if I had even opened my mouth, I was sure one would fly out. I just could not eat a thing at breakfast. I simply sat in the grand hall and watched the hands on the big clock kiss the numbers goodbye as they passed them by. The seconds once full producing minutes and minutes once full producing hours. I suspected that if Mr. Frank saw Jessie, inevitably, he would immediately pull her aside and try and persuade her not to take us by telling her that we had broken some royal rule or other, and therefore we were no longer permitted to go.

Breakfast had been and gone, and now it was almost time for lunch, yet there was still no sign of her. I moved to sit by the large single- pane sash window in the grand hall, and wished-for Jessie to present herself.

I began to daydream about distant lands and happier times that were eagerly awaited, when suddenly I came up with a series of chilling scenarios of how the holidays would pan out if she did not show up if and we had to remain here. Slowly returning to reality, I looked up to see the silhouette of what looked like two figures in the distance, possibly a man and a woman moving hesitantly towards the house, locked deep in conversation, their outline drawn by the rays of the sun now warming the earth as it seeks its favorite position in the sky. As they came nearer, I could see that the woman was, in fact, Jessie and the man walking with her was indeed Mr. Frank. I think I began to pray, not that I even knew how to, but it must have been something like 'Dear Lord, please *make* him let us go!'

Clearly, he was trying to talk her out of taking us away for the Christmas holidays. He was trying to talk her out of it by telling her what we had done, lying to her even about how naughty and bad we had both been. He informed her quite emphatically that we had been found guilty of stealing, which was simply not true. In truth, he knew that we had not stolen a single thing. In truth, he knew that we had purchased those sweets, and we had the till receipt to prove it. So exactly what were we guilty of? Thank God, Jessie did not suffer fools lightly. She was a very wise and wonderful woman.

Mr. Frank 's demands were so pathetic and unrealistic that even the police had attempted to talk sense into him, but he was not having any of it; he wanted us punished, hurt even.

Clearly, he was a man who completely hated children, utterly despised them in fact. Thankfully, all his words had fallen on closed ears. Thankfully, Jessie was having none of it. As I hid behind the curtain in the reception, I could hear her say

'Well, I gave the girls my word and I never break my word to a child,' she said sternly. 'I never go back on my word,' she stated quite emphatically. Jessie was not letting up, and he knew it; she had successfully managed to draw his integrity into the equation and so he had to give in to her and, eventually, he did; after ninety-six long minutes, he did. She came directly over to me after seeing my head bob out from behind the curtains whilst he sent the staff to go and find Odette. Mr. Frank then went immediately and directly into his office and closed the door behind him.

'Quick, quick!' came her anxious whisper. 'Get your things together as fast as you can. I don't want the old fool to change his mind again,' she said. 'Meet me in the car when you're ready,' she added.

'OK,' I answered. Upon hearing those words, I ran upstairs, like a bat out of hell, pulled open my drawers, flung open my cupboards, and started stuffing items of clothing into just two small, white plastic bags. This was the usual mode of transportation for luggage belonging to the looked after kid in those days to assist in the moving of their clothes and possessions from A to B and from B to C. The type you would usually use for rubbish. I did not have much, so it was not really that difficult, and in all of five minutes, I was done. With items overflowing from out of the tops of my bags and my quarters a mess, I ran out of the room, down the corridor, up the stairs, along another corridor turned right into another, down the stairs on the west wing, along a short corridor, down more stairs until finally reaching the main reception area, – what a maze!

I was rather hoping that no one would see me as I left, but just then, Mr. Frank came out of his office and gave me one of those 'I wish you were dead' stares as I breezed past him before retreating back into his office, like some kind of deceitful reptile recoiling into its shell. Only God knew exactly what he got up to in there and what work he did, if any. Apart from plotting his next onslaught against the children.

Christmas at Jessie's

We jumped into her shiny new sports car. It was her Christmas from John. The top was down. The sun was shining. We knew we were about to experience something very new and out of the ordinary. That forbidden fruit, I believe they call it, – *happiness... emm*. We all threw our heads back and laughed at the methodology of our escape, as temporary as it was. But deep down in my heart, I wanted it to last forever. I wished we could have stayed with Jessie forever. Unusually, Christmas came and went rather quickly, and that year was no different. It was our first Christmas away from our Dad since we were babies and the start of many more that would follow.

We played Monopoly almost every day of the holidays. We also helped Stacy, Jessie's niece, build her model ship; it was mammoth: I had never seen such a massive lump of plastic before. All cut into pieces of different shapes and sizes for you to stick them back together again. It required the use of our fine motor skills and such accurate precision.

Stacy loved making models, but guess what? So, did I. That was at least until we got into a disagreement of course, and I, I broke it.... At the time, I could not understand why Odette was so incensed to the point of actual tears or why she was speaking to me so unsympathetically. What had I done? I mean, Stacy had started it, but according to Odette, it was, of course, just all my fault. It was always all my fault. I was never allowed to react or respond to anyone about anything. I just had to take it. All the time I had to take it, whatever was thrown at me, no matter what was thrown at me. But guess what? I could not, I was already carrying too many suitcases and now I had dropped one.

After things had calmed down, Odette quietly explained to me that if we got into trouble, Jessie may decide that we could not stay with her ever again, and perhaps that would mean not seeing her ever again too. Odette was so nervous of being rejected, and so nervous of good things ending. She told me to go into Jessie's room and apologize for what had happened with Stacy.

I can remember the scent of the room even to this day: it smelt of what I now know to be cheesy feet and cigarettes; I guessed John's cheesy feet and Jessie's cigarettes.

John was tall, dark, and very funny. He was also a teacher. He taught in an 'all boys' school somewhere in London. Jessie was still teaching at our old primary school in Tottenham. She had taught both me and Odette and was instrumental in making sure we got into the top classes in our secondary school, even if that for me meant working through every lunch hour after a speedy lunch and having extra lessons during class time.

I was always happy to be in her company. I felt safe in her presence and content in her space. We spent the rest of the holidays visiting members of John and Jessie's extended family, for which there was an endless supply of turkey and mince pies, all offered up like sacrifices on the altar, only without the praise, followed by the infamous old black-and-white version of Oliver Twist, which appeared almost simultaneously on the screen of every home we visited.

After about the 3rd house and the 3rd set of relatives and the third serving of lunch I was all turkeyed out; I felt like I was going to burst. I was so glad when Stacy spoke up and said she was going to be physically sick if she ate another thing. Looking back, perhaps there was some hidden meaning or hint that I should have been paying attention to or perhaps even a prophecy of what was coming my way.

We would end each day playing Monopoly late into the night. I always bought the electric company, the water company, and the railway stations. John commented that if ever the light company was selling shares, we should take advantage of it. He was under the firm belief that we would make a lot of money from it; and he wasn't wrong either. Ironically, I always seemed to purchase Old Kent Road and Whitechapel and usually won the game. I had no idea that there really was an Old Kent Road or that one day I would actually travel down it.

Our time together was all going so well: a cloud short of heaven. *But all good things must come to an end, right?* And eventually, that day came for us to return to Grimshaw Hall or, rather, Alcatraz as I preferred to call it.

On the last morning of the last day, I remember pottering around the living room. I was looking at the items above the fireplace for the last time. I wanted to remember every feature of the front room just as it was then, a treasure to capture and store in my heart upon which I could reminisce when I closed my eyes. Then suddenly, I realised that Odette was missing.

'Where's Odette?' I asked casually. Jessie gave some lame excuse that she had popped out to drop Stacy off with John... 'I mean, John has taken her to pick up something,' she said, trying to not attach too much weight to her incoherent excuse. Then John suddenly reappeared but without Odette. However, at that point, I had not noticed that Odette was still missing. Jessie began to whisper to John and then made the announcement that we were leaving right away.

'Hurry up, love, get your things,' she said.

'OK,' I answered, still none the wiser. I loved hearing her use phrases like that; it made me feel as though I was really cared about, even if it was just for a moment. I felt as though I was really cared for with love running right through my veins... just in that moment; I could testify that someone cared about me. I ran to collect my bags from Stacy's room; it didn't register that Odette's bags were not there.

'We're in the car, love,' hailed Jessie, exiting through the front door. I followed them straight out and climbed into the car only to realize that Odette was not with us.

'Where's Odette?' I questioned, trying to remain calm.

'Oh, I can't do this,' said Jessie bowing her head. John reappeared and began to try to comfort her. Still I had not clocked on to what was about to happen. To what was unfolding with me right in the middle of it. At first, there was just the three of us: Jessie, John, and me and then suddenly we three became four, when a mysterious woman appeared from out of nowhere. She was wearing a full-length beige mac, square one-inch heels and an Auburn bob, with a large handbag that matched her hair color. I had never seen her before, and now she was also getting into Jessie's car and without asking. She never even introduced herself throughout the entire journey, but it was obvious she was from the SS. We were all in the car now but still without Odette. Something strange is going on, I thought.

'Where's Odette?' I asked again, now filling up with anxiety as we slowly began to move from off the forecourt. No answer came back. 'Where's Odette?' I asked in a slightly louder voice as panic began to set in.

'Listen, love,' Jessie began, '... it was decided that...' she began again, 'she... she's not coming, darling.' She ended her sentence with a sad quietening in her tone.

'Noooo! Noooo! I screamed. 'Noooo! I don't want to go back there!' I sobbed. 'I hate it there,' I cried. 'They are gonna kill me!

'They're gonna kill me!'

'What do you mean?' Jessie was puzzled.

'They beat me up there!' I shouted, crying again even louder. 'Please, Jessie, please, I beg you... please don't do it... Don't take me back there!' I pleaded, I begged, and I sobbed, whimpering like some broken animal.

An eerie silence fell upon the interior of the car, but no one was answering me. My continuous sobbing eventually broke the silence. As

Jessie began moving the car, I tried to open the door to jump out. I was eleven years old and was about to jump out of a moving car. In that moment, I no longer cared whether I lived or died. But Jessie quickly used the central locking system to lock all the doors.

After studying the locking mechanism, I was able to override the system and then I managed to open the car door again. I was going to jump and had every intention to do just that. I looked down at the ground moving fast under the wheels of the car and then Jessie turned around to see from where the draught was coming. Upon seeing the car door half open she slammed on the brakes, and the car jerked as it came to an almighty stop! Everyone was thrust forward. John quickly got out of the front of the car and jumped in the back and sat beside me on my left. I also had the strange woman on my right, so there was no possibility of executing that plot again. Jessie moved the car forward. I continued to plead and beg her not to do it. Then in a moment of madness, in sheer desperation, I moved the gear stick, almost destroying the gearbox of Jessie's lovely new sports car, soft top included.

'Nooooooooo!' Jessie screamed. 'Hold her John!' she shouted. 'She's going to destroy the f*****g gear box!' she mumbled.

With that, the strange woman threw her full weight on top of me, almost breaking my legs in the process. I let out an almighty yelp, followed by a scream. Jessie turned to see what was happening, at the same time almost colliding with the oncoming traffic. In her disbelief, she shouted, 'Get the f*** off her! What are you doing? You don't sit on a child!' she shouted.

'I was not sitting on her!' the woman replied.

'I f*****g saw you. Don't you f*****g lie to me,' shouted Jessie.

'I wasn't,' said the woman.

'Yes, you were!' I screamed back at her.

'No, I was not,' replied the woman again.

'Yes, you were!' I screamed even louder.

'Yes, you were!' interrupted John. 'Look, we all saw you, right with our own eyes. What, are we blind?' he added.

'Oh, sorry, was I sitting on her?' she now retreated.

'See, this is what they do to me there!' I blurted out with tears streaming down my face. What was I saying? It was true this had happened on one occasion. *But was I prophesying as to my own demise?* Again, a blanket of silence fell and quietened the voices in the car; again, you could have heard a pin drop. Jessie and John did not know what to say, how to say it, or even whether they should respond.

'Please, Jessie,' I whimpered. 'Please don't take me back there,' I cried. 'Please, Jessie, please don't let me go back there. They are gonna kill me, and she knows it!' pointing at the woman with my chin as my arms were now being tightly held, one by John, the other by the woman. I repeated my sentence until I had no more voice to speak and the tears of bitter discontent crashed into each other as they raced down my cheeks. At the same moment, Jessie pulled over and tried to calm me down.

'Look, darling,' she said gently, 'if you don't go back, they won't let me see you anymore.'

'Not without Odette, not without Odette!' I screamed with my half worn-out voice. I cried, I sobbed before screaming again. I instinctively knew that without Odette, I was everybody's game; I didn't stand a chance.

'OK, right!' said Jessie. 'Where is her sister?' she asked the woman. The woman did not answer.

'Well, can we get her here to calm Jacqueline down?' Jessie asked.

'No,' replied the woman.

'Why?' asked Jessie, her patience now wearing thin.

'She's already gone,' replied the woman.

'Gone where?' asked Jessie, quite annoyed now.

'I don't know,' said the woman.

'What do you mean you don't know?' Jessie responded quite tersely.

'I mean... Trent... I think,' said the woman trying to sound responsible.

'Did she know what was happening?' Jessie asked. Complete silence fell again, but this time the woman did not answer.

'OK then!' said Jessie. 'Can we call Odette or get Jacqueline to call her as soon as she arrives back then?'

'Yes!' snapped the woman, this time answering quickly. 'I think we might just be able to arrange that!' she added.

'I don't want might, I want definite!' demanded Jessie. In that moment, I just wanted Jessie to really tell the woman off for creating this entire crazy messed-up situation.

That day something more of me seemed to break away, deep from within the very pit of me. I didn't know what; I did not understand why; I did not understand any of it. It was positively the worst day of my life up to that point. This was Christmas on fire, and what a way to end it! Speaking of bangs, this was certainly an explosion. When I got back, I just ran inside: no goodbyes, no hugs, and no kisses; and no, I'll see you later, it was just all too painful. By the time I had plucked up the courage to look out of the window, even the tyre tracks had gone. That was the last time that I saw Jessie and John in that lifetime: right then, right there, in that moment, I never knew if I would ever see them again. I cried myself to sleep for the next few nights that followed.

It must have been whilst I was sitting, listening to the radio that it dawned on me that in all this time, it was Jessie who had been our fairy godmother, and now she too was gone. It was hard not knowing whether I would ever see her again. I had never felt so alone; not only did I not have Odette, now I had no Jessie either and all my rescuers had completely abandoned me too; they had all conveniently disappeared: no one to call me and no one for me to call.

The four months that I spent alone at Grimshaw Hall were more like four years. It was the longest period of sorrow, grief, and despair, that I had ever experienced in my young life, and up until that point, it was the longest period that I had ever spent alone. I had never been without Odette for more than two weeks before, – and even that felt as though it was the longest period of my life, – and from the standpoint of a child, it was perhaps the most traumatic. I had no idea of how long this separation was going to last or even if I would ever see Odette again... I already had one dead sister, although unbeknown to me then.

Return to Alcatraz

We arrived back at Grimshaw Hall, just in time for lunch, but I wasn't hungry. In looking back, I find myself being questioned by yours truly, asking the same old questions over and over again. '*Why didn't I say goodbye to Jessie and John? Why did I treat them so badly?*' The truth was, I just couldn't say goodbye. I felt so let down, so betrayed. It was all too painful, and more so to say goodbye; it just felt as though to say goodbye was to remove all hope. I mean how do you say goodbye to someone who had been so perfect, so ideal! It just seemed so final, like 'The End'. I couldn't bear it.

I went up to my room and stuffed all my belongings back into the drawers and cupboards, from which I had pulled them. I sat on my bed and looked out of the window. Even the name sounded like a prison, but this time, it was different: this time I was vulnerable. This time I was alone. I sat there thinking about how much I did not want to be here, yet, all the while, in my mind's eye, seeing no other alternative. I had no vision, no imagination, and no picture of better times ahead.

All hope was gone. Here I was, I had left home to be with the only person whom I knew and loved and whom I knew loved me; yes, to the point of sacrifice, and now she was gone. What was I going to do? They took the shoes from runners, so I thought I would pass on that option as the floors were hard and cold, like the mindsets and personalities of our charge hands, and even if I did run, exactly where would I run to? I had no idea where I was exactly or where they were keeping Odette.

Eventually, I had to conclude that, in fact, I just had to accept it. I had to stay where I was. Something more of me had broken away that day. Nevertheless, I just had to get on with it.

I sat there for a while, in deep thought, looking out to the grounds which extended on to vast lands that appeared to go on forever, until they disappeared into the mist. That was when I noticed them; my eyes became fixed upon some smartly dressed magpies in the distance. They were walking bold as brass upon the grass, head up, chest out, tail out straight, smartly dressed as if having a great debate about something or other.

A magpie is an interesting bird of just two very bold colors, black and white, but when in flight another color appears within the fan of the tail; it's almost a turquoise with hints of blue and green.

In fact, it's really quite beautiful. I remembered the nursery rhyme which was tied to the bird. I had learnt it whilst at the Lodge:

'One for sorrow, two for joy, three for a girl, and four for a boy, five for silver, six for gold, seven for a story never to be told arhhhhhhhh,' and I don't remember the rest, only that they always travelled in twos, and if you ever saw two together, that was supposed to be good luck.

So, don't worry if you think you can only see one, the other is usually not far behind.

However, for me, more importantly, they became a point of contact for 'hope', a hope that I would one day get out, that one day I would eventually leave this place. And each time I saw even just one, I would think about getting out.

I would think about a better life, and I would start believing, hoping, willing even, that soon that day would come, when just like the bird, I too would fly away and be free! I continued staring out of the window, my heart hoping, lost in thought, locked in a trance, until the aroma of supper found its way across the hall, up the stairs, along the corridor, turning left into my bedroom.

Of course, it failed to waken my taste buds though, probably, because the food was always so bland and lifeless. Completely devoid of any seasoning or expression or even care added to it.

In contemplation of what to do next, I decided to go downstairs to the TV room and wait there. If the Scorsese brothers were in a bad mood, I wanted to be the first to make my speedy escape: a quick exit back up to the girls' dormitory; where the boys were strictly forbidden from entering and they rarely broke this rule, knowing full well that if they were caught, they were done for.

There were no locks on any of the dormitory doors, so your bedroom was not a secure place of safety, and if you had to make a run for it, you would have to learn to fly, *yes I did say fly*, up a short flight of steps consisting of about five or six steps and continue running to the bathroom where you could lock yourself in. An act I had rather well managed to perfect even with members of staff hot on my heels. I got so good at getting up the stairs I found I could make the jump in two.

On one occasion, I even managed to get up the steps in one jump, run around to the bathroom and lock myself in by bolting the door. It was Flannigan who was hot on my tail that day. He kicked it so hard that the screws which held in place the lock shot out a quarter of the way.

I was standing directly behind the door. One more kick and that lock was certainly going to come flying off. I moved away from the door and crouched down beside the bath; all the screw heads were boldly protruding. I knew instantly if he kicked it again, they would come flying out and the door would swing wide open. I closed my eyes expecting Flannigan at any minute to come bursting in and start attacking me. Strangely he didn't; he didn't kick the door again, he just whacked it with what was I'm guessing the back of his hand, threatening me as he went away.

I waited a long while before re-opening the door and coming out again. Upon arriving back, I learned very quickly that two of the three sisters had already left Grimshaw Hall. Apparently when their mother had learned of Mr. Frank 's determined decision to have us all prosecuted she removed two of her daughters immediately. She said *her daughters would have never done such a thing if they weren't led astray.* I thought you don't know the half of it, lady and you certainly don't know your own daughters that's for sure. It was harder for her to get the other out but eventually she did.

That evening there just happened to be a good film on, which we all managed to settle down to watch quietly, without any hiccups, tantrums, or fallouts from the brothers.

The Scorsese brothers were indeed a crazy bunch; they loved action, and their approach to solve life's ups and downs always included their fists, feet, heads, and sometimes their teeth, even I had managed to receive the odd bite or two during our short yet rather deep acquaintance. They were every bit the dirty street fighters, the ones you never hoped to meet, not even on a sunny day.

They had no regard of whether you were a boy or a girl; they didn't care if you were big or small, or if you wore glasses; there was no special treatment afforded to anyone by the Scorsese's – if you were earmarked you were just gonna get it.

Cross the Scorsese brothers and you had three times the trouble. They all varied sizes: Martin was the eldest and the tallest; he mainly used his fists. Dirk was the smallest and the youngest; he punched and kicked and spat and bit and even pulled your hair right out of your head. And Desmond was the middle brother and the roundest; he was the main biter of the family, and God help you if he fell on you. Anyone who Dirk couldn't handle, Desmond would handle; anyone who Desmond could not handle, Martin would handle, and if the situation ever arose where two or all three were required, they would happily rock and roll with you or whoever was game.

Desmond loved trouble and just about managed to have a fight with someone every week without fail, including me on the odd occasion. I hated the Scorsese brothers explicitly, and it was thought almost every other child in that place also thought the same, except Shirley that is. Just to be in the same room with any one of them was a suspense thriller ready to unfold. However, to be in a room with two of them, any two was a bloody nightmare. *And all three?* Well, that was just too much; you were probably signing your own death certificate.

Eventually, the staff decided to separate the boys; in so doing, their strengths and weaknesses were made visual, and their trouble was greatly reduced.

January was the start of the New Year, and for this academic term, the staff had elected to invest into an art and crafts program for the children. I remember being able to re-create everything I looked at in the new arts and crafts book. It was remarkable. I had no idea that I was so creative. I didn't really know how I would re-create everything from the pages of the book, not even knowing whether we had all the materials required, however, all the children marveled at my accomplishments, but these were brought to an abrupt end by Desmond and Dirk, who on purpose knocked them to the ground before completely destroying them under foot.

They were so typical in their course of destruction that you could practically predict what they were going to do next. However, there were only four projects that were worth any effort in the book, and after their completion, I was bored again.

After some time, we began having lessons in the outside trailers. It was a nice break from being couped up in this massive eerie house all day. We would endure about 45–50 minutes of academic subject matter each day, using the remainder of the morning to play chess or other board games. We would have a tea break in-between, where we would all congregate in the main hall, spending about fifteen minutes eating biscuits and drinking hot tea before having to return to class. It was a life saver if you had missed breakfast; by 10:30 a.m. you were guaranteed a hot cup of tea or coffee with biscuits both on tap until the end of break; so, that was one good point. There were also a couple of pool tables that would be set up in the hall, so we could entertain ourselves whilst the fifteen minutes passed; so that was a second good point.

I remember there was one occasion, during tea break, when the boy they called Oscar, suddenly, and without any hint or warning, threw himself on the floor. Apparently, it was recorded somewhere that he suffered from fits. However, none of us had actually seen him have a fit before in all our time spent with him. But I will never forget that day when suddenly without even a hint that there was anything wrong, he threw himself on the floor and started shaking. We went over to him and leaned over, not sure if he was joking or what, as the demand for attention in that place was rife... It didn't seem real to me; then he started frothing at the mouth. But in some strange way, they looked more like tiny saliva bubbles. I noticed he was incredibly careful not to bang his head whilst on the floor or on the leg of the table. Then someone said, 'Get up, Oscar, or I'm gonna kick your arse all over this hall.' I think it was Martin, and so with that, he jumped up and then it was time to return to class again.

One of my pastimes that I did enjoy was building model planes, which were then put on display in the glass cabinet in the small foyer area, just inside the trailers. They were kept under lock and key, so there was no way that the brothers could destroy them. Usually, the sessions ended with us playing board games, and chess was still my forte.

The games became so intense; they would often overlap into the start of lunch. For me, having been a champion player since age seven, it wasn't too hard to conclude every challenge successfully. I found it refreshing to be out of the main house, which gave me the shivers right down my spine from the moment we had arrived. I almost hoped the renovations of the art room would take forever, so we could spend as much time out of the main house as possible.

Once the art room had been completed, we moved all the artwork back in. I remember, for one arts session, we had a qualified tutor who had come in specially to teach how to make clay models using molds.

On the day in question, we were making authentic Chinese chess pieces from clay, formed out of an old-fashioned quick drying mix. This was then poured into rubber molds, and after a short while, we could peel off the rubber molds and leave them to dry. We were all given new chess boards as well, so there was no expense for us at all, and we could use the pieces to play chess with on the boards.

There were three or four choices of molds to choose from. I selected the real authentic ancient Chinese molds because they were so lifelike; with the naked eye, you could see all the graphic details, every line. I thought they would look stunning in black and white, so I elected to choose these colors; they were also easy to paint.

Once they were dry, they looked so real to life, even if I did say so myself. I remember that I had just finished painting the last piece, when in walked the big, fat, bully... Shirley, with her sidekick, Sarah, in tow.

Shirley was fifteen now; she was one of the oldest children at the estate and was still one of the biggest; and she was certainly, without doubt, one of the meanest. She was indeed true to her name: a big, fat, bully, and everyone was afraid of her, and you probably would not be wrong for thinking that she was born that way because she was totally devoid of any degree of remorse or sorrow after terrorizing and hurting the children.

The staff never did anything to stop her, neither would they ever bother to help whoever it was that she was battering half to death. With one steep blow, she swept her hand across the table, knocking over the fragile pieces and smashing two of them beyond repair as they fell to the hard-stone floor below.

'Hey, what are you doing?' I shouted.

POW! The next blow made contact with my face. Blood began to trickle down from my nose.

'Are you crazy?' I demanded.

POW! Another slap hit me at full speed across the other side of my face. For a moment, the room went foggy, but I held my focus by locking my gaze on to the droplets of ruby red blood that sprayed out across the room like droplets of red rain, only they weren't falling from the sky – they were being sprayed out from my nose and mouth as the force of her slap spun my head around to the left. I kept seeing it over and over again in slow motion; it was reminiscent of the boxer in Raging Bull, except that on this occasion it was happening to me: I was the one who was being hit.

Shirley and Sarah began to laugh out loud. My nose was now running blood from both nostrils like a tap that could not be turned off; it was everywhere: even my mouth was filled with the red stuff. 'What did you do that for?' I shouted.

'POW!' came the third blow without reason or warning.

'Right!' I said, raising to standing and storming out of the room. I marched directly into Mr. Frank 's office. I barged right in pushing the door wide open without knocking, my eyes filling up fast with liquid. He was unmoved, unemotional, and unconnected. He remained seated and silent as if watching a show, not even budging so much as a millimeter from his desk throughout my blood spattering speech.

I was offered no first aid, and no assistance, no towels or tissues, and no kind words. Mr. Frank was completely unperturbed by the events that had brought me to his office and not in the least alarmed by the state of my bloody nose and mouth.

The blood ran out and made its tracks down my face, before jumping off the edge of my chin and splattering down, on to my glorious white T-shirt as they landed. Their attempt at suicide no doubt. Mr. Frank only rose to stand once he thought I had finished.

'Well?' he said.

'Look at me!' I screamed. 'Look at the state of me!' I screamed again.

'And so?' he answered without a portrayal of even an ounce of emotion.

'Well, aren't you going to do anything?' I spluttered, spraying out even more blood everywhere as I spoke.

He looked straight at me. His eyes narrowed as they locked on to mine in a motionless stare without any words. I looked in through the windows of his soul, but it was still and dark, waiting for him to say something, anything in fact, yet he continued just looking straight back at me, still not speaking. Then it came … as cold as ice…

'Close the door on your way out then?' There it was, as simple as that, completely devoid of anything else. He just dismissed me without any compassion or even the slightest bit of concern. I screamed out in my loudest voice for all and sundry to hear that this was it! I vowed right then and there in that moment to kill anyone who ever put their hands on me again.

'I said close the door on your way out!'

It was quite apparent that he was just not interested; he wasn't bothered, and he did not care. Your guess is as good as mine as to what type of outfit he was running, or rather, clearly wasn't and why. I left the room and ran upstairs to the bathroom and locked myself in again. I washed out my mouth and blew the blood out of my nose. I lay down on the hard cold floor feeling a mixture of emotions and fell asleep.

Before the girls had all been separated and scattered, we would often meet up in our bedroom and listen to the low-down on the different members of staff.

'So, what's the story on Mr. Frank, then?' I asked inquisitively. 'Is he really all there or what?' He always seemed to be gliding through the building as opposed to a normal person walking. In casting my mind back, I could hear the girls retelling the chilling story about what had happened some years before. Apparently, he had locked a young girl in the bedroom opposite ours. This was a spare room at the time, but from that moment on, it became known as the '*lock-up*'. Incidentally, this was no ordinary case. This child was known to be claustrophobic, but that didn't matter, he did not care. He threw her in that room anyway, with no curtains, no light, and no covers. He slammed the door shut behind her making sure he locked it before walking away, revealing no indication of when he would return. She screamed and screamed and screamed to be let out, but no one came to release her.

In her panic, fueled by anxiety she broke the large pane of glass, which sat directly over the door. This was a feature all doors had above them back then, except it was not toughened glass, neither was it crossed with wire. It was just normal single pain glass; it was a little over a meter square in size. She then began to climb up on top of the furniture in the room, with the intention of climbing through the window, after she had broken the glass. Upon reaching the top and managing to exit about halfway out, she slipped and fell, her body slamming to the floor in the twelve-foot drop from the top. As she fell, a piece of the jagged glass had caught her arm, piercing the skin quite deeply, tearing the flesh downward all the way to the wrist. She was wounded badly by the glass and lay there screaming hysterically, all the while her heart pumping out the blood.

The girls were too scared to move; they lay there crying and screaming in their beds, hoping, wishing, willing even, for someone, anyone to come and help, but no one came. Eventually, someone plucked up the courage and pushed the fire alarm in order to raise the alarm. Mrs. Frank was first on the scene. She came running up from her flat, which was directly adjacent to the girls' sleeping quarters.

They said that when she saw the girl, she began screaming for someone to help, the girls still too afraid to move from their beds. Then she ordered one of the girls to run over to the boys' side to get Big Benn, another staff member, who was on sleepover duty that night in 'A' Wing, the boys' sleeping quarters.

Whilst Mrs. Frank was waiting for Big Benn, and holding the wound, they said her husband came up with his rather large sheepdog to see what all the commotion was about. They reported that he had strolled along as though he was without a single care in the world, not even batting an eyelid at his wife or the victim both on the floor. He did not lose a second of his concentration by becoming distracted by what it was his wife was trying so hard to do.

In her panic, Mrs. Frank, now covered in blood as she had been holding the wound with her bare hands, screamed at him to call for an ambulance and to get the first -aid box. However, Mr. Frank just carried on walking without saying a single word, without giving so much as a glance.

'Get an ambulance!' she screamed. 'Get an ambulance!' Mr. Frank did not even bat an eyelid; he just kept on walking, without even looking back.

'That's it!' she screamed. 'I want a divorce, you bastard!' her voice screeching after him. Even that did not cause him to turn and look back or even change his tempo or pace. A few moments later Big Benn arrived on the scene. He had not even had time to tie up his dressing gown; it was flapping behind him as he ran along corridor after corridor and jumping up and down staircases. It stood opened, over his pajamas as he tried to absorb the scene.

Upon coming back out of his own shock, he shouted for the girls to pull the sheets off the bed to put pressure on the bleeding, which Mrs. Frank had been holding all the while with her bare hands, too afraid to let go. Every piece of her clothing was touched by the girl's blood. Big Benn ran back to the office as fast as he could to call for an ambulance, his dressing gown still open, following fast behind him. It did not take long to arrive; the flashing blue lights lit up the darkness as the overbearing sirens screamed up the drive.

The ambulance men marching in formation stopped to bind up Angela's wounds; they scooped her up onto their stretcher and drove off with her into the night. Angela never did return to Grimshaw Hall, not even for her clothes, and no one in that place ever saw her again. And so, the sorry saga went.

Rumor had it that Mrs. Frank also left that same sad night. She left her clothes and Mr. Frank, ... well I'm guessing he received his divorce papers in the post. Of course, for him, it was business as usual. It was just as though nothing had happened at all. It was as though nothing and no-one moved him. He appeared entirely devoid of any emotion whatsoever: It was difficult to assess why.

When I woke up from off the bathroom floor that same evening I went to my room and cried myself to sleep once more. After a while, Sarah appeared with some morsels of food. Yes, the same Sarah, who had threatened me with all the violence from her much older friend Shirley, the estate bully, when I had refused to steal a pair of tights for her from the sweet shop, the day we went carol singing. And now she had done it anyway. In this instance I no longer cared who was on my side or who wasn't.

A pattern began to forge itself into existence, and we started to meet night after night at about 10 p.m. after lights out. Sarah would signal me to come up to her room where we would eat from the same plate and drink from the same cup. After which I would allow Sarah to touch my long, wavy hair, which I had not combed for days. Her gentle caress caused me to sway gently, uninhibited, until eventually I fell backwards upon Sarah's bed. Sarah continued to stroke my face and neck; before long, our lips touched together, as we became lost in our own world of puppy love, schoolgirl passion and motherly affection. The latter being the powerful missing ingredient in all our lives. But this was not my first kiss, neither was it to be my last.

Each night, we would meet in Sarah's room after lights out. We shared nibbles of food and half cups of juice that had been diluted with too much water. We would stroke each other's hair before caressing each other's skin in a meaningful way and holding and hugging each other. Our meetings continued right into the night and were repeated night after night until it all came to a dramatic end. We were caught by Big Benn. He stood at the top of the stairs and roared like the king of the jungle ordering us back to our own beds in our own rooms. Everyone was so afraid of big Benn; when he spoke, you literally jumped out of your skinny skin, skin; and everyone obeyed him without question or argument. At times, his voice appeared as loud as thunder and when he yelled it was nothing short of a volcanic eruption, if not louder; it went right through you, it shook you and brought you right back to the land of the living, *if you know what I mean.*

A few days later Sarah also had suddenly disappeared, it was as abrupt as it was swift. There were no goodbyes and no farewells; she was just *girl gone*, and I was sure her arrival had probably been the same as ours, sudden and unexpected.

After Sarah's departure, it was back to the drawing board for me. I did not let anyone else into what was now, my world. I deliberately failed to interact with the others, keeping me to myself. I refused to communicate, even forgetting the sound of my own voice.

It must have been just two weeks later that I found myself being dragged by my t-shirt out of the recreational room, my hair had got caught in with it and I was being slapped around the face and punched in the head and upper torso whilst being called every name under the sun worthy of some disobedient dog. A struggle ensued, and we both fell to the floor; it was a scramble to see who would get on top first as I attempted to wrestle my way out of his grip. In a matter of seconds, before I knew what was happening, I was being dragged across the floor of the recreation hall again, this time backwards, and was being pulled up the staircase that led to the girls' dorm, by… Mr. Flannigan, another child hater. He threw me hard into my bedroom as I slid across the cold shiny linoleum floor, he slammed the door shut sharply behind him.

Coming to a halt in the center of the room and gathering my bearings I quickly scrambled to my feet and ran back to open the door, but alas, Flannigan was now holding the door handle firmly in the upward position so that it could not be pulled down in order to disengage the latch and open back the door.

I had absolutely no idea of what I had done or said to offend anybody. The truth was it was the damn Scorsese brothers again! Apparently, they had got into some kind of argument with each other and were going at it like cat and dog. We were just standing around watching yet another frightening brawl unfold as it usually did in that place; and Flannigan, well he just did what he did best. He attacked the child closest to him, the child standing on the end of the line, which on this occasion just happened to be me. This happened again, and again and again and again. I lost count trying to keep score. The simplest thing would send him off the edge.

On one occasion, he even managed to rope in Fat Miz, whom I actually liked and whom I thought liked me, mainly because she used to read me Beano stories, and other bedtime stories whenever she was on the night shift. I felt as though I could relate to the slow pace, gentle tone, and rhythmic dance of her voice. It really made me feel calm inside, sometimes to the point where I would actually fall asleep.

I hated to go to sleep in that palatial room all alone; it was so eerie and so cold and so daunting. However, on this occasion, Flannigan also got the not-so-big Jan to participate. I only knew normal-sized Jan from a distance because she worked mainly with 'A Group'. She drove the new Rover. It was brown in color, with beige interior. There was ample space inside, and you could see your reflection in the shiny hub caps. It was really quite evident that she felt immensely proud of her new car and was keen to show it off at every opportunity, as she was forever offering people lifts in it.

Jan was of medium height and build, probably about twelve stone, if you're looking for a number. She had one of those new perms everyone was raving about, leaving her almost grey lifeless mousey hair bouncy and curly. It hardly seemed the type of color for a woman – the car I mean. A couple of times she had also given us a lift back in it upon seeing us walking back from the shops.

Perhaps she felt she had more to offer the adolescents than the youth. I did not really know her reasons or her motives for working in such an establishment, mainly because she seemed too well-to-do to be there, and she spoke in a very la-di-da accent too.

Perhaps she had some epiphany with philanthropy, and this was her contribution, to 'do good' and be a 'do gooder' – *who knows?*

Flannigan continued twisting and bending my arms up behind my back. As I struggled, I could feel his nails cutting into me, piercing my skin with each contact. When he saw her, he called out to her to come and help him play her part in his plan. Strangely, and without even asking any questions, she too began to pull at me, grabbing at my clothes, her nails also cutting into me. They lifted me up and carried me up the stairs by my hands and feet, like some disobedient upside-down donkey, dropping me several times back first on to the hard wooden steps as we went up the stairs.

Completely unaware of what was about to happen next, I could feel myself fast filling up with fear and anxiety all over again. I had no idea of what I had done wrong or what they were going to do to me next. As we all entered my bedroom, I was still struggling. Flannigan began pulling me by my long hair. I could hear it ripping from out of my hair band. My lovely new T-shirt was also stretched until it ripped. They were twisting my arms so tightly that I thought they would snap out of their sockets, because that was exactly how it felt. I could feel their nails piercing my skin, but I had been here before, and Flannigan knew it.

Suddenly, he just lifted me up and threw me on to one of the beds in my room, as if he were fed up with sorting out the washing. It was the one by the wall nearest the door. Ironically, this was the bed I used to sleep in when I first arrived; we had had a full room back then – now it was only me who slept in there.

Flannigan started to bend my legs back up behind me all the way to my buttocks whilst holding my arms with the other hand. Then he told Fat Miz, who looked like she was about 21 or 22 stone heavy, and Jan, who was about 12 or 13 stone heavy, to sit on me. At first, they refused and then he started screaming at them hysterically. Fat Miz tried to calm Flannigan down, but no one had witnessed this degree of craziness before. He screamed in complete hysteria. 'Hey!... hey! I will f#@*#%*g beat her up if you don't do what I say,' he screamed. I continued struggling, almost managing to get free before Flannigan started punching and kicking me in the back of the legs, upper thighs, and buttocks. They did what he said without further hesitation; they followed his instructions to the letter.

I was screaming, 'Help! Get the police! Get the police! Somebody, anybody, help! Get off me. He's killing me!'

No one came; there was no one there to hear, no one to come to my rescue.

As their weight crushed me, pinning me to the bed, my screams of help became blotched out by the warmth of my own breath coming back at me each time I tried to lift my head up from off the pillow to gasp for air. It was as though everything went into slow motion as they repeatedly bore their weight down upon me. I seemed to be screaming without sound.

Whatever noise I could muster was hindered by the proximity of the white puffy pillows and the warmth of my own breath as it splashed back against my face; now sinking even further into the pillows.

Each time my face was held pressed into the pillows, it was just for that little bit longer and inwardly I prepared myself for death. I closed my eyes to darkness as if to welcome in the abyss of the unknown, every so often hearing Fat Miz say, in her broken accent 'Hold on, let's just check…, yes, she's still breathing.'

They say your ears are the last to switch off before you die... Trapped in the darkness, my mind flashed back.

The year was 1973. A friend had decided to come and knock for me so that we could walk back to school together. We were on home lunches, so the Conservatives were in. She had told me that she would do so even though I had specifically asked her not to, but she did anyway. This was one time I prayed that Dad would say, 'I am sorry, but she is not allowed.'

I mean, that is what he would usually say, wasn't it? But on this occasion, oh no, he thought it would be a promising idea and surprisingly he said yes. But somehow, I knew this was all going to end in tears, and those, clearly being my own.

Just as we reached the point where we should have turned right, heading in the direction of our school, my friend just happened to remember that she had forgotten her trainers, which she needed for games, that same afternoon. I could not believe it and after a very brief, verbal tug of war, we ended up turning left, so I guess she won.

Unfortunately for me, Dad just happened to be watching from the living room window. He saw us as we turned left, back into the flats, instead of turning right across the open green spaces, failing to enter the pathway which led all the way down to the school.

He saw me, despite my desperate and constant efforts of ducking and diving behind every wall, every person, and every parked vehicle, which were so few and far between, making all my efforts appear in vain. I guess he must have been foaming at the mouth upon witnessing this bold demonstration of outright disobedience, so much so that he sent Odette marching straight down to the school and ordered her to wait at the gates for the sole purpose of simply summoning me back home to the flats again.

Sometimes, when you know or suspect that something bad is going to happen, you begin to hope that it will not. The little hope that I had, as derelict as it was, quickly evaporated into thin air upon seeing my sister standing there at the school gate; I knew before Odette had even opened her mouth that I was busted.

'Dad wants you to go home!'

'W-why?' came my crumbled response.

'Dad wants you to go home,' she repeated.

'Come with me?' I pleaded.

'I can't,' she responded.

'Please,' I begged. Inside I just wanted someone anyone to defend me against him. She shook her head and slowly walked away, as if to distance herself from the trauma about to unfold.

I began to take my time on the short journey back to the flats. Dragging my fingers along the wall as I went, trying not to think about what sad fate lay ahead; yet wishing desperately for something, anything to happen right now to separate me from my immediate expected forthcoming demise.

In that same moment, I heard footsteps running up pitter patter, pitter patter behind me. Meet Andy: Short for Andrea. She was about my height, perhaps a little on the plump side; she had straight blonde hair and sea green blue eyes, and it was her who had very kindly got me into this mess in the first place.

My stomach began to tie itself in more difficult homemade knots. I knew without doubt that this was indeed bad news, and this was gonna be very, very bad. As we reached the lift, I told her not to follow me any further. As I climbed the eight flights of stairs, mumbling to myself and still mumbling as I walked along the balcony stopping at the front door of 58. I gave it a gentle, tap tap upon the ultra-thin-line stainless steel letter box, which was glistening in the gentle rays of the afternoon sun.

I knocked in the remote hope that Dad would not hear the door, or if he did, that he had somehow miraculously changed his mind or that he had gone back to sleep even. As those thoughts whirled around in my head, the door swung open, and I was met by an angry bitter man, whose large hand reached out and pulled me in, my feet departing from off the floor as he gripped the scruff of my clothes, causing even the cotton to scream as it separated from the fabric.

My body, now conflicting with the laws of gravity, was forcibly brought back down to a crash landing onto the linoleum floor covering with a thud, his side of the threshold. It was almost as if I had been ejected out of the passenger seat of James Bond's car and my parachute had failed me. I landed somewhere down the hallway, past the halfway mark on top of the plastic carpet protector.

I collapsed in a heap on the floor by the living-room door. As I got up, he ordered me into the front room. I tried to stop myself from shaking and wetting my pants, but I couldn't. He ordered me to remove my dungarees with a blast; I could not control the shaking. Dad was firing questions at me like bullets being spat from an automatic machine gun.

'Why did you go that way to school?' he screamed. Believe me I had asked myself the same question – why had I gone a different way to school when he had already told me which way to go? I attempted in vain to answer him, and at the same time, I was also attempting to open my dungarees as my hands continued shaking uncontrollably. I knew what was coming, which only sought to increase my fear and anxiety.

In that same moment, I felt an almighty whack that connected with the back of my hand! Then again, another whack! This time it made contact with my shoulder. The buckle on my dungaree flew open. 'I said to take off your clothes!' he shouted. I began to plead and beg with him not to beat me, but he picked up what I believe all you chippies call a 2 by 4, and with every blow, I literately went flying around the front room like the ball from off the squash court, crying as I went.

'Do as you are told!' he shouted.

'POW!'

'Yes, Daddy,' would follow my whisper of a response.

'POW!' another hit

'Do as you are told!' he screamed.

'POW!'

'Yes Daddy,' I said again.

Then again another 'POW!'

He was hitting me with every word. He was screaming and yelling and shouting; I couldn't keep up with everything he was saying – a lot of it was so incoherent. He had a habit of speaking really fast particularly when he was angry.

It felt as though he was holding a bat and I was the ball. I don't know how long it lasted, but the final blow sent me flying over the sofa that was situated by the wall in the far-left corner of the room; we had been standing near the center of the room. I landed front side down behind the sofa, the wind knocked right out of me.

After hitting the floor with a thud, I did not know whether I could move. I had no idea if I could even stand up. But I knew quite intuitively that I could not physically take any more of this. I believed without doubt that this was it. It felt like that feeling you get just before you fly, just before the plane enters the other side of the force and breaks through the gravity pull barrier.

In that moment, I honestly believed that if Dad hit me again, I was surely going to die. I just knew that I could not take another hit. My arms were bruised repeatedly, and ruby red droplets began to gently pierce through and stain my white T-shirt; my entire body felt numb with pain.

My fingers were so fat and swollen I could no longer bend any of them. My hands and arms were now decorated with scratches in addition to the bruises. I lay there on the floor, unable to move.

Completely out of breath, Dad ordered me to return to school in exactly that same state. I couldn't move, not even to obey his command. My hairclips were broken, my hair was a mess, and my clothes... they were all over stretched and disheveled. I looked like I had been in a fight alright - with some wild animal.

How on earth did he expect me to return to school looking like that?

I was a mess; eventually I did manage to get up. I cried all the way back to school. I knew I couldn't tell the teachers. How would I even try to begin to explain what had just happened? They simply would not understand this Caribbean mentality, already installed in his mother's home, and reinforced by the church. He was simply doing to his children what had been entrenched into his very being, into his DNA.

I remembered frequenting the toilets so many times, just so I could cry. I was sure my teacher knew, but it must have been grace that held her from calling me out me in front of the class...

As I came back to consciousness, I found myself still on the bed, still at *Alcatraz*, still having the crap being beaten out of me. It felt as though I was literally having the very life squeezed out of me. I was certain that this was it as it was becoming harder and harder to breathe, harder and harder to inhale. In my mind, I questioned why they were doing this to me and what had I done to any of them to warrant such a savage atrocity? Had I not left home to escape this sadistic brutality?

In truth, what became abundantly clear was that the staff knew that any complaints would fall on deaf ears, bearing that in mind they were free to do as they wished to whomsoever they chose, which on this occasion happen to be me.

There were no checks and balances and no audits either, so they could literally do whatever they liked, knowing full well that they could get away with it.

Clearly, it had been going on for some time. As the load bore down on top of me, I could not hardly breathe any more. My face was pushed so deep into the pillow as Fat Miz bounced up and down on my upper back, and neck, and head; *yes, her arse really was that big.* As she became tired with having to lift her own weight up and down, some twenty stone plus, the down bounces began to last longer and longer. As my head went down into the pillow again, I could feel my struggles become weaker and weaker. I tried to lift my head up for what I believed was perhaps my last breath, but I could not. Now with what I believed was my dying breath, I forced out the words, 'You're …gonna …kill … me!' before sinking my face back down into the pillows and closing my eyes, I prepared to go through death's door. I had no hope of being able to lift my head up again, now heavy with the weight of Fat Miz on top of me I closed my eyes to die. Strangely, my mind went back again; this time, it was 1967.

I must have been two, going on three, I remember drying up the dishes with my sister who was making me laugh out loud. We were in the kitchen of a large house in which Dad had rented two rooms: one for us and one for him and his new wife, Mordecka. We were laughing as we happily carried out our chores: just being children. As the laughter began to fill the house like a warm, fragrant incense, Mordecka decided that this was just not acceptable, and with that, she came bursting into the small pantry type kitchen like an icy torrential wind. We both froze in our shoes.

'Who is making all that noise?' she demanded. Of course, Odette was quick to point the finger at me. Totally unaware of what was about to unfold, with that, Mordecka grabbed me by the scruff of my clothes, like how one would handle a wet cat. There was no time to answer or respond; she pulled me up to her room, where she took her hard-back plastic slipper and began to beat me senseless; she hit me as I ran all over that room and she hit me all over my body. It was pain like I never knew existed, totally excruciating, and each contact blow was so loud it rang out in your ear like a bell with no chime. I had no idea of what on earth I had done or what was so terrible, that it warranted this degree of craziness. At one point, I flew from one bed on to the other, which was some distance away, still screaming with every strike, crying the words 'no, no' with each hit – crying and screaming and screaming and crying. When the beating finally came to an end, I could do no more than just lie there, my body shaking, whimpering like an injured animal.

As my mind returned to consciousness, and I was back in my bedroom again, the shouting began to slow to a halt. Fat Miz lifted my head with her chubby hand, and eventually, one by one, they got off me and left my room. No checks, no care, and no first aid.

I cried myself to sleep that night. The next morning, I was still coiled in the fetal position and still dressed in the same clothes. The bedding damp with a mixture of tears and saliva, soiled with mucus that had hardened on the pillows. I did not go down for breakfast that morning. I did not change my clothes. I did not have a bath or even a shower. I did not watch TV or sit in the sitting room. By evening I was very hungry. I slipped into the dining room and sat down, hoping that no one would speak to me. No one did. From that moment, onwards, I became very introvert. I completely avoided conversation and life began to center around the radiogram in the grand hall, which was just turned low enough to hear. The only other place I could be found was in the still quietness of my own bedroom which I shared with no one.

Eventually, the bruises and scratches healed, my tears dried up, but the trauma would remain as a gaping wound for many years to come, and the scars of my emotions would not be so easily healed. I would come to the realization of that, some 32 years on, in my journey. It would be only then that I would come to realize the toil that all these unwarranted attacks would have upon my character, my personality, my body, and my mind, and the subsequent cost of trying to heal the pain in a futile attempt to try and distance myself from the memories. I had no idea of all those who would be injured in the process. I had no idea that's what hurting people do; – hurt, *themselves and others*. These people were my rescuers; they were my saviors, yet they were also, at the drop of a hat, my consistent, faithful abusers.

The attacks lasted the whole of the winter, well into the spring. My repetitive cries and screams for help all fell on deaf ears, and I would always be left alone to nurse my own wounds and cry myself to sleep. The SS continued to ignore me, never taking a call, never calling me back, and never answering the messages that I left, time after time; and the other staff, well they all did what they did best – absolutely nothing, not a thing! I couldn't work out whether they were all in it together or merely just collecting a pay packet. The kids would often have this conversation. We all decided to tell our own authorities, believing that someone somewhere must be able to do something, but no one did. No one ever did.

After that night, I never saw Jan again; none of us did. Rumor had it that her behavior had got the better of her, and her conscience was stuck in reverse to the point that she was not able to deal with the aftermath of her own thoughts; perhaps she too became haunted by her own nightmares? Whatever her reasons, she left.

I always wondered how she had managed to live with herself. In all these years, I couldn't help but wonder how it had been for her, how did what happen back then affect her or did it? Had she been able to put it all behind her? Had she just stuffed it under the carpet like a true conservative, or had she continued to carry around the guilt and regret of it for all these years, hoping for redemption?

It wasn't long before Fat Miz also soon followed suit. But, up until her departure, quite bizarrely, I continued to ask her to read to me at bedtime, each time that she was on night duty. Perhaps it was a sick thing to do, I don't really know, but it was the closest thing to normality that I could get; it was the best I could make out of what was an already intrinsically warped and very messed-up picture of care afforded by the State.

We never discussed what had happened that awful day, even whilst she was reading. As I made myself comfortable in bed, I found great comfort in the repetition of the slow pace of her voice, which when combined with the warm, tranquil tones, contributed greatly to my own rocking like motion, deep within the depth of my soul; despite the fact that she, now my pacifier, also doubled as my brutalizer.

The stories had to be at that slow pace; they had to have a real rhythmic feel to them, like the swaying motion of a pendulum, or like a rebellious wave creeping repetitively up to cross the shoreline, or like a gentle breeze carefully swaying the leaves on the branches of a tree. I guess for outsiders looking in it was indeed a crazy kind of therapy. Nevertheless, the worst was still yet to come. And the clock was ticking, tick tock… tick tock…tick tock.

To this very day, I remember the garden incident as though it was yesterday. I guess as long as I live, I shall never be permitted to completely forget it... I mean, how could any of us?

It was one fine day, in spring. The morning was brisk, crisp, and bitterly cold despite the sun putting in the odd appearance. She was peeping out from behind the clouds intermittently, totally oblivious to the fact that we would be in desperate need of her warmth.

At 9:30 am, we were all summoned straight from the breakfast table out into the garden. I don't think any of us had actually finished eating, and many of us were not even wearing any day clothes yet let alone outdoor clothes. Others were still quite clearly in their nightwear, and no one was wearing any hats, coats, or gloves. We were all completely unprepared for garden duty that day. But you guessed it, Flannigan was on duty.

Well, it could only have been Flannigan. Who else was capable of making such ludicrous demands? Only him! He believed that he was always politically correct. He had to be the one; no one else was that insane, to frog march approximately nine half-dressed, half-fed, half-awake, children out into very freezing conditions to dig the garden and plant bulbs. None of us were wearing our Wellington boots, and we were all sinking into the soft, moist fertile earth beneath our feet; some of us were even falling into it as we tried to maintain our balance, whilst lifting one foot up to push the spade that was too big and too heavy into the ground.

The morning was very chilly, becoming more so with every passing hour. None of us had on even an iota of warm clothing, and the cold was beginning to take effect. We were just kids. As the early morning became late morning, the temperature failed to rise, and we all began to feel the effects of exactly how harsh spring could actually be, as beautiful as she was.

We tried as much as possible to rub-warm our little hands together, in-between shoveling to stop them from becoming numb, this time from the cold. As we plucked up the courage, we asked, one by one, if we could put on a coat or hat or even get some gloves, anything, just as long as it would keep us warm. It was then that the crazy threats came firing back, as if from a Magnum 45, advertising the lock-up as his trump card – yes, I mean literally. Conveniently, there was one on each side of the dorms: one for the boys and one for the girls.

The lock-up room was adorned with incredibly high ceilings, intimidating windows, that were bare and did not open, that were equally as high and almost reaching the ceilings. In hindsight looking back perhaps they were deliberately kept that way as a convenient method to torment young vulnerable minds with the night's shadows as darkness fell.

Empty cabinets and closets with squeaky doors were all ill positioned in the room, and a cast iron bed without any linen appeared to add to the drama. And the bed frame may or may not be accompanied with a mattress. But in any event, there were always no sheets, no pillows, and no blankets, not even in the wardrobe.

You would be held in there at Flannigan's pleasure, until Flannigan said so, and the other staff, well, they all just went right along with it. No one dared to comment on his actions or his decisions as crazy as they were, they simply pretended that they could not see. Whatever atrocities Flannigan wanted to inflict upon the children, he did so. And he did it so well in true professional style. It was as though he thoroughly enjoyed it: unleashing his utter madness on those who were young, vulnerable, and helpless.

Every child was a target; every child was a victim and every child had a case to be answered. Only God knows the truth about what they had already endured and had to escape from, only to find themselves right back in the thick of it, right in the middle of yet another real-life nightmare, and at the mercy of a real-life mad man.

Broadly speaking all children were not being taken into care because they were bad, disobedient, or out of control. In reality, many of them were in care, to be protected, and should have been protected, respected, and cared for; perhaps even loved a little.

Red was the first to leave us, kicking and screaming and shouting as he went. He was wearing only his slippers and dressing gown, under which he was wearing just a vest and a pair of pajamas bottoms, however, now half covered in mud. As Flannigan grappled with him, he fell into the mud and got all muddy again and again.

'Please, Flannigan!' he screamed. 'I ain't got no more clean pajamas, arrrah.' He sobbed. Brutal Flannigan began dragging him by the scruff of his dressing gown. Red was now pleading, as if for his life, to give him a second chance. We all felt really sorry for him, especially when he started begging and crying like a baby. Real tears began streaming down his face. We all looked at Flannigan, perhaps to remember what the face of mercy did *not* look like. There was none; for many of us, this was our first lesson on mercy. Flannigan was in his element; he was enjoying himself far too much.

The word *compassion* simply did not resonate within his limited or rather profane vocabulary. Every other word was usually a swear word of some kind or a common slur. The truth was, he really did not care, which was evident by his actions in dragging Red, a 12-year-old boy, across the wet muddy grass in front of his peers and into the house. Red's screams could be heard all the way across the grounds before finally disappearing within the confines of the brick walls inside the estate. Now barely audible there was a short pause then an almighty outcry. I felt annoyed and angry.

After a while, Flannigan returned and immediately started shouting at us to dig faster and harder.

'Put your backs into it,' he screamed! But now I too could take no more of the cold. And eventually, I left my gardening post as the weather was now unforgivingly cold. I mean, you could feel it on your chest every time you inhaled. The sun had not yet reached her favorite spot in the sky from where her faithfulness was guaranteed to beam down rays of warmth that would warm up the earth and all those in it; until then, it was, quite frankly, simply colder than I could bear. I could feel the cold setting into my bones, and it took my mind back to home life again.

Suddenly, I was back in my parents' house, it was night-time, and I was freezing cold. I had no covers because I had given them to my sister, who had no mattress or covers. I felt that I could not allow her to lie there half naked, with no covers to keep warm, I just couldn't. Sometimes it was so cold, I would beg her to lie on the edge of the bed, just so we could share the cover; one very small, very thin blanket, but she wouldn't, she couldn't, she was too afraid. Sometimes I would lie at the very edge of the bed, so we could both try and share the blanket and keep warm, but it didn't work, it was too short.

I remember always having to pull my very thin nightdress down over my knees, taking on the fetal position, in a futile attempt to try to keep myself warm, after having given her all the blanket. I would tuck my knees right up tight to my chest to try and achieve this, even pulling my arms back through my nightdress. At some point, I think Mordecka had cottoned on, so for no apparent reason she would begin to do random midnight raids at all hours of the night. When it suited her she would kick off, criticizing and condemning us with every word; and after a torrent of verbal abuse she would then demand that Odette sleep standing up in the bathroom all night, or sleep in the bath tub, or even sleep sitting on the loo all night long.

My mind now returning to the garden, having dropped my spade I began to walk back across the wet grass in the direction of the large house. Through the gasps I could hear the stamping of fast feet, stamp, stamp stamping, stomp, stomp stomping up behind me. I turned to see who was there, only to be grabbed by the scruff of my T-shirt caught in with my hair – Flannigan pulling it up half over my head, my midriff now exposed to the elements and an audience who half began to jeer. He then dragged me across the remaining grounds through the soft wet grass and damp soil, now evidenced on my clothes. He continued pulling me on to hard surfaces, bashing me into the frame of the narrow glass doors as he pulled me through them and into the building. Now I was the one screaming.

As we entered the building I slipped and fell on to the recently polished wooden floor that had been gleaming up at me. Flannigan wasted not a second of this opportunity, diving on top of me and saddling me as if I was his bucking horse or something. As I twisted and turned to try and wriggle myself free, he began to commence the well-known head-banging process; the only thing was, it was my head he was banging on the floor. He was pulling my hair which had got caught in with my T-shirt. I could hear it tearing in his fingers again as we wrestled. In-between bashes, he was screaming and swearing undiluted profanities at me, bellowing at me, telling me how much he hated me. I tried my best in sheer desperation to shout back,

'You're killing me! You're f*****g killing me!' But it was of no use. He would not let up. At one point, he must have got cramp in his leg or something, and it caused him to ease up for just a couple of seconds. I seized the moment, punching him as hard as I could in the back of his nuts with my knee.

'You f*****g little shit!' he shouted, easing up even further. In that tiny window of opportunity, I conjured up every ounce of energy and flipped my legs up and over my head, causing his arms to become twisted in the process, forcing him forward and causing him to let go of me *(thank* God *for gym class)*.

'You f*****g little black b****,' he screamed. We both looked at each other, him ordering me to come back over to him, and then we turned, and both looked at the door. We looked back at each other, both searching for that flinch, which screamed deep from within – *'Run!'* And in true form, it became a mad dash for the west exit from the hall. I knew if I could just get through the door first, I could get a head start up the stairs, and it was just possible that I could make it up all four flights of stairs on the short narrow staircase which led up to the girls' dorm; but it was past the dorm, along the hallway and up another flight of small stairs, along another short corridor and into the girls' bathroom, where I could lock myself in, that I was heading for. That was the only place in the entire estate where it was safe.

In the scramble of madness, my wet plimsoll had come off from my right foot, but I could not stop now, I could not look back, I didn't care. He was running, I was running, faster and faster, we were neck and neck now. My mind was focused on the slender gap directly in front of us, where it was clear that only one of us could pass through at a time. We accelerated in speed. We both could not fit; one of us had to go faster, one of us had to go first, one of us had to retreat.

Have you ever wondered what the average speed of a human is? With that thought in mind and with no intention of stopping, I leapt up into the air like a young gazelle as my slender body, somehow by sheer millimeters, curved around in front of Flannigan; slicing the atmosphere with my physique, I made it through. Flannigan, on the other hand, crashed recklessly into the door, banging himself rather abruptly into its frame. We both landed on the floor simultaneously just inches apart.

I looked up; he was not in front of me, he was not on top of me. I got up and began to run, just seconds ahead of him. I was halfway up the first flight of stairs when, looking over my shoulder, I could see he was hot on my heels, but at the last quarter of the first flight, he lunged at me, grabbing my right ankle in the process. As I reached for the top step, with one almighty yank, I was right back there with him; he applied his full body weight to my underweight figure, making struggling difficult, if not painful, with the steps under my back. Slapping both my wrists together, he pulled me to my feet and began to drag me up the stairs, banging me into the walls and steps as we went with him ahead of me.

When we reached the top, he continued pulling me along the corridor, stopping at the 'lock-up', where he held my thin bruised wrists with one hand whilst he unlocked the door with the other. I attempted to struggle free in the moment, only to be met by his nails piercing deeper into my skin as he deliberately scratched down my arms with his long nails. If ever I had wondered why they were that long, I certainly knew now. I knew in this same moment that he was crazy. Was this what leaving home was all about... meeting crazy? I thought I had left her far behind. With that thought still pondering, he opened the door and threw me in to the room, causing me to crash into the bed frame as I slid along the cold slippery linoleum floor. He slammed the door shut behind me and locked it with the key. I scrambled to my feet and began to bang on the door, screaming and shouting, 'Let me out! Let me out!'

'Shut up' came his answer! I continued shouting and screaming at the top of my voice, now husky, but no one came, no one could hear me. These walls were nine bricks thick. This was a detached Victorian estate, which never had any problems of complaints regarding nuisance or noise; every room was completely soundproofed, which meant unless someone was standing right outside the door, no one could hear you, not even when you screamed with all the energy from your lungs. Nobody really cared anyway.

Flannigan had, earlier that morning, placed the large chest of drawers outside the room in total apprehension of how his planned-out scenario would unfold. It was certainly clear that this entire fiasco was completely premeditated. He had planned it ever so timely that whosoever he locked in the lock-up room that day would not be able to escape and more to the point that I would not be able to climb up and break the glass on top of the door frame as I had done on so many previous occasions.

A fter sometime of banging and shouting w ithout being answered, I looked through the keyhole, surprised to see that Flannigan had left the key still in the door. I looked around the room to see what I could use to try and push the key out of the hole and on to the floor, and then drag it under the door. Miraculously, there was a single wire hanger hanging in the closet, almost concealed amongst some wooden hangers. I took it out and began to untwist it. I opened it out, and after bending the tip at one end, managed to steer it through the keyhole, pushing the key out of the lock. It dropped to the floor the other side of the door. It all seemed so easy; I could practically taste freedom.

Unfortunately, thoughts of instant freedom were short lived. My continuous attempts to pull the key inward towards me under the door all failed, primarily due to the separation of the two dividing pieces of the linoleum floor. The key had conveniently lodged itself quite comfortably between the two separate pieces directly under the door. I could not believe it. No matter how hard I tried, I could not get it out: it was stuck and so was I.

Filled with righteous anger and sheer frustration, I began to throw everything in the room around, including the bed frame, wardrobe, and small bedside cabinet. Once I had calmed down again, I realised that it sort of resembled the scene from an unlit bonfire: the only person missing was the guy; *perhaps in this case that was Flannigan*. I climbed up it to see whether it would hold my weight. It did; it was a success. *All I needed now was to break the glass above the door and then my escape was imminent,* or so I thought.

Picking up the bedside lamp from off the floor, I rushed to the top of my man-made mound, and as hard as I could, I gave the glass an almighty whack, and it cracked. *Yes,* I thought, as I quickly jumped down from the heap of furniture, which was now beginning to give way from under me. I repeated the process again. The glass had cracked badly but was not broken. I needed to break the glass in order to escape.

I piled the furniture up again and went charging up my makeshift mound. I swung the lamp and hit the glass again – 'crock'. This time the glass broke, and a single slice fell to the ground, with a smack, on the other side of the door. It shattered into fragments as it hit the floor. I jumped off and went up again quickly in order not to lose momentum.

This time, there was a gaping great hole in the center. Easing myself to the top, held on by I don't know what, I began to pull out the pieces with my bare hands, which quickly became bloody from the sharp edges now cutting into me. Some of the surrounding pieces were jagged. The task now was to dislodge the glass on the bottom of the frame to make enough space for me to climb through.

As I looked out through the broken glass, it was a long way down; Flannigan had deliberately pushed the chest of drawers about five feet to the left of the door. This would have been ideal to break one's fall, but it was too far to the left of the doorway, my right peering out from the broken window. I had no idea whether I was even capable of swinging out of the frame far enough to miss the slices of jagged glass that remained in the frame. I wasn't even sure if I was capable of landing on top of the chest. In my opinion, there was no miracle known to mankind that was gonna swing me far enough right to land me on the chest of drawers, where it currently stood. *But I had to go for it,* I thought.

I climbed up, placing one foot on the door handle and the other on the slender rim of the light switch. I reached up to the ledge and pulled myself up almost a quarter of the way through the frame, when suddenly I lost my balance and slipped back down, scratching my arm on the glass as I slipped, crashing to the floor finding myself still on the wrong side of the door. My hand was bleeding badly.

I looked around for something, anything with which to apply first aid. I found a forgotten pillowcase in the cupboard, tore it open and wrapped it around my hand. I went up again this time with refueled determination and continued to pull out more of the glass. Eventually, there was enough room for me to squeeze through. As I looked out, down, and to the right, I could see that the chest of drawers, which was ideal to break my fall, was still too far away from the door:

Well, of course it was, I mean no one had moved it any nearer in the last ten minutes, I told myself sternly. *If only I could reach it,* I thought.

It must have been sheer tiredness and exhaustion that caused me to sit down on the edge of the bed frame and just gather my thoughts as to how this was all going to pan out. And time tick-tocked on by.

I must have closed my eyes for what seemed like a moment, only to be woken by the clatter of plates against glassware and the jingle of cutlery. The scent of melted butter, sinking into burnt toast mingled with the fragrance of hot tomato sauce that oozed out from the steaming spaghetti.

'*emm,*' I thought. 'It's *tea time.' I wondered whether anyone was going to come and get me?'* I had missed tea break and lunch and had only half-eaten breakfast before all the madness began... Or were they just going to forget me? I had been in the lock-up for almost seven hours now. Clearly 'no' was the answer that floated back in the dense atmosphere of this spiritual unrest.

Suddenly, I could hear the sound of pitter-patter footsteps coming up the stairs. 'Oh no, who is this,' I questioned? '*If it's Flannigan, I'm really dead now,*' I thought. I climbed up my makeshift ladder again and popped my head out of the half empty frame to see whose head would be emerging from the top of the stairs. *Oh, thank God,* I thought as I gave a sigh of relief; it was only Marley, just little Marley. She came stomping up the stairs and along the corridor, rattling the contents of the tray, spilling the water into the spaghetti as she waddled towards me. The tray was clearly too heavy for her, but she had just about managed it with undiluted resilience and sheer stubbornness. Truly an asset to the cause was little Marley. '*Well done,*' I thought! I began to call her towards me 'Marley, Marley,' I called! I began to frantically pull out more and more pieces of glass imbedded deep within the frame, piercing my hands even further in the process.

I had every intention of pushing my body through the hole, jagged with glass. I had every determination to get out whatever the cost. I managed to slice up my hands even more as I continued, but I cared not; actual freedom meant more, whatever the price. Eventually, Marley came over to the door but not without a display of anxious hesitation and fearful reservation. I told her to put the tray down and push the chest of drawers towards the door directly under the window frame. She said she couldn't.

'Marley, do it,' I screamed!

She began to cry. I now had the timely task of having to calm her down before anxiously beginning again to coax her into thinking that she was the greatest and that this was her big opportunity to be known by everyone as the person who had helped me escape. I began to worry that Flannigan would join us before she had finished pushing and I had physically managed to escape.

However, this was her opportunity to be famous, at least in our world anyway.

'Marley, no one will ever bully you again!' I said, encouraging her further. 'Err... because you are a very brave little girl,' I affirmed, thinking of what else I could say to encourage her. After much coaxing and persuading and, of course, some bribery, which benefited solely Marley, she agreed to help me. I told Marley to stand behind the door to my room as I knocked out some more large pieces of the glass with the lamp.

'OK, Marley, you can come out now!'

'Don't tell Flannigan I helped you,' she pleaded in her usual squeaky little voice.

'No, of course, I won't.'

She put the tray on the floor to the right of the door, knocking over the drink as she did so. 'Oh no!' She began to cry again, thinking I would be upset with her.

'No, no, don't worry, Marley, it's OK. I didn't want the spaghetti any way. Don't cry, OK.' I assured her. Marley eventually calmed down and agreed to help. She went over to the chest and began to push it with her little hands, but it was of no use; the chest was far too heavy for her. She could not move it. I began to shout at her to push harder, but she could not. She almost began to cry again. Just then Marley had an idea! She laid down on the floor and began to push that big old chest with her feet, and yes, the chest began to move. I couldn't believe it, first one centimeter and then two, then three, four, and five; And then Marley farted, and we both burst out laughing, so that took more time and anxiety was rising.

It was difficult for her to control her bodily functions as she tried to work at pushing and breathing in unison, but it *was* moving.

'Great Marley!' I said. You're doing great, just great!' I shouted. Just then my makeshift hill began to collapse, and I tumbled to the floor again. Marley became afraid and ran away with the job only half done. 'Marley!' I called. 'Marley, wait, please wait!' I pleaded. But Marley had gone. 'Damn!' I said, disappointedly, and I had cut myself again too. Frightened half to death by the crash, poor Marley had gone for good.

I quickly rebuilt the mound up again, this time without any hesitation, without any further thought, with one foot standing on the top of the mound, I pushed up on to the slender light switch, which proudly protruded itself, approximately three and a half millimeters out from the wall, as if to be hesitantly introducing itself to the room. I continued pushing up again, raising my right leg up to my ear, breathing in pure determination like some incensed fire-blowing dragon, easing my body out through the half-emptied frame with nothing except sheer resolve to assist me.

Glass piercing my hands, now hooking on to my shirt and jeans, as if in an attempt to hold me back, I rocked on to the frame, the jagged glass stabbing me in the shoulder as I went. It sliced into me and down my arm as I went through the gap, swinging my body out of the frame and round to the right, hoping to make it on to the chest, to break my fall, which I did, just for a flash before falling off the other side and crashing on to the floor.

I lay there for a few moments whilst my senses returned to me. I opened my eyes to find myself lying there quite still, wondering whether or not I had broken anything; or even more importantly, whether or not I was still alive.

After a few moments, when the stars were no more above my head, I rose to my feet, walked over to the tray, picked it up, and went into my room. I sat down on the edge of my bed and began to pick at the tired, dried out, value supper. The last time I ate was at breakfast, which starts from approximately 8:30 am. It was now 6:35 pm. I did not realize how good cheap spaghetti and dried-out fish fingers could taste even with extra water added. As I sat there, my mind drifted back.

It was 1974, the summer before our departure. The Osmond family sibling band were riding high in the charts along with Lena Zavaroni and the Bay City Rollers, with Crazy Gary Glitter in the background. I would see Gary later. And the clock was ticking tick, tock...tick, tock...tick, tock...

Then it came; Dad had suddenly done a complete U-turn from any kind of outside play – 'No!' to playing outside ever again. Just like that, we were not allowed to play outside anymore. He gave Odette the Holy Bible and told her to learn it off by heart. She read it cover to cover. He gave me a book called '*Listening to Jesus*'. I think it had been given to him by the Jehovah Witnesses, who occasionally visited. If he was bored, he would permit them to stand at the door and entertain him, sometimes even inviting them in for a coffee if he was having a melancholy moment. He had told me to learn my book, 'Listening to Jesus', off by heart too; and in my panic, I did. All 125 pages of it.

Dad didn't really understand religion or even faith for that matter and the difference between them. This meant that he was unable to have a fulfilling relationship with God the father through the son, with the help of the Holy Spirit. Therefore, he was unable to be led by the Spirit and as a result he was not able to teach us his children correctly. It was not long after that that we were running late on our return journey back from school, out of breath; we decided to take the lift. We both knew that we should not have taken the lift because Dad had given us a very clear and specific instructions never ever to take the lift, but on this occasion, we were tired from running just to be on time all the time. We felt we couldn't make it up the stairs, so we took the lift. We believed it was the only way to make it home on time.

We stepped inside and pressed for fourth as we tried quickly to retrieve our breath. The lift ascended slowly up from ground to first through to second and passed third, stopping at fourth; we thought we were home and dry until the door of the lift opened, and who should be standing there on the other side? We could not believe our eyes when the door peeled back squeaking as it did, only to reveal Dad standing right there on the other side. We were well and truly busted now. He stared at us with such piercing black eyes, disgusted at our blatant disobedience. Odette said she was sorry. I looked down and said nothing.

'When I return home, I will cut ya oll backside!' He hissed. *(That's a good beating to you and me.)* I remember we were huddled in our room like two runaways hiding in the shadows, as we waited anxiously for his return. I began mumbling something or other; at one point, I think I was even praying. Then Odette spouted out.

'According to the Bible, if we ask and pray for anything in the name of Jesus, whatever we ask he will give it to us.'

'*R-R-Really?*' I said full of surprise. 'So how do we pray then?' I asked returning to my state of panic.

'I don't know,' she answered.

'You must know,' I replied anxiously. 'You know everything.' So, I began to pray how I thought I should pray but was still a little unsure about things.

'Dear Jesus,' I said. And stopped. 'Dear God,' I continued. 'Please, please, do not let our Dad beat us when he returns,' I said out loud.

'You have to say, "In the name of Jesus", she said.

'OK, Dear Jesus, Dear God, please, please, do not let our Dad beat us when he returns, in the name of Jesus.'

'Is it at the beginning or the end?' I asked slightly baffled.

'I don't know.'

'What do you mean?' I asked, even more baffled.

'It doesn't say.'

'OK, I will say "In the name of Jesus" at the beginning and at the end.'

'In the name of Jesus, Dear Jesus, Dear God, please, please, do not let our Dad beat us when he returns, in the name of Jesus.' I prayed with all my energy over and over and over again, wringing my hands as I prayed. I squeezed my hands so tightly that one of the water bumps on my finger burst, releasing its transparent liquid. I was so nervous and so anxious at the same time. My stomach was in painful knots. I prayed with my entire being. I prayed with all of my energy. I prayed until I was exhausted. I prayed for well over two hours.

By the time Dad had returned, it was almost dark. We were now sitting in the dark too afraid to turn on the light. Remarkably, he did not call us to come down to see him, and he did not come up to see us either. That evening, we received no beating and no beating the following day either. The prayer had worked. Thank God! Thank you, Jesus! The prayer had worked. Unfortunately, though, just two weeks later, the beating was delivered (*I guess I must have prayed the prayer of postponement, ouch!*). However, somehow, we were able to withstand it. It was certainly short but definitely not sweet.

After returning to the present I realised that the thought of prayer had never even entered my mind. I placed the tray on top of the chest of drawers; I was determined to stay in my room that evening. I had no idea of what Flannigan would do to me next if he saw that I had escaped; and all the mess that I had caused. I decided to push all the broken glass under the door in the hope that no one would notice that it was missing from out of the frame above. I pushed the chest back to its original position and straightened it up before returning to my room and closing the door behind me.

I don't recall ever seeing the cleaners, yet the place was always spotlessly clean, never even so much as a cobweb in sight. I could be more relaxed once I knew they had been and swept up all the bits of glass. Remarkably Flannigan did not return to check on me that evening nor the following day.

Evening became night and night soon returned to day, when the call for breakfast came around once more. Again, I slipped in amongst the other girls as though nothing was wrong, as though nothing had happened, as though it was not I who had been dragged across half an acre of garden, across the hard ground, through the hall, up four flights of stairs, along the dorm corridors, and thrown into the 'lock-up'.

Despite sitting down to breakfast, I found that I was not really hungry. I found myself increasingly more and more retreating into myself. I seemed to spend my days further and further away from my peers, who had betrayed me more than once. I ate less and less, yet no one noticed; for Lent, I gave up all biscuits, puddings, and desserts; I lost a stone in body weight, but still no one noticed. I guess, the truth was no one really cared. It felt like no one was really there, or perhaps it was I who was not really there.

One Saturday, I decided to pluck up the courage to go to the shops alone. I had found a couple of 2 pence pieces on the floor and one member of agency staff had given me a 10 pence piece. Hoping I would remember the way there and back, without getting lost, I set off on my journey as soon as I could, after breakfast.

I tried to take in as many landmarks as possible so that I would not lose my way. Without spending too long inside the shop, day dreaming on things I could not afford I made my purchases and left. I had brought some chewy worms and, whilst deep in thought, I began to chew them as I slowly made the walk back to the estate.

The weather was bright and not too cold. The sun had intermittently popped out its face from behind the white and grey clouds, but appeared hell bent on playing cat and mouse. I must have been walking for not more than about five minutes when the sound of screaming sirens could be heard in the distance. It was an unfamiliar sound in this neck of the woods. I listened to see whether I could establish which type of vehicle they belonged to. As the road came out of the bend, I could see smoke in the distance. A part of me wished that it was Grimshaw Hall that was on fire. *Wishful thinking, I think they call it..*

As I turned into the long drive, it became more apparent that, in fact, the smoke was actually coming from the estate. Filled with elation I increased my pace as I walked up the drive; however, I was bitterly disappointed to see all of it still standing there, fully intact. As I got nearer, it appeared that the smoke was in fact coming from the right and to the side of the estate; it was pouring out from behind the wall. Fast filled with inquisitive interest I walked around the high wall and stood behind it, not sure what to make of the picture that awaited me.

To my complete surprise, and utter shock - I saw Flannigan; he was just standing there, a mass of black hot ash surrounded him, his face, and clothes also sooty. Red had come out and began to try and salvage things, anything. He had found a '*hot note*' it was a not too badly burnt £20 note: *a lot of money back then*. I had never seen one of those before. Red tried to comfort Flannigan with sympathetic words of comfort. Flannigan was mumbling in a dialect we could not understand. He was like a man who had lost his mind. The fire engines had already departed now. They simply put out the flames and left.

Apparently, Flannigan had been frying some sausages. The oil had become too hot; he turned around to pick up a tea towel, and in one second, the cooker was alight and in another, the entire caravan was ablaze, and all his belongings had gone up in smoke with it. I stood there looking, staring, shocked even, trying my best not to smile, yet inside, feeling completely justified. I believed with all certainty that it was a sign from the Lord God Almighty... We all did.

Flannigan had to try and quickly salvage what he could before the skips arrived to take the rest away to the dump, and they were already on their way. The mess was spoiling the look of the place; *apparently*. Everything he owned was in that caravan – his whole life. I think he only managed to save one thing, can't remember what, oh yes, it was the clothes on his back, and to make matters worse, he had no insurance, neither did Mr. Frank, and so another argument ensued between them. It wasn't long before the rumors began to circulate that this was indeed the 'Wrath of God!' Every time Flannigan raised his voice or stepped out of line; the Scorsese brothers would blatantly remind him. '*Served him right*,' we all thought, but no-one spoke it.

Still traumatized by the events that had gone on, I began to find solace in music and started to spend my evenings sitting by the radiogram in the upper hall. Despite having a permission slip just in case, the notorious Flannigan ever decided to kick off, I would always vacate the area prior to the bedtime call; I did not want to provide him with any excuse to attack me. But sometimes no matter how hard we try to prevent something from occurring or happening the inevitable will always present itself for testing. And yes, there was this one rather particular occasion, when Flannigan, who had not been on evening duty for some considerable time since the fire, had now suddenly reappeared back to work for the evening shift.

I could hear his high heels clogging down the corridor and his squeaky voice ordering the children up to their dorms. In a panic, I looked around for somewhere to hide but my saving grace, the larger than life sofa, had already gone, replaced now by a much smaller one, with no secret compartment in which one could completely hide.

'*What am I gonna do now?*' I thought. Sheer panic fast filling me up. I was convinced he would see me if I decided to hide behind the giant curtains that stood either side of the giant windows. Looking around, there was nowhere to hide. The sound of his clogs getting louder as they got nearer; And just in that moment, as he walked past me, I closed my eyes and willed myself invisible, dead even. I would have given anything not to have been there in that moment, anything to have disappeared, despite even having my permission slip with me.

He called out to me, but I did not answer. Trying not to breathe even; I told myself I was asleep. I could hear his footsteps moving closer and closer towards me, and he continued to call out to me. Still I made no movement, no sign, and gave no answer. He spoke again, this time bending right over me. His strong, coffee-smelling breath, mixed with tobacco, spread out over me, covering me like a thick blanket. Trying hard to control my own breathing, I began to breathe it in. Just then, the boys from 'B' group appeared and then - the strangest thing of all happened. Flannigan picked me up and held me in his arms, like a new born baby. I could feel his warm breath on my face and his heart pounding against my ear, now close to his chest.

'How could this man who was so cruel now be so kind?' I questioned, not really expecting an answer.

'What's wrong with Jacqueline?' asked the Scorsese brothers, in total trepidation. They tried to congregate around me as I lay lifeless in Flannigan's arms. Flannigan did not answer, and I did not move a muscle. The Scorsese brothers began to chant.

'Jacqueline is dead, and Flannigan has killed her! Jacqueline is dead and Flannigan has killed her!' I must have been very convincing, I guess.

'Shhh!' he said, with full emphasis upon each letter. 'She is sleeping,' he continued. But they were not having any of it; they continued to chant and heckle until Flannigan threatened them.

'Listen, right? If you don't get ready for bed now! And I mean right now! Then just wait and see what will happen when I get back, and I mean it!' he added.

'Oh no, no, no!' they cried as if suddenly remembering what he was capable of. 'We're sorry, Flannigan, we're sorry.' Oh, so not *the three little pigs.*

'We're sorry.' They begged and pleaded and begged some more.

'Right, go and get ready for bed right now!' ordered Flannigan quite emphatically. 'I will be up there in five minutes,' he exclaimed starkly. Flannigan carried me up the next night and the next and the next, and every night after, when he was on duty.

It was like some warped pleasurable dance we had both signed up to. But somehow, it felt nice, comfortable even, despite being just for a moment in his arms, the warmth of his chest, the proximity of our bodies, the contact. I wished it was real, this was what I pined for. He would lay me down ever so gently upon my bed and then summon Fat Miz to get me into my pajamas. She would obey him without question, even if she had to stop what she was already doing.

I continued to skip tea and lunch and snack, just picking here and there at what I wanted. Looking back, I was sinking deeper and deeper into myself. Each evening I continued to meet with the radiogram, not really listening to what it was saying or the songs it was singing. In my mind, I was miles away, and just before bedtime I would retreat into the fetal position and deliberately fall asleep. Each night, I was carried to my quarters by Flannigan. Before long, big Benn also joined in the dance if Flannigan was not on duty.

One evening they had both arrived to take me upstairs. They were both saying I will take her up; this verbal tug went on for a couple of minutes, but it was Flannigan's persistence that won out in the end. He said he had something to retrieve from the flat over in the girls' dorm so of course Big Benn conceded. However, I was quite sure that Flannigan was lying...

During the days, I was made to join in with what we now recognize as extra-curricular activities, and those included horse riding, roller skating, and swimming; these usually took place on Saturdays. Chess and arts and crafts took place daily and with camping occurring at Easter. This was Gordon's brainchild, a mental desire to take us all on a camping trip, in the middle of nowhere and in the pouring rain. It was also his futile attempt to bond with us, his goodwill gesture at friendship.

Gordon was also on the tall side, yet not quite as tall as Big Benn, – no one was as tall as Big Benn. Gordon had an oval face, which he kept clean shaven. He had grey eyes, which although never really connected with you, always appeared to be shining. He kept his mousey hair now turning silver in a style from his youth, despite it thinning slightly on top. He always wore ridiculous jumpers and brown corduroys that were clearly too short for his long legs. It was Gordon who would sit on the children once they were caught after attempting to run; and it was Gordon who would take away their shoes. I don't think he ever thought about what the impact of his weight had upon their usually very thin frames, but this was how he dealt with runners; and no one ever questioned him.

Back at the campsite and again we weren't really equipped for it; any of it, in fact. We had a hole in our tent, through which the rain came, and yes, you guessed it, it was my sleeping bag that was positioned directly underneath it and it was my face the rain came in on every morning. However, I think I felt even more annoyed by the fact that there were no decent washing facilities, the toilets stunk of pee wee and the showers were in a terrible state, which meant I had to remain in the same clothes for an entire week because I was never gonna use them. I think we peed in the bushes mainly. By Friday I could feel my skin itching; I wanted to go home if it was at all possible to ever call it that.

Nevertheless, Gordon was still convinced that this was a '*good*' bonding exercise for all of us. I for one hated it with every fiber of my being. Of course, there was an upside to this event, which was that we found some wild ponies for our amusement.

We attempted to ride them bare back, but not knowing whether or not they would buck us off, we didn't dare to stay on for too long. It was really only me who succeeded though, riding horizontally, as you do, across the pony for all of five feet or so, before also jumping off, not fully trusting it to stay calm.

At the end of the week, we were so glad it was finally over; we had made it and now we are going back or so we all thought. However, beggar's belief, Gordon was now saying that he wanted us to extend our one week stay to two, – *was he crazy or what?* He was really pushing for it now. He went through the group one by one, trying his best to really put the pressure on us and make us feel guilty if we didn't give him the answer he was looking for. However, you can never have too much cold food, wet sleeping bags, and nowhere to wash or change, so we made our objections very clear: an unequivocal *no*! So, we packed up our belongings folded down our tents and commenced the long drive back. We arrived at the estate just in time for tea.

The Big Dive

It would be usually a Saturday when we would visit the swimming pool and horse-riding stables, we would alternate our time between the two, however, on this particular Saturday, we were going swimming. Those who did not have swimsuits could visit the '*room*'. It was always kept locked but behind its walls lay an Aladdin's cave.

There was every single item of clothing that had ever been invented. I mean, there were jumpers and coats and slippers and dressing gowns, and wellington boots and hiking boots and raincoats and macks and T-shirts and socks and thick socks and jeans and pants and vests.

In the center of the room, stood a high wooden table; it was piled high with more clothes, then there were the shelves that went around all the walls of the room, from the floor almost reaching the very high ceiling. I stood there my mouth ajar. '*Who brought all this stuff?*' I thought, and '*exactly who wore it because it certainly wasn't us?*'

There must have been enough clothes to last an entire family of kids a lifetime. I had gone up to the room because I needed a swimming suit; I didn't have one, I had never had one of my own.

Gordon, who was facilitating this event, had ordered that everyone was to attend this trip to the pool, so I had to go up to the room to get one. In truth, I had never seen so many clothes, all in one place before; I mean, they even had swimming goggles. My eyes were dizzy with the magnitude of it all.

I had a choice of three types of swimsuit, a deep navy blue one, which did nothing for my complexion really: a dark green and white one – again, very boring. I knew that wouldn't suit me either; I mean, I felt glum just looking at it, but then there, over there, poking out from the mound of clothing on the center of the table was a bright, summery, pink swimsuit, it was as though it was calling out to me. It was so bright and vibrant and truly complemented the very color of me. It had my name all over it, so this was the one I picked. I couldn't wait to try it on. I was also given a pair of slippers and a dressing gown. I had been freezing my butt off all winter without reason, but now, it was spring, and I had slippers and a dressing gown.

Each Saturday, that it was a swim day we would attend a different pool in a different location. On this occasion, we were visiting an Olympic-size swimming pool. It had two diving boards. The pool was massive. Of course, I had never dived before and had only just learnt to swim in the bathtub at home not even twelve months prior. Nevertheless, after watching the older children do it, I told myself that I too could dive, and that was the same story I told my peers who raved about my swimsuit; apparently, the colors looked really cool against my skin tone.

'Don't worry, it's not mine,' I said, reassuringly.

'Is it from the room?' Red asked.

'Yes,' I nodded. 'I will have to give it back at the end,' I added. Everything was always returned at the end; this was fast becoming the story of my life. I may not have been living on borrowed time, but I was certainly, living with borrowed clothes.

Interestingly, it was only the boys who had noticed that I was wearing the most stylish swimsuit in the pool; it boasted all the colors of sun, sea, and sand with splashes of pink for good measure; but for now, the boys were suddenly my best friends, *as temporary as that was.*

The conversation had steered on to the diving boards; it was dominated by those who thought they could dive from the top board. For me, it was an opportunity to prove myself once and for all. *Anything to get these cronies off my back*, I thought.

I made out like it was no big deal. Those who thought they could, lined up, and those who dared, walked the plank. I was about eighth in the queue. One by one, they reached the top only to retreat and come back down the ladder; knees knocking and white with fear.

The high board was sixteen feet above the water line. One boy had already tried to make the run back to the ladder from the board but slipped off and fell side first into the water below. I closed my eyes not able to witness him just miss the side of the diving board below. All the while I was trying to talk myself into it. Before I knew it, it was me. I was up. It was my turn. I climbed on to the first step of the ladder that went all the way up to the highest board and continued to mount the steps one at a time.

'I can do this, I can do this,' I kept whispering to myself. Once I had reached the top, I walked along the board as if walking the plank. I walked right to the end and looked down. I could not believe my eyes. What was I thinking by saying I could do this when really it was just too high? Clearly it was too high. I was so high up that I felt like I couldn't breathe. This was so much higher than standing on top of the headboard above my bed and jumping off, a well-known pleasurable pastime event whilst still at home. But this was so much higher than standing at the top of the stairs and going down it in my brothers bath tub. It was even higher than standing on top of the window ceil and jumping over the headboard on to the bed.

Suddenly I was afraid. Suddenly I couldn't do it, I wanted to turn back. I looked down at some of my peers who had made the jump before me. They were looking up at me and began to jeer at me. I walked back to the ladder. The jeering got louder. It felt as though the entire pool was watching me. I felt red hot and afraid. The jeering and laughing got louder and louder. In that same moment, I ran to the edge of the board, jumped up and off, high into the air. Keeping my body completely rigid, as straight as an arrow as

I made my rapid descent; getting the wind knocked right out of me in the process. I could hear myself saying, 'Why did I make this jump? Why did I make this jump?'

In the same moment, my stomach went up to say 'Hi.' to my mouth. With one hand, tight against my side, the other holding my nose, nails digging into my skin, I speared at the water, causing it to open up and let me in. I penetrated the water deeply, like a spear into soft soil. My problem now was how to get back up to the surface without drinking the water. I found that if I did not panic, the air in my lungs naturally carried me up near to the surface; from there I only had to tread water until arriving at the top. It sounds simple enough; however, it did take some time to master this technique.

That board was sixteen feet above the water. What a triumph, what elation, and what a splash! I had made it! Now I was an eleven-year-old to be reckoned with, because I was the only one from 'B' group who had made the jump. The other two who also made the jump were from 'A' group; desiring to continue to build confidence, we three repeated the jump until it was time to go.

In hindsight, looking back, I think I enjoyed the horse riding most, perhaps more so because horses are my most favorite animal. I felt as though I could really connect with them despite having a bit in their mouths to control the direction in which they went and a saddle on their backs as a stark reminder of their captivity. However, once out on an open field they were free to run, even if just for a moment. When I was riding out there with them, I felt that freedom, even if it was just for a moment. For me, it was the state that was the bit in my mouth causing me to arrive wherever it was they wanted me to go; and for now, it was Grimshaw Hall that was the saddle on my back.

The upside of these activities was that, apart from being pleasurable, they allowed us to forget, for as long as they lasted, who we were, and where we had come from. It allowed us to forget what was going on, in our traumatic and often turbulent lives and to some extent, it helped to distance the pain of being forced to live a merely clinical existence in a clinical loveless bubble.

The same existence I am sure my elder half-sister had experienced before meeting her own premature death, some eleven years earlier; she had not even made it to her fifth birthday, and those that came before; I was positive she did not celebrate even one of them before going down to an unknown grave.

Daily practice caused me to excel even further at chess, but it was not here that I learnt.

My training ground had been at the Good Sandy Lodge, first rapping my small thin knuckle-bitten fingers around the beautiful, sculptured, wooden pieces at the tender age of just seven. Here at Grimshaw Hall, I could add to what I had already learnt there.

Sandy Lodge was a relatively delightful place compared to this. What I liked best about it was their policy on violence; they had a zero tolerance to it. Dr Sootu would go absolutely crazy, and I mean crazy, if the boys ever hit the girls, let alone the staff, who would probably be fired on the spot. *Why couldn't everywhere be like that?* I thought. Of course, the girls did get away with hitting the boys. Well, that was a different story, they usually deserved it. Paul Smith, in particular, to name but one. He would always tease me to the point of no return, which I utterly hated, and yes, it most certainly was me who bent his brand-new football boot in half, pulled out the laces, and flushed the right one down the toilet. When he found it, he squealed like a baby pig; I couldn't understand it really, – I mean, - *it was only a shoe...*

I was the undefeated chess champion at Sandy Lodge, which perhaps in the circumstances was rather ironic really, because in my mind, in my emotions, deep down in the pit of me, I had already thrown down the gauntlet; I felt beaten: mentally and physically defeated. I felt pressed down and utterly oppressed in this unkind and unforgiving foreign land and I just wanted out.

Perhaps even more sinister was the fact that I had no idea of what was being formed in my psyche. I had no idea of what patterns were actually taking root, deep down in the pit of me or what was being knitted together in my organs, or what would be the form of it, or what this would grow into and what would be the far-reaching ramifications of all of this? What if in the years to come I would one day find 'me' on Oprah's sofa trying to dissect it all and compartmentalize it all? Would I tell her the whole story, the real-life ugly truth or would I be prepped and told only to say the not so dreadful things, the not so sad things. I was convinced that Oprah would want the whole truth and nothing but the truth. The reason for my thinking was that I knew without doubt that Oprah is a woman of integrity, and I respected her for that. I had no idea of the kind of fruit that it would bring forth. I had no idea of the effect of what was now shaping me, or that I, the real me, was all the while being ebbed away at, perhaps I was becoming lost in the thick of it. Perhaps I was just becoming lost in the system. Only time would tell, and the clock was ticking, tick, tock... tick, tock.

Later, I would somehow come to learn that these people, these charge hands from these agencies, or rather institutions and establishments were perhaps themselves lost in their own bitter, twisted, turmoil of a less than perfect life. But right now, in this moment, they had become an essential part of our own lives. My life, and this was my story, it was the making up of me. I would also someday come to understand that they, as sordid and as warped as they were, represented 'family', 'my family', and the day was coming when I would come to wonder where they all were now. I had no words for prayers back then, but if I did perhaps it would go something like this.

'Oh, Dear LORD Abba Father of light, omniscient, omnipotent, omnipresent God, reach down your hand from heaven and save these, your children. Save the children who have been tortured with violence, humiliated with abuse, starved of love and affection, and denied all manner of respect. Oh, Abba Adonai Shammah,

Jehovah Rohi, the Lord who heals, send forth your Word that is sharper than a two-edge sword and that can separate sinew from flesh and bone from marrow, and with that Word, heal their scars, heal their wounds, mental emotional and physical too, and bless them, oh Lord, I pray. Lord, that you would draw them into your everlasting family, your everlasting bosom of love and grace. Shower them with your mercy, embrace them with your compassion, flood them with your love, surround them with your peace, and allow them to see your glory in the name of your precious son, the Lord Jesus Christ. I pray. Father your promises are yes and Amen! I heard they are shooting through the air just waiting to be caught so I snatch this one down now, in Jesus' name, Amen!'

Clearly, I had no prayers back then. I knew none, but if I did have just one, then I'm sure it would be something like that.

The fall finally arrived, with it bringing the season of beautiful spring. She had adorned herself in an array of vibrant and refreshing blossoms of subtle pinks and pure whites, set against a back drop of royal blue skies and dotted with marshmallow clouds.

This was a new season and it felt like a season of new possibilities had opened up, positive possibilities. There was something different in the air, and it felt good. I realised very quickly that I loved spring and all its offerings of striking beauty and tranquility, for me the New Year began here, and the magpie was my renewed hope.

Being out of the grey city and away from the jungle concrete, now surrounded by green pastures, enabled me to have a deep appreciation of the seasons, noticing all their colorful changes. The different birds, the beautiful flowers, and the full blossom on the trees all conspiring together to do their part in creating an ensemble of beauty, and yes it was good. It was pleasing to the eye and edifying to the mind and the inner man.

Spring was definitely on my side; indeed, it was my most favorite time of year. It gave true meaning to the hymn, 'Morning has broken'. We used to sing it at primary school during assembly. It boasts all the elements of freedom, peace, joy, and happiness. It draws on all the characteristics of a better life and rewrites the ingredients; a life more than this, a life worth living. I loved to sing it. It gave me hope of a real future, a good future... but right here right now, - this was not it. How was I going to capture it and step into it, if at all? Clearly there was going to have to be some miracle and on a grand scale.

Eventually, as all the children began to take their permanent leave of absence from this God-forsaken place, it came down to almost just me. Then out of the blue came one of my rescuers; she had been there on the day of my exodus from the farm all those many moons ago. Clearly, a lot had happened since then, and I think that by now, I was indeed a very different person, more so because of everything I had endured. Albeit, unbeknown to me then, I had picked up something new, a different spirit, a spirit of depression and one of rage, pure uncontrollable rage. I would find out much later what a fight I actually had on my hands, and the weapons that I would need to overcome them, and the clock was ticking, tick tock...tick tock.

Valarie Gene came abounding over to me one more time, like some untamed Labrador. All the natural curls in her hair bouncing in unison with every flat-footed step that she took. Her big breasts leading in the dance of bounce from under her grey overstretched jumper, that was really too small; perhaps caused by being over-heated in her washing machine, followed by being half spun to death on the spin cycle that was really going too fast and then roasted in her dryer 12 minutes over the recommended time. She brought with her a north-westerly breeze that blew without thinking and I was not happy to see her, neither was I impressed.

I had not seen Val since she had dropped me off or rather dumped me at Sanquingay Park with her colleague the previous year, some seven months prior to the events that had led to her untimely presence now. I realize this because it was her as well as her colleagues who had ignored my pleas to get me out of this place, as well as the receptionist, and Jeanie, the boss of them all. And it was Val who had failed so bitterly to return even just one of my calls, each one desperately pleading for help, or even to answer any of my left messages; Jeanie included. It was her colleague who had sat on me in the car to keep me from escaping on the journey back to Grimshaw Hall, after Christmas break.

In hindsight looking back perhaps the SS in all honesty did not know what to do, so they did nothing. In the years that followed I would come to learn that this was not an isolated case and a ransom was to be paid.

Clearly, Val by her body language, had forgotten all that had gone on, as she came bounding over, grinning from ear to ear, as if to indicate a '*happening*' celebration of some kind. She began to inform me of what *they* had all decided and what *they* had all planned for me. According to Val, my next mad stop was going to be an all-girls boarding school in Hastings. *'The hell it was!'* I thought. Looking straight into her eyes, without wavering, without flinching and without even blinking, and speaking directly into her inner man, I said, 'If you think I am going to any boarding school, you can think again, because I'm certainly not!' The words came out more like a blast. Val tried not to shudder.

'Well, there is nowhere else for you to go,' she said shrugging her shoulder towards the heavens, as if she had done all she could.

'If you try and send me to any boarding school, I will run away every single day, and I will make your life a complete and utter misery!' I said quite emphatically.

We all knew the reputation of such institutions and what kind of things went on in those places. According to us they were demonic, and this was where I drew the line. For me I had had quite enough of Oliver Twist at Christmas break, – I didn't feel I needed to physically re-live it in order to believe it.

'You cannot force me to stay there!' I snapped.

'No one is forcing you,' she replied timidly. 'But we are all out of options now,' she added.

'Well, you better think up some new ones,' I demanded quite abruptly!

'Well, it appears that you and your sister are going to be with us a while, and this is where we send children who are going to be with us a while,' she said in a super soft voice, as if it was her tone that was supposed to make me conform.

'I don't care,' I slammed! 'I'm not going there even if you force me, and if you send me there, I will make your life a living hell,' I shouted! '... and I will run away every single day,' I said even louder!

It was there, we believed, that girls were bullied, beaten, oppressed, and tortured on a far greater and more excessive scale than even what I was currently experiencing at the estate, which was clearly bad enough.

'Now go away and tell your string pullers that!' I shouted in my loudest voice ever. Val, knowing full well she was out of her depth and without even the slightest objection, hopped off across the massive green garden, hands still deep in pockets, as though they were stuck or something. She then hobbled back through the garden door and disappeared inside. After a while I could feel the change in temperature; it had dropped quite significantly now becoming cold, almost resembling the permanent atmosphere inside the house. I decided to go back inside and wait for her on the stairs to the girls' dorms. I kept walking across the hall and along the corridor through the main hall and up to the lounge and back again, backwards, and forwards in order to keep checking that they were still in their meeting; I had lost all trust in Val, I didn't trust her for a minute. I was surprised when she found me again, patiently waiting for her on the stairs, back over at B group, as I didn't even tell her where I would be. I half expected her to leave without saying a word. I mean what she had done up until now? – absolutely nothing.

'You win,' she said. 'You win, you're right, no boarding school for you.'

'So where then?' I demanded to know refusing to let her off the hook too easy. 'What then?' I demanded. 'I have to get out of here now,' I stressed! 'Now! I want to leave now!' I slammed!

'Be packed and ready to go on 23rd,' she answered.

The 23rd April was exactly three weeks to the day if she meant it.

'I'll be ready,' I affirmed, a smile almost etching its way across my face, yet still not convinced of her word. She rubbed my shoulder as if I was suddenly her new-found best friend as she went, but I quickly shrugged it off; my response was automatic. I couldn't help but feel that she had been nothing more than a complete let down in the months that had passed. She had not called me once during my entire time here, neither had she visited me, not even once. She had done nothing to protect me from the crazy wickedness that existed here in this place and that was permitted to thrive here, on a daily basis, neither had she even attempted to arrange a single visit or call with my sister.

It was because of her failure and that of her own superior, Jeanie Rudders, who, between them, had failed to do anything about the goings-on at Grimshaw Hall. Many children had suffered so much physical, emotional, and mental abuse; and for many it would take a lifetime to heal and perhaps in some cases even take a life, and all for what? In my mind, they just drank tea and coffee on tap, ate biscuits from a tin, wrote poorly constituted notes that had no real meaning as they were based largely on personal opinions as opposed to being constructive or truthful - or even meaningful with an intended positive outcome. They drove their family cars to distant places, or sometimes taking the train, staying just five or ten minutes before making their excuses for their abrupt departures and all for what? I thought because they couldn't even protect a fly in a square tin box.

As I counted down the days, I expected the worst and hoped for nothing. I just couldn't allow myself to believe it. I could not allow myself to trust her, not until that day arrived and not one moment before, not until I was in it.

Meanwhile, back at the *ranch*, Shirley had now turned sixteen. She was told quite ardently that if she dared to put so much as a single finger on any child younger than herself again, the police would be called, she would be arrested and charged accordingly. *Too little too late,* I thought. It was rather a small recompense after what appeared to be her life long reign of terror in that place.

A few days passed when more good news came to my ears. Out of the blue I received a phone call. It was Odette. I remember her voice sounded so tiny, she sounded so far away. We didn't speak for long

'How are you?' she asked.

'Ok', I answered softly. 'Where are you?' I asked.

'I don't know, somewhere called Trent,' she answered lowering her voice. I had never heard of such a place.

'Can I come there?' I asked.

'I don't know,' she said.

'What's it like there? Do they have brothers and sisters there?' I asked anxiously reaching out to hope.

'Listen, I'm going to ask if I can come and visit you,' she said reassuringly, sensing my anxiety rising.

'Really,' I answered, sounding more enthusiastic. 'When?' I questioned, almost not being able to contain myself. To see Odette again would really make my day, I thought. I felt I desperately needed to be in her company, to touch her, to hug her, to embrace her in my arms once more. My world was so empty without her; I had never felt so desperately lost and so completely alone. It was different to when she left home before because that was for only two weeks. I knew she would be returning; but this time was different – our separation had lasted 4 months so far and neither of us knew when we would be reunited or even if we would be.

'I don't know,' she said.

'How will you get here? Will someone bring you? Will they bring you? Will they bring you in the car?' My bombardment of questions had begun.

'I will find out and let you know,' she added. She sounded more like the SS than herself. 'I have to go now but I will call you again soon,' she added.

'When?'

'I miss you.'

'I need you. I need to see you soon.' My words were uncompleted as the line went dead followed by its tone.

She had gone. I was overwhelmed with sadness again. She never did visit me, neither did she call back to speak to me throughout the remainder of my stay. We were not given money in many of these places, so you had to really creep up to and befriend the agency staff in order to beg them for two pence for the phone. The regular staff would always say they had no money, but sometimes the agency staff would give you money; that was until they were corrected by the regular staff.

When asked, remarkably no one at Grimshaw Hall knew the telephone number of where my sister was, neither did they know how to access it. So, that was it: I couldn't call her either. That was all I had to remember her by at that time, a two-minute phone call. I had no idea when I would see her again or even if I would ever see her again. I would close my eyes and remember the sound of her voice replaying her words over and over in my mind just to gain some comfort.

No one told us a thing about our future or how long a child could expect to stay in Grimshaw Hall. Apparently, it was some kind of assessment center. The maximum period of time one could expect to stay was approximately 6 weeks. This time frame had long passed by now. However, it had become normal procedure that everyone overstayed their assessment time, me included.

Leaving Number 10

Leaving Grimshaw Hall was the tenth move in eleven years, not including the double dips or rather the places that we went back to twice and a stop to Huddersfield which I vaguely remember. In any event it had never been a home for me, so there was no love lost there, no tears to cry and certainly no long goodbyes. I could not wait until the day arrived for me to leave here though.

However, given the reputation of the SS for their long string of endless disappointments, all on tap I might add, I didn't want to get my hopes up. I couldn't help but wonder whether she would in fact keep her word by physically turning up to deliver me from my Egypt.

I decided to proceed with caution. I found that after visiting the internal shop and handing back everything that had been loaned to me, I was back down to nothing again, I was left with practically nothing to pack, barring a white shirt with a missing button and the clothes on my back, which had all been my sister's hand me down uniform from Darlington Bassett Grammar School.

Remarkably, all the clothes that had been lavished on me were all apparently on 'loan' and had to be returned. I was not permitted to keep a single thing. Not a thing; it didn't matter that by returning everything I would be left with nothing bar the shirt with the missing button and my uniform. Of course, I did want to lie and say that the hiking boots were mine; they were indeed the most comfortable pair of walking boots that I had ever worn in my entire young life. In truth, they were the only walking boots I had ever worn. They were the first pair of boots that were not hand- me-downs, I know this because they were new right out of the box, and I was the first one to wear them. The swimsuit too, was so bright and pink; it really suited me. But I just couldn't. It all went back. About now I just wanted out and hey, I had been here before vis-à-vis my exodus from number 58... There was no love lost here.

The forms were all signed, and the boxes ticked; a short wait later and we were finally given the OK to leave. I could not believe it. I was grinning from ear to ear. Anyone would have thought I had just won the lottery or something; perhaps I had, but that's another story. We loaded my plastic bags into the very large, very spacious boot and got into the car; we closed the doors in unison not even looking behind us as we mounted the long drive out.

The sun was shining down on us as if in agreement with the decisions that had been made long before that day and stayed with us as we embarked upon our journey to collect Odette from a place called Trent Cross. This was another faraway place I'd never heard of. We arrived there shortly after an hour of nonstop driving. I had never been to Trent before. I mean not even in passing, at least not that I knew of. I had only managed to speak to Odette just once during her stay there and that call lasting no more than a couple of minutes in what seemed like an eternity. It felt good to be finally meeting her again... Or so I thought...

Upon our arrival, we appeared to have stumbled into what looked like unorganized chaos: a child was running through the reception area, another hot on his heels. Then an almighty Crack! Whack! Bang! Wallop! The child behind had just thrown a great big tub of what looked like hair grease at the child in front. It crashed into the rear of the head of the child in front, breaking in half on contact when it hit the floor; the child in front followed the tub by also crashing to the floor. Then Bang! Wallop! The second child ran over and disciplined the first child further, armed with green flip-flops. Remarkably all this unfolded in the presence of a member of staff who had witnessed the entire show in all its glory, yet without even a blink of intervention, not even a word. But then, surprisingly neither did Val.

However, that second child, the one with the perfect shot, was Odette, my sister, a twelve-year-old girl, and that first child, now on the floor, was a fifteen-year-old boy who thought it was OK to touch girls anyhow, anywhere, anytime. But clearly it wasn't, and Odette was going to physically prove it, one way or another, he was going down; and he did with a bang.

Years later, Odette was to reveal the ugly truth of what really went on in that place.

In truth, I never really knew why they had separated us anyway. I mean, we were already in separate social rooms, meeting up only at mealtimes and bedtimes. It was interesting to see that they did not take it upon themselves to separate any of the other sibling groups into different houses or even separate the girls in the dormitories according to age. I mean, we were not loud or boisterous or show-offs or aggressive or anything; we were every bit the opposite, in fact. To my mind there was just no need for us to be separated, no reason at all. But that was how the very system that was set up to protect you operated. In truth, it did no more than to wear you out and tear you down, weakening you at every turn, ultimately set to destroy you by ebbing away at the very spirit of you, draining the very life out of you, stealing your joy and your peace; your reasons for wanting to go on. They knew full well that if they separated siblings, they were easier to break; after all, aren't all children vulnerable?

Trent Cross was indeed a huge place, so much so that it took some time to locate the authorized individual who had the authority to sign the papers for Odette's release. However, after some time, which although included sudden squeals and loud outbursts from strange children, she emerged. Odette came too with her small plastic bag of emotional possessions.

Now three in number we all bundled into the car, the engine roared as Val overturned the ignition and we drove out of the drive and off the premises. Inside I wanted to cheer, I was so elated.

We were heading to a place we had never heard of before; a place called Hampshire and a village called Waterlooville. We were leaving again: another house, another town, another people, or rather people group: strange people. In any event, there was no love lost in this hard land as this had certainly never been home. We were both just so glad to be together again; or at least, so I had thought.

Sadly, something had happened in our period of separation. There had been a change. A shift in the atmosphere, a br-eak-ing of the bond, a sn-app-ing of the cords. We were no longer bound together in love, too much had happened. Odette's heart had hardened, and I had become filled with rage, only I did not know it then; but the clock was ticking, tick tock...tick tock...tick tock...

Val did not speak too much about the place which we were now travelling to. Perhaps so as not to put us off I guess, as she knew full well that we were about to get the shock of our young lives; *what on earth could possibly go wrong now? I thought.*

Our journey continued on and out of the big city, where built-up areas were soon to be traded in for green open spaces and the miserable people masses for peaceful animal colonies, and where grey skies became perfect silent blues, and hard dominating dreary grey clouds, transformed into white fluffy cotton balls.

We recorded horses, sheep, and cows along the way and some very, very large houses, all with exceptionally manicured gardens. These were half the size of full length football pitches, and that was just the front.

The warm sunshine accompanied us throughout the journey, as if like a comforting umbrella of peaceful protection. If it was, clearly it was too little, too late? I guess it could have been, but only time would tell.

After napping and sitting, and opening and closing, the window in order to find the most comfort in the rear of her car, Val enquired whether we would like to stop at the Little Chef for something to eat. Well, the mention of food was indeed every child's main pastime. '*Never say never to a burger, chips, and shake,*' I thought.

Back then, Little Chef was indeed in its glory days, at the height of its fame so to speak. It was always a good place to stop and eat on the go: the burgers were a real mini meal in themselves, so beefy, so succulent, and so juicy; the buns were freshly baked daily and toasted to golden brown perfection and served warm: never burnt, never stale. The onions were soft, sweet, and tender, and the chips, well, they were a light crispy crunch and salted to total perfection: a master class for foodies on the go.

Little Chef had mastered its milk shakes to sweet precision; banana flavor was my favorite and still is, in fact. They were absolutely marvelous; they used generous helpings of ice cream to make it, so it was really ice cold with added banana flavorings; then they were whisked until creamy and frothy, served in a long, tall glass, from which you drank using a long straw: Every child's fabulous food heaven.

Whilst eating our food, we tried to quiz Val even further in the hope of obtaining more information, about this new place in the country, which we were now destined for. However, Val was not revealing too much; she was being very careful to only reveal just enough to keep us hanging on in there. At age eleven and twelve, we could not really understand the purpose for all the secrecy and suspense; perhaps it was the fear of putting us off what we were about to walk into. Strangely though, she kept repeating the words,

'Oh, if only you knew what I did to get you here! Oh, if only you knew what I did to get you here!' She kept on mumbling it over and over under her breath. I could not make any sense of it; it was like a mystery in itself. Then she would go really quiet and look down. She seemed forlorn, sad even. Then in a very low voice, she gave the first indication that she would no longer be our man on fire; not that she had been great at her post or anything or had actually even been on fire. In fact, she had been quite the opposite. However, this was probably the last time that we were ever going to see her in this lifetime.

'Why?' we asked anxiously.

'Why? We don't want you to leave,' I said, scraping up the last morsels of my warm apple pie and ice cream and speaking with my mouth half full.

'Well...' she said, pausing, 'I, I'm leaving,

'Leaving where?' we asked simultaneously.

'I, I'm leaving the department,' she said quietly, still stuttering.

'Why?' we asked again, with an almost apprehensive empathy.

'If I...' She stopped. 'If I...' she tried again. '... don't leave... Well... I'm sure, they will sack me anyway...' Stopping mid-sentence before she had said too much, she added, 'I guess I don't have a choice really.' She continued in a mumbled voice. I did not understand the words she was using. It was all Morse code and a bit like *cloaks-and-daggers* or a *who done it! Like Miss Marple meets Poirot,* I thought. However, Odette did. She always understood because she was way more intelligent than I was.

I mean, at the age of five, she could recall her alphabet forwards and backwards as well as tell you the corresponding letter to the number, and of course, she could count past 100 and then in reverse too, coming all the way back down to one again; and at age ten, she had already read the Holy Bible from cover to cover.

Odette would explain it to me, at least fifty times until I got it. I thought, as I licked out the remainder of the banana milkshake from the long slim glass, using the green and white stripy straw to slurp out the last bits of froth. The over spill of droplets of which had neatly aligned themselves together with the earlier tomato sauce stains already present down the front of my lovely white shirt. *Just one of my little party tricks, even to this day,* I might add.

Dad always said I did not know where my mouth was; of course, that was not entirely true; everything I ate just seemed to jump off my spoon at the last moment *somehow.*

After stuffing our faces full, we got back into the car and quickly fell asleep for the last leg of the journey. The road, long at times, took us through a place called Devil's Punch Bowl and up to a place called Petersfield out the other side, and along through a cluster of little villages called Clanfield Horndean and Cowplain, before arriving at a small village called Waterlooville. We pulled into the entrance of an old Tudor house, slightly set back from the road. This was Acorns?

Acorns

Upon our arrival, we pulled on to a large newly tarmacked driveway. To the far left of it sat slim trees with busy branches stretching over the small lawn. On the other side of the house, there was more shrubbery, and trees that were positioned directly in front of the house, which almost concealed it from the road.

I think the idea was that they should blot out the noise from the road. Back around to the rear end, there were more flower beds, shrubbery plants, and four fruit-bearing trees, two apple and two pear.

A single-level garage with the space for two minibuses was included in the extension. It was a two-floor extension, which boasted a large music come-play room on the ground floor, immediately next door to the garage. On the first floor there were three bedrooms and two bathrooms; one on-suite and the other for sharing.

The new extension was connected to the main house via a door that led up a small staircase and a long a short narrow hallway. It was only accessible from the first-floor landing, meaning there was one way in and one way out.

Impressively, the driveway was wide enough and long enough to easily complete a 360-degree turn in a large vehicle such as a mini-bus, or something similar and still have enough space for parking.

After dismounting from Val's vehicle and waiting patiently at the front door, which was oddly located at the side of the house facing east, we were all shown into the visitors' reception room. This was the first room on the right, directly opposite the staircase which stretched out on to two levels like the branches on a tree.

The reception room was a very posh- looking room, well dressed in a comforting décor of pastel lemons and primrose whites, warmed up with the natural browns in the form of the very hard wicker seating with matching coffee table. It was adorned with rectangular extra thickened glass as its centerpiece and polished to high perfection. Reflecting briefly on my earlier relationship with glass, I quickly looked away.

Overall, the room boasted an appearance that was exceedingly pleasant to the eye, creating a sense of light and space. Oddly, though, it did smell rather musty, a bit like death warmed up or something. Strangely, I think we all felt a little uncomfortable in that room, even after we had settled in. *Don't ask me if anyone ever died in there because I have no idea,* although it was not the norm for people to die in reception rooms. And I had absolutely no idea whether or not ancient bones lay buried under the floorboards either. Perhaps a more tailored explanation for the smell was that the windows faced north and east as opposed to facing south, so it didn't really receive the full benefit of the sun which it desperately needed, and the windows were never opened unless sister was having the room spring cleaned, which wasn't very often.

Apparently, the sisters were praying, or so I thought I had heard someone say, but I was not really sure what that meant. *'Sister, what sister,' I questioned. 'Whose sister, sister who? My sister is with me,'* I thought. However, it did not stop me from asking my sister rather peculiarly whether she was going to pray. I could not make any sense of what I had heard. *'What kind of set up is this anyway?'* God only knows what Odette thought about it all. She moved over to the window and began staring out of it. The sun was still shining; it was as though the day was beckoning for us to come out and play, as if in celebration of our arrival.

'Please can we go outside please?' I pleaded.

Eventually, Val answered, 'Yes, OK. But then just for a little while,' she added.

'Yes, yes!' I shouted, without listening to the last part of her request. We ran outside, full of excitement, and just at that same moment, the resident children returned from wherever it was that they had been and came out with us to play as well. We practiced hand stands in the grass and then posed together for photos. We had not yet noticed that all the children in this household were pale in complexion, barring one, he, a boy was mixed race.

However, the biggest shock was yet to come once the sisters arrived. There would also be more shocks, and they would inevitably continue right up to enrollment at the local schools; But for now, we were having fun.

Again, the papers were signed the tick boxes ticked, and we exchanged our goodbyes. However, this time, it took a little longer than usual. This was the last time it was expected that we would ever see Val again. We walked together through the garden, which circumference the entirety of the house, with her trying her hardest to say goodbye and with us trying our hardest to get back to the excitement. Eventually she left, and we waved her out the gate as she made the long drive back up to London.

We were then shown around the house by a girl called Tess. There were so many rooms to remember. Finally, she showed us to our sleeping quarters, which we would share with her and where we could unpack our half-filled plastic bags of odd bits and bobs, select our beds, and then wash up for tea.

Our main concern at that moment was exactly who was running this joint? And whether or not they beat up on kids or even permitted the use or threat of violence against them? In short, was this a place from where we would have to run? Tess assured us categorically that there was no violence here, but she also told us the joint was run by two sisters.

'What do you mean sisters?' I asked. 'Sisters like me and my sister?' I enquired further, not trying in the least to be smart.

'No, they're not, but some are,' she answered. Well, I was really confused now.

'They are nuns,' she said.

Clearly, I could not quite get my head around this statement, bearing in mind that up until this point, I had never even heard of the word, title, or phrase 'nun' before then, nor had I ever seen one in real life. However, I did see that film, where the beautiful Audrey Hepburn became a nun for a short while, before leaving the order and her vows, and skips off into the sun set with her on set leading man, gets married and lives happily ever after; or so the story goes. Albeit it was enough for us that there was no violence here.

When they arrived, I could not believe the way they were dressed. I tried my best not to stare at them. They were wearing beige looking dresses, which I learned were called habits. They had a piece of cloth on their heads known a veil. These were usually black in color, but could also be beige, grey, or blue; depending upon the order they represented, or at which stage they were at in becoming a nun. Sister was another interpretation for the name nun.

Our room was situated at the end of a long narrow hallway. It was adorned with a deep green olive carpet, the hallway that was. The walls were painted over in white, divided by a dildo rail also painted in white gloss. At the end of the hallway stood a window covered with a beautiful white net curtain, directly below it stood a little wooden table upon which sat a small china vase inside fresh cut flowers from the garden outside. I would come to learn that the flowers would always be there. And I would come to the realization that I hated it. It was all so perfect. What pretense, what pomp I thought. My life was far from perfect. This little innocent table would become my punch and kick bag for every moment of frustration over the next two years that I remained at Acorns.

At the other end of the hallway was a toilet with painted pink walls. Even the ceiling was pink, and the lamp shade, which was really too small for the light bulb was also pink. The seat and cylinder were jet black which seemed to clash with the pink. I hated this toilet; it was so cold and dark despite being painted pink. I always felt so uncomfortable using it. The window was always left open so there was always a cobweb or two and the spider that went with it somewhere in there. Quite coincidentally, it sat directly above the reception room. I think I used it perhaps once during my entire time at Acorns. *Creepy room.*

There were three beds in our room. I called it the sunshine room because the sun came bounding in every morning in spring and summer, she never knocked, and she never left until nighttime. The sunshine really made our room so bright and light and very warm.

My bed would be the one next to the window and Odette's next to the door. The third bed was for Tess O'Malley, the youngest of the three of us. Hers was positioned in between the wardrobe and the wash basin.

Tess was residing with her older brother, Toby. She was smallish in stature with a basin haircut, just like her brother's, in fact, except hers had been permitted to grow out at the back a little.

Toby was much taller than Tess and much stronger too as I would later come to find out. She, like her brother, was covered in face freckles, which I had never seen before, at least not to this magnitude. Tess quickly brought us up to date with her family tree, and we established that they also had an older sister, Tia. She too had once been a resident at Acorns; in fact, she had just flown away the previous year.

Of course, she did come back to visit her siblings whenever she could, which remarkably was not that often, considering she was a single person with no responsibilities, such as children or a husband or even a pet or anything; and when you come to think of it, she did not live or work that far away either. I guess, once you left, you just did not want to look back over your shoulder, not even for your own siblings, if you could help it; you just wanted to keep on going and simply forget.

We changed our clothes and went down for tea, where we met the other occupants of the household and were introduced to them one by one. Gino was the eldest; he was a long, tall, cool drink of water, and very handsome with it; a Greek god, some might say. He had auburn wavy hair that kissed his shoulders at every opportunity, particularly when he moved his head, which was very often; Toby would often tease him for it. Although he was always sweeping his hair back behind his ears there was nothing boyish or la fem fatal about him at all; Err... yes, he certainly did look finger-licking good, and of course, Odette had noticed that too.

He was a strong Italian stallion, who, after the departure of his two elder sisters, was residing alone; both his sisters now lived in Portsmouth, where they shared a small house together, and Carminella, the older of the two, was destined to be my godmother in less than a year to the day: only we didn't know it yet.

Toby was tall but not as tall as Gino. He always wore a polo neck jumper regardless of the weather. Then there was Aaron; he was the youngest of all the children residing. He was a mixed race, very temperamental young man; he could switch at a flinch, fly right off the handle, just like that and for no apparent reason. He was so annoying that Sister Black would often take the long wooden spoon to him and smack him with it. Of course, to hear that, your intuitive reaction would be one of complete disapproval horror even. However, after an hour with Aaron, you too would be begging her to take out the wooden spoon and to use it on him.

Then there was Jill, she was the helper to the nuns and would assist with the bedtimes, bath times and food prep. Jill was really nice; she was very quiet, a little shy even. She had short brown hair which she kept in a bob. She always wore brown over the knee skirts. Her blouses always completely covered her up and were only ever one of three colors, yellow, beige, or white. Over the top of them she wore a cardigan. These too were also one of three colors, yellow, beige or cream.

Monday to Friday supper was always served in the kitchen at the long table. It was at this table where speech impediments were corrected, and language was practiced until perfected. In other words, it was here that we learnt to speak the queen's language at the direction of Sr Bea. By the time of our departure we would end up speaking all plummy and toffee nose.

We went downstairs for tea and met the other children. We also met and were introduced to the two sisters who ran the joint. Sr Bea and Sr Black. I really had never seen anything like it before and had to keep picking my jaw up from off the floor. They were dressed in cream over the knee dresses, which flowed out from the waste and they each wore a black veil on their head, secured with a hair band that was also attached to the veil.

That night we ate a simple supper of cold meats, potatoes, and two veg; all washed down with milky tea and plenty of bread and butter. After the kitchen, had been cleaned and cleared, it was prayer time. We had no idea of what this entailed or even what it meant; our religious input up until that point had been very confusing if not completely warped. Nevertheless, it was a religious ritual, religiously performed by the nuns who clearly believed it did some good. They demanded that it had to be attended by all the children every evening, Monday to Friday.

After tea, we would all congregate in the TV room, where we would all kneel down and say many, many prayers, and we, the newbies were expected to join in, which we did, for a while anyway. For the first time, my knees really pained me, but I daren't complain I just kept it to myself. The session would last approximately thirty minutes before we would disperse into our groups for homework.

Our homework sessions were undertaken in the dining room. It was a cluttered room with overflowing side cabinets on every wall, and an array of clutter on top of each one. Light white nets covered the large sash windows, which were positioned in the center of the wall facing across from the door; they looked out on to a small section of the south-facing part of the garden.

Directly below the window lay a beautiful well-kept flower bed. It was filled with elegant roses standing tall and slim wearing deep red petals the shade of blood. The roses were accompanied by the Delphinium.

These were the sun seekers. Standing at around 5 feet in height and wearing mainly pink, with the odd purple petal for boast, – they always made me stop and stare. I guess subconsciously, I felt they somehow always looked out of place, the purple ones I mean; like me they loved the sunshine and therefore were strategically positioned where they could lap it up like thirsty dogs. Also, amongst them stood the Lupine standing at approximately three feet tall; they were the late bloomers arriving at almost the end of spring. They were dressed in subtle yellows and sometimes in orange with the odd pink dotted here and there. These were followed by the Foxglove also standing at 5 feet.

The gardener had carefully selected them in only cream, which had the effect of toning down the flower bed as he had selected quite a few of them. They stood in amongst the Delphiniums and the Lupines ensuring that they could take full advantage of the partially shaded areas; being pale their petals were quite sensitive.

They arrived on time, at the beginning of each summer with a life expectancy of just two years; ironically, that also would be the entire length of my stay, – unbeknown to me then. And it was these very heads that would eventually roll after being severed by my very own hand, following another meeting of where suddenness and calamity collided birthing another fit of rage. I would storm out into the garden pick up a switch and from left to right and right to left I would swing my arm until all heads were neatly off, now laying on the ground. And it was this window through which I would later make my subtle entrances and sudden exits.

On the remaining wall, there was a hatch which opened and locked from the kitchen side, and it was through this that Sunday dinners and puddings too, would be passed and positioned on the antique dinning, table. It was positioned in the center of the room and boasted a hidden compartment so that the table could be extended to include larger numbers when we had extra visitors; but that was not very often.

All the pieces of furniture were antique from some gone by era or other and were finished in an ugly, dark, mahogany, varnish giving a real gothic feel to the place; each piece standing boldly, as if claiming its position as of right, upon the awful burnt orange linoleum floor, which was beginning to sever gracefully at the join; that ran down the center of the room.

There was another door in the dining room which led down to the laundry room. It was partially blocked with all sorts of stuff and therefore, never permitted to be opened. However, you could still see whether or not someone was in there via the frosted glass panels on the door.

One entered the laundry room through the cloakroom, that was left out of the dining room and left again. It stank to high heaven of pea wee, the cloakroom I mean, as did the laundry room. The culprit of the stench was the cat-litter tray. Unfortunately, there was no ventilation and the tray was not emptied on a regular basis hence the smell. Opposite the cloak room was the conservatory which housed several bikes, one of which was destined to become mine.

Parental visits were usually carried out by the mothers, who visited even less than the older siblings who had now left, perhaps maybe once or twice a year at the most. In truth, most of the kids usually got really messed up after a visit from their mother; and it probably took the best part of a week and sometimes even two, to have them calm right back down and put themselves back together again. Their emotions that is, no drugs included.

I guess it was a combined effort really, the sisters plus the other kids to whom this task would be entrusted; but it was usually left to us, the kids, to pick up the pieces and counsel each other back to the land of the living. As the nuns, just didn't have the patients or the time.

On that note, I guess we were the lucky ones then as our parents never visited us; they never wrote, and they never phoned. We had never seen our mum since that day at the nursery, and now nine years on, I could not even remember the outline of her face. I never had a chance to run my fingers over it; to touch her face, to hold her, to hug her, to memorize her sent. I had nothing to remember her by, except her spirit. But this would one-day change, unbeknown to me then, and the clock was ticking... tick... tock... tick... tock...

We seemed to fit in quite well with the other children here, and the life and trauma of Grimshaw Hall seemed firmly behind me, or so I thought... Until that day, when Sister Bea came up to see me, she seemed quite nervous not her usual self. Her countenance filled me with anxiety once more. She said we had to go somewhere, but she couldn't say where. I was not getting a good feel feeling at all. We were not to go to school that day; instead, we boarded the train back to London and were taken straight to a court; can't remember where.

For us to remain in the care of the Local Authority, we had to become what they called 'Wards' but this was not *Jandice and Jandice*. We were going to become 'Wards of the State'. And of course, Jeanie wanted this to happen quite quickly so that we could remain at Acorns, because a child could stay there until they were seventeen or eighteen and usually, they did. She wanted us to settle down. *But at what cost? You had to have a reason a good reason to make a child a ward of the state and because dad would not sign us away the case had to be presented as if we were being taken away.*

When we arrived at the courthouse, we saw Dad, his wife, our brothers, the younger one who was still in the pushchair, and our sister. We went over to say hello to Dad, but he completely ignored us, turning his back on me as I was in mid walk of walking over to him. I felt so embarrassed, so shocked, so ashamed. It was as though he never knew us, and Mordecka, well, she just turned her back to us too. She had to stand up to do that, she looked silly facing the wall whilst sitting on a bench that was fixed to the wall, I thought. When she did rise to face the wall, she was actually standing too close to it. I was convinced she was going to start having a conversation with it.

Bobby just stared at us from where he had positioned himself in the corner; it was as though he had already been warned not to speak to us. As soon as Corina recognized us, she immediately came bounding over to say hello but was sternly summoned back midway. The baby didn't have a clue as to who we were. He was so young when we had left. I could only remember seeing him once, and that being at the hospital at the time of his birth. I remember that day as though it was yesterday.

We had to keep going in and out, and in and out of the court for the entire day, it felt like no one really knew what was going on; and it was true, no one did. We had to become wards of court, but no one knew the grounds for doing this, for making this happen. In my case, I was the one who had left home, and Dad wasn't saying a word.

On one occasion when we went in, and the clerk said,

'Well, if we charge them with theft, then we can make them wards of court because we can take them in on those grounds.'

'I'm not sure that's quite right,' said the lady Judge. 'Don't children get a warning or a caution for a first offence?' she asked speaking to the clerk.

'Err... yes, madam, but if we withdraw the caution and charge them with theft then they can become wards of court under that ground.'

'I'm not sure I like the sound of that, Mr. Cursor,' she said.

'That's the only way provided they plead guilty,' he replied.

The Judge then called us back into court again and explained the situation to us before instructing us to plead guilty. But I refused; we hadn't stolen anything. So, I was sent out again and then told to come back in and then the judge tried to talk me into pleading guilty, but I refused; I had done nothing wrong.

'Well, they don't actually need to answer.' Said the clerk.

'Are you sure about this, Mr. Cursor? I don't feel very comfortable about this at all,' she added. So, on that day, we were both charged with offences, we had not committed at the direction of the clerk and by so doing we became Wards of the State. There was no following of protocols with us. The English girls, on the other hand, were nowhere to be found; they did not even turn up to court. Even to this day, I can hear the judge's voice saying,

'Are you sure about this, Mr. Cursor? I don't feel comfortable about this at all.'

I guess their mother knew the great importance of having a clean name. We would later come to learn the damning effects and the treacherous repercussions of this injustice, just twenty-three years later, and the clock was ticking, tick tock...tick tock...tick tock.

I felt really down when I returned to Acorns; it lasted a good few days this time. Dad had kept his distance on that day. He said he never wanted to have anything to do with us ever again, and by his actions, it was definitely true that he meant it.

'Nice,' I thought. His words were so final and completely backed by his actions, he never wrote, he never called, and he never visited; And we never expected him to either. We were certainly not hanging on to any kind of false hope as far as family relations were concerned. Sister said we did not have to go to school the following day if we didn't want to. I spent the day in my room, but Odette decided to go to school. Another layer of depression was added to my bowels. I suffered with extreme constipation for the rest of my time at Acorns. Sr Bea would often introduce me to different potions to try and help relieve my pain and discomfort, but none of them really worked.

On that note, there was no comparison between us and those children with pent up emotions running riot through their veins, which clearly exploded each time their mothers visited. We were certainly not affected, or so we thought. Our only visitors were the SS, which, in this case, was Val's replacement, Mrs. Lolita Brown. She had relaxed well into her mature figure. She wore extremely thick milk bottle-bottom glasses and always dressed in some combination of frumpy schoolgirl greys or browns. She persistently insisted on taking us out to dinner once a month, (*what a nuisance)*, and always on a school night, which subsequently meant we were tired for school the next day.

Once she and Sister even got into a ruckus about the timing of it all; she was running extremely late that day, I mean, evening. We had not eaten, and it was late very late. We were pacing the floor walking up and down the corridor in our going out clothes. Of course, she won; still, once we were out, it was nice to be out. I guess it did not overly concern anyone because the following day was usually a Friday. However, our outings did give us our first taste at experiencing both Indian and Chinese cuisine. It couldn't really be anything else given that it was all the choice boasted in the village.

I guess it was not really that extravagant, and if my memories serve me correctly, both employed very poor DIY cooks, so it was nothing to write home about either. We were always usually the only people sitting in the restaurant apart from, maybe one or two other business gentlemen at most. I remember always staring at them rather discreetly, desperately wanting to be rescued even then, and not really caring by who; just so long as they were gentle and kind. The men were always dressed in really smart suits, occasionally one or both would look over at us and I would stare back trying not to be obvious.

After a couple of days of settling in, we were advised about schools. Odette was to commence the Pressing Reed Grammar School immediately; the following week, Sister Black took her out to get all the pieces for her uniform to the handsome tune of one hundred and fifty nine pounds and ninety nine pence. She had not had so much spent on her in one go before, ever, and certainly not in cash. I think she was glad to have some much-needed attention for once. In that moment, she was happy, so that's all that mattered, I guess.

Unfortunately, my outcome was not quite so simple; it included Sister Black deciding that I too could go to Pressing Reed, *now,* or if I wanted to,

I could finish the year out at St Mary's, the local primary school, situated just the other side of the fence, in fact. Tess was currently there, and so was Aaron. Tess was in Year 4, and Aaron was in Year 3.

It was Sister Black 's thinking that, given I had missed almost all of my first year at secondary school, perhaps it might be more advantageous for me (*I'm sure*) to start at Pressing Reed later in the autumn, at the start of the next academic year. I knew there was a catch in her presentation somewhere; however, I was just not sharp enough to figure it all out back then.

'Go to Pressing Reed now or later, go to Pressing Reed now or later...' was all I could hear in my head... I guess the lack of uniform should have been a clue, or rather a no uniform policy required for St Mary's.

Interestingly enough, what she failed to mention was that there were no children of color at St Mary's Primary School, neither were there any at Pressing Reed for that matter (just a small fact, which might have held some benefit in my coming to a decision about the whole thing). Later, I did, of course, find out that the truth was that she did not want to spend more than three hundred pounds on school uniforms in one go, primarily because the summer holiday period was just around the corner. It was already booked and already paid for, and she did not want to dip into the money she had set-aside for spending, because the SS had a reputation for being extremely slow payers; even back then.

Reading between the lines, what she was really saying was,

'I want you to go to St Mary's, OK!' just not in those exact words. I was eleven, about to turn twelve that year, and given that I had already started secondary school in London, to me it didn't really make any sense to revert to primary school and then commence secondary school all over again. However, in a bizarre twist of events and all the pressure applied, I stupidly agreed. I couldn't really understand why she kept raising her voice each time she asked the question...? As the kitchen began to fill up for evening tea, I became increasingly more embarrassed to answer her.

All the children wore their own clothes at St Mary's, so there was no initial outlay required there then. Of course, Sister Bea knew exactly what Sister Black was up to with me being the guinea pig of it all. Nevertheless, given the fact that I did not have any of my own clothes, some expense had to be laid out in respect of items needed for everyday living, such as T-shirts, skirts, shirts, jeans, that sort of thing. Items such as socks, pants, and vests, they appeared to have in abundance in different cupboards that were located high up.

We often had to go climbing about, scaling the high wardrobes, looking for clean knickers; of course, it was always my shoulder and my head my sister would be standing on, to assist her efforts in reaching the underwear. It was hard for the nuns to understand that we changed our underwear every day and that it was important for us to do that; this was how we had been taught by Dad and we wanted to continue with it, despite him not wanting to see us ever again. In the end, the SS had to get involved to really bring the message home. Anyway, after that, they began to allow us to keep some clothing in our room, but our cupboards were still quite bare and we still never had enough knickers; somehow, they would just disappear after the wash, but once we found out where they were kept, we would secretly help ourselves.

After supper and prayers, we were expected to join in with Gino and Toby for math's, no questions asked. The subject was taught by Mr. Smith. I would meet his daughter later at the start of the new academic term when I would join Odette at Pressing Reed.

Odette and Mr. Smith would frequently lock horns, clashing over his teaching methods, or rather his *lack* of them. It would usually end in one of them storming out.

Rumor had it that he had applied for the headship at St Mary's primary school. But he had been over looked because of his age. His second blow came at his failure to secure the deputy headship at the local grammar school. Both disappointments he had taken rather badly, and now being told he couldn't teach was perhaps a little more than he could bear.

When the day arrived to finally meet my peers at St Mary's Primary School, I could not believe my eyes; as the door to my new class swung wide open, my eyes ran around the room once and then a second time, only to be met with all these little white faces, staring right back at me. I could not have dreamt this up if I had tried. I had no idea of exactly how much I was going to hate it. I despised the feelings of being constantly on show. *'Exactly where were all the little brown children?'* I thought. I had never felt so exposed in all my young life: the feelings, the thoughts, the emotions were absolutely awful, overbearing in fact, and I hated every minute of it. But most of all, I hated it. What on earth had I signed up to?

I never saw Tess or Aaron during my short stay. I spent most of my time crying some mornings in the toilets, with even more mornings refusing to get up and get out of bed for school at all. I got away with it most days; however, Monday was sheet- change day, and I was not a happy bunny at having the sheets ripped right off me amidst pleasant dreams of better times, in better places, that had certainly not gone by; and those that I had yet to discover.

I would try every trick in the book, including having my sheets tied to the under springs of the frame of the bed, a trick I was forced to learn at Sanquingay Park; however, in that case, the course of action was taken to prevent the boys from ripping the covers from off of me. In the end, I would jump into my sister's bed and stay there until about 11 or 11:30 am. I would then creep into school and hide out in the toilets until lunchtime or until I was found and taken back to class or even frog marched before the teachers, whichever came sooner really. Surprisingly, though, the class teacher never even realised that I was missing, or if she did, she never showed it.

Usually, they would assume that I was not feeling well, and of course, I would just go right along with it, so they would send me home or to sickbay from where I would just sneak back to the house as none of the doors were ever locked. I would just sit on my bed in my room until home time.

Of course, it all came to an abrupt end, when something called communication was improved between the parties. Now I was stuck and unhappy until one fine day, the most popular boy in the school began to talk to me and kept on talking to me; it was really awkward at first. I thought it was some kind of joke, with me being the butt of it. I remember always looking around for the punch line. But it was real, and it was upon his association with me that every other child in the school began to accept me for who I was.

They too began to treat me with kindness and respect; they began to welcome me, which, in turn, made me feel accepted, and this was a good feeling, I think. Wherever I was, whatever I was doing, he always came to find me and sit next to me, which although boosted my own confidence and ego, it totally annoyed his own admirers.

I did have a wonderful class teacher who was very sympathetic and compassionate. Her name was Mrs. Joel. We did not use first names back then, but titles were no barrier. She always offered up k ind words of comfort and encouragement; she was indeed a very special teacher. It was as though she saw right through me, right into my aching heart that was burnt black with pain. I for one had holes in my soul, gaping holes.

It was as though some part of her connected to some part of me, perhaps she had a connection to pain. I didn't know for sure. I mean I didn't understand any of it back then. I just felt that she understood me, for me, and for me, at that time, this was enough. We got on so well that I even invited myself over to her home to hang out one Saturday. She looked shocked at first, and for a moment I thought she would say no and then even if she did say yes, perhaps the nuns would say no, so I did not want to get my hopes up, but she got back to me.

'As long as it's OK with your guardian, Jacqueline,' she said softly. After all the yeses were in, we arranged it for one Saturday. I wasn't allowed to mention it to the other children in the class. I met her daughter and her husband and her dog. She had a very nice house and I got on really well with her daughter. It was as though we had the same kindred spirit.

On the day of my visit, we went to the pictures, and when we returned home, we played all her board games. We ate home-made hot dogs with fried onions which I loved and drank home made lemonade. It was nice to forget for just one moment that I had stepped out of a clinical, loveless existence, even if it was for just a moment.

Subconsciously, even back then, I was searching, my heart was searching. Strangely though, despite her pleasantries and that of her husband, who only really made a flying visit, her house did not feel like a home as nice as it was. There was something very cold dwelling predominantly in her living room; it just did not feel like home. Something was missing. I did not understand it back then. I was just a kid. I was too young to work it all out.

Mrs. Joel's daughter and I after playing all her board games and making all the puzzles, played mental games, and thinking games from the afternoon right into the evening, which we really enjoyed, far better than the TV.

Kids back then were not preached to or educated by the TV for hours on end. They educated themselves and were preached to by parents and teachers and the church, which, in my case, were a bunch of nuns and of course the priest on Sundays. Soon it was time to go, Sr Bea came to collect me; it had been a wonderful day.

I loved playing board games growing up; my favorite games were Cluedo, which I always won; the strategy is to always ask your opponents for two of what you already have. I usually won at Monopoly too and didn't do too badly at Scrabble either. I loved it when the twins came over. They were great board game lovers too. They always brought lots of chocolates and cakes with them when they visited. Sister Bea would allow us to take just two chocolates at a time, until we saw Toby taking pure handfuls behind her back.

The twins played with such passion. Of course, they weren't really twins; they were a young married couple who were young at heart and who had also once lived at Acorns. They had met each other at Acorns, which added to the sweetness of their story. Religiously, they returned as often as they could, usually once every three months or so and Sister would always get lots of wonderful things for tea, which we would have in the living room at the large round table by the oval window, which fitted neatly in the space. I also managed to enhance my chess skills even further and learnt to cycle really well too.

I was given an old bike which Toby helped me fix up. We were all out on the bikes that day testing whether or not they were road worthy. As I went down the hill on mine Toby decided to do a U-turn on his with no hands in the middle of the driveway of course. I started to pick up momentum on the decline; once it became absolutely apparent that we were going to collide. I pressed the brake, only to find none – they did not exist. I had no brakes. oh no I thought. By the time I realised that I was going to crash into him it was too late. I could not even call out to tell him to get out of the way.

Crash! Bang! Wallop! Right into Toby and his bike. Upon making contact I found myself flying through the air before crashing back down to the ground with a smack and seeing stars above my head. Both the bikes ended up entangled around Toby. However, this would not be the only time that we would collide. Toby came over to help me up and we hobbled back up the hill and in to the house together. I was surprised at how well he took it, and how compassionate he was towards me. I had half expected him to kick off or something.

Speaking of bikes, it wasn't long before I had two, one of which I painted orange and then later sold, to one of the neighbors' children for the handsome sum of £30.00; her dad did make me sell it to him though.

At Acorns, things seemed to run very smoothly until the arrival of the Baileys. They were a brother and sister duo. Both were of medium build, boasting honey blond hair and very blue eyes. Saul was the older of the two and he was very, very funny. Sabrina was the younger one and the more secretive of the two. She didn't say much, and it was very hard to know what she was thinking. I would come to learn later that she was the one with the issues and I think Saul tagged along to protect her or at least try..

The nuns were very much into their daily rituals and religious routines which were almost military. Breakfast was at 07.15hrs Monday to Friday, with school departures commencing from 08.00hrs finishing by 08.30hrs.

Upon our return home, we would be expected to polish our shoes and place them in our respective cubby holes in the conservatory, which stunk to the skies of pee wee, there was no ventilation down there and it was often a while before sister would get round to emptying the litter tray.

Supper was religiously served on time, the same time every day, always at 5:30 pm sharp. We always washed our hands before tea, which was taken in the kitchen at the long white table. At supper, you had your language corrected as well as your manners tailored, and everyone had an opportunity to talk about the highs and lows of their day, and we laughed at each other. This must have been a good attribute as it was one of those things that I continued in my own life, with my own children in later years. Albeit we were not really permitted to laugh out loud at the table, but after Saul's arrival, this rule was going to be hard to maintain as it slowly began to make its way directly out of the window along with many others – even Toby the loyalist couldn't manage it.

After supper, we would take it in turns to dry up the dishes, followed by evening prayers; but again, with Saul in the room, this was another ritual that completely went up in smoke. From that moment onwards, life at Acorns was 'gonna be a blast'. From that day onwards, every prayer meeting was going to be a comedy piece: you could not have paid more to see a better show.

All of us would be laughing and rolling around the living room floor in stitches, trying to hide behind pieces of furniture that were too small to conceal us, in the hope that sister could not see us laughing at Saul's jokes and short sketches; even the loyalists Gino and Toby could not contain themselves.

We would all literally burst into laughter mid-sentence and try our best to conceal it. Raspberries were going off left right and center. Once they were blowing everyone would start laughing out loud; And on one occasion we even caught Sister Bea laughing too.

'Well, they say laughter is good medicine for the soul, don't they?'

Unfortunately, not all the sisters were able to see the funny side of life, and it wasn't just the starch in their habits either.

Most of the time though, Sister Bea was quite serious. She was petite in stature, but her feet pita pattered very quickly across the floor to take her to wherever she was going.

She always wore a house coat, which although she said was to protect her habit, I could not help but feel there was a permanent barrier between her and us. She had other idiosyncrasies, which I found utterly irritating, such as washing out the tin cans every time they were emptied. She would so carefully peel off the outer labels and wash the inside to a perfect shine.

'Why are you doing that?' I would ask irritated by her actions. 'is it going to be used again by someone?'

'She thinks Heinz is going to come and get it out of the bin and refill it with baked beans and say oh thank you very much we really needed that can.' Saul would joke and everyone would burst out laughing.

'One day they are going to be recycled,' she would answer enthusiastically.

'Oh, who told you that?' I asked.

'No one, I just know it so I'm getting prepared for it.'

'Yes, but it's not now, is it, so you're wasting your time.'

'Not really.'

'So is the rubbish man saying thanks then when he picks up the rubbish?'

Of course, that question got me one of her funny looks, only it wasn't funny. And with that I would walk away, and the argument would lay dormant for another day.

Saul and Sabrina were the only two children in their family, and their story was unclear. I remember Sister often reminding us not to question the children on their stories, but once we got to know and trust each other, we all volunteered up the ugly truth of our presence anyway.

Saul was like a walking comedian – everything he experienced he turned into laughter and made a joke out of it. He ignited life. We needed him, and it was great to have him on-board. He made life more bearable. After church he would say grinning,

'You see the wine, yea, how much do you take?'

'Oh, just a sip,' we would all respond in humble agreement.

'What about you?' I asked. 'How much do you take?'

'Oh, I take mouthfuls, I do,' he answered boldly. 'After I've had it, there is always hardly any left! He gives me a look, he does,' Saul continues, 'then he has to go back to his little cupboard and fill it up again. You should see the look he gives me when he looks at me. Like this he does.' Saul would make his eyes go funny in portraying his example of the priest.

'So, how much bread do you take?' I asked.

'Oh, complete handfuls,' he would laugh. 'Well, I'm hungry in I,' he replied. We would all laugh too. 'And you see the basket. You know, when you're supposed to put the money in, I take it out. I take handfuls, I do.' He laughs again. Once I got a fiva.

'Oh, that's for the poor, you know,' Tess piped up. We all laughed again. He had jokes on everyone and in every situation, which often earned him a couple of blows from Toby and a deduction in his pocket money from Sister, but it deterred him none. I appeared to be his only fan, or perhaps, we just had a similar sense of humor. He wasn't bad looking either as guys go. I really adored his mannerisms, and I loved his humor; it was my daily 'make me feel good' medicine and I needed it.

In hindsight, it was evident that kids in great pain will often cover it over with a blanket of great humor. They will try to suppress the pain with it.

Eventually, the daily prayers did come to an end, more so after our joint protest that we did not want to have them every day. What the Sisters failed to understand was that for kids like us, who had been through so much, prayers without understanding was like rubbing salt in the wound. We had no idea of what it meant to pray, or even how to pray; it simply felt like a ritual that gave only them, any kind of benefit, and the kneeling down really made my knees hurt.

Although they took our objections on board, it was not without perfect resentment and absolute disdain, an eternal marker against each one of those who had initiated and voted for change; clearly Odette and I were, no doubt, at the top of that play list. We would now have them only on Mondays after supper.

The next thing to go was Mr. Smith's Math's lessons; these were taught on Mondays and Wednesdays. They would usually involve a degree of screaming and shouting, and of course door slamming, mainly from Mr. Smith. In fact, only from Mr. Smith. It was a bit like severing the old soul ties with hot irons, if my memory serves me correctly.

Nevertheless, it had to be done. He was teaching us Math's, which did not even, in the slightest, relate to the school syllabus, and he was refusing to provide any methodology to his logic or conclusion in arriving at his answers, which annoyed Odette to the core and frustrated Toby and Gino, who really just wanted a quiet life, so never complained. In any event, he had to go...

'Bb-bub-bb-bub-bb-ba and its goodbye from him,' we all said with the voice of Tweety Pie, *who today still stands so proudly on the back of my eldest daughter's bedroom door, which she hand-painted herself just before her final year of secondary school.*

Sister enrolled us both at girl guides in her attempt, I think, to make us *better people*. Our leader was very nice and friendly and always invited us up to her home.

I guess the strangest thing of being back together with Odette was that we could not stop fighting, arguing, or falling out. Perhaps we had just been apart for too long? Had the cords that had once bound us together so tightly in love, now been completely severed... forever? We had both taken on the passive aggressive stance and so would clash at every turn.

Odette had absolutely no interest in my ideas or my suggestions, or anything I had to say, for that matter. It really irritated me rather immensely. Neither would she allow me to play Diana Ross in any of the dance shows we put on for the nuns. They were always planned, choreographed, directed, produced, and edited by Odette, with Odette always playing the leading role; Odette was always the star of the show and we were always the back-up singers and the back-up dancers.

The nuns loved our performances so much that they even invited the other nuns from the convent to come up and watch. I loved the applause. It made me feel good inside. It made me feel confident to the point where I too felt that I could also be Diana Ross as equally and as good as Odette, yet she was not having any of it, and the other two girls, well they just went right along with her. Whatever she said, they did, which sent me into such a rage that I began to demonstrate the worst temper tantrums ever; even I didn't know that I was housing such demons.

On one occasion, I turned Tess and Sabrina's room completely upside down; it looked like a bomb really had hit it. In one moment of madness, Tess's favorite ornament was broken. All this and for what – just because Odette had refused to allow me a turn at center stage. Tess and Sabrina had failed to back me even though they had said they didn't mind me playing lead. I hated the bossiness of Odette in that moment. It was always her way, or the highway and I could not stand it any longer.

Once I came to the realization of what I had done, I thought Sister would really be mad with me and expel me, excommunicate me, and pack me off to somewhere else. I was afraid, but when she came up and saw the mess she didn't; she just sat with her arm around me, talking to me, explaining to me all the disappointing things about life, and in particular, that if I did not always agree with friends and family, that was OK. It was here that I learnt that it's OK to agree to disagree; And that was safe. I felt safe.

I felt really bad for wrecking their room; it was a complete wreck. It looked like a tornado had passed through it or something. After helping me fix the beds back and making them up again, Sister Bea said she would keep them downstairs whilst I tidied the room back up.

However, it wasn't long before Tess noticed that the crystal glass ornament was missing. She was a collector of crystal ornaments; it was one of the first things she had told us about herself when we shared a room with her. When she enquired as to its whereabouts, I remember Sister blamed herself.

'Oh dear, I must have dropped it when I was doing the dusting,' she said.

'But you don't do the dusting,' Tess said insistently.

'Arrh... yes... (pause) but you know, sometimes I do help Mrs. Nicknameus,' Sister added coyly in her very Irish accent.

I knew then in that moment that Sister Bea had my back, and so I did not want to disappoint her by letting my temper loose again. That was barring one trifle and all the crockery in the house. *'Oopsy, Sorry about that...'*

We soon came to realize that every child in every place had a history, they all had a story; even the house we lived in had a story, and sometimes when they were not busy, the nuns who knew it would tell it.

Interestingly, the land upon which the school now stood was land that once belonged to Acorns. It was surrounded with grounds which went on, almost forever, from the rear, all the way down to the little brook in fact. It was beautifully adorned with apple and pear trees, which completely covered the land upon which the new primary school now stood. The grounds were divided by a driveway, which, to the right of it, was adorned with the most beautiful blossom trees; people would go there to take their wedding photos. When the blossoms were released it was truly a fairy tale scene, really beautiful.

Next door, which now boasts the priest's house, was the milking house; the entire site, in fact was a sort of mini farm; they had cows and pigs and hens and all sorts. But more importantly, all the food was derived from and grown on the farm or from farms within five miles.

Acorns belonged to the convent, which stood at the end of the long drive. The convent was attached to the church and later became attached to another place called Mansion Heights View. This was the extension that had been built on to the rear of the convent. Not really sure where the 'View' part of the name had been derived, because the building was not really tall enough to secure a pleasant view of anything. It was situated at the bottom of the hill. Nevertheless, on a scale of grandeur, it was to be aligned with the likes of baby mansions. Boasting 15 well-proportioned rooms, two with added accessories for cooking, I would find out more later.

A small brook ran at the bottom of the front garden, which was separated by the short drive way, which no one really tended to. It was almost hidden by the shrubbery that sat in front of it. I would often find myself going down there, just to be alone. I would lie down on the grass, amongst the wild free, growing flowers just to get away from it all really and get lost in my own made-up world of daydream; little did I know someone was watching.

After the sale of the land for the planting of the school, there were only two apple trees and two pear trees left, standing in a severely reduced garden. Conversely, a gate was erected within the garden fence, which opened straight into what were now the school's grounds. The deal was that we could enter and play there at any time we liked, without further permission. We had a lifetime easement over the land.

However, in practice, there always appeared to be thousands of excuses as to why it was not practicable every time I wanted to go there. Nevertheless, as soon as the new dew appeared on the ground, no one could stop me from opening the gate and tiptoeing barefoot upon the first new dew.

The cold fresh dew against my dark naked skin looked like diamonds in the sunlight; it was so beautiful and so gentle. I would run up and down, barefoot in the grass, my feet and ankles becoming speckled with droplets in the process. I would continue until Sister's untimely voice interrupted my fun, ringing out like an annoying bell, calling, 'Time for school! time for school!' – the evidence of what I had just done holding steadfast to the hem of my skirt.

Unfortunately, for me Sister Bea was not always 100 per cent in agreement with my antics. Such as the time when I crept out of the house in the middle of the night and began rolling around in the snow in just my pajamas. I didn't mean to lock myself out, the door just closed too quickly behind me. Truth be known, I had no idea of what I was doing. In one moment, I just lay there looking up at the diamond-cut stars stitched into the night's sky; all the while, my pajamas were becoming more and more saturated from the warmth of my body, now melting the snow. Then suddenly, there seemed to be a great light beaming down upon me, yet it was not emanating from the sky above. It was being projected from the bedroom window, Sister Bea's bedroom window, where she was now staring down at me in complete amazement, shock even. '*Oh no*, I thought, *how on earth am I going to get out of this one?*'

In a flash, Sister Bea was at the kitchen door, and there were more bright lights.

'Come in! come in!' She said, 'You'll catch your death!' She took me into the living room and stirred up the big open fire again, feeding it some more twigs and sticks to get it going a little. In truth, I was numb and could not feel a thing.

'What were you thinking out there all by yourself?' she asked in her deep Irish accent pulling up a thick blanket over my shoulders. Of course, I could not answer. How could I possibly answer? How could I even begin to make Sister understand what it was I was doing? My main concern was – what would Sister do now? I mean, clearly, I was well and truly busted; but who would she tell? Was I now to become the laughingstock of the entire village? One by one different scenarios made their presentations in my mind's eye, as Sister rubbed my back warm again, before taking me back upstairs, tucking me into bed, switching off the light and going back to bed; it was three in the morning. I never heard her speak about it again; even Sister Black never mentioned it either, so in that moment, I honestly thought I beheld Sister's trust. And so, I was able to relax a bit, at least for a while anyway.

Once we got to know where things were Sister would allow us to travel to the shops on our own. I could often be found in Boots the chemist. All its displays were housed in cabinets of bright lights, an allurement all of its own. However, on this occasion I was in the tin food section in the process of picking up a tin of baked beans, and contemplating whether or not I should steal it, '*don't ask me why*?'

Suddenly I felt a strange hand on my left shoulder followed by the words 'I thought I recognized you.' I turned around quickly only to see Mrs. Pepper-mount whom I was absolutely convinced I had left behind at Darlington Bassett all those many moons ago. Perhaps what was more bewildering was the fact that she was acting all friendly and nice towards me, like we were forever long-lost best buddies, or something; And that we were just reunited. She was now proclaiming what a God-forsaken place Darlington Bassett was, and how it was driving her crazy, and how she was so glad to be out of it. According to her, she had come down here to look after her sick mother, whom she had been pushing around in a wheelchair outside until she recognized me. How she saw me I don't know. In any event she felt that she absolutely must come in and speak to me.

I was guessing, '*is this an attempted apology after the way she had treated me?*'The only word I could find to answer all of her questions put together was '*a certifiable Yes*'. I had no real idea of why I had picked up the baked beans. I watched her leave the shop, '*perhaps for the back of her head*', and make her way back over to her mother, whom she had left unattended and diagonally parked on the pavement, practically blocking the constant flow of people traffic. People were now complaining at her when she came back out, but she just shouted back at them, telling them to shut up!

I waited until she was gone, before making my exit and returning back to Acorns, without the beans, using only the back roads not really wishing to bump into her again. I never saw her again, after that. Thank God. *Of course, I have forgiven her now.*

Spring term finally passed, and summer came, with it bringing the sunshine and the flowers into full bloom. We had after-school club in the last term, which was really cool; it was an outlet for most children. I got to try out badminton at which I found I was exceptionally very good at and my tutor positively commented. But I lacked concentration and needed a coach. I could not keep to anything in fact and perfect it, and not having a mentor or someone to guide me and encourage me didn't help matters either.

One girl at club brought in her brand-new bike and we all lined up to ride it, but it was clumsy me who ran her over with it, *by accident of course.* Oddly, she did not say anything, so I don't think she minded too much.

In the last week of the term, we enjoyed the sports day in which I came first in almost everything I entered until I sprained my ankle in the 100-yard dash; I never told anyone though, I never complained.

One of the best things that happened during the last few days at the school, was that our Year 6 was selected to receive a special silver plated 25-pence coin. This was in celebration of her Majesty Queen Elizabeth's II Silver Jubilee. Mine would be stolen exactly thirteen years later and the clock was ticking, tick tock, tick tock, tick tock.

I loved looking at it, it was so shinny and big and it came in a lovely dark blue case held in place by a crush velvet seat.

At the end of the last day, it was a total relief, mentally and emotionally; nevertheless, the worst was still yet to come.

Southern Ireland

The summer holidays had arrived, and we were now preparing for our trip to Ireland.

Just before the start or our vacation, Sister Black would ask me to collect up all the fruits that had fallen off the trees in the garden and then to climb up the ladder and pick any ripe fruit from off the branches that were about to fall. Sister Black had brought me a new red and white top and a rah-rah skirt to match. In truth, I was a jean girl, but it was the swish of the skirt that really encouraged me to wear it; and yes, I did notice Toby looking at me after seeing me in a skirt for the first time. Some of the fruit from off the trees would be put out on the table so we could help ourselves; the rest would be packed into boxes and loaded on to the van to take with us for our holiday. This was another ritual carried out every year before the commencement of our departure; of course, Sister would make all the usual suspects. Stewed apple, apple sauce, apple pie, and apple crumble, sometimes with pears too. And it was not long before I too began to try my hand at pastry. I started with apple pie for Sunday dessert, which everyone absolutely loved.

Our first holiday at Acorns was to the mid-west of Southern Ireland. We had never been on a real holiday abroad before, where we would actually cross the sea, so this was a real novelty to us. I felt that all my prayers sent up to heaven from our tiny little room on the Broadwater Farm Estate were finally being answered one by one.

However, our excitement was overshadowed by anxiety, regarding the existing problems consuming Northern Ireland at that time. After a lot of reassurance, mainly from Sister Black, accompanied by diagrams, including geographical maps, we soon became settled with the idea. At least, until something new occurred in the news, or was said out of turn, which would then cause us to become unsettled and rather distressed all over again, and she would once more attempt to resettle us, reassuring us that was not the part we would be visiting. And so, it was decided that we were not allowed to watch the news and she made sure that the TV never showed the news if she was around.

Eventually, the day came when we were to depart; oddly, though, we left very late in the evening. Sister Black at the wheel, she drove all night all the way to Holly Head without stopping. It was here that we were to catch the very last ferry crossing. Her idea, of course was that she believed if we left in the dead of night, we would wake up in Ireland, ready to start the new day. Yea, right! What she had failed to factor into her little equation was the fact that eight tired children would very quickly become eight miserable children, which, indeed we were, after having been woken up at twelve midnight to get out of the minibus in blustery conditions and take a seat on the upper deck of a very windy ferry, that was freezing cold. The seats were cold, and hard and very uncomfortable too; taking these factors into account, which when added to the fact that we were all very tired, did not make way for very nice little children either.

Once we came ashore in Ireland and touched down on Irish soil, the sisters soon found out that they had eight very hungry children, as well as two bulging tyres desperately in need of repair. After refueling the van with petrol and providing nourishment for eight hungry children, plus the added unplanned expense of two new tyres, we set course again to find our all new five-star luxury house in the country. *Wow! We could not wait!*

We were now becoming really excited at the very thought of it. I for one was imagining the built-in pool and add-on tennis courts, and everything else it was said to boast. Uncontainable eagerness, mixed with excited enthusiasm, was imprinted on everybody's face. Our venue was to be the highlight of our stay, and we could not wait to get there if we could just find there. It was because of this that we were able to suffer every other discomfort on the journey. We sung ABBA songs until we knew them off by heart, and the tape began to literally melt from the heat.

For those of you who have not already been, Ireland is a very funny place. At the end of every road you would find a sign, pointing in the direction of your destination, and at the end of that road, you would more than likely find yourself back on the same road upon which you started again; not any nearer to where you actually wanted to be. Your only recourse was to phone a friend or, failing that, to phone back home and speak to someone, anyone in fact, who had actually been there and who knew the roads or to follow someone who was driving to it or through it... *fat chance of that!*

After a period of witnessing Sister Black becoming completely stressed out, in her futile attempt at map reading and following sign posts simultaneously, asking for directions and then following the wrong road signs, we all began to throw suggestions at her of what we individually thought she should do; unfortunately, these did not go down too well either. It was late afternoon before we mistakenly stumbled upon, quite by accident, our luxury holiday pad. We all cheered, out of sheer relief more than anything else.

In total naivety, we all began to help unload the minibus, only to come face to face with the full knowledge of the awful truth. What shock, what horror, what disappointment, and it just kept getting worse! We all soon came to the dramatic realization that our luxury five-star holiday home was in fact some old, dilapidated house that was in an absolutely filthy state; the make-believe pool was in fact a rather large lake. It ran out in front of the house, taking with it at least three victims every year without fail or so the sorry tale went. The tennis courts were no more than overgrown lawns, boasting worn-out nets now trampled to the ground, with evaporating white lines.

Back inside the house, and the mattresses were all soiled and stained right through, and there were cobwebs everywhere. Everything and every room in the house required some kind of super deep cleaning; even I didn't have the tools for that, but the buck didn't stop there... welcome to the bathroom, which looked as though mud itself had taken a bath and forgotten to clean it or perhaps cleaned it with more mud. Even the nuns were repulsed at the sight, and that was certainly saying something.

When we asked how we were going to take a bath, they revealed that there was a convent nearby, and they would ask whether we could use their facilities on a weekly basis, for the duration of our holiday. It was in this moment, for the first time, that we began to eat up all our nun jokes; it was at this time that we were all thankful and relieved in our own personal way that on this occasion and in this instant that they were in fact nuns, and it was because of this fact combined with the complete boldness of Sister Black that we all got a free bath.

There was just one tiny hitch: Sister Black and Odette just seemed to keep on getting into a tizzy about something or the other for the entire duration of the holiday. Exactly what the problem was, I could not be sure. Nevertheless, it all came to a head one bath time. We had all had our baths now, and we were just drying off and grooming our hair, and creaming our skin when suddenly, there was a lot of pushing and shoving going on, even some raised voices; at which point the shouting commenced.

It later transpired that Odette had become somewhat incensed at the way in which Sister Black would continually fuss and fret over the long honey-blonde hair of Sabrina. Well, Odette needed the comb. There was only one, and Sister Black had it. She could not understand that we all needed to use the comb. Odette picked up the comb in-between twists, and when Sister Black went to snatch it back, a struggle ensued; of course, Odette won.

Truth be known, Sister Black was besotted with everything about Sabrina. She had eyes of deep turquoise blue and skin as pale as snow; she was your all-time favorite English rose. Sister Black 's doting and fretting over Sabrina was really too much and did not include anyone else, yet everybody noticed to the point that even Sister Bea had to make a comment. *I mean, she wasn't a doll or something.* And when considering in some thought, her warped obsession, it certainly was, I believe OTT (over the top), which I am sure was against the rules of engagement or something. I mean, Sister was obsessed to the point that she found herself, as we all did, rather bizarrely, making ringlets in Sabrina's long, golden hair after every bath time, using, you've guessed it, brown paper bags torn into strands; these would be twisted on themselves and tied around the hair to secure the ringlet in place, and it took forever.

I had a traditional afro, so it was shake and go for me. But Odette was not about to go out in front of the boys without first grooming her own hair; she had her pride you see, which was huge for a young Caribbean girl, more so when going through puberty. In any event, after receiving no response from her repeated questions directed at Sister Black, requesting the comb, of course she took it by force, and of course there was a struggle, and of course, Sister Black 's fingers were red, and well, rather twisted with imprints of the comb's teeth now as the only evidence that she had once been holding it; and of course, with Odette winning out in the end! I think this was the second disagreement Sister Black and Sister Bea had concerning us in as many months; '*oh dear, honeymoon period over then I guess.*' But, Sister Black, determined to have the upper hand, set out her plan in her own mind's eye. Deep down, she had a real spiteful streak, and I would come to find out that even after thirty years later she still had not mastered it. She still had not managed to discipline the flesh despite all her prayers and confessions.

We managed to tour quite extensively, during our stay, taking in places like the breath-taking views boasted by Tipperary, all the window shopping in Cork, hill climbing the big Brandon not far from where we were staying and the show-jumping in Dublin. The hands-on favorite was Eddy Mackin, and he didn't disappoint, stealing the show as per usual; another item on Sister Black 's bucket list and only God knows how many times it appeared there. Of course, she was, herself, equally besotted with the overall appearance of Mr. Mackin as she was with Sabrina, for he too had blond hair and blue eyes, a small man of athletic build in tight pants and long boots... Emm...need I say more.

We walked quite a lot throughout the trip, particularly enjoying our midnight walks which we carried out in pitch darkness, followed by delicious midnight snacks and a cup of hot chocolate upon our return.

Every day, for lunch, we shared a picnic of assorted sandwiches, crisps, biscuits, fruit cake, and very hot tea. Lunch always ended with the use of bad language blurted out by yours truly, me of course. It was the best I could do after having yet another cup of boiling hot tea thrown all over me by the delightful Sabrina. This was her usual jerk reaction after seeing yet another spider. *What did she expect...? I mean, we were outside for goodness sake.* Nevertheless, Sabrina was frightened of everything in the insect kingdom; and her reflex action was second to none which evidently meant that whatsoever she was holding in her hand at the time of a sighting would inevitably be jerked upward and outward, landing on whosoever was in front of her, which on this occasion, happened to be me. No one ever said, 'Oh, Jacqueline... Are you OK? Did she burn you, Jacqueline?' or 'Are you burnt?' Oh no, the only response I ever received was, 'Do you have to use that language?'

'Well yes, I did.'

After picnic number three and the third cup of boiling hot tea being thrown on to my leg this time, I demanded that Sabrina was to sit as far away from me as possible when she was eating or else, I was really going to kick her head in. In the end, she would say, 'Please, Jacqueline, please, can I sit next to you? Look, I don't have a drink.' So that was her compromise.

We did eventually manage to fix the net on the tennis court in the backyard or rather, I say we, but it was really Toby and Gino who did it. I met and befriended some of the locals, me being me, they would always invite me in for a cup of tea every time I visited their house. We were also given access to one of the rowing boats, which we were permitted to use to cross the river over to the small island in the center of it. I never actually got to visit the island, I always seemed to miss the boat when the others made the trip.

There was one occasion when the tide was up, and it was absolutely impossible to see where the bank ended and the water commenced, particularly because of all the floating leaves lying still pretending as if they were on dry land. On that occasion, Odette was the last to board the boat; when she placed her foot on what she believed to be the bank and then raised the other to board the boat, she began to sink rather rapidly. Gino, in utter panic, let go of the ores. They sank to the bottom. And he began grabbing frantically at her without success as she sank. It took all of five seconds before she had completely disappeared in the dark murky water. I just stood there mouth open wide. Then with one mighty strong arm, he lunged down deep into the water, grabbed hold of her hair, which was in a neat bun on top of her head and pulled her up out of the water, wow! She came up crying. I stood on the bank mouth still wide open. He pulled her on to the boat and tried his best to comfort her like a baby in his arms but in her upset mood she jumped out of his lap onto the bank, stormed into the house, and went upstairs. Once in the bedroom, she tried to have a strip wash at the sink. They both blamed each other for the mishap, but I think they both secretly enjoyed the bodily contact, as brief as it was. I saw the way he looked at her, and I noticed the way she looked back at him too.

The other thing we fished out of the lake were eels. We brought them into the second kitchen and tried without success to cut off their heads.

Every time they squirmed, we would run out of the kitchen, screaming, waving our hands above our heads, *as you do.* It was interesting that neither Toby nor Gino, the two biggest and the two strongest alpha males, were unable to help; suddenly all their machismo had completely evaporated. In the end, we placed the live eels in the freezer and forgot about them.

I think we climbed Brandon Hill exactly three times during our stay in Ireland, and the views appeared exceedingly more beautiful with each climb. In-between climbs, we would visit the beach, try out the home-made ice cream, and even visited the pub. Children were allowed in the pub, at least this one; anyway, we were all given free fizzy orange juice and a free sweet from the sweetie jar by the landlord... *I think you call it - bliss...*

Unfortunately, on the third occasion that we climbed Brandon Hill, all did not end as well as we had expected or even anticipated. Somehow, perhaps even accidentally or on purpose, I don't know which, we managed to lose the nuns. We came down Brandon Hill, and they were nowhere to be seen – even the van had gone. For some strange reason, we thought we should go back to the house, and so we found ourselves hitch-hiking all the way back to our holiday home in Montgomery.

It was in this moment, we discovered the true extent of the generosity of the people in Ireland and, in the same breath, the terseness of the nuns. We did not even have to pay for the lift, which was good. the first truck took us to the end of the long road that led to the road which connected to the town, which joined the road, and at the end of which was where we were staying.

We walked for just a short while before the next vehicle carrying a young couple offered to stuff Tess, Sabrina, Odette, Aaron, and me into the back before happily driving us all the way to the road from where we would endure a short walk, bringing us up the short drive to the house where we were staying. They were a very happy and kind couple, and they talked all the way.

When we finally arrived back, we had not been there long, if all of five minutes, when we heard the nuns' mobile come *stretching* around the corner. '*So, they can drive,*' I thought to myself turning to see exactly who it was behind the wheel. Of course, when they came over to us, voices were raised, as if guns a blazing. You could have raised the roof, and of course, it was all Odette's fault. Surprisingly, for the first time, I now knew how she felt at always being blamed for everything and everyone else's failures. Five years of always being blamed by my parents and now this? The thought alone was enough to make anyone pack up and leave. Almost spontaneously we all began to stick up for her, because we had all made our own decision to leave; we could not find the nuns and the nuns' van was not where we had left it; or so we had thought.

What we did not realize was that we had come down the hill on completely the wrong side; even the nuns had not noticed. Of course, the nuns rebelled, and we all ended up in the doghouse, so it was a very long time before tea. And, of course, Odette would not eat again. Back then, that was how children made their point by the willful, deliberate, abstinence from food.

The next day, sadly, was the day of our departure. Yes, we were all a bit melancholic because unanimously we had all felt the sincere warmth of the Irish hand extended in such friendship and with such love, and we all felt that we had received so much more; it was real, and we all felt that it was very tangible too. We had found no racism here and no prejudice either; none of us wanted to leave. We cried on the boat going home, except the older boys that is, and I think we all must have thrown up too. At least once any ways.

Starting Over

Once we arrived back, it was only a few days before I too would start at the *same* local secondary school as Odette; it was a grammar school back then, which opted for conversion during our time there. In the very same week, I also entered into puberty, which was really awful. We had to ask Sister for towels, which was even worse because you had to make sure no one was listening, and sometimes Toby would jump up and say, 'Ha-ha I know what you said, I heard that.' I would always beg Odette to ask Sister for me, because I just found the entire process so demoralizing and humiliating to say the least.

Unbeknown to the pair of us the same second, we got back, secret evil arrangements were being made to have Odette packed up and shipped out to Mansion Heights View by Sr Black.

When the move actually happened Sr, Black told everyone that it was because we kept on fighting, but in truth, it was because she herself kept winding Odette up to the point where Odette would always retaliate. Sister Black said it was for three weeks whilst she herself was set to be away on her own holiday. However, after about week four, I think I began to ask questions; at about six weeks, it seemed clear that Odette was not coming back, and no one was talking. Apparently, she was going to remain at Mansion Heights for the rest of her time as a Ward, or so we thought.

Mansion Heights had a completely separate and distinct set up compared to Acorns. There was a certain degree of equality and mutual respect afforded to all the girls there, by all the nuns and this transcended throughout the entire structure of the house; it was really no surprise that she did not want to return even after Sister Black had. I guess it was Sister Black who ended up with egg on her face again then. Of course, once she left, it was all really hard again, at least until Sister Bea and I devised our own method of communicating without speaking. I would leave a note under her door, and she would place the goods under my pillow. This worked really well, at least for the remainder of my stay anyway.

Secondary school was again filled to the brim with more strange faces; it was only Odette and I who offered up any color to that place, not forgetting the t wo Spanish sisters and the one black boy who was in year 10 and practically on his way out. However, it was us who were the lucky ones, if the Spanish girls managed to reach Odette's complexion after a long scorching hot summer in Spain, then there would be four of us who would be classified as non-white. I guess it took the heat off of us until winter, when their tans would once more begin to fade.

School was a complete and utter nightmare. It was the thorn in my side marred with racism, prejudice, discrimination, inequality, and oppression, all thrown into the mix. Our work was constantly marked down, we were never praised or encouraged for anything, and everyone called us names, including the teachers.

The series *'Roots'*, by Alex Hayley was on at the time, so you can just imagine the language and the fighting that accompanied it. I could have killed Alex with my bare hands; I hated that show, with every fiber of my being. Every day I was met with phrases like – 'You Nigger!', 'You Blacky!', 'kunta kinte!' or the all-time favorite 'You Black Bastard!' which was very common back then.

Every week, I was in the deputy head's office because I had retaliated by punching someone. It got to the point where he would just say, 'OK, what have you done this time?' or 'OK then, see you tomorrow,' or 'See you later, then.' It was from that moment on that my visits to his office became fewer and farther between until quite miraculously, they stopped all together.

Sister Bea wanted us to take up as many hobbies as we could, so before she left Odette and I joined the Girl Guides. She even allowed us to visit the youth club, but just once. And it was really once too many because after just one taste, I wanted a constant repetition. I wanted more. It was only held once a week on a Tuesday evening at the local community hall.

Children from all over the area would attend; the hall was massive, and I wanted to go every week. The music set me free, something inside me would come alive, it was my doorway to freedom; nevertheless, Sister Bea was not having any of it. We wrestled over the issue for about three weeks before I threw in the towel. I'm positive she regretted ever opening that can of worms and I'm sure she wondered what on earth she had let herself in for because when she tried to close back the lid, she had a real fight on her hands.

Just before Odette's departure, Sister Black had asked us both whether we would like to stay at Acorns permanently. Well, of course, we did; crazy school kids and teachers aside, we felt safe there. Then she dropped it...

'Well, if you want to stay here, you will need to become Catholic,' she said. Of course, we had no idea what she was talking about. It all sounded gobbledygook to me. Odette looked at me, and I looked at her in pure bewilderment.

I don't think either of us really understood what we were letting ourselves in for, and the nuns were not very good or open to the idea of explaining anything in any kind of depth, so none of it made any sense either, not to me any way. Sister Black showed us a scripture in the Bible and would point to it saying,

'There, that's what it means...' and '...that's what you say.' Sister Black had given us an ultimatum if we wanted to stay at Acorns. We would have to become Catholics. I could not understand what the crap was going on, but I felt I had no choice, and I'm sure Odette, more than likely, felt the same. I remember feeling so uneasy about the whole thing.

'What on earth was I signing up to?' I thought.

Odette went around, asking all the other children if they were Catholic to which, surprisingly, they all responded 'yes'. But it was Aaron who was the only one able to offer up an explanation that even remotely made any sense, about the whole thing. It was all really double Dutch to me. But somehow, we both felt tired of that feeling of being constantly on the move, we needed to settle somewhere, and perhaps this was a step in the right direction. So, we said an unequivocal yes to the whole shebang.

Our catechism lessons commenced immediately as did the search for four sets of godparents. We had to have two sets each. God only knows why, it's not like you're ever gonna see them again after the big day an' all. No one really takes it seriously.

Odette asked the Girl Guides' leader, to which she immediately agreed with huge tears streaming down her face. She said she was so over the moon and always hoped that someone would ask her such a question – meaning she really saw it as an honor to be asked such a question.

The intention was for us to take our first communion in time for the Archbishop's arrival. This had been scheduled to correspond with the special harvest event in the Catholic calendar that occurred in late autumn, if, of course, I could just behave myself until then. He came every year around that time, so the gear up was on and the preparations had started. By now Odette had secured both sets of her would-be godparents, but the search was still on for mine.

Unfortunately, as life would have it, I was not able to take my baptism and Holy Communion with Odette as I had been naughty again. By this time, Odette had already moved to Mansion Heights on a permanent basis, so it was thought best that we should take them separately anyway. I found it really irritating to be second guessed all the time.

In any event, I seemed to have located mine in the eleventh hour with the help of Sister Bea; she took me over to see the church cleaner, Lenny, and of course, Sister had already asked her behind my back, and she had agreed, also behind my back, so when I came to ask her, when I finally managed to get the words out, she just said yes. The second godparent was Gino's sister Carmelina. She was a lovely girl. She had such a vivaciousness about her that was infectious as it was attractive. The irony of it all was after this big day, I saw her only once more and then never again, and I never saw Lenny again either, despite the fact that she only lived just two doors away.

They never remembered my birthdays or sent me Christmas cards, they never called or came to visit. What was the point of all that palaver and performance and dressing up? I thought when clearly by their actions they hadn't meant a single word of their declarations which they had made before God.

To be a godparent is to make a promise before GOD that you will help bring this child up in the ways of GOD and step in if the parents can't be there or are not there. Being a godparent is more than just collecting certificates with names on and repeating declarations you have no intention of ever keeping; *isn't it?*

With Odette now at Mansion Heights I hardly got to spend any time with her at all and once Jeanie got wind of it, she stepped in to save the day by ordering that a visit be arranged ASAP. We had not seen each other in well over eight weeks now.

When we finally did meet again, we were only permitted twenty minutes, and we were not allowed to be alone. It felt as though we were in trouble again, only this time no one knew what we had done wrong; including us. Odette seemed very distant, not caring at all about what was going on or what was happening to us; we seemed to be drifting further and further apart or perhaps she had just become very good at camouflaging her feelings or perhaps this was her tipping point. *This was another characteristic of the looked-after child.* Perhaps it was all part and parcel of the experience, the journey, the ride.

Eventually, I was permitted to visit Odette every week, after Sunday lunch. I found it quite pleasant to visit her at this time of the day. I would walk down the long drive way from Acorns by myself, taking in the scenery of the small primary school on my left and the blossom orchard on my right. It was a quiet time of day. When I arrived, they were all about to settle down to the Sunday matinee. They would set up plates of cheap cakes, biscuits, and tall pots of really bad coffee, with a few bags for tea lovers, which you could help yourself too during the film. Odette only drank coffee, so each time I visited her so did I.

We always had to say our goodbyes before evening tea. I didn't like having to leave or say goodbye because it made me feel as though I was being pushed out; rejected even. But I never told anyone how I was feeling, I would do no more than to stuff these emotions into my already bulging suitcase on life.

Odette never said much at our meetings. I remember beginning to feel always as though I was a burden to her, yet I loved her so much, and so desperately wanted to be with her all the time; she was everything to me: mother, aunty, teacher, protector, dentist, doctor, sister, and best friend. Albeit I never felt as though any of my feelings of endearment were ever reciprocated, at least not in the same way that I held her in my heart, which piece by piece was breaking.

She hardly spoke to me on any of my visits, yet I still settled into the routine of their Sunday-afternoon teas, which were far from high tea at the Ritz, but it was the best they could do with what they had. The sequence of events that unfolded never changed. After the movie we would kiss and hug and say our goodbyes exactly in that order. I would, of course, then leave without a fuss or even one word of objection and walk back up the long drive to Acorns alone. I think the horrid truth became quite evident that I was in fact her Achilles heel, the thorn in her side, still very much intact.

Gradually, my visits decreased, becoming fewer and fewer, until eventually not at all. No one noticed, not her, not them, and certainly not Sister Bea; and no one complained. I think I had become somewhat tired of drinking really bad coffee, eating processed cakes and sweet biscuits, whilst watching the boring black and white Sunday afternoon matinee.

However, there was one very good advantage of not having Odette with me full time, under the same roof. I fitted very neatly into her shoes. Now I called the shots. I told the girls what to do, where to go, and when to do it. About that time, we had two more new arrivals. They too were sisters, but there was in fact three of them. The eldest being in her teens had moved straight to Mansion Heights. I would have my encounter with her later, but for now, life continued with Bella and Annabelle. And I would wait just seventeen years to hear her trumped-up announcement accusing me of leaving her out and, wait for it, *bullying* her of all things and then she would sock it to me with her really rude hosting skills, or rather lack of them. I felt horrified at the news as true as the former part was – I mean, if my memory served me correctly – wasn't she the one who was just too slow and too awkward and too much of a tell-tale to roll with us, *the girls?* And wasn't she the one who wanted her Barbie dolls to accompany her everywhere she went? The decision was unanimous: all the girls felt the same, including her own sister. In any event, she always appeared content in her own little world of Barbie land. *I hated dolls.*

The nuns did have some pretty strange festivals, though, which they always wanted us all to join in with them and celebrate. One was midnight Mass; this happened every year in the Catholic calendar on 24 December.

On Christmas eve we would be sent to bed early; then we would be woken up around 11 p.m., get dressed quickly, and run down the long drive to the church. Our pews were always reserved for us, second row from the front and to the side of the altar. *This did kind of make me feel a little special. More so when someone sat in them by mistake and had to be asked to move, it was then that I felt famous, even if just for a moment.*

We had no idea of what was going on in the ceremony. In one moment, we could be standing the next sitting then standing and singing, then standing and praying. We would place the money given to us in the basket, mainly coppers really, sometimes five pence pieces, and pass it on. I know now it was supposed to be our tithe, but no one explained it to us back then, so for much of the time, we were just left in the dark and really confused with what was going on; at least I was anyway.

We would say the 'Our Father', 'The Creed' and the 'Hail Mary', all of which I can still remember by heart even till today. We would listen to the priest's message and then take part in the Lord's Supper followed by the grace before returning back up the hill to the house, filled with excitement at the thought of opening all our presents. And possibly thanking God that it was all over because it made absolutely no sense.

I think I was really too tired to appreciate the entire goings-on or the true meaning of Christmas, but I do remember that for my first Christmas at Acorns, I received twenty-three presents in total. It was the most presents I had ever received in my entire young life. I was clearly in my element. I felt as though I was floating. It was my best Christmas so far. *Thanks GOD!*

The New Year came in, and I was signed up for ballroom dancing and ballet as well as still attending the Girl Guides. I had the same instructor for ballet as ballroom dancing, which were held on the same day, a Friday, and in the same place. Sr Bea would drive me down and pick me up afterwards. I found I was very good at dance. However, when my tutor realised my potential, without telling me, she decided I should take on some extra lessons at no extra charge, but of course, I saw it as a punishment.

To my mind, I was already missing half of my favorite TV programs, especially the first fifteen minutes of *The Professionals*, and now, she wanted me to miss out on something else.

'Well, oh no,' I thought. 'I am not.' I said to myself. I explained that I was unable to come on any more days or do any more hours to which she became rather incensed and said quite emphatically.

'Well, if you do not accept these extra lessons, do not bother to continue to come at all.' I was really quite shocked at her somewhat stark response.

'Fine,' I thought; as I stormed off behind the last two girls, who had gone before me, telling her exactly the same thing and also jacking it in then and there. At no time was I able to understand her point or see her generous proposal as a compliment, and no one was on hand to assist me in my limited understanding either.

Teachers were not very good at giving appraisals back then; neither were they very good at explaining exactly what they meant by their statements, which usually appeared as arrows of criticism and always fired straight to the heart. They could not give a compliment if their lives depended on it. So, the request to take extra lessons was easily seen or rather interpreted as a punishment, especially when accompanied with the words,

'Well, if you don't want the extra lessons, then don't come back!' And being as stubborn as I was back then, my answer was always going to be the same.

'Well, fine then!'

In later years, it was indeed another decision I would come to regret. I mean having a natural flare for dance, clearly, I would have really benefited from the extra tuition. However, I still do remember some of the steps and can often be seen dancing the waltz on my kitchen floor with my youngest daughter, who, like me, also has a passion for dance.

New Shoes

Sister Black also left Acorns not long after Odette, in fact. I heard she took a leave of absence, but I couldn't help thinking it was to improve herself. In any event, it became an indefinite sabbatical. And whilst she still occasionally came to visit, she never returned to stay, at least not in my season anyway.

There is a time in every young girl's life when she will need new shoes and I was no different. I cannot begin to tell you of the elation it brings to a girl or a woman when it is time to buy *new shoes* and by the time Easter arrived, I was really in need of new shoes, and so after school, I went with Sister Bea and Hannah, the new home help, to see if we could get a pair in the village.

Hannah had replaced Jill; she was a lot younger than Jill and it showed in more ways than one. She was noticeably overweight and said the most stupid things, all of the time. Her greasy hair was kept back in a low pony tail and she kept a white coat over her normal clothes attempting to be like Sister, but I think it just annoyed the children than to assist in her bonding with them.

We went to every shoe shop in the village, four in total. I was exhausted. Thankfully, the style that I wanted, that I had dreamed about, could be purchased in the last shop, only, just my luck, they did not have my size in stock and would not have it until the following week, on Wednesday. Of course, this infuriated me to the very core. I needed new shoes, and I wanted them now!

Sister left the shop early as she had a prayer meeting at the church every Monday evening, so she did not want to be late. I was left with Hannah to walk back down to the house with.

Hannah tried her best to talk to me, but I was not in the least bit interested in what she had to say. Truth be known I found her so patronizing, to say the least, all of the time and today I was not prepared to tolerate her at all.

The gap between us began to increase, with me lagging further and further behind. It must have been about four houses along, the gap that is, when in one of the front gardens, they were doing a lot of renovation work;

the front yard was definitely a construction site. Upon seeing it, and in total frustration, I pulled off my shoes and threw them deep into the heart of the construction site. Then I walked the rest of the way home only wearing my socks. I marched right past Hannah, who did not even notice a thing. But Sister was no dumb blonde.

That night, I went to bed feeling very pleased with myself believing my actions to be rock solid and completely undetectable. I sank satisfyingly into the covers, knowing full well that in the morning, I would have no shoes to wear to school and ultimately would not be able to go.

'*Ha ha!*' I thought to myself. 'Stick that in your pipe and smoke it!' I thought again. I was so keen to see what Sister was going to do about it. Exactly how was she going to handle that! Either she was gonna have to write a note for trainers or a note to explain my absence, and I couldn't wait.

When the morning came, I got up, got dressed, with the intention of heading downstairs feeling very proud of myself, in my mind holding up the banner of victory; I was absolutely elated. I swung open my bedroom door to go down stairs for breakfast. I stepped out of my room, only to get the shock of my life.

'Oh, my goody gum drops!' It was a like a car coming to a sudden halt with screaming breaks. I gasped. My mouth fell wide open as there, right there sitting on the floor, parked right outside my room was the very same pair of shoes that I had thrown deep into the construction site, now shining, staring right up at me, gleaming even.

'*How did she know?*' I thought. '*I hate you,*' I thought. I put on the shoes, and without speaking a word, I ate my breakfast and went straight to school without speaking a single word to a single person.

That night, Sister Bea and Hannah had mounted the fences and trespassed onto private property to relocate my old shoes, and they had found them. Sister cleaned them up to a perfect sparkle before parking them right outside my bedroom door; I had never seen them so shiny. *Of course, it was one to her nil to me.*

The following week though, I finally got my new shoes. My uniform was now complete, my ego intact, and now, according to me, I was the coolest dressed kid in the school with the smartest uniform, or so I thought.

The year skipped on by, and eventually Hannah was asked to leave. It was no surprise really, more so after her final stupid remark, where she had informed me that I would never make it as a dancer because of the color of my skin. In that moment, I felt so crushed, so hurt and so disoriented; it was as though I had had the rug pulled right out from under me. Upon hearing her remarks, the other children were so incensed at her comments; they all bitterly complained and so she was asked to leave. Apparently, her choice of words were at times unacceptable, even to Sr Bea.

After Hannah, we had a new helper called Simone; she was of real Indian descent which I thought made her more interesting as a person. Except, just like Hannah, she was of no help with homework. However, Saturdays did become more tolerable as we learnt to cook different things in the kitchen. Our culinary efforts were stretched to include home-made bread, scones, doughnuts with jam inside and baked rice pudding. The jam doughnuts were a very messy operation. The sugar and jam went everywhere. Albeit they were very tasty. The house felt like home as the smell of warm bread filled the hallways. The rice pudding on the other hand refused to set, which was rather annoying.

Sunday afternoons would once more become filled up with visiting Odette again at Mansion Heights. It seemed as though no one was bothered except Jeanie who insisted we continue with our meetings; even from London her strong-arm commanded authority. I would join in with them in watching the afternoon film and having afternoon tea, usually accompanied by cake and biscuits. Just as I had convinced myself that I was a burden to her, she began to show me around the house including her bedroom. I felt as though she cared again which was nice even if it was just for a moment. Her room was all different shades of green, each one complementing the other.

The walls were painted in a light spearmint, her duvet was one shade up in willow green, the curtains were deep grass green, and her carpet was rich jade. It was always spotlessly clean and very cozy. I loved just to stare at it from the doorway. A couple of times, she even invited me in and allowed me to sit on her bed but only for a few minutes though. With this gesture, I felt that perhaps she liked me again even if it was just a little. Afterwards, we would go back downstairs to watch the rest of the film and have more tea and cakes. We never really got to talk much, but she would always end by saying,

'Please, be good. Then you can come and join me here, OK?'

'OK.' I said, convinced I could make her happy.

That was all I wanted, just to be with her again. I loved her so much, I wanted to be with her all the time. But she no longer felt the same about me. I was so blind I couldn't see it.

Jeanie did arrange for Odette and me to see separate FPs. It was her final attempt at happy families but went down like a led balloon. She believed that children should be raised in families; so, we went for a weekend, just one, in order to please her. On arrival our meeting was cold and distant, nothing really took off. They didn't speak and I didn't speak there was no real connection on an emotional level, it was almost like meeting the ice queen, for me anyway. Perhaps I didn't give it long enough. Perhaps we should have given it another try.

By January 1978, I found that I too had outgrown Acorns along with all its inhabitants. According to Rudolf Steiner, children go through a 'coming out' stage, which commences at any time around the ninth year becoming fully developed by the twelfth year. It is in this cycle that children begin to form their own identities and personalities.

At age twelve, perhaps, I was a little late in not being able to fully verbalize what I was feeling. I only knew that I felt emotionally stifled. Just like a bird needs to spread its wings and fly I also needed to express myself creatively, and here at Acorns I felt I was being held back. I felt bound despite Sister giving me some small token of independence, in giving me my own bedroom. It was in fact her own old room, which was on the other side of the house. It backed on to the road. It was noisy and dark allowing hardly any sunshine. She did add on an extension to my bedtime and gave me a pocket money pay rise of a whopping five pence per week. Albeit, it just wasn't enough, the feelings of freedom of expression were still missing.

So, one fine day, right out of the blue, I just made up my mind not to go to bed at 9:30 pm or 10 pm or even 10:30 p.m. On one occasion, it was after eleven before I even began to feel tired enough to retire, and that was not before Sister Bea had already taken me up to bed several times prior, in the end, resorting to some considerable force, by dragging me along the cold antique floor tiles covering the corridors and bump, bump bumping me up the hard stairs. I loved it; I was in my element, sliding along the cold, slippery tiles, but not so much the bump, bump, bumping me up the stairs; that was largely somewhat painful.

One of Sister Bea's motives for moving me out of a shared room and into my own room was that she believed that it would help me to feel more mature, more grown up, and perhaps even assist me in acting a little more mature too. But the truth was I hated it. It was much colder than the large sunshine room that I had become so accustomed to, as it was north facing, so it was never adorned with bustling sunshine; the sunshine did no more than merely tease the window with a glimpse of its rays just as it was about to dive beneath the equator. It was a much noisier room too; I could hear very clearly the sound of the road which would keep me awake for ages each night.

I think one of the most annoying things was that Sister Bea would just go right ahead and make all these room changes without ever consulting you first. Every time we had a new person there was a room change but she never asked or consulted with you. She never empowered you by bringing you into the discussion that was clearly all about you. I can't tell how many times Tess changed rooms, backwards and forwards and backwards again.

I am sure she was equally fed up with it as I was, and Tess was the one who moved the most times. We never told her though, we never complained, but it was really annoying to return home from school only to find all your belongings packed up and moved into another room. I was sure Sister Bea thought she was doing some great good service, but the truth was she wasn't – it was all very disorientating and somewhat upsetting; at least for me anyway.

Perhaps this was the final straw in my world that made me decide I wanted to leave; I don't know. Perhaps in hindsight, looking back I just wanted what Odette had because that was what I did best, or perhaps I was just growing up, or rebelling, or simply giving back some of what I had been on the receiving end of, for the past twelve years. Who knows? The only thing for certain was that it was time for me to move on. It was time to leave what once had been home, at least for the past twenty months or so.

Ballroom dancing had already collapsed and ballet with it. I guess it was inevitable really, given it was the same tutor an' all. Deep down I had always wanted Sister to sort it all out because I did actually enjoy it but never actually told her. But I wanted things to stay as they were, with no extra lessons. Now there was nothing really to hold on to, the anchor was up, and my ship was drifting. Perhaps I was just bored. Tess did ballet, and it was really after seeing all the attention and memorabilia being lavished upon her that naturally I felt that I wanted some too. So, I asked if I could go as well. Sister Black sort of put up a fuss in the beginning saying I was too old, but backed down after Sister Bea piped up in my favor *(Of course I wasn't sure if her support wasn't because she just wanted to get me out of the house or whether she was really being genuine, but I didn't care; it worked).*

I had never done ballet before, so I was placed with all the little children to learn the basic steps, which I actually did not mind. None of the children could take their eyes off me. Yes, I was the only person of color in the room, but I did not mind this time around. Our teacher would speak to us in French and walk around with an exceptionally long ruler, which she used for tapping whoever she thought was out of alignment or simply not trying hard enough.

All the usual suspects would frequently be reduced to tears. Many of these young flowers would more than likely cut their dance tuition short as soon as they could persuade their parents to agree; others would silently depart with a chip on their shoulder; probably very few would remain until the bitter and often bloody end, holding on to some warped belief that they too were the next Anna Pavlova or Darci Kistler. Fortunately, for me, I followed directions rather well – I had had a lot of practice living with Dad, so there were never any recalls or repeats where I was concerned.

I had perfect lines in both my arms and legs; I guess being double jointed helped. And when it came to the ballroom, I seemed to have a natural flair; however, she would never say,

'Hey, listen, Jacqueline, you are really good at this...' or 'Well done at that' or 'You did good today!' She never praised anyone for that matter, she never gave an ounce of encouragement, or her stamp of approval to any of us. You could dance your pretty golden shoes off (*yes, they really were gold in color*); it was as though you were dancing for nothing and no one. So, when she demanded, I took extra lessons I intuitively saw it as a punishment for which I wanted no part. Of course, I do regret it now, but back then, I didn't understand any of it, and she didn't help either; no one helped me to understand anything, and I didn't care either. Only Odette helped and we were separated now, although this time by consent – hers not mine – no one asked me how I felt about yet another separation.

The Girl Guides followed suit with violin right behind that. *On this point, my advice to all you parents is 'Please, do not let your child give up on their hobbies but rather encourage them to continue and see them through to the highest level where they too can become tutors in that discipline if they choose to.' It certainly beats an early-morning-cleaning job or blip-blipping the produce at the till in Tesco in order to get them through university.*

Inequality

Upon the arrival of Bella and Annabella, I was made to share with Bella at first, whilst Annabella was made to share with Sabrina and Tess. Bella and I got on relatively well and even took up walking to school together. It was one of these journeys to school that was to change everything forever, even between us.

On that day, Bella had been reading the newspaper and stumbled across an article on a kidnapping. We began to speak on the topic at length with passion and emotion, saying what we would do if ever we found some... err... kidnappers... as you do, when surprisingly she announced her idea that we should hunt down some kidnappers, and in a bizarre twist of fate, we ended up boarding a train to Brighton whilst on our way to school, convincing ourselves, *as you do*, that it was all alright because we were going to catch kidnappers; *err... how crazy an idea is that? What were we thinking?* Perhaps that was just it: we weren't.

There were several routes to school, and one was right across a train crossing where the train would slow to a halt and we would get on it, still believing in the integrity of our story. We chatted all the way non-stop to Brighton. When the train pulled into the station, we suddenly realised we did not have a ticket, and it dawned on us that we were not going to be allowed through the barrier without one or in this case two; Suddenly our intentions to catch kidnappers evaporated as quickly as they had developed.

I allowed Bella to do the talking because she had an aunt in Brighton whom she believed we could visit, at least up until the point that they threatened to call the police and have us locked up, that is. *This always seemed to be a trump card of any adult back then.* In any event, it was at this point, without any prompting or hesitation, that I told them exactly who we were and where we had come from and what we were attempting to do, which yes included catching the kidnappers.

After the tears of laughter had been wiped away, and the sound of laughter had died down, they came up for breath to ask their next question. Bella startled them further by pulling out the folded piece of newspaper, which she still had in her school bag. They laughed at us again until their faces were red like beetroot. I told them our names and that we lived with nuns in a convent. They started laughing again. I told them that our names were stitched on to the collar of our shirts. With that they peered down the rear of our shirts to find that our names were really stitched on to our clothing. *Thank you, Sr Bea.* They had not believed us until physically seeing it with their own eyes.

The next step was that they had to get the number for Acorns, which was tricky because it wasn't listed, so we had to ring the convent to get the number for Acorns, so the nuns could meet us at Havant Station and pay for the tickets. What an embarrassment! Now everybody in the village was going to know of our exploits as crazy as they were. We were now the laughingstock of the entire village. Sister Bea tried her best not to laugh upon meeting us.

'Kidnappers indeed.' She said under her breath.

'Ok, ok!' I whispered under my breath.

Toby and Saul, well, they were not going to let us live any of it down... ever. We had become the butt of every joke, even being mentioned in the priest's Sunday-morning sermon. *'Beam me up scotty!'*

When we arrived back at school the following day, we were both supposedly put on report for two weeks. I was made to sit in the chilly hallway by the main entrance, adjacent to the principal's office, because I was the naughtiest, the worst, the leader – it was freezing there – whilst Bella was permitted to sit directly outside her classroom door, in the warm, and which, in fact, only lasted for four days as rumor had it. My punishment on the other hand lasted the full two weeks. I was absolutely freezing. No one ever mentioned the disparity in treatment, not the teachers, not the nuns, not Bella, no-one.

I kept a tight note of the days as I counted them down from ten. I just kept telling myself, 'You can do it! You can do it!' It was freezing sitting adjacent the main entrance door; each time it opened, it took me ages to warm up again. I was reminded of my life back on the farm with our parents again and how cold I was there especially at night and now I felt as though I was reliving it all over again; in truth, I felt that I just wanted to run away. Sister Bea made no comment about the disparity in our treatment. She knew, yet she said nothing, and she did nothing; somehow, deep down, that made it even worse, another arrow to my heart. Perhaps that was the moment I simply drifted away from them all. Nevertheless, I would reveal my hand of disappointment at a later date.

Climbing the Roof

One of my most exciting exploits at Acorns was climbing on to the roof of the garage with no more than a drainpipe, a window ledge, and a fence for assistance. Now you know you could not put all your weight on the drainpipe; otherwise, it would just break away from the wall and you would fall off it. Neither could you put all your weight on the window ledge; otherwise, you would most likely slip and also come tumbling down. You had to gauge it exactly right or else, *Crash! Bang! Wallop! Ouch!* However, once I mastered it, what a pleasant view, seeing all the way down to the convent; what I didn't know was that they too could see all the way back up to me. It was a good place to hide from Sister too.

On one occasion, unbeknown to me, I was being watched by one of the nuns, apparently with X-ray eyes, and yes, all the way from the convent. Of course, she told Sister Bea, who of course announced it, as if making an important announcement over the tannoy, to be released over dessert at Sunday lunch. Mealtimes always seemingly appeared to provide an excellent platform for dumping you in it. I mean I was quite happily enjoying a handsome slice of home- made apple pie and custard, made by yours truly. It was whilst inserting about my fourth spoonful into my mouth and savoring on the flavors of the apples that had been soaked in and simmered with cloves and warming spices combined with the texture of the butter rich short crust pastry, when the announcement was made public; well, I almost choked half to death on the pastry.

My eyes quickly darted around the table trying to clock everyone who had heard her comments, and after thinking on my feet, I thought about asking the question of whether my accuser had known for certain, without a shadow of a doubt, that what or who she believed she had seen on the roof was in fact me?

Holding on to that thought, I decided to play my cards close to my chest, at least for as long as I could anyway. I looked up at Sister Bea, who was refusing to make any eye contact with me. What I couldn't make out was why. Then I looked at Toby, who was sarcastically tut-tutting and shaking his head as he scraped up the last mouthfuls of my home-made apple pie and custard on to his spoon and placing it neatly into his mouth and licking his spoon. '*Oh, why don't you just shut up?*' I thought, as I gave him one of my drop- off- your- chair looks.

'Err...Doesn't she wear glasses?' I asked.

Sister Bea, now having to think for a moment, made no comment. 'For all she knows it could have been a fox or a dog or a cat or anything,' I said assertively.

'Or you,' said Toby. Everyone made a quick head turn to look at Sister sitting at the top of the table who made no comment or gesture. It was as though I had won, at least for now, anyway.

'Well it wasn't me,' I snapped. *Of course, it was.*

'Perhaps it was you,' I said, referring to Toby.

'Yeah... right... it was me,' he said in his rather deep voice, which had recently broken.

'There you go, Sister it was Toby,' said Arron. Before long everyone was accusing everyone, and Sister had lost control of the table.

'Err... can I leave the table, please?' I asked, ever so politely.

'Well, now,' came the softly spoken Irish response. 'We will all leave together,' she added. I couldn't bear it. Saul had now joined in the banter with Toby, and I was the joke of the table, of course. But Tess had my back, though. Good old Tess.

'I think it was you Toby,' she said, 'dressed up as Saul.' Now the whole table erupted in laughter. Touché one nil to the girls I thought. Sister could not gain back control.

'You wait,' said Toby gesturing at his sister.

'Jacqueline, will protect me said Tess, won't you Jac?'

'You touch her you have to go through me,' I said reassuring her.

'You touch her you'll have to go through me,' he said mocking me. 'Now that should be interesting.' Little did we know that those words would come back to test both of us.

School continued to be an absolute pain. It was a real living nightmare. The young games teacher was the only person in the entire school who seemed to be nice to me. She gave me her number and said I could call her whenever I needed to. I did once but I never said anything, like a lemon. Whenever Sister Bea and I had one of our blow ups I would walk down to the village and sit on the bench that was parked right in front of the phone booth.

'How do you tell your teacher that you wish you wasn't here?' I thought. 'How do you tell your teacher that you wish you were dead?' I thought again.

I was exceptionally good at games, and this helped take the edge off the other subjects; but they never made me the captain of any team despite my proven ability. It was for this reason that I made up my mind that if they did not make me the captain of the netball team, I would drop all sports altogether – even my peers commented on my ability and felt I should be captain.

I had played the game since I was about eight going on nine and was very good at netball, in fact I was very good at most games, especially ball games, even if I do say so myself.

When the school Olympics came around, they wanted me to compete in the heptathlon, because no one knew how to throw the javelin, the shot put, or the discus; they could see the power in my arms I guess, but I refused outright, so we had no score for any of these events, and I somehow felt justified.

Clearly, in hindsight, looking back, perhaps I wished I had helped them out but more for me than for them. If I had known that I could have used my strength as a bargaining chip perhaps I could have done so, using it for my benefit to help me get to a better life. I was also very good at contemporary dance, and I remember we had to choreograph movement to the tune Green Onions by Booker T. and the M.G.s.

I used abstract robotic-like movements with Sulia as my partner. It was a hit; the games teacher loved it; she was ecstatic. Just like that she wanted us to perform the dance for the school talent show which was next on the school calendar and coming up in just a few weeks. We would perform it to the entire school and then again in the evening to the parents. I also auditioned for a solo piece where I would perform dance and mime by the Aristocats called 'Thomas O Malley' and it was also accepted. I was on cloud nine. For The first time, I felt empowered to do something on my own that I had complete control over and at last I felt accepted by my peers.

Poker Face

The event would be attended by all mums and dads plus the nuns of course. I was pleasantly surprised when Sister Bea said she would attend. There were to be two showings, so everyone had an opportunity to attend. I had watched Odette do it several times before at Water Farm Primary, and it was a success then. I asked whether she minded me repeating the piece now. I had captured the very essence of it in my mind.

Sister Bea helped me to make a long fur tale for authenticity. We stitched odd pieces of fur together, which we then stuffed with odd bits of sponge; finally, I stitched on two pieces of cord to the end, with which I would hold the tail in place from my waist.

On the night Odette penciled on my whiskers and a cat's nose for authentic effect and I was good to go. The children screamed and roared with elation after my performance. The school loved it, and for the first time in my young life, I felt a sense of achievement, a sense of satisfaction; it was as though I had arrived. Now they accepted me for me. I was on a complete high, only to come back down to earth with a hard-harsh thud after overhearing Mrs. Malanoska, one of the geography teachers, saying to Mr. Brunswick, her sidekick,

'Well, we can't have that now, can we?' Her face was full of utter disgust.

'Oh no! No, we certainly can't,' came his suck up response. No words could express how depleted I felt in that moment. Those evil insensitive words had pierced me so deeply that night it was hard to breathe. I was crushed all over again. The pain must have been so evident upon my face because even my peers were asking me what the matter was as we lined up for the third performance. I was just some little kid just trying to do my best; she had always been a spiteful *cow* anyway.

She hated the idea of migrants coming to Britain, who were not of British descent; it didn't matter if you were first generation born here or second or third, if you were not of British descent she hated you and she made it crystal clear that you were not welcome. It made no difference that your parents had actually been asked to come to help build back up the British economy. *Talk about gratitude.*

Mrs. Malanoska always wore really tight white trousers or a white trouser suit, which, by some bizarre twist of fate, she had managed to stuff herself into and shut up the zip. I was just sorry it didn't go all the way up past her head. And yes, her bum really did look big in this! I always wondered how she never managed to burst the zip, the stitching of which appeared always to be screaming holding on to the material for dear life on the brink of bursting either side of the zip. She was always in tow with her little sidekick, Mr. Brunswick, a smaller man of thin stature. Whenever you spotted her around the school, there he would be, always eating up all her comments of propaganda, prejudice, and discrimination.

She was one of those teachers who unreservedly believed that children of color should not be permitted into the school and had no right to attend. In truth, most of the teachers did not want us in the school or even in the country, for that matter. Clearly the climate had been made worse by comments like, 'they will take your houses and your jobs.' And the infamous Enoch Powell speech. It did not matter that our parents had come over to support their economy or that we were born here. It felt as though they hated us, and the British government never officially welcomed us and to this day they have never apologised. And many of them were determined not to teach us a thing, and if we got it, they would just mark us down or put us down anyway. They never encouraged us apart from Jessie and she was long gone now; I mean I had no idea whether I would ever see her again. However, there was the young games teacher, at least she was nice, it was as though she really somehow understood. Then there was Mrs. Malanoska who was always ready to pour out her home-made venomous propaganda on anyone who was remotely interested or ready to listen.

They called us names at this school, usually under their breath, but sometimes, 'You Black Bastard' would just slip out, like on the day when the children were pushing in the lunchtime queue, as they usually did. Only on this day, dear old Mr. Jackson happened to be in the queue too, and one would think after seeing what had happened, he would be quite capable of handling the situation, but oh no, he simply turned around and blamed me. He didn't look for anyone else, he didn't ask any questions, but he just blamed me, demanding I go to the back of the queue. I left the line completely; he followed me outside, calling out to me as he tried to catch up to me, but without success. I had no lunch that day; I was starving.

Mr. Jackson lived in the village and was a friend of the nuns or so he pretended to be. Whenever he had seen me with the nuns in the village or at church he would always stop and chat like he was the good Samaritan or something; but his true colors were out: he was a fake. And the next time he saw us in the village and stopped for a chat I walked off and left them to it. I knew sister would think how rude can I be, but I didn't care, I knew exactly what message I was sending and why. After that incident, I think I stopped trusting adults, full stop. I don't remember whether I told Sister though.

My grades were really low again that year. I think I came in the bottom three for Math's. The class would always laugh out loud when the grades were read out. By the end of Year 3, I think I had completely stopped caring.

Math's was taught or rather screamed by the piercing Mrs. Babel. Rumor had it that she was in the middle of a bitter divorce and as a result she was left unable to determine when she was in the middle of a Math's class or when she was warring with her hubby. Most of the kids would become so distressed, they would leave the class in tears, one by one. It was just old tack for me, though; I had been here before. However, it was not long before we were rescued by another teacher from the class opposite to ours and Mrs. Babel was eventually replaced.

I spent most of my first two years bobbing between the lower Math's class and the GCSE Math's class. In all honesty, I preferred the lower Math's class; it was calmer and less stressful, but the question was how to stay there because as soon as I felt relaxed, my grades would automatically improve, and then I would be moved back up again, and as soon as I became distressed, my grades would deteriorate and I would be moved back down again. This yo-yo going back and forth continued almost until I left.

Aberystwyth

I was glad when the holidays came around again. It was the least stressful time of year for me. My second holiday with Acorns was to Wales. This time, we were going to stay in a little old farmhouse; Sister had planned that we were going to drive all the way there in daylight, which made more sense and she made sure that we had plenty of refreshments on board so there was less mumbling, muttering and complaining this time around. I had purposed in my mind that it was going to be just great.

Odette and Gino would not be accompanying us on this holiday as they had already departed along with Sister Black, which was a good thing I thought. Sister Black 's departure I mean.

There was no TV, no phone, and no radio, but we did have a barn and unbeknown to any of us then in this summer holiday Cupid would fire his arrow once more. As we unpacked and moved in familiarizing ourselves with the house the moans of discontent rang out as the disappointing news spread regarding no TV. The good news was that we all had clean beds and a clean bath, in fact the entire house was clean, warm, and cozy.

We sat down that evening to a humble tea of cold meats and new potatoes washed down with milky tea and finished off with fresh fruits. We could not wait to scout out our new surroundings to see what we could find. We all noticed the barn opposite. We also found cows in most fields and a bull home alone in another; there was so much cow poo everywhere it was a task in itself not to step in it, – unfortunately, Arron was not so lucky.

As soon as night fell, we would all go for a midnight walk which you would not be wrong for thinking was really a favorite past time of Sister Bea. It was pitch black out there, I mean there were no streetlights, but Sister did have a torch. I was convinced that we would get lost because Sister did not even have a map or anything. We must have walked just over a mile before finding ourselves right back at the house again. After piling into the humble country style kitchen, we all settled down to warm hot chocolate with marshmallows; *emm lovely.*

Each day after breakfast Sister would take us out on an excursion of some sort and we would have ourselves a hearty picnic before returning back to the cottage again before tea. One afternoon the farmer had left a message for us to lend a hand in the barn if we wanted. It was Sister Bea who encouraged the boys to lend a hand, and after helping to unpack the picnic and tidy up the kitchen the girls soon followed them over.

Once all the hay was stacked up, we took it in turns to throw each other off and before long we all began to wrestle in the hay; it was crazy funny, I mean we had a blast. This was the summer holiday that our bodies would collide. I would be deliberately dropped from the top of the haystacks by Toby and then he would land on top of me and then I would land on top of him. He was staring right up at me, and I was staring right down at him, nose to nose, yet not really knowing what to say or do, but there was a feeling in the air.

Had Cupid shot his arrow, who knows? What was clear was that suddenly I became aware of my sexuality as had he. We both had felt a connection, it was like electricity shooting through our veins, yet neither of us was prepared to speak about it. From that moment on, we could no longer look at each other when seated at the table, we would completely avoid making any form of eye contact. It was as though our nakedness had been exposed.

As the holiday drew to an end, we spent our time visiting little towns collecting up ornaments and souvenirs as we went.

I would always save my pocket money each week after the Christmas present buying season was over. I found that if I did not spend a penny from December to July, I would have a whooping £23.40 to spend on holiday; and I am sure I never spent it all.

When we arrived back from our holiday, Toby and I had another encounter, where Tess and I were throwing water at each other; Toby walked right into my line of fire and got a little wet to say the least. Of course, he wanted to get me back and dared me to come over to his level. Always up for a challenge I obliged him. He grabbed me, and we began wrestling in his room in the dark. The door was wide open, so the option for screaming was always available, but I didn't, I didn't even attempt to, even when he straddled my torso; I think we both had been trying to put bubbles into each other's mouths when suddenly he began lifting up my T-shirt. He placed his clammy adolescent hands on top of my firm, pouted, naked breasts. I was unable to move or struggle free as his knees were pinning down my arms. The words '*I'm gonna kill you*' seemed to fade with every inch that he made in moving his face towards mine, as if to kiss me. We were almost nose to nose and lip to lip; when I turned my face to give him my cheek, he bent down towards me and whispered in my ear

'I think you should leave my room.' With that he slid off from on top of me. 'Go,' he said, 'just go!' then he cried out 'errrr.' I got up and ran back to the girls' side, pulling my T-shirt down as I went. I met Tess on the top landing, but she was not sure where I had come out from as my back was to the bathroom door.

'What happened?' she asked.

'Nothing,' I answered, my mind drifting back to our encounter and wondering whether she could see the evidence written all over my face.

'Supper time!' called Arron. 'Supper time!' At the tea table, I noticed Toby could not look at me, he was refusing to make eye contact with me, but neither could I look at him. I'm sure Sister noticed something, but she said nothing. Tess looked at me and then looked at him then looked back at me again. Every time I tried to concentrate our encounter together would interrupt me and come bursting into my mind. I knew she knew something had gone down, so I later told her that we had a fight to keep her off the scent. We sort of kept out of each other's way from then on, just smacking each other as hard as we possibly could on the bum or back whenever the opportunity arose.

Leaving Acorns

That year had been rather a difficult one regarding my relationship with Sister, more so than the one before as Sister Bea and I were now clashing at every turn. I felt she would never listen to me, or if she heard part of what I was saying, she would make the rest up and try to convince me I had said something that in fact I had not. I felt she was constantly and deliberately contradicting me at every opportunity. I found this extremely frustrating about her, and it caused severe tension in our relationship more so because it left me feeling I always wanted to make her express an emotion, a feeling... or something – basically anything to let me know she was real and not oh so holy, that she was really down to earth. Eventually it got to the point that whenever we fell out, I would just stop arguing with her altogether.

Whenever she upset me or contradicted me from that moment on, I would wait and wait and wait, like some predatory wild cat. Then out of the blue when she was least expecting it and of course when she was always in the presence of that all important person, at that all important meeting, or had an important guest round; such as the insurance man, it was then that I would lovely up beside her making her believe all was well between us and it was then suddenly without word or warning, I would pounce lunging at her veil as hard as I could, causing it to slide right off her head exposing her hair to whoever she was in the meeting with or entertaining. Of course, they never understood what was really happening or whether this was in fact part of the meeting, or if they were really in the meeting or just daydreaming; I'm sure that the insurance man thought this was some sort of play or something and even until this day is waiting for the ending, whatever that is.

I could see his speech went right out of the window, and sister well she absolutely hated it, she would go all red in the face. I am sure if she could, she would have definitely said a bad word or two right then in that moment or whacked me really hard, if she had not trained her own behavior so well, that is.

The insurance man would begin to stutter and lose his train of thought until he had stopped talking altogether. I'm sure she could not believe the cheek of me. She would try to give me her evil eye, but I would throw my head back and laugh out loud, as loud as I could before running off and sometimes slamming the door just for added effect.

I would pull off her veil so many times for just one offence from her. And when I saw Lucy, that cat upon whom she would lavish all her love and attention on, I would usually drop her accidentally on purpose over the balcony or out of the first-floor window from my bedroom into the rose garden below, *Poor Lucy.*

On one occasion, I simply forgot that I had deliberately locked her in the bathroom cupboard, until Sister mentioned at supper, one evening that she had not seen her and began asking us all one by one if we had seen her. It was then that I almost choked on my milky tea, suddenly remembering where I had left her. Everyone began to ask if I was ok. I realised if I coughed some more, I could in fact ask to be relieved from the table, whereby I could seize the moment and let Lucy out of the cupboard before Sister launched a massive manhunt for her; of course, if found she would know intuitively that I had placed her there. The difficulty now came in trying to open the lid; I mean I had no idea as to whether she was going to pounce out at me once the lid had been opened.

My plan was to stand back as far as I could and open it with the broom handle. It took a few attempts as the stick kept slipping out from under the lip of the lid. I could hear supper coming to an end as grace was being said. Then with one mighty shove, I forced open the lid with the tip of the broom. But Lucy did not come out, she just sat there purring at me. The hot water pipes ran through the cupboard so it was as snug as it could be, and Lucy was certainly very comfortable. I had to physically lift her out in order to get her out: *fat cat.*

When the day finally arrived for me to leave Acorns, there was a big meeting where unanimously all of the nuns, bar one was adamant that they did not want me to go to Mansion Heights. As far as they were concerned, they saw it as a type of treat. They were all in agreement that I was a naughty little child and therefore I should not be rewarded with treats. *Truth be known, I think I was just a child who was misunderstood. I was a child who needed love, mentoring and encouragement in order for me to make it through this life successfully. But above all I needed love.*

Not going to bed on time, coming back downstairs after lights out, and having Sister Bea drag me along the cold tiled floors all the way back up to my bedroom, and pulling her veil off in public all spilled out at the meeting, which, although was all about me, ironically, I was the only person not permitted to attend it. The only one not permitted to speak up in my defense. The only one not able to challenge the accusations put so neatly against me; and to add insult to injury, Sister Bea even told the SS about my midnight stroll alone in the snow, probably trying her best to imply that I was not all there in the head or something: as Jeanie later interpreted it to me. I thought this was the ultimate betrayal.

'how could she?' I thought. Nevertheless, Sister P was certainly not put off in the slightest; she still wanted me to come to Mansion Heights; even I was shocked. *'Was there nothing I could do to put her off?' I thought.*

Sister P loved a challenge; she would always rise to them all one by one and excel every time, GOD really was with her; I guess.

What everyone would give up on, she would not, and of course, she always got her way and would always win in the end. For Sister P, I was that challenge; she told them she had made a promise to me, that day down by the brook when she had met me there, and she was not going to break it, no matter what. This was the day that I knew that Sr P really was a woman to be reckoned with, she was a woman of integrity and her word was her bond. She had made a vow to the LORD and she was going to keep it come rain or high water.

Unfortunately, I was unable to go straight to Mansion Heights directly from Acorns, just as Odette had done. The main reason was that there was no room: all thirteen bedrooms were occupied as well as the two bedsits, which were located on the ground floor. I could not believe it. I felt as though I couldn't wait. I wanted to go now. I wanted one of those upstairs bedrooms, which would be adorned with fresh paint, with my very own towels, my very own linen, and my very own colors; each room was identified by its own color. I wanted to do my own washing in the laundry and clean my own room myself on room day; I wanted to take responsibility for my own clothes as opposed to having to beg for clean knickers or having to go hunting for them butt-naked, or having to risk climbing up into high cupboards in an attempt to try and locate them. I wanted to win the tidiest room competition every week. I could see it now all in my mind's eye. I was so close I could taste it. But I had to wait. I had to be patient. Therefore, I had no choice but to return with the SS back to London, at least for a little while anyway. *Surely, I could handle that,* I thought, *I'll just hitch up with Jeanie for a few months, not a problem,* I thought. *Then I will return to Mansion Heights to be with Odette.* It was that grass, I believed, that really did look greener, or so I thought, on the other side.

Little did I realize that the nuns at Acorns had joined forces with others from the convent and they were all actually plotting against me so that I would never be able to return, ever! If they could have got a signed petition going, I'm sure they would have; And this dance was being led by sister Josephine.

You see, in truth, I really was the black sheep, the real wild child: the one who walked the corridors of the convent unannounced; the one who was seen abseiling from off the garage roof; the one who refused to get out of bed in the mornings; the one who was seen rolling around in the snow at 3 a.m.; the one who smashed all the dinner plates including dessert plates, cups, and a trifle right into the floor. I was the one who voiced out her opinions loud and clear for all to hear; I was the one who publicly removed the veil without warning or consent; the one who dropped the cat over the banister. In fact, I was the one who would just not do as she was told. The one who was caught smoking and burnt the bedspread. This was me. If there had been a flag called rebellion, I am sure that I would have been waving it.

The Year of the Child Conference

The plan was, I thought, that I would hang with Jeanie for a few weeks; Little did I know that Jeanie had her own plans. During that time, she took me and the king's daughter (*from some tribe in Africa*) off to Leeds for 'The Year of the Child Conference'. Jeanie had connections with Leeds and had even purchased a house there, now making a grand total of two for her portfolio.

At some point, during my transportation, I had developed a throat infection which was getting worse by the minute. I had been invited to speak publicly at the conference which seemed more and more distant as the infection worsened.

This was my first public-speaking experience, which at age just thirteen was a remarkable feat by any means. It was rather cool I guess, and the food wasn't bad either. We stayed four days and three nights. By the third day, the infection had reached the stage where I was prevented from speaking or swallowing completely, so I was unable to eat at all and had lost about half a stone in body weight by the end of it.

It was not until Saturday morning, the third day, that Jeanie decided to take me to the doctor, who prescribed some sort of red potion, which, when drunk and gargled, really did do as it said on the bottle. By lunchtime, my voice had returned, and by the evening, I could swallow again without pain.

On the last night, there was a disco after all the speeches, accolades, credits, and appraisals had been given out. Once the word had been given for the dancing to commence, couples began to shyly fill the floor. As I stood on the sideline, I began to look around at all the smiling faces; I guess seeing all the smiling faces made me smile. My eyes automatically stopped at the eyes of a young man subtly locking on to mine and who, without hesitation, smiled at me. I immediately looked over my shoulder to see if my instincts were correct – '*was he really looking at me, I thought?*' In the few seconds it took for me to turn my head back, he was walking across the hall in my direction. As he stopped right in front of me, he held out his hand and asked whether I would like to dance. I looked from side to side over my shoulder before coming to the realisation that it was in fact me he was talking to. I took hold of his outstretched hand and stepped out towards him.

Close-up, he was not much taller than me; it was easy to think that we were a couple as we appeared to fit like a glove. He was of slim stature, he had medium length brown curly hair, his skin was pale, and he wore round lense spectacles. He was dressed very smartly in a three-piece grey tweed suit, but he had taken off his jacket.

He held me ever so gently as we floated around the floor. All my ballroom dancing skills seemed to kick in automatically. I had not experienced anything like it before, but then, I was only thirteen. As he talked about the conference, I felt myself enjoying being in his embrace; as the music tempo slowed, his arms brought me in a little closer. I could feel the warmth of his body, breathing next to mine. I had never been held in this manner before. The last time I had so much as half a hug was upon my return home from Sandy Lodge and that, as scary as it was, was from Dad. Before that moment, I had not experienced such an intimate embrace or the emotions that accompanied it.

Clearly, I must have experienced a closeness from my mother, as a baby, I mean, before I was snatched from her arms. As tender, yet unfamiliar his embrace, I closed my eyes… for what seemed like only a matter of moments, and as the music played it was then that I was reminded of these three things: 1) I was just thirteen years old, 2) this was a grown man, perhaps almost twice my age, and 3) Jeanie would go absolutely crazy if she were to walk in now or even ever get wind of this. The third of which, I was absolutely certain. This thought was like a bolt of light. With all this information being processed, ticking over in my brain, my eyes suddenly opened, I broke abruptly from his gentle embrace, like the needle on the arm of a record player being dragged across the record, and told him I had to go.

'Thank you for the dance,' he said shyly. 'It was really nice to meet you and speak with you.' I simply smiled and walked away, not looking back. I felt like Cinderella having to leave the ball before the clock strikes twelve, but in this instance keeping both my shoes. However, in that moment, something more had happened. There had been a transfer of emotions.

I now realised what it felt like to experience tenderness and gentleness, and what it felt like to be held in a warm embrace. My encounter had clearly awoken my desires to wanting more. I had gone through Pandora's box, and now there was no turning back and no undoing of the already *done.* From that day on, I would pine to experience the touch of gentleness and tenderness and I would pine to be loved. But there would be one more such encounter and the clock was ticking, tick tock, tick tock.

There was no hugging or expressions of affection in the places that my rescuers took me to, not even from them: in fact, there was no physical contact, no words of endearment, no words of encouragement, and no 'I love you', or 'You can do it,' or 'You're gonna make it.'; it was just all so cold and clinical, in its purest form there seemed to be no hope. I had no coach and no cheer leaders.

That night, I shared my experience with the king's daughter, who teased me without mercy, threatening to repeat all to Jeanie first thing in the morning. I practically had to beg her not to, now finding myself having to completely retract my tale of '*could it be love*' and what could have been, promising her that, in fact, the entire encounter was no more than a fabrication of my mind. Finally, she relented accepting either my retraction or my plea for leniency – whichever it was, I was relieved.

As a child, the last thing you want is trouble amongst adults. Yet that is the very thing that adults teach children, and by the time they reach their teenage years, they appear to have mastered it rather well. When I think about it, I didn't really know who he was. He could have been some hairy teenager in his late teens, who had just dressed up for the conference, or perhaps he too had just left the SS coming of age, or perhaps he too was a member of the SS; And I had no idea if he knew who I was either - *just a child.*

Abandoned in Cornwall

The next morning, we rose early to make the long drive back down to London. I remember packing up the rear of the small blue car with my pillows and duvets. Well, I for one was certainly going to be comfortable, '*I thought*,' as I slept for most of the journey back.

It must have been about two days after our arrival back in London, that I felt I was beginning to settle back down into Jeanie's rhythm of things, when out of the blue she said I could not stay at hers, of course I was absolutely crushed.

'Why not?' I meowed.

'Because there is no one here to look after you,'

'But you're here,'

'But sometimes I'm not, sometimes I get back late,'

'But Zachary is here,' I stated sheepishly.

'Don't be silly. Zachary has got his own life; I can't expect him to look after you,' she replied.

My eyes filled with tears as her words sounded so final. It was the war of the *Buts* and clearly, she had won. I couldn't believe it. The next day we rose early to board the London to Cornwall train. Another town, another house, another people. And I hated it. Every last minute of it.

Surprisingly, they met us on the platform and Jeanie did the brief introductions before making her excuses. Meet the Garfunkel's – another set of FPs – they lived in a small town near Truro right on the coastal line. *Jeanie and her damn FPs,* I thought. She was blooming well obsessed with them. She never asked me for my consent, my approval, or even consulted with me about what I wanted. As far as Jeanie was concerned, I had no voice, no opinions, and no views. I was just there, an irritable stain that could not be erased. She must have been planning this for days I thought, only she never said a word.

It never occurred to her that there were clear cultural differences as well as differences of race and color. But that was Jeanie all over; she always thought she knew what was best in everyone else's life but never asked them what they wanted or if they were happy, and she never listened. She was becoming complacent. But it was soon all to come to a horrid end and the clock was ticking, tick- tock, tick-tock, tick-tock.

The reason why she had managed to get them to meet us at the station was just so she could jump on the next train back to London, which was leaving in... err... well, exactly seven minutes. How rude really. Talk about killing two birds with one stone; she was killing me in the bloody process. This was Jeanie in her element, at her most self-absorbed.

The introductions were just about half exchanged before her sudden 'I have got to get my train' departure speech; I think I must have really hated her in that moment. Here was a thirteen-year-old child being left at the station on the platform with two complete strangers, and there was Jeanie running down the platform her fat arse trying to keep up as she tried to catch the next train back to London to attend her next meeting. Wow! Whatever next? Thanks, Jeanie. *Your simply the best!*

We made our way to their house, which consisted of a short drive followed by a short walk to the center of the woods. I hated it already. I just wanted to cry. They had two dogs which, despite being different breeds, one an Alsatian and the other, a small terrier, got on relatively well.

Their house was situated in the middle of the woods, almost two miles from the village, whose quaint little shops poured out right up to the coastline. I would later read about their flooding from the storms and the clock was ticking, tick tock, tick tock.

The house was freezing cold as it had no central heating. The only form of heat was produced from a wood burner, and it was only when that was lit that the house was able to warm itself up; only then could you actually get out of bed.

I laughed when their daughter informed me that she would cover her bed with all the coats in the house and sometimes she would put on all of the clothes that she could find in the closets before going to bed at night, she really made me laugh and it was then that the ice broke between us and we became *team*. But the cold was no joke, and it was not long before I too followed suit. She was a real bundle of joy – you couldn't help but love her.

They had a modest TV without a functional aerial. This severely restricted the number of channels received, and most of those were very fuzzy. This, on top of living with strangers, really irritated me. It was not until after the ice broke with the dad when he discovered that I too could play chess that I began to accept the situation I now came to find myself in, and life became a little more bearable.

It was here that I was able to sharpen my chess skills further, beating both daughter and dad individually and together. Often the daughter and I would team up and play against the dad together. We were similar in age and hit it off rather well. Her name was Rosy, she had really pale skin and masses of brown wavy hair; like me she was thin in stature and she was every bit a real doll, very kind and compassionate. She spoke right from the heart; Rosy was real. We were able to speak about everything. She shared with me half of her entire stamp collection and half her coin collection. She was a real sweet heart. *Where are you now Rosie I want to kiss your cheek and say thank you!*

Her dad Tom was so knowledgeable on all things stamps and coins. He would explain the story behind each coin and each stamp. I found it all so interesting I loved a good story.

During the days Rosie would attend school, Tom would go to work, and I would be left home with the mum. She never spoke to me which made me very uncomfortable. I would count the hours down until Rosie returned from school and she would tell me all the goings on and fill me in on all the dramas.

The first day she took me to the village with her. She tried to explain that the distance from the house to the village was one mile. The time needed for the average person to walk one mile would take twenty minutes; it was a straight road from the forest. But is wasn't. It was ten minutes from the house to the road and twenty minutes from the road to the village, so it was thirty minutes in total. In the village, there was a post office, haberdashers, bakers, and butchers with the post office doubling up as a convenient store. I guess for most, life revolved around the village. This was where you became up to date with everyone's life and what was going on in it.

After I had mastered the short walk from the house to the village and back again, completely unaided, I was all 'bored' out with life at the house, partly due to the crazy mood swings of Rosie's mother and partly because there was absolutely nothing to do. But I never complained. Of course, at age thirteen, I should have been in school myself, but somehow Jeanie had got it into her fat head that it didn't matter so much, and therefore no real emphasis was placed on it. In fact, I missed so much school, quite unnecessarily really, during my secondary education; it was no wonder that my subjects no longer made any sense to me.

After just three weeks of staying with them, Rosy begged her parents if I could attend her school with her. Her mother was silent on the matter, so she had to really beg her dad to speak for the both of them. She was like a dog with a bone and would absolutely not let up, so in the end, he agreed not forgetting to tell her to ask me whether I actually wanted to attend with her.

Despite being a bit hesitant with my response, partly because of the stark reminder of my frosty reception already received from Pressing Reed, following my yes, a part of me was already bracing myself for more of what I had previously endured in Hampshire. However, after collecting up all the yeses she needed from this end Rosie now had to ask the school whether it was ok for me to attend, which had to be reconfirmed by her dad.

I was filled with excitement and anxiety at the same time, waiting for the answer. Once Rosie returned home to say that the school had accepted, that I could attend if I wanted to, and I did not have to wear a uniform. I could not believe it; I could not wait to start.

The following morning, I too rose early to board the grass-green double-decker bus, which sped along the slender country lanes before arriving at the school gate delivering us all safe and sound; the same bus would also bring us home again when school finished at 3:30 pm.

Here, in Cornwall, what I received was a completely different reception; in fact, they treated me more like royalty; somehow, I was famous just because of the color of my skin, a stark difference from my reception in Hampshire. Upon alighting, we would make the short walk back to the house from the road and through the woods.

Clearly everything seemed to point for me to stay in Cornwall; I mean, I got on so well with the daughter and the dad, the school loved me, but the mum, well, the mum was a strange cookie; she would often have these dramatic temper tantrums and for no apparent reason; I could not work them out, the cause that was. Thank God, she only did them when the dad was there. Suddenly there would be a scuffle and you would hear Tom stop and drop whatever it was he was doing to go over and calm his wife down. On occasion, you would even hear things crashing in the kitchen.

No one ever commented on the commotions, not even me. I think but for her obscure behavior, perhaps I would have stayed.

However, in later years I would come to regret this decision, to leave them I mean. Back at the house though, if we were not playing some board game or analyzing our stamp and coin collections, we would embark in a little wrestling. Both Rosie and I would jump her dad. I loved it. He would have to use all his strength to stop us getting him down on the ground. We had such fun until one day the family dog, the large Alsatian, was out from his usual resting area, a fact that no one had noticed.

As I held on to the arm of Tom and jumped up towards him, the dog ran at me, jumping up at me and snapping on to my arm with his big open mouth, all his teeth intact. They were very, very sharp. I felt them go right through the fabric of my jacket and scratch my arm. Thank God, I was still wearing it. We all shook with shock.

In one split second, Tom threw his daughter from off his back and beat the dog off me, and then beat him some more after the dog finally let go. Thank God, I was still wearing my jacket. Tom kept asking me if I was OK and then kept inspecting my arm and hugging me. I kept reassuring him that I was fine. In truth, I was really afraid, of the dog, but right there, in that moment, just for one moment, I too felt like Tom's daughter. Thank you, good sir. *Where are you now Mr. Tom? I just want to say thank you and I love you guys.*

Just as I was beginning to settle down, it was time to leave again. Out of the blue, as per usual, I was given the instructions that I was to pack up and be ready to head back up to London within the next two days.

'You do still want to go to Mansion Heights, don't you?' Jeanie asked down the end of the telephone. The line was bad it was really crackling.

'Yes,' I replied slowly, seeming unsure in my response.

'Because you can stay there if you want to, but I need an answer now,' she added. *Well of course you do Jeanie.* I didn't have time to think or to weigh things up or talk things through with anyone or anything. I couldn't think. So, before I knew it, I was on the next train out and making the long journey back up to London alone. I did not even get to say goodbye to my new-found school friends or to Rosie. I knew she would be sad. I didn't even have her address to write to her or to say thank you to Tom and his wife who, despite her infirmities, was an exceedingly good cook.

Rosie, Tom, and I had all really bonded so well; she was so kind and compassionate. I knew she would be upset at finding me gone like this, it was just not fair; it wasn't fair on any of us. I arrived back in London at the end of the day, tired, hungry, and fed up. I made my way straight over to Jeanie's house in Hornsey because she didn't make the train station again; I should have known. Nonetheless I knew the route by heart now once I got to Crouch End. I followed the left fork at the tower, then took the second right by the swimming baths, and then right again. Thank God, Zachary was there to let me in. Otherwise, I would have been waiting outside for Jeanie until well gone after ten that night; she was working late again, as usual.

Zachary had himself been with Jeanie since he was a young teenager when his placement had broken down badly. He had been so traumatized by it all. Jeanie said there was something about him it jumped out at her and she just couldn't let him go and so he ended up with her. She had encouraged him through his GCSEs and his flair for cooking had really shone through. He went on to complete his City & Guilds at college; and now he had a top job, working as a chef for the Metropolitan police.

Back in the 1970s, they were still operating under old law where a policeman was unable to make purchases of food whilst on duty, so they still had in-house kitchens.

Zachary worked in one of those kitchens and was based at Holborn Police Station. He was just seventeen: tall, slim, and very handsome. He owned a Yamaha 250cc. He had a best friend, Wilson, a white boy, who was always coming around and hanging around. Nevertheless, I had a secret crush on Zachary. I would sit and chat with him for hours, and he would make me laugh till my stomach ached and tears of laughter burst from my eyes. I would spend all the free time I had in his company, where my feelings only grew stronger. I even started smoking just because he smoked. On that occasion when he asked me if I smoked.

'Of course, I do,' I answered.

'So, what do you smoke?' he asked.

I had no idea what it was that I smoked.

'The same as you.' I smiled. Up until that point I had never smoked in my life. With that he went to the shop and bought a box for him and a box for me, number 6 Blue, and I had carried them off with me back to Acorns just before I left that place. I guess I just did not want to be left out or feel left out; I wanted to have as much in common with Zach as possible. Secretly, I was infatuated with him, but no one knew it, only me.

After two weeks back in London, Jeanie called me in to her study for a chat. I guess she spent a lot of time in there because she even had a bed in there. She asked me whether I still wanted to go back to Hampshire and move into Mansion Heights.

'Yes, of course, I do!' I responded with absolute certainty.

'Oh good, oh good,' she said. 'I was just checking. Well, would you be ready to travel in the next few days?' she continued.

'Really?' I asked, quite surprised.

'Yes,' she answered.

'Err, well, yes,' I said, trying to ascertain why she was telling me this now. 'Why?' I asked apprehensively.

'Well, a vacancy is going to come in the next couple of days, and they are asking if you still wanted to go,' she said.

'Ye-ye-yes, I want to go,' I affirmed stuttering as I tried to get all the words out quickly. I packed up my things and in the next two days, she dropped me off at London Waterloo, again this time to make the long train journey alone back down to Hampshire. She had arranged with someone, I didn't know who, to meet me at Havant Station. I just about had time to say goodbye to Zachary. In truth, it really felt as though Jeanie could not wait to see the back of me or perhaps, she just did not want the responsibility. Her life was all about work.

Once I arrived at the other end, the nuns were there, waiting to greet me at the station, with big smiles running across their faces. They came right on to the platform, calling me from the top of their voices; talk about embarrassment! It was a short drive back to Mansion Heights in Waterlooville, and it was a lazy hazy Sunday afternoon with the sun just beginning to set. We entered by the back gates. I had never seen them open before, they were electric.

In a way, I was thankful that I did not have to drive past Acorns, but it was only a matter of time before the judgement, ridicule, and gossiping would commence. Upon my arrival, my luggage was placed in the hall, and I was brought into the lounge just in time for afternoon tea, which was always accompanied by over processed cake. After tea, I was taken into the office. The door remained open, so I gathered I was not in trouble. Sister P asked how I was and how the journey had been.

'Well,' I answered. 'Good,' I added nervously.

'All right then...' She paused. 'Would you mind having one of the bedsits on the ground floor for the moment, as the bedroom is not quite yet ready?' she asked.

'No, of course not... I mean, no, I do not mind,' I answered, fumbling my words, searching for the right words. That night I moved straight into bedsit 'A'. The ceiling was really high, and the room was long and slender. I felt very isolated away from the others all the way down there. I was thankful I only had to sleep in there a few nights or, so I was told. I was given a key so that I could lock myself in at night and sister could be content that I was safe.

'No matter what happens do not open your door.' she said.

'ok, then.' I responded.

Bedtime was still the same, up to our rooms at ten and lights out at eleven. We could go to the disco on Tuesdays and to the club on Thursdays, and if you had a boyfriend, you could go out with him on Saturdays, and he could visit you on Sundays after lunch up until supper time, and he could call you on Wednesday between 7and 9 pm. Although I was not allowed out alone, I felt I had more options than what I had previously experienced at Acorns.

Approximately four weeks later, I moved upstairs to the first available room. All the rooms were identified by color, so I was in the yellow and brown room. I had brand new golden matching towels; they were super soft, and I had a set of three. I had starched yellow and brown bed sheets and duvet covers, with matching bright yellow pillowcases. We changed our sheets every two weeks here, and we each had our own room day where we would do all our own washing, ironing, hoovering, and the dusting of our rooms. If you didn't have a Saturday job, you were expected to carry out chores on the weekend too.

We were awarded £2.00 per week in pocket money – of which 50 pence would be placed in compulsory saving, and 50 pence was automatically placed in our toiletry account, so that you could purchase items at a discount. Each girl had a toiletry book and a pocket money book: all entries were recorded, as was all expenditure. You also had the opportunity to earn an extra 50 pence each week for having the tidiest room of the week from Monday to Friday. Well, up until now, Odette had been the *queen of clean*, but I was hot on her heels and determined to beat her and take her crown.

Once every three months, Odette and I were also given £30 from the SS to spend on clothes. I was a very good saver and learnt not to spend my pocket money, so when the holidays and Christmas came around, I would have a lot of money to spend on souvenirs and presents, approximately £26.00 for each occasion.

Being a WOTS was not all bright lights and sparkles, in fact none of it was. Of course, you did get to meet some really genuine people but there was an irritating downside too, like having your money and possessions stolen.

I think that had to be my most serious pet hate. What I found even more remarkable was that when it occurred and you did report it, you followed the rules, you went through all the correct procedures but no one would ever do anything about it and you never got your stuff back, so you inevitably had to take the law into your own hands.

I arrived at Mansion Heights with two brand new bras from Marks & Spencer: one white, one black, same style, same size, same pattern, yet quite miraculously they disappeared right from off the rack, out of the laundry room, simultaneously, on the same day the first time I washed them. My first port of call was always to ask my sister what I should do and who I should ask; of course, she came with me to re-search the laundry room, but it was to no avail, there were no bras anywhere to be found in the laundry room. Her instruction at that point was to inform the nuns, who in turn told me that I had to bring it to the meeting.

Every Monday, after supper, we would have a meeting. It was called the 'Monday Night Meeting', and everyone had to be present, no ifs, no buts, no maybes and no excuses or else. It was here that the girls and the staff both got to voice their grievances and air their concerns, make their complaints known, and have their questions of uncertainty answered and their anxieties reassured; notices were given, and apologies were made.

I had to bring up the disappearance of my bras, they were brand new and I had to ask each girl individually whether she had seen them. What was clear, crystal clear, in fact, was that the bras had not got up off the line all by themselves and walked away of their own free will, intellect, or volition. What was clear was that they had to have been helped and that help had to have been deliberate.

The question was, by whom? I was deeply upset because my whole life I had always had my things taken from me and for most of that I had received more hand-me-downs and second-hand clothes than new ones; for once, I had something new, and I wanted to keep it. Clearly, the nuns were of no help in this situation. They could not understand how I felt about having my things stolen, and I could not believe it. They were of no help whatsoever and did not appear bothered in the slightest. But then, perhaps it could have been that they just did not know what to do, in which case, they did nothing and said even less. I was so incensed to the very core of me.

Friendship in Tatters

Upon my return to Waterlooville I slipped right back into Pressing Reed - just in time for what only seemed like another round of mental and emotional abuse with some freshly baked torment and brutality all thrown into the mix; it was as though I had never been absent at all – they simply picked up where they had left off. *Oh, but don't worry; it was me serving up good-size helpings of brutality.*

Oddly, I had befriended a girl called Sulia Sulti, initially in our first year at the school. A group of us had befriended her, in fact. Sulia wore what I called doctor's spectacles, which at all times sat across her half-freckled face, except when she was sleeping, I guess. She had short brown hair that would have made it into a bob except for the disobedient waves that sat around her forehead. She was quite petite in stature, which I'm guessing was out of choice rather than out of neglect, and with her teeth she kept her metabolic rate up exceedingly high, by keeping her nails constantly short.

Sulia, was the youngest of four in her family and clearly suffered from what they call the '*youngest child syndrome*' or in her case, the '*fourth child syndrome*'. She was unable to get all the attention that she craved at home and therefore forced her points, her opinions, and often herself on anyone who would give her the time of day at school, which I for one found really annoying.

She always had to be talking, always had to be heard. For me, although being the eldest in my year, she was by far the most childish and certainly the most irritating – not sure whether this had anything to do with her being the youngest in the class, and possibly the entire year.

Every Thursday afternoon we had history; during this season, we were studying the Roman Empire. Unfortunately for me, my table was right next to hers, and if it was not one thing, it was certainly another.

Our history teacher was as eccentric as they come evidenced by her choice in dress and backed up by her orange hair, which was sometimes red and looked as though it was constantly on fire. Surprisingly though, she also taught us for art. She was very excitable and very highly charged; only GOD knows exactly what combination of pills she was taking.

I remember, on one occasion, Sulia wanted us to play a game, whereby we had to say something, anything in fact, that was true about the other person, to the other person. I agreed, and she went first.

As she began to fire her insults at me, I began to sharpen my pencil with ease, as I listened to her remarks.

'You orphan!' she blurted out. Not being able to contain myself, I burst into laughter.

'You orphan!' she stamped again. And again. I laughed harder and harder. Once I was able to catch my breath, I had to inform her that in fact I was not an orphan, and both my parents were still very much alive and well. I continued laughing, still sharpening my pencil, even sharper and sharper, all the while the lead inside becoming longer and longer with an undeniable razor-sharp point.

My intention was to do some shading in on the Roman pot I had drawn in the lesson before. Mrs. Crabtree had asked that we pick some Roman pots to add to our piece on Roman history.

'Right, I believe it's my turn then, is it not?' I confirmed.

'Ok,' she said trying to hide her defeat.

'You spoilt little brat!' I said quite emphatically and still laughing.

'You blacky!' she retaliated. I stopped and thought and laughed again, still harder as I continued sharpening my pencil.

'You spoilt little brat!' I repeated emphatically.

'You nigger!' she snarled.

'Sulia!' I said in total shock, bringing my pencil sharpening exercise to a dramatic halt.

'I'm going to tell on you,' I assured her, immediately rising up my hand into the air to summon Mrs. Crabtree over to our table. Even this statement did not call her to remorse or repentance; for from out of the mouth speaks the abundance of the heart.

Mrs. Crabtree was plump in stature, adorning herself in gipsy-like clothing, on some days she had short messy red hair on others it was orange. Although she doubled as our art teacher her countenance and weirdness was the same in both classes. I remember all the time asking myself if she was for real expecting her at any moment to start to speak and act normally, but she never did. In one moment she would be speaking to you then suddenly out of nowhere she would burst into what seemed like uncontrollable laughter and for no apparent reason; you would be waiting for the punch line or for her to bring you in on the joke but she never did and it was impossible to understand the conclusion of her instructions, which were always rather frustrating to say the least.

My arm remained in the air all the while, still holding my very sharp pencil in my raised right hand. Unsatisfied with my response, Sulia tried to reach for my arm but without any success as I was able to hold her back with my left hand; in that moment, perhaps filled with sheer frustration and possibly fear of getting into trouble and even worse being suspended, she was now seething with anger and dived down head first, my left arm still on the table, my wrist exposed. Her mouth opening as she dived, her eyes closed, her mouth opened even wider before sinking her big ill, ugly, odd shaped looking teeth deep into my left wrist, making contact directly with my skin, as her jaws crunched down teeth first, piercing right through my soft smooth skin. Her eyes gleaming, her mouth drooling, and refusing to let go like some wild dog whose jaw was now in lock down.

The pain felt wet as it intensified and cold as my flesh opened up to greet the temperature of the room. It was as though the pain was marching up to my brain like a defiant army demanding a response but not one that involved making some simple yet formal complaint. Nevertheless, I willfully and deliberately refused to give Sulia any indication of my situation. I did not ask her to stop. I did not ask her to let go. I did not shake my wrist from her out of her mouth. I waited patiently, yet in vain for either Mrs. Crabtree to attend to me or even for Sulia to release me from her jaw; neither happened. The pain intensified, it was almost unbearable; then - just like an airplane - falling from the sky, I brought my right hand down from up there where I had been holding it, with one swooping motion, clutching the pencil firmly on its descend, like a warrior holding a javelin, sending the long razor-sharp lead tip deep into her hand, causing it to snap off at the nib. Instantly, she dropped open her mouth releasing my wrist, which I then pulled out of her mouth and examined it. With her ill-formed over-sized crocked teeth, she had managed to sever the upper epidermis; my wrist was now bleeding but so was her hand. I looked at my wrist and looked at her and made no comment.

'I'm telling!' she said.

'And so am I!' I assured her.

'And you will be the one to be expelled from school, as you know that biting is strictly prohibited and so is name calling,' I added. Screwing up her face and now sulking, she thrust her hand in the air to request permission to go to the toilet so she could attend her wound.

She called me later that evening to inform me that she had had to have a tetanus. When I told Odette of all the madness, she advised me to tell her that I had to have a rabies injection. In truth, I should have had a tetanus injection too, but I did not bother to write home about it; I was a warrior.

Life at Mansion Heights View

Life went on as usual at Mansion Heights as did all our routines. We would each be split into pairs to do the washing up after supper, depending on the number of girls residing. This factor would also determine the frequency as to how often we might be on washing up, drying up, putting away, wiping down the sides, sweeping the floors and tidying the dining room in a five-week cycle. I was paired up with Brandy; she was an English kid, tomboyish like me and we were about the same height and build, and we worked well together as a team; in fact, we held the record of just twenty-five minutes for after supper clean-up time.

When it was your turn on the washing up, you would wash up every night Monday to Friday for a week then the following week another two girls would do the same until the banner came around to you again, which at the most was once in five weeks and at least once a month. We also had weekend chores that we did on the weekends, and these would rotate once every three to four weeks. But as all the older girls took up Saturday jobs, Odette included, we seemed to have more and more to do on the weekends which was very tiring. At times, my back would be aching from the hoovering: but I never told anyone, I never complained.

On Thursdays, we frequented the football club, which hosted a night of dancing every week from 7 p.m. until 11 p.m. We had to be home by 11 p.m. sharp, so this would mean we would always miss the last dance. Of course, once we got on the dance floor, we would show them how to dance with rhythm, a crowd would quickly form around us, and we would have them eating out of the palm of our hands. It was as though we were doing a performance and we loved every minute of it, all the attention and everything.

Sometimes the music would be so good, we would compete against each other to see who had the best moves and if the DJ was in the zone, then he would definitely go five or ten minutes over time, which meant we would undoubtedly leave late and have to run all the way home as fast as we could; it didn't matter though. Sister may have given us one or two chances, but after that, it was all over, and punishment was eminent. And the punishment always lasted as long as she wanted it to – indeterminately. A month was usually about right.

I remember one night, there was a young black boy who upped the stakes; it was hard to keep the attention and the spot light that night, but I think we just managed the edge. When it was time for us to leave he wanted to escort me home; he spoke all the way as we walked down the hill and around the side of the convent not even coming up for air; He could have been walking with his own shadow for all he knew.

As we approached the back door, he pulled me into the shadows under the kitchen window and began to kiss me. I had only ever been kissed once before, by a boy, and this was not nice at all, and it was about to get a whole lot worse. Suddenly, he started to put his hands all over me, touching my groin without my consent. I hated every second of it. I felt so uncomfortable, but at the same time, I felt paralyzed to do anything about it. Inside, I was praying for it to stop, but he wasn't. Some of the girls passed us chatting as they went but they couldn't see us in the shadows. I kept telling myself, *'Move, Jacqueline, move, move now!'*

The second he moved his lips from off of mine and loosened his grip on me I stepped out into the light; I could hear all the voices filling up in the kitchen. I walked quickly up to the kitchen door and entered without looking behind me. Everyone was being loud as they came in sharing the highlights of the evening.

'What's that?' said one of the girls as she looked through the window. I held my breath waiting for him to be spotted and the ridicule to commence.

'It's nothing,' said Odette.

I thanked God silently that no one had seen us; what an embarrassment! I made small conversation before retiring upstairs to my room. I washed my face and had a strip wash before brushing my teeth quickly and jumping into bed. I never wanted to see him again.

Monday to Friday breakfast started from 7 a.m. It always included a choice of cereals, toast on tap, and sometimes eggs x2: scrambled, boiled, or even fried, on or off toast as you liked it, and tea and coffee as much as you liked.

As the week ticked on by and Thursday came around again, we went back to the club. On this occasion, I learnt that this boy actually had a girlfriend who had just had a baby. I learnt this in the space of approximately three minutes whilst checking my make-up in the powder room. It was as though the girls in there were speaking another language, except his girlfriend wanted to tear me to pieces; apparently someone who knew him had seen us leave the club together and had reported back to her, and she was absolutely fuming. Later Odette would inform me that a shakedown had occurred in the girls' toilets that night. Those girls left the club early that night and did not return for a long while, probably to allow things to cool down between them and our girls. What a scoundrel of a boyfriend! I thought.

Supper was always at 5.45 p.m. precisely, and it was on this day that I was asked to round up everyone for tea. As we flowed into the dining room, Sr P noticed that Kiara was missing. I was asked to go and see if she was upstairs, which I did. I looked in both the bathrooms, but she wasn't there, I looked in the shower room, but she wasn't there either, then I knocked on her bedroom door and after a few moments she opened it.

'Yes, I've just got out of the shower and I'm getting dressed, tell sister I'll be down in a minute.' When she opened the door, I noticed that she was only wearing a bra on her upper half and a towel on her lower half. It was a black bra. I could see quite plainly that it was the same black bra that had gone missing from off the line in the laundry room how many months ago. In fact, it was my black bra! She was wearing my black bra!

'Hey, that's mine,' I said. 'That's my bra!' I shouted. Immediately she slammed the door in my face. I tried to open the handle. But she was holding it tightly. I banged on the door some more, still shouting.

'That's my bra,' I shouted. 'You thief, and I'm telling Sister P!'

Hurriedly, I returned back to the dining room and reported the theft, naming Kiara as the culprit. Still no reaction from the nuns, not even so much as a twitch to my allegation. I mean no one even went to see if I was telling the truth. I was really fuming now, ready to take matters into my own hand; and I knew exactly how I was going to handle it.

After a long time, Kiara came down to supper; she was very, very late. Sister P completely ignored her; she was good at that. I made up my mind I would never speak to her again. My sister whispered in my left ear and told me never to leave anything in the laundry room ever again, and from that day, I was careful to follow her advice.

After supper, for those who had homework, they would be expected to do it, except there was no help from the nuns. They did not understand it; I'm not sure whether the thought to enlist competent tutors to help and support those of us who had homework and who needed support ever entered their heads; I for one needed help. Clearly I was still suffering from post-traumatic distress syndrome, but no-one knew it back then not even me.

It was remarkable that whilst in London, I sat in the second to top classes for Math's but upon moving to Hampshire, I had dropped right down to the bottom classes. I had no idea whether or not this was the effect of having been out of school for two periods, one of ten months and the other of four months or whether I was suffering post-traumatic stress from my time purely spent at Grimshaw Hall: for some strange reason, it no longer made any sense to me.

By the end of the third year, I had done better than my peers for English including some of those currently in the GCSE classes, so inevitably one would think that I would be moved back up. The irony was I did not want to move back up, because I knew that my English teacher would do whatever she could to put me back down again at least it felt that way; there was no encouragement for us, no appraisals, no guidance no nothing. You would often overhear public conversations of discontent at our presence, the air was thick with it and you could have cut some atmospheres with a knife.

I was really glad that the nuns had allowed me to bring my bikes down from Acorns to Mansion Heights; on top of which, I had been given one more, so now I had three. I would often ride the short distance of approximately 1.5 miles to the school, the hardest part being the part up the hill, around at the halfway point. The ride back down was of course always exhilarating though; downhill all the way: *Yippee!...*

Kiara did not go to the same school as us. She went to the school next door. It was a non-denominational school, which meant, they were of not connected with or to a religious denomination. You didn't have to be a catholic to stay at Mansion Heights and you did not have to have a religion to attend that local secondary school, however, you did have to wear a uniform, a deep purple uniform. It was truly ugly.

At home, we kept our bikes altogether in the same bike shed. Today was the day that I had taken my bike into the bike shed by myself usually sister would take it there for me, as I would usually forget. On this day I had met Kiara there and it was also the day that she had supposed she was going to flex her muscles of adolescence upon me. Unfortunately, I wasn't prepared to accept any of her rubbish that day; the thoughts of her stealing my bras were still fresh in my mind and my response to her arrogance was one short, sharp, extra hard punch. My fist loaded with all the frustrations of life making full contact with her right cheek. I remember she yelled as she went down, taking a row of bikes with her. And after calling me a few derogatory names, *as you do*, in the process. She then went in playing the sympathy card, running to tell the nuns what had happened. I for one did not care.

Quite remarkably, again they did nothing, and said nothing, no expression, no words, no nothing. I felt anxious; I was convinced I was in trouble, big trouble. What happened next was even more remarkable. Kiara, unbeknown to me, began to make her bruised cheek look even worse by adding make-up to it, all the way up to and including her eye. Surprisingly, Sister P did notice this and absolutely hit the roof, shouting at her, almost frothing at the mouth, as she ordered her to leave the table immediately and go and wash her face. Sr P seldom raised her voice but when she did it wasn't nice. In truth, I had not even noticed. When Odette explained it to me later, I just laughed at her silliness, but I was glad she had been told off even if it was a bit late in the day. I guess I felt almost justified.

Setting My Hair on Fire number 1

After the Saturday morning chores, which would have usually included hoovering the sun lounge, front room, dining room, and study or music room, or the main reception hallway, all three of the downstairs loos, the laundry room and laundry stairs, or the kitchen, dining room and pantry. All three areas would be shared equally between the girls who did not have a Saturday job, which usually came down to just me and Brandy; and if Brandy was spending the weekend away, would come down to just me. It was a lot to do and I would usually feel tired and even hungry afterward. Incidentally, it would usually be about lunchtime by the time all the chores were also finished; and on Saturday's we could make our own lunch, which we were encouraged to do. *A forward step into independence,* I thought.

On this particular Saturday, I had decided to make a full English breakfast for lunch. This would include x2 slices grilled bacon served crispy, x2 slices of toasts, x2 eggs, over easy and baked beans seasoned with course ground black pepper, mixed herbs, and melted butter. Visualizing the food in my mind's eye confirmed the fact that I had indeed made the right decision for my menu, which would all be washed down with a homemade banana milkshake. I decided to grill the bacon to arrive at that crispy finish I really loved.

We always used tappers to light the grill and they were always kept by the side of the cooker, in the drawer or on the window ledge, but after looking in all the usual places and not finding them there I decided to tear a strip of newspaper with which to light the grill. Merrily I blew out the piece of paper to a glistening glow, and then dropped it into the long chestnut brown kitchen bin that we used for the rubbish.

Kiara had been on kitchen duties that morning and had very cleverly lined the bin upward with newspaper, an act that she had repeatedly been asked not to do by Sr Coco. In the split second, it took for me to realize what I had just done, I turned only to see the bin now ablaze. Orange flames danced out of the top of it, and like some demented person, I began to blow at the flames using only my mouth.

Ironically, in my head, the only voice I could hear was my teacher from my home economics class, promising me faithfully that one day I would set the kitchen on fire because I kept leaving the tea towels on top of the cooker. Well, that day had come. I blew harder and harder *as if that was really going to do anything... da.* Then I began to shoo the flames away with my hands, *as if that was going to do anything da da.*

Then another brain wave, I thought I would pick up the bin inferno and place it outside. *Great idea*, I thought. As I opened the door, the flames swept back, leaping into my face and hair. I dropped the bin, slammed the door shut again, and began to put out the flames from my hair; at the same time, I now began calling for Sister P to come to my rescue.

'Sister P! Sister P!' I screamed at the top of my voice. There was no response. 'Sister P! Sister P!' I continued screaming.

In my desperation, I pulled out the fire blanket from off the wall where it had been so carefully wrapped and neatly placed, never once having cause to leave its position, and continued screaming for Sr P's help.

'Sr P! Sr P!' I began to wrap it around the bin, like some confused matador teasing the bull, *'da...' What possible good was that going to do?* A simple question in hindsight, I'm sure, still screaming frantically for the assistance of Sister P,

'Sister P! Sister P!' and all the while still wrestling with the bin inferno, my eyes frantically scanning around the kitchen, looking for anything that could lend support to my unfortunate event; my teacher's voice was firmly ringing out in my head.

'If you keep placing the tea towels on top of the cooker then you will surely set it on fire and possibly the entire kitchen too.' As I looked over at the sink I saw 2 empty milk bottles sitting quietly on the window ledge, I put down the bin, walked over to the sink, picked up a bottle and began to fill it with cold water, I walked back over to the bin, the flames still dancing out of it and quite calmly emptied the cold contents into it; immediately, the flames ceased before being reduced down to nothing.

The bin shriveled down into a heap of melted plastic on the floor, as if it had finally retreated in defeat. I ran out of the kitchen across the hallway and burst into the living room. I was sure I was covered in soot and smelling of that burning smell you get after a fire, all the while still calling out for Sister P.

Unfortunately, she had not been able to hear my cries for help as she had been deeply engrossed in the movie, *The Marx Brothers,* being shown on BBC1 for which there were no ad breaks, so no tea breaks.

I moved right in beside her and whispered in her ear that the bin has just caught fire and had been on fire; with that she literally jumped up out of her armchair and fled to the kitchen like a bat out of hell. Of course, she was extremely upset about the bin so much so that she forgot to enquire as to my own wellbeing, and then said, 'Well you will have to buy it back, *dear*.' God, how I hated that word.

I could not believe it! I had just had the ordeal of my life, and all she could think about was me replacing the damn bin.

'I will make the necessary deductions from out of your pocket money until it's all paid off.'

'What?' I thought to myself; I could not bloody believe it; now I was infuriated as well as traumatized but said nothing as usual. She made a point of telling me that the bin had cost £5.25 pence.

When Sister Jay and Sister Coco learnt about what had happened, they could not stop laughing. I, on the other hand, could not see the funny side of it at all. But as the story got more and more publicity, my reviews were mixed. Nevertheless, they both agreed that it would not be fair for Sister P to penalize me further by making me replace the bin.

Thankfully, they both also agreed that had Kiara not lined up the bin with paper, it would not have gone up in flames as it did, and therefore, she was partly to blame, more so because Sister Coco admitted that she had personally instructed her not to repeat this behavior just two weeks before.

The good news was that I did not end up having to pay for the new bin, however the downside was that I became the butt of every fire joke for a long while thereafter, which was also rather annoying to say the least; however, things soon died down with the change of seasons.

My Birthday

I celebrated two birthdays at Mansion Heights – my fourteenth and fifteenth. Sister P had a rule that whenever it was someone's birthday, everyone had to give them a present and a card, and we always had a cake. I remember when it was Angela's birthday, I thought I would give her a handmade tapestry of an exotic bird. I had decided on using all the glorious colors of the rainbow. I had even brought a frame for it and had managed to get a piece of glass in the village which had been cut specially to fit the frame. I ran all over the village for different-colored treads as my supply ran out; I stitched and stitched yet did not seem to be making any ground. I asked Sr Jay if she could help but she said she was too busy. I could feel myself becoming more and more stressed as the week of Angela's birthday fell upon us and I found myself stitching the tapestry every evening after school in my desperation to get it finished on time.

The more anxious I became the more frantically I pushed the needle into the fabric, the more I stabbed my fingers with the needle and the more anxious and worried I felt. It suddenly dawned on me that this was indeed a mammoth task, and at day three of the countdown, I did actually think that perhaps I might have bitten off more than I could chew. I became so overwhelmed with emotion but there was no one to help, and I had no more money left to purchase a different present. I had no choice but to continue. I had to keep on keeping on, working at it. When I came home from school, I went straight to sew again; I sewed so much, my fingers went numb.

The night before, I even turned my lights back on after lights out – a risky game with dire consequences if caught. But to turn up without a present would bring humiliation, embarrassment and possibly punishment, a fate I favored not; I pressed in sowing harder and harder, faster, and faster. Stabbing my fingers left right and center. And when the day of Angela's birthday arrived, immediately after school I went straight to sow again. Now I could smell the aroma of supper making its way along the corridor and up the stairs and turning left into my bedroom. I had recently changed over rooms. I was now in the lilac room situated right next to the stairs. What a mistake. It was cold and dull. The sunshine never entered this room due to its geographical position.

It was just 4 minutes 45 seconds before sit-down when I pulled the last thread through. I pushed it back through the fabric and back through to the other side cut the green thread from the needle and tied a secure knot. It was finished. *Phew!* What a relief. I had finished just before sit down. I quickly assembled it in the frame and then realised that I had no wrapping paper or Sellotape. Four minutes to go and I managed to find some used brown crinkled parcel wrapping paper. I wrapped it around the gift holding the folded edges in place with my fingers until I could locate some tape, 2 minutes to go before I had to settle for pink fabric plasters. It looked absolutely awful, but it was the best I could do in the circumstances. For the first time, I felt what it was like to be really stressed trying to work to a deadline; thank GOD, I made it.

When I arrived down at the dining room it was one minute before sit down, I added my present to the existing pile on top of the sideboard and took my place at the table. I was the last to be seated and Angela left my present, which was the biggest until the end before opening it. It was certainly the biggest and the heaviest too. When she opened it, she couldn't stop smiling? Everyone gasped in awe; it really did look very expensive. She told me afterwards that it was the best present that she had received, and she liked it the best. I could not believe my ears; clearly, it was not my best work, but I somehow felt relieved and proud at the same time, and perhaps more of the latter because I had actually made it with my own fair hand and felt somewhat elated at her comment.

Today, however, was my special day. Three of my school chums attended, as well as all the girls in Mansion Heights. My sister made my cake, – a very moist, very decadent, very chocolate sponge with jam, and chocolate butter icing in between each layer. I had four tiers that year, so the cake stood quite high on the plate; it was light, chocolaty, fruity, and very delicious. Everyone commented on it. Seeing how wonderful her cakes were, perhaps that also encouraged me subconsciously to start baking on a regular basis.

I think we both had the baking-cooking gene passed down to us from our gran and our dad. He did a lot of the cooking at home and always baked the best Christmas cakes ever. I guess when you bake a sponge, you are looking for that 'melt on the tongue' texture, which is so light and fluffy that you just want to savor the moment whilst taking in that special memory before allowing it to slide down your throat. By holding it on your tongue and pressing it on to the roof of your mouth was the softness test.

I probably perfected the art of making apple pies to the point that I could almost do it with my eyes shut. To that extent, baking the layer cakes and decorating them became my next challenge. And I do remember quite vividly that there was this one occasion when I had succeeded in making my first ever five-tier, fresh-fruit-and-cream gateau, which was destined for our afternoon tea and matinee the following day, our normal routine after lunch, when in walked Sister P, whose first words were not 'Hi Jacqueline how you doing?' or 'That looks nice.' but rather 'I hope you're gonna clean up this mess.' And she gave me one of those looks, you know the one where you snigger, and your upper lip quivers up because you're so annoyed but don't want to show that you're really annoyed. OK, OK, so I was a messy cook, but was that statement really called for? It pierced me to the core and instantly I became offended and incensed.

Fair enough, I would be the first to accept that I was not the tidiest cook in the world, but had I not always cleaned up the kitchen to a pristine sparkle after every one of my baking events? Was I not the new queen of clean? I looked at the cake, and in a blink of an eye, I witnessed my left-hand smash it to pulp on the table. In that same moment I took a deep breath in, bringing my heart rate back to normal and thought, *how could I now cause her the same annoyance that she had just caused me without getting into any trouble?* It was then that it happened, that it came to me. I would finish the cake to complete perfection, and then I would give it as a gift to the old dears over at the convent. I needed to get my timing just right. I had to make sure I knew exactly where Sister P was and how long she was gonna be there before making the short journey over to the convent. I walked across the small courtyard and entered in by the back door with the cake in hand; it was massive and very heavy, but it looked stunningly beautiful, like a wedding cake in fact. Each layer was covered with raspberry jam and vanilla butter icing. The outside was covered in soft lemon butter icing with fresh fruits to decorate the top. It looked mouth-watering, so beautiful, even if I do say so myself; '*Eric Lanlard, eat your heart out and lick my fingers too.*'

I found my way over to the kitchen of the convent and handed the heavy cake over to Sister Agregayous. A round woman, small in stature and always dressed in grey. She was so ecstatic that she took me and the cake into every room on the ground floor to show it off to all the nuns; they were all praising me and thanking me. It was at this point I told them that in fact the cake was a gift from Sr P who had ask me to make it especially for them as a token of her love and appreciation for them all; well by now they were all completely speechless. After the tour of the lounge she took the cake in to the kitchen where it was parked up until their afternoon tea also on Sunday. Well, if ever my name was mud, it had certainly been changed to beautiful that day, at least in the convent anyway. I certainly felt every bit the best child ever born. I returned feeling justified and elated. I even cleaned up the kitchen to a glittering sparkle before settling down to watch some well-earned TV.

That afternoon, Sister P asked whether the cake was in the pantry. I didn't answer, so I guessed she was assuming it was. I think she was really looking forward to having a nice slice with her Sunday tea. When Sunday arrived, we got up, had breakfast, went to church, had lunch, and were just about to sit down to our usual afternoon tea and cake, when Sister Coco came bounding over to ask Sister P whether she had had a slice of the lovely cake over at the convent. '*Oh crumbs,*' I thought silently, time for me to make a quick exit. I left the front room and went upstairs and began counting the seconds in blocks of tens until I felt that it was safe to return back down again.

Sister P immediately rushed over to see the cake, only to be met by all the nuns who were praising her and thanking her for the cake and telling her what an excellent job she had done with me. I told them that Sr P loved them all so much she had asked me to make them a special cake as a token of her gratitude and love to them. As angry as she was, she could not show it. She didn't speak to me for a week after that little episode. But I still felt justified. – One to me and nil to her I believe.

Setting my Hair on Fire No. 2

The next episode of me setting my hair on fire would occur a short while later. It would be after church so thank GOD for small mercies. All the girls had left the building already, but I wanted to light a few candles and would stay behind to do so. There was a queue, so I had to wait my turn. When I came before the candle stand I was surprised to find it packed, so much so that people had now resorted to fixing candles in between the candle holders and it was very warm up there, even more so as I bent down to pick up a candle; in so doing I stopped half way before fully returning back up to standing. It was in this moment that something remarkable happened...

Whilst I was down there deciding for whom I was lighting the candle for and had them in my mind's eye, I stood up and closed my eyes to pray for them at the same time wondering why it was very warm. Upon convincing myself the heat was coming from the candle stand I stretched out my hand to light one of my candles. It was in that moment that suddenly my head was being swished and swayed from side to side and backwards and forwards; as I turned, I was met by the words of a tall stranger who said, 'For a moment there I thought you were ascending down from heaven like Jesus and the angels!'

'What on earth is going on,' I thought.

In that same moment Sr Coco then appeared at the door and began to hurry me up. I looked across the pews at her then back at him then back at her. Not fully understanding his words. I lit the rest of my candles, said my prayers, and returned to the minibus in which everyone was engrossed in their own conversations. It was then that I put my hand in my hair only to grab a handful of burnt hair, and upon so doing realised that when I bent down to pick up the candle it was my hair that had caught alight. No one noticed as they were all too engrossed in their own conversations. And to tell the truth I felt rather embarrassed at the entire situation I mean how on earth was I going to live that one down. However, it did not take too long before my hair grew back; ready for the third hair fire episode just four short years later, and the clock was ticking, tick, tock...tick, tock...

The Isle of White

That year we spent our holiday in the Isle of White. I had never been there before, so it was definitely another pin on the map for me. We drove to Southsea, like sensible people, at a normal hour of the day, which did not take too long, and then took the hovercraft over for the short crossing followed by a short train ride to the area in which we would be staying.

To our surprise, our journey finally came to an end with a long, tiring uphill walk, up which we each had to lug our own luggage. It was really hot that day; the heat was scorching, which made travelling to the hotel much harder and seemed to add to the weight of our cases. No one knew where the hotel was exactly, and we had no map with which to reference from where we were.

When we finally happened upon it, we were so thankful to get out of the heat. We were all sweating buckets. We had already picked our room partners, with whom we were sharing, before we had left Waterlooville. So, upon arrival, it was just a matter of being allocated our rooms and collecting our room keys from reception.

I was sharing with Brandy. We partnered really well when at home, so it only seemed natural to partner for the holiday too. During our stay on the island, the nuns had arranged for us to attend an array of activities to keep us, as far as possible, occupied. Perhaps the most interesting was the assault course and the least interesting was a couple of boring walks; we also visited the funfair, and the beach, with all of us trying our hand at swimming in the sea, which was really cold.

We visited the assault course twice during our stay as it was so good, and I got sprayed with mud from head to foot when spiraling down the zip wire and whisking through the muddy puddle on the bottom, which completely ruined all my clothes. I ended up showing off my panty loo loos to *all and sundry* as Sister would say, still it was great fun.

At one point during the holiday, most of the girls were in one room chatting away, and I don't remember whether the conversation was getting out of hand or heated or anything, but I remember just getting up and going out for a walk; no-one noticed that I had left the room or the hotel. I walked up one road and seemed to walk so far that I had no idea where I was. I remember looking to my right and seeing the sea, and the edge of the cliff then in the next moment I felt so overwhelmed with wanting to give up on life to the point where I just lied down on the road. I couldn't think about the pain of being run over because I had never been run over before. I remember lying there with my eyes shut tight as if willing myself out of my present life. I was overwhelmed with thoughts of not wanting to go another day in my present existence. Suddenly, I could hear the motion of a moving car coming towards me. Thoughts swirled around in my head that this was it. But then, for what seemed like no apparent reason, I heard a scream. It seemed to be coming from the direction of straight ahead of me. Then I heard the quickening of fast-moving feet coming in my direction. Suddenly they stopped. I could feel the warm breath of a stranger on my face as he checked for my vital signs. His voice raised the alarm for a call for help.

'Call an ambulance, she's injured!' said the man.

With that remark fear struck me. I didn't want any trouble. I didn't know what to do so I got up and ran away, but they ran after me, calling out to me to stop. I didn't answer. I just kept running. They kept calling for me to stop as they chased me and then they began to name call. *As you do.*

'You Black Bastard!'

I didn't answer; eventually I outran them. I could not understand what had happened, what had gone wrong.

That evening, I went out with the girls as normal, as though nothing had happened and as we sat drinking and chatting and laughing at the competition in the bar we had come to frequent, it dawned on me as I looked at them one by one that none of them had any idea as to what had happened to me earlier that day. I looked normal to them, but they had no idea of what was wrong with me, – nor did I for that matter. I couldn't put it into words back then, but I realised later in life that I was simply trying to escape my life even if it meant going through death's door. I was suffering from post traumatic distress, only I didn't know it then.

As the years passed, I never told anyone, not even my sister what had happened that day.

We spent the remainder of our holiday at the beach during the days, where I tried my hand again, or rather my feet, at surfing on my surfboard, that I had inherited from I don't know where. I had spent several days proudly painting it and repainting it, before the holidays, in some dull golden oil-based color, which had bubbled at the sides, but upon entering the water both me and the board just kept sinking; however, it did double up greatly as a sun lounger as hard as it was, and it helped to keep the sand off my towel.

We spent the last few evenings of our holiday frequenting the local bars and clubs providing they were all free entry of course. Our drinks were usually brought by strangers with whom we would chat to briefly before taking to the dance floor.

At the end of our trip, it was back to Mansion Heights. We would remain there for two days before we were repacked and ready to meet the 'Portsmouth to London' train; Sr Coco was driving us down to Havant Station on time to catch the 1:20 pm arriving at 3:50 pm.

We had been invited back to Jeanie's again, which we really enjoyed, funnily enough. It was very relaxing there probably because there were no rules and no restrictions, although we never took advantage, and we had Zachary to make us laugh. I guess our staying with Jeanie was becoming a bit of a habit, nevertheless it was a good one, one that I didn't want to give up, so I never asked any questions. At the start of the visit I was booked to spend four days with Flavia before re-joining Odette. As much as I loved seeing Flavia and having a good laugh with her I was becoming increasingly board with her mother's religious program.

In comparison when back at Jeanie's we laughed and joked constantly with Zachary, and when he had time, he would cook me his signature dish. Lean minced meat, fluffy buttery mash, and sweet petit pois finished in a lovely onion gravy, – absolutely delicious! *Jamie Oliver eat your heart out and smell my breath too.* I asked Zachary whether he made this dish for the chief of police to which we all laughed. Of course, we would frequently tease him, asking him whether he would have to take the food on his bike to the chief of police if he had been called out on an emergency. Everyone erupted in more laughter. I also asked him whether the chief of police had given him the siren to use so he could get his lunch on time. Even Zachary was laughing at that one.

Nevertheless, Zachary would also give back as good as he got. He would mock us all back by taking the mick out of us, in particular the way that we spoke, – after two years in the shires both our accents had become very lardy da. It was always non-stop laughing whenever he was home. He would call us up to his room, and the jokes would begin, and the laughter would reverberate throughout the house seeping into every room. It was absolutely contagious.

Whenever I visited his room, I noticed that he would always have romantic love songs playing. He said that he liked to unwind with these playing in the background; they would help him come down from the high of his day. He would always point out the solo piece being played by either the sax or the piano. It was really nice to have a completely platonic relationship with someone of the opposite sex whom I trusted implicitly and who respected me and treated me, always, like a lady. I felt completely safe, relaxed and at home in his company. He never made any advances to me or at me and he never spoke to me in a derogatory manner or used foul language ever. I could totally be my silly self with him – I could be the real me, the crazy me, the messing up me, the falling in the mud me and he was absolutely fine with me. He accepted me for me. In Zachary's presence life was bearable again.

Zachary was of mixed heritage, I think. I never asked him to be sure. He was tall, slim, and wore his hair in an Afro, which, when you touched it, your hand just fell into it because it was super soft; however, unlike my uncle he didn't use Daz. He was always in long skinny blue jeans, a black leather jacket, and black boots. His mode of transport was a Yamaha 250cc, and he smoked Number 6 blue and of course, so did I. At least until I managed to burn a hole in my bedspread upon being caught by Sister all those moons ago. Sometimes, do you ever wonder why you do the things you do? It was the story of my life back then.

I mean after getting caught by Sr Simone, she said she was going to allow me to break the news myself to Sister Bea. Sr Simone was a nun in training, and she was waiting to take her final vows, so her veil and garments were slightly different to those of the regular nuns. She was very tall, very slim, and always appeared to be laughing even when she was talking.

Each time I would approach Sr Bea in an attempt to break the news I just couldn't. I couldn't tell her that I tried to smoke a cigarette, or that Sr Simone had caught me, or that I had burnt a hole in my bedspread. After two weeks of trying, I think the most I managed to get out was 'I... I... I'm sorry.' She filled in the blanks. Thank God. Surprisingly, I was not punished, I was not rebuked, she just asked me to give her the cigarettes and the lighter, which I did.

It was during this holiday that my world came crashing down to earth with a bump. Strangely I hadn't seen Zach all day. Then suddenly I heard him come shuffling in and joking up the stairs with his mate, Andy, and someone else. I didn't recognize the third person. Thinking no more of it I freshened-up and stood outside his door ready to knock on it when I heard the laughter of a female voice followed by Zach and Andy. I couldn't believe it; in that moment I felt so crushed, so stupid, so embarrassed. Immediately I returned to my room and cried myself to sleep. They were in the room next door. I could hear them laughing together and then it went quiet. I could not wait to get back to Hampshire and forget the entire affair.

The Turning

When we returned back to school for the start of the new term, we learned that we had Sr Grey for our form tutor. She was of a different order than that of our nuns and to some extent the rivalry was quite evident. It was the start of the third year. Our class had moved into the main building on the west side. It was darker than our previous class and all the desks were positioned in such a way that our backs faced the windows. You would not be wrong for thinking that perhaps I could or would command a degree of favor from Sr Grey given that I lived with nuns and she was also a nun; however, you would not be more wrong.

I remember one-day Sr Grey decided to label everyone through color identification by the shade of their skin. I am not sure whether this was some sort of game or whether it was a form of mockery of some sort. But clearly being in a predominantly pale class each member could expect to be classified as such; until it got to me that was. 'Well what color would we say Jacqueline is?' she asked the class.

'Blacky!' shouted someone sitting behind me and the class erupted into laughter.

'Dark!' shouted another.

'Darky!' they all shouted out and the laughter started again.

'Nigger!' someone else shouted out.

'Less of that,' snapped Sr Grey quickly. But isn't that what she really wanted to happen? I thought.

'Well I think Jacqueline is more coffee colored,' she added, trying to take back control of the class as it got too loud.

'Is that with or without milk?' another child asked. They all jeered again.

In all honesty, it felt like she really just wanted to describe my skin color just so that she could publicly label me, I guess it was her way of insulting me with my consent. However, I refused to take part by deliberately refusing to comment or to add to any comment that was made. Her little game did no more than to trigger a further barrage of insults with 'coffee colored' fast becoming my nickname for most of the first term in the third year.

In hindsight, given that all the other children in the class had pale skin, I am convinced that she deliberately and willfully just wanted to make the statement out loud. I guess it was her way of putting in her 2 pence by name calling without saying 'you this' or 'you that.' To her, it was probably a subtle way of making a racial slur against me, but for exactly whose benefit, I was not really sure. I think you call it political racism, you know, where someone wants to make a point about color without actually making a racist remark but with all the derogatory racist undertones attached.

I continued to excel in woodwork, metalwork, home economics, P.E., and English, despite never really being credited or appraised by any of my teachers apart from my P.E. teacher. Somehow it felt that the decision to mark me down was not completely universal. I could see it in some of their faces, in particular my woodwork and metalwork teachers, who would try to give me high marks, but never full marks. If asked why? I am sure they would not have had the answer.

I really enjoyed technical drawing too; it was a quiet class and one where I could hear myself think. However, it wasn't long before I gave up trying after being completely and utterly publicly humiliated for, according to teacher, using the wrong pencil. The teacher shouted at the top of his voice, 'Well you'll never make it as an architect will you.' I felt absolutely humiliated, so ashamed, so embarrassed, so crushed. This was exactly what I didn't need. Apparently, I had used a HB2 instead of a HB. *Gee thanks, Sir.* I dropped it the following year. However, I continued to shine, standing out in dance and games.

To be or not to be suspended

It was just coming up to spring again when we found out who was going to be our personal tutor, for the following term. It was then that I decided that I would leave altogether and let the SS know from now, so they could start to make their plans. I decided to go to the phone box to make the call. Upon my arrival, there was a queue. When my turn came up I had about 5 mins before the bell, and afternoon classes would resume.

Two girls had joined the queue behind me and were chattering so loud I could not hear what London was saying. Then they started tapping me on the shoulder and speaking to me whilst I was trying to speak to London. They were making it intensely difficult to hear what was being said by London, which was completely frustrating. This was a crucial time for me. I had found out who my personal tutor was going to be in year 4. A Mr. Propretus. If this information was correct, I knew I didn't stand a chance. Even the pale skinned children knew he was an outspoken racist. I felt I had to make a decision and quick. I decided to leave again.

A form tutor is supposed to be a person you can confide in, aren't they? A form tutor is not someone who is fluent in crude, cruel, racist jokes, And certainly not to a child.

I was making a collect call to London to tell my rescuers that I had decided I was leaving home ... again, but I was unable to tell them the reason why, more so because little Miss Noisy and her buddy were making so much noise standing right behind me. The SS had already failed to hear my cries of help despite being screamed from the top of my lungs whilst at Grimshaw Hall. In truth, I doubted very much that they were going to start paying attention now, and I for one certainly wasn't about to start holding my breath, not at this point anyway. Of course, she just tried to talk me out of it and kept asking why. I felt as though I really couldn't go into detail right then and there.

The bell had gone, and break time was over. I had already waited 20 minutes for the phone and now I could no longer hear a thing, given the fact that these two songbirds were making as much noise as they possibly could, and had now added tapping me on the shoulder in order to hurry me up and laughing with it. When I got off the phone, I turned around to see only one of them still standing there.

'What do you think you are doing? 'I asked her angrily, as I grabbed her by the scruff of her shirt.

'Err...err...nothing,' she promptly answered. I could see the fear in her eyes as she tried to put the entire blame on her friend now gone.

'Well don't ever do that again,' I screamed at her, grabbing her by the scruff of her clothes, pushing her to one side and snapping her neck chain in the process.

It took an entire term and a bit to find the other girl, but I was in no rush and a few of the class were also keeping an eye out too. I was in my sister's class when the word came that she was coming into the block. We just had to hope she was coming up the same stairwell that we were standing at the top of. I ran backwards and forwards until I could confirm exactly which staircase she was on.

Once it was confirmed I stood at the top of the west staircase and waited. As she mounted the last staircase, I took a run and jump, jumping down the stairs, my right foot connecting to and making contact with her torso in one sharp swoop. Losing her balance, she slipped down two steps, almost losing her balance on the third; then allowing herself to collapse in a heap on the floor on the last. Back then, teenage girls were very different. If they were not showing off, believing they had one over on you, then they were exaggerating the consequences or rather the effect of the symptoms of you having had the upper hand over on them.

In that moment she started screaming for all and sundry to hear, screaming for her friend to get a teacher, any teacher. She was hell bent on playing the victim, and oh my goodie gum drops was her performance going to demand an Oscar that day. Oh boy! Was I in trouble now? I kept my cool. *I don't care,* I told myself.

Registration was starting. The roll was now being called out by Sister Grey. She must have called out about four names from the register when our door opened without warning followed by my name being called out, summoning me to go to the principal's office. I knew what this meant. I took my coat and picked up my bag as I knew that I would not be returning, at least not that day anyway.

I went down to the main entrance area and was about to knock on the door when I was stopped in my tracks by the shouting coming out from behind the other side of the door.

'Was that Sr P?' I asked myself. I thought I recognized her voice. Yes, it was Sister P... She had already arrived, and she was screaming at the top of her lungs at...at ... eventually the office door opened; to my surprise it was Sister Mangot the principal who had been standing behind it and she now appeared to be ushering Sister P out, who rushed past her briskly.

'Come on, dear,' she said as she extended her hand to open the main door for me and we both walked through it. We got into the nun mobile, and in silence we made the short drive back to Mansion Heights. I never really knew what went down that day, but I came away knowing that she had my back. It's only now as an adult, in hindsight, looking back that I was able to piece together the missing parts of the puzzle.

When we arrived back, I wasn't sure whether or not I was in trouble or on punishment or what. I did not know whether I had been confined to my room. For a while it did feel as though I was walking on eggshells so I tried as far as possible to keep out of her way, believing that I had let her down and she was now disappointed, until oddly she broke the ice by making suggestions of what I could do. Once she saw I was getting comfortable, she said,

'Let me know when you are feeling ready to return to school dear.' Deep down, I didn't want to. I felt as though I just couldn't face another day of it. In truth, I just did not want to go back there ever again. If it wasn't the children dishing up abuse then it was the teachers, and if it wasn't the teachers, it was the children. It was a vicious cycle, and I was fed up with it, I was fed up with all of them. To my mind my education was finished - ruined. After three years of abuse, I had given up, I had thrown in the towel. And I was ready to walk away for good. And never to look back.

Three days later I returned back to school. It was something she said right in that moment which helped me to understand that she had been sticking up for me in that office. She had been screaming on the side-lines for me. Sister Mangot had wanted me expelled or, at the very least, suspend me. She wanted to do whatsoever she could do to ruin my name, my report, and, if possible, my entire life; without any thought or consideration for what I had had to endure on a daily basis from my peers as well as her teachers. For the past three years it had been hell on earth for me, in her establishment and what was worse was that she did not have a single thought whatsoever of what I could become. Neither did she care, not a single iota – none of them did. The blinkers were on and the shutters were down. But this child would not forever be, one day I would become an adult and tell the story, the whole story.

That day it was Sister P who was giving Sr Mangot, the head of school, a very real, up close, and personal reality check. It was one which clearly left a very bittersweet taste in her mouth and one she was not prepared to swallow, at least not yet anyway.

Back at school no one commented on my three-day sabbatical, so life just continued as normal. I was still not speaking to Sulia and it really felt like she got her just desserts when Dani had her birthday and deliberately refused to invite her. I mean when Dani invited me, I wasn't really sure because I was not really on speaking terms with any of them. When Dani spoke to me on my own she explained that she was sick and tired of the way Sulia treated everyone and wanted to teach her a lesson, *well how could I refuse...*

During the build up to Dani's party she kept telling Sulia each day, from about the Wednesday, that she had something very important to tell her and only her. Every day Dani would add a bit more drama and suspense, just enough to keep her interested and then on Friday she asked Sulia whether she would be in on Saturday evening around 6pm. 'Yes of course,' said Sulia absolutely beside herself as if expecting to receive something amazing.

When Saturday evening finally arrived, Dani called Sulia and put her on loudspeaker.

'What are you doing,' asked Dani? Harriot and I kept very quiet listening alongside her.

'Oh, nothing much just watching TV,' said Sulia. 'W hy, what are you doing?'

'Oh well, we just went to the pictures.'

'Who did you go with?'

'Harriot and Jacqueline,' replied Dani, 'and now my mum's making us some yummy hot dogs with tomato sauce and onions, I love onions with hot dogs, and then we are going to have popcorn and ice cream and then watch a movie.'

'Oh, are you having a sleep over too,' She asked?

'Err, are we having a sleep over girls,' Dani asked raising her voice?

'Yes, we are!' we all shouted down the phone.

'And you're not invited,' said Dani!

With that Dani and Harriot began to roar with loud laughter. The line went quiet. Sulia did not speak another word and after a few moments she hung up the phone. Well, I was speechless, but I do believe that Sulia got her just desserts, even if it was long overdue. Well '*if that ain't socking it to ya*'. I didn't stay over that night. I was not aloud. Sister came to pick me up just after 10 pm, and I returned home.

I spent my free time continuing to ride my bike around the village on the weekends, but that also came to a dramatic end, when after misjudging a pit I came up off it; and whilst flying through the air I failed to let go of the handle bars, which successfully connected with me, stabbing me right in the center of my groin upon making impact with the dirt. I lay there on the ground trying to get my bearings. Once the stars had evaporated, I tried to get up. I could barely make it to my feet for the pain was so great but there was no one near to help so I had just had to get on with it. Slowly I managed to walk back to the house. I felt I couldn't tell the nuns; I was too embarrassed. The only person I was able to speak to about my ordeal was Odette. She checked me over and confirmed that no serious injuries were evident. Still, I wasn't able to wear jeans until the swelling went down which wasn't until several days later.

The remainder of the term ticked on by really quickly and before we knew it, the Christmas holidays were upon us.

Christmas 1979

We had the tallest tree I had ever seen, and it was real; it was beautifully dressed in all its glory boasting tinsel and shiny balls and the girls were encouraged to take part in dressing it, I think Odette did most of it. She was very creative. Sister P made a point of the fact that every girl had to give a present to the other. Her request caused the tree to become packed solid with a sea of presents overflowing from underneath it. The dining room was tastefully decorated too, with holly, mistletoe, and glitter.

The table was dressed immaculately with red tablecloths and white napkins held together in elegant silver rings, the very best. Expensive crackers and more tinsel added to the style and panache that caused the table to stand out. Sister P had put out our best cutlery and our best crockery, and oh my gosh! the food was amazing! We had everything. You name it, it was there. Roast turkey, roast chicken, roast lamb, sausages in jackets, roast ham, roast potatoes, boiled potatoes, mashed potatoes, vegetables that went on forever (peas, broccoli, carrots, cauliflower, cabbage, sprouts), cheese sauce, mint sauce, bread sauce, Yorkshire puds, and gravy. Not forgetting all the desserts, including Christmas pudding, home-made minced pies, ice cream, jelly, lemon sorbet, vanilla cheesecake, chocolate, and cherry gateau all served with cream, brandy cream, and or custard; the choice was yours.

I think Odette had joined in and helped with the cooking as she loved to cook. Sister P had invited over Father Paul, our local parish priest. He lived in the house next to Acorns, at the top of the drive. He seemed nice enough if you needed a chat or something. Sister P had him sit right next to her. We giggled secretly. He was handsome compared to Father John and much, much younger.

We washed down all the food with glass after glass of lemonade, Coke, Cola, white wine, and sparkling wine. The main course was followed by an extravagant cheese board accompanied with bulging grapes, finished off with coffee and port. One by one, the girls opened the top button on their jeans in an attempt to make more space for the food to go down, and then one by one, we excused ourselves from the table not being able to eat another thing. I'm sure we all slept exceedingly well that night.

The day after Boxing Day we were set to return once more back up to London. We boarded the fast train at Havant station, which would only make four stops before reaching London. Sometimes there would be an unscheduled stop, factored in to the journey where we would be held up for as long as half an hour before continuing on the journey. The holdup would usually occur between Guildford and Woking, one of the frequently used excuses for the holdup would be '*sorry ladies and gents there's something on the line.*'

Before coming into the station at London Bridge, we would often be signaled to wait several moments on the tracks for a platform to become vacant, before pulling alongside it and being able to disembark.

Whilst we were waiting I could see the top floors of old buildings made from old bricks. I would wonder where we were, and what was below. I could hear the chatter of a multitude of voices raising like a vapor to reach my ears. It was as though they were speaking another language. It was the sound of many voices. Cutlery warring with crockery, dominating the sound, all clashing together, probably being spilled into the dishwasher.

In a moment, the atmosphere had changed as the aroma of foreign spices filled the air, a mixture of east verses west. Just then as the pictures filled my mind the train moved along the line and pulled into the station.

We would be staying at Jeanie's place again. We would meet up with Zac and visit all our usual haunts. Swimming, shopping burgers and shakes and perhaps even take in a movie or two, that sort of thing. I remember when GREACE came out we saw it five times. The queue almost circled the cinema. We just could not get enough of it. That good feel feeling. We tithed to the memorabilia and sung the songs for a good few months that followed. In those days pretty ladies visited you in your seats and brought to you your refreshments.

With the arrival of the New Year we returned to school for the start of another new term. It snowed that winter. It was cold yet beautiful.

Surprisingly, Val came up to visit us. We had not seen her in years. She didn't stay too long but took lots of pictures of us in the snow. They were powerfully striking, despite being in black and white. She told us she was leaving the UK for good and just wanted to see us one more time before she left. I thought that would really be the final time that we would ever see her again. But in fact, only I would see her one last time in London, as she returned to remove her last bits from her flat. Odette refused to see her on that occasion.

Spring Break

The first term ticked on by really quickly and before long Easter was upon us. It would be then that we would return to London for Easter break and our usual routine would begin to unfold, I would always spend the first few days with Flavia and her family before catching up with Odette back at Jeanie's.

Flavia's family were very much the overly serious Seventh Day Adventists, extremely committed and zealously religious. They commenced their ritual from sundown on Friday evenings, so all the cooking and cleaning had to be completed before dusk. Her mum was really strict about everything being done on time, and then even stricter about nothing being done throughout the entire duration of the Sabbath. As I got older, all the restrictions and rules and religious religion became too much; it felt like wearing an itchy woolen jumper that was ridiculously too small in summer and not being allowed to scratch or pull it back to its natural shape.

Thinking back, it must have been during the early part of 1979, when Odette decided she wanted to visit our Dad. For me, well, after his performance at court, I had almost succeeded in entirely erasing him from the contours of my mind, along with all his other children and in particular... his wife.

Apparently, the SS were supposed to have organized a visit, but each time Odette made enquiries, she was given the same information that '*someone else was dealing with it*' and '*that they would come back to her once they had an answer*'; I think you call it 'passing the buck'. *Not cool.*

In truth, the SS had had an entire year to arrange a visit since they had been put on notice of Odette's intention, but had failed bitterly to do anything about it, so it was on this trip that Odette had decided to take matters into her own hands and visit them herself without sending them prior a letter, or notice, or warning that she was coming.

After my return from the Featherstone's I thought the plan was still that we would meet up and go straight from Jeanie's. However, at the time, she had not told me of her plans', so I was the last to know what her plans were. We had not seen him since the court date some three years earlier and had no idea of how the day was going to unfold or more importantly how well we would be received if at all. I guess she was just hoping for the best. I guess that's what teenagers do, hope for the best. 'Oh, great,' I thought, somehow, I had a really bad feeling that this was not going to end well. In the last minute, she asked me to accompany her. I did not have time to check in with my emotions, so I just followed her.

We arrived at the flats at approximately 2:30 pm, walked along the balcony to number 58, and tap tapped on the thin, slender letter box. I guess subconsciously we were both hoping that Mordecka was not in. There was no answer, so we knocked for a second time and waited nervously. Still there was no answer. We were about to leave, when we were sure that we heard footsteps coming along the hallway in the direction of the front door. Remaining in our position we knocked again, really hard this time. Then we heard it again, more footsteps. Odette was certain she saw the blinds move, yet no one opened the door. After about thirty minutes or so, we decided to leave. Odette did not speak or look at me, which usually meant she was absolutely incensed. She power walked all the way over to Uncle Matthew's house, Dad's older brother, whom she hoped still lived in Kitchener Road.

I was surprised she remembered the way even after all this time; I had to jog just to keep up. I could feel her disappointment, it was so thick, it was tangible. When we arrived, they opened the door immediately; we could not believe how happy they all were to see us again. Odette explained the situation to Uncle Matthew, who immediately got dressed, bundled us into his car and drove directly over to the flats. He banged on the door with such ferocity that the entire door and its frame began to shake; this time, it was just a few minutes before Dad came to the door. After peeping through the blinds and seeing his brother, he slowly opened the door. We were kind of standing behind him, not entirely sure of the temperature of our reception. It was upon seeing us that Dad walked off without saying a word. Uncle Matthew followed him into the kitchen. We could hear him begin to reason with Dad. They were in there together at length, at times shouting at each other. Then we could hear Dad; he was crying... I felt really awkward, not really knowing what to do.

After about thirty minutes or so, he came into the living room and sat down with us. His eyes were all red, his lashes still wet. It was evident that he had been crying, but neither of us commented on it. I had no idea of the pain he must have felt each time he had to leave us; or the pain he must have felt when we left him. Perhaps my departure was even more traumatic as it was not planned, it was not aforementioned, and he did not see it coming. Albeit each departure was an emotional tear. And the day was coming when I too would stand in his shoes, and have my own heart ripped right out of my chest; and the clock was ticking; tick.. tock... tick ..tock.

In that moment on that day there was so much I felt I wanted to say but couldn't; and many, many years would pass before I would find the strength or the courage to speak out. But for now, the cat had definitely, got my tongue. We sat there for perhaps a little over an hour, making small talk about school and where we were living, but not really talking, if you know what I mean. Dad could not imagine how far Hampshire were because he had never heard of it, neither had he heard of Waterlooville; he had no idea where in the UK they were and on a geographical point neither did I;

therefore, it was not easy to communicate to him where we were in relation to him geographically.

At this point, Uncle Matthew left because he had to prepare for work that same evening. He still worked as a baker, just like Dad did. As the time arrived for us to go, Dad asked whether we could return to see him again. This made us very happy. I guess we both felt we had been sort of accepted back into the fold in some way again, at least by Dad anyway. Quite automatically, we both agreed that at our next holiday, which would be after the summer holidays, we would definitely return to visit him and our siblings again.

As we reached the second-floor balcony of the flats that sat adjacent to ours, we looked up to wave our last goodbye, only to see Mordecka moving along the balcony in what appeared to be in some Darlek-like motion. Unpleasantly shocked, we quickly dropped down our waving arms and continued walking without looking back until we were out of sight, not wanting her to notice us. As I coyly looked back for the last time, I witnessed her disappear into the flat without looking in our direction. I felt somewhat relieved that she had not noticed us. Part of me knew that she would most certainly be responding with some crazy like action if she found out. We had not come to see her anyway and neither did we want to. *Of course, this was unforgiveness but neither of us knew it back then.*

When we returned to Jeanie's I was happy to learn that Zachary and his girlfriend had finally broken up. Selfishly, I enjoyed his company all to myself and now the door was open again, so we continued to meet up after he had finished work. Our evenings would once more be filled up with telling jokes and listening to music until bedtime.

It was about this time that I noticed that Zachary's friend, Andy was always hanging around. Up until now I had never been formally introduced to Andy. But he was the same Andy who had set Zach up with his first female encounter and broke my heart.

It was slightly annoying always finding him there with Zach. I mean when I wanted to be alone with Zach. I wanted to speak with Zach alone and I wanted to laugh with Zach alone. Zach was my friend and I wanted our meetings to be just me and Zach. Then from nowhere appeared Maud who had also become Zach's friend. Strangely, without me even realizing it, I was appointed by Maude as Andy's girlfriend. I could not believe it, and she appointed herself as Zachary's girlfriend. *How did that happen?* I thought. I mean I was right there, I didn't go anywhere, did I? Who made her the boss? I thought.

Maude was a black girl, of African descent. I remember she had a really flat tummy and immediately below that a pair of body builder's thighs, what you alpha males call *fit*. Me, well, I had no shape, at least not yet anyway. Maude always wore her hair scraped back and stuffed into the same old ponytail, using the same old hair band, held in place with some sort of greasy gel like mixture, as if in a futile attempt to prevent even one strand of hair from escaping. She was quite neurotic in her personality really, and she walked and spoke in exactly the same neurotic way. If you stopped to think about it, she would completely get on your nerves.

Andy was blond and had very clear, watered-down blue eyes. He was just over six-foot-tall and not really my cup of tea. His hair was always parted from the center of his head down to his forehead and quaffed at the sides just making the flick over his ears. Quite pathetically, I just found myself going along with things because I guess that was what I did best; her suggestions, I mean. However, I was in puppy love with Zachary, had been for years, and Zachary, well, he was none the wiser, but I never said, *'Well, actually no, Maude, I don't fancy Andy and in fact I'm in love, Zachary, so I guess I' ll be going out with him now, won't I; thanks, all the same though.'* I guess it was weird how both Zachary and I never questioned the arrangements; neither did Andy come to think of it.

We all just went along with it like zombies really. We became a foursome to dances and to the pictures and for just hanging out at Jeanie's, but there was nothing serious happening, not between me and Andy, anyway. I had no idea that Andy was a virgin too, back then partly because he went on like he was so knowledgeable and experienced in all areas of sexual matters, but in truth, his experiences were the same as ours – zero, apart from Zachary that was: no thanks to Andy.

At the end of the Easter holidays we returned to Mansion Heights as usual but then totally unexpectedly and quite out of the blue, Andy began to write to me, and then, well, I was the talk of the town. I felt so embarrassed.

All the time I had been in Hampshire, I had never shown any evidence of a love interest before. I mean, no one had shown me any attention apart from this one guy, who I danced with one time at the youth club. In fact, he was Kiara's boyfriend, and she had ordered him to dance with me to one of the slow tunes – it was the very long version of 'reunited and it feels so good'. He had big, bouncy blond curls. He was not much taller than me, and remarkably we connected like a hand in glove. His touch was gentle, I mean so gentle, and his embrace was tender and kind, I could feel the tenderness of his soul, and I wanted more, but he was taken.

That night he gave me a lift on the back of his bike. He had a Kawasaki 350cc. It was massive. I held him tightly as I sat on the passenger seat behind him. His body felt good. It was firm and strong, and I wanted more. He took me several times up and down the long drive that ran at the side of the house. Until the neighbours turned on their front porch lights, and it was time to go. She dumped him shortly after for some ugly mutt who also had a bike. I wish I could have told her that I would not have minded dating him. *Where are you now John? He was beautiful, he had a beautiful soul and we fitted like a glove. I think he joined the army.*

However, now I was receiving mail from a guy whom I did not want and whom I did not care for. None of the other girls received mail from their boyfriends as their partners all lived locally. Suddenly, according to them, I had arrived.

All rumors and concerns about me being the only gay in the village had finally evaporated. Still, I was not sure that I wanted a full-blown public relationship lived out in front of everyone or all the attention that went with it. The letters started flowing, and the phone calls followed, but I did not know how to perceive it all; I mean I was only 14.

One day a very strange letter arrived, asking whether he could come down for a visit. I'm sure I nearly died of shock. Sister P was sitting right there; she must have seen me flinch. She began to question me about the contents of the letter, so I showed it to her. Surprisingly, she was full of elation. I asked her how this would work as I reminded her that visiting times were only on Sunday afternoons from 2:30 p.m. to 5 p.m.

Clearly it would be unreasonable for him to travel all that way for so short a time and then to have to return the same day. Sister read the letter and was so moved by the sincerity of it that she immediately wanted to meet him. 'Leave the matter with me,' she said reassuringly.

Sister P put the word out in the church whether there was anyone who lived locally and had a spare room to host a male guest for the weekend. Within three days, we had a response. It was from the Selinkies, who also lived on the hill just around the corner from us about halfway up. I went with Sister P to go up and meet them. They were from eastern Europe; they had a very nice house. It was very tidy and very clean. The guestroom had just been freshly painted so it seemed comfortable enough, they seemed sincerely hospitable and were so happy to accommodate Andy. When he called on the following Wednesday evening, I told him of the good news, and he decided to visit on the following weekend.

I was really surprised yet, at the same time, very humbled by their meekness and very thankful too. Now I felt like I had arrived. I felt like one of the girls. I had my own real boyfriend. I kept wondering how to act. But something was wrong; I did not feel as relaxed with him as I did with Zachary. *What was I doing?*

Andy arrived early Friday evening, and we hit a club in South sea, right on the sea front, or rather it hit him; the poor boy only went out to the toilet and was jumped by five boys, who objected to interracial relationships to the point that they felt they had to express their objections with fists. When he returned, his clothes were ripped, his hair disheveled, and he was covered in scratches and bruises; he looked as though he had just done five rounds in the ring with Mick McManus. When I realised what had happened, I could not believe it. I called the girls over and told them what had happened; they immediately went looking for the boys.

I had never known white guys to get attacked for dating black girls, I had never experienced racism on this level before, I mean had they not seen Loving -v-Virgina; had they not heard the story? We immediately got a taxi and left. The next day, he came over, and the nuns handed me linctus to wipe over his bruises. It was good for taking the color out of them. That afternoon, we shared a light tea together before he retired back to the Selinkies to get some rest. I think he was in a lot of pain and somewhat shocked. It seemed apparent that he had never experienced racism on this level before, in fact he had never experienced it full stop.

Little did he know this was what I had to deal with on a daily basis. Oddly, my knuckles never became sore and neither did I suffer any scratches or bruises; apart from the time I was thrown into the bushes, by some giant whilst on the way back from the village.

On that day, I was surprised to see that I had three teenagers behind me. All of a sudden they seemed to appear from no-where. The two girls thought it would be a promising idea to taunt me with racial names, whilst I was on the short walk back from the village. Although I managed to wrestle the two girls to the ground, the boy that was with them just picked me up by the scruff of my neck and threw me in to the bushes, the thorns made for an easy landing, scratching me as I struggled to free myself. I didn't tell anyone about it, the nuns I mean. What was the point; and I'm guessing they also attended our local church on Sundays.

That Saturday night, we both had an early night. The following day we went to church as per usual; I looked out for him but didn't see him. We had our lunch as normal, but I still didn't see him. I felt I didn't want to ask because I didn't want to appear worried. After lunch, there was still no sign of him. Sensing my anxiety, but without me knowing Sister P called over to the Selinkies to see if everything was ok with Andy. We both knew he would be leaving at some point that day and heading back to London. They said he was fine; he had just been out for a walk.

He gave the Selinkies a lovely set of fine bone china cups, accompanied by a beautiful hand-written thank-you card – an expression of his gratitude. He also gave the nuns a beautiful thank-you card too. Right then, at that moment, I was very proud of him. He certainly knew how to say thank you. *Many people don't.*

Before leaving, he asked me whether I would take a walk with him. He told me that he had something to tell me. He was carrying two bags full of gifts, so I knew it was not all sad news. I asked the nuns if I could go out with him, and surprisingly, they agreed. I was surprised as it was after visiting time. As we walked slowly up the hill to the village, the temperature had dropped a little, and it became quite blustery. We sat on the bench next to the phone box on London Road.

It was the same bench that I had on so many occasions sat on. It had become my bench of languishing, of sadness, and of tears. I would usually sit there after some dramatic disagreement or other with Sister Bea. I would sit and stare at the phone box or stare up at the stars and then look at the cars that drove past before looking back at the phone box. I would pull out from my pocket a neatly folded piece of paper that my P.E. teacher had quite diligently given to me, on it her number. I always kept it in the same coat pocket... and after some time, I would call the operator and ask to be connected to South Sea 555373.

Mrs. Hughes was a nice P.E.. teacher: she was the younger of the two. Deep down, I wanted her to rescue me, but I was unable to say. I thought she could be like Jessie, I guess, but she didn't know how or what to do and even if she did, she couldn't. I had cried so many tears of wanting to be rescued on that bench. And right here, right now, with Andy, I felt that I did not want to sit on that bench because even as confused and messed up as I was, this was a happy moment.

'Can we move from here?' I asked.

'Sure, where do you want to go to?'

We walked down to the next bench in front of the library; this was the library that I would borrow books from, forget about them, lose them, find them months or even years later, then find myself having to sneak them back in again and put them back on the shelves, without being notice. *Thank GOD for book amnesty.*

The bench was set back away from the road, so it was a bit quieter there. I sat down, but Andy was still standing. He showed me the gifts he had brought for the Selinkies and the cards which he asked me to sign too. Then he made some small speech, the words of which I could not understand at the time. All the while I was looking up at him, he was looking down at me, the wind blowing away his words, which became lost before reaching my ears. I was freezing as the wind knotted up. He looked rather cold as well. When he had finished, he handed me a small box, identical in size to that of a ring box. I was much taken back because we had not known each other that long to be exchanging gifts, I thought.

In that moment, I became slightly afraid, hoping it was not a ring – praying it was not a ring even.

I was not sure about Andy at that time and certainly had no intention of marrying him or even being engaged to him for that matter. I positioned the box between us, and slowly I began to peel off the paper. I was looking at him, and he was looking at me, in my heart the pressure was mounting. After removing all the outer wrapping and packaging I looked down at the little black box. It was the same shape and size as a ring box. I looked up at him, trying to find a smile.

'Go on, open it then,' he said, in almost-uncontainable excitement.

The spring was relentless as I tried to pry it open, holding my breath as I tried to reveal its contents, hoping not to be shocked. However, upon doing so, it provided the stand for a beautiful 22-carat gold chain, attached was a 9-carat gold crucifix. Unbeknown to me then, I would receive this exact same gift again just twenty-one years later; but not from Andy, and the clock was ticking, tick, tock…tick, tock…tick, tock...

In that moment, feeling quite relieved that it was not a ring, I was not exactly sure how to respond, other than to say, 'Oh, thank you.' I was not sure whether my face would reveal enough emotion, though, if any, for that matter. As I had not had much experience with this type of thing. I guess; it was an awkward moment, at least for me anyway. He took the chain out of the box and gently fastened it around my neck. It would remain there for exactly three short years before being ripped off in a single fit of rage and the clock was ticking, tick tock ...tick tock.

But right here, right now, he told me that he liked me and wanted to get to know me. I was just fourteen. *What was there to get to know?* I wondered. I did not know how to respond or how to react to this rather heavy information. I had no words to exchange with him. No gestures of endearment to return to him. Still, if I could hold on to just one thing – it was that he liked me and that was a nice feeling to know even at this immature age, that someone liked me.

The wind was really starting to pick up momentum, the litter, leaves and disused plastic bags that had all gone astray now joined together as if in the dance of ring a ring a roses. The wind swooping them up off their feet at times as they all appeared to rally around, forming a circle the temperature dropping even further.

We gathered up our things and headed back to the house, walking briskly against the push of the wind, it now pressing up against us. After escorting me safely home, he took a taxi back to Havant train station, taking the Portsmouth to London, departing at 9:20 pm.

After his departure, we continued to write to each other, and we would also speak on the phone every Wednesday night between 7 and 8 p.m. for approximately 15 minutes. I remember feeling that I did not want to get too attached, as I did not know what the future would hold. I had no Idea of how to express myself emotionally or even physically, because up until that moment I had not yet learnt these things. Little did I know I was still suppressing all the turmoil from Grimshaw Hall, and the clock was ticking… tick, tock… tick, tock...

However, for now although it was nice to be 'one of the girls' and fitting in, as far as having a boyfriend was concerned, this was all still completely unfamiliar territory to me. It was unfamiliar ground, which emotionally I was not yet ready to uncover or explore even. I was never attracted to Andy, neither did I feel attached. I mean, I didn't know him the way I knew Zachary, - in my heart, I guess I was still secretly still in love with Zachary.

Final Semester

Back at school, exam time was fast approaching as were the holidays; I could not wait, my mind kept drifting off towards a state of relaxation; it was hard to retain my concentration. Thinking about exams I had no idea of how to prepare for them, mainly because I had never been taught or supported in this area of my education. In the years that followed I would later come to discover that I was suffering from Post-Traumatic Stress Disorder and had been throughout my entire time in Hampshire. Of course, this was completely unbeknown to me at the time. I had no idea why I did the things I did or said the things I did.

Perhaps everything I had been through up until that point had a cause and effect, the far-reaching ramifications of which I would learn later in life. The entire platoon was just a time of stress on top of stress on top of more stress, but I didn't know it then so I could not verbalize it; I could only act it out. But this was a new type of sign language not seen before and no-one could understand it. Throughout my entire time at secondary school I had scored really badly. I had no idea of what was wrong or what had happened because I was not a kid who found learning incredible difficult, I could not understand what had changed since being at Darlington Basset.

In fact, I had scored in the bottom 3 percentile at the end of the first year, and I was at the bottom 5 percentile at the end of year two. Each time the scores were read out, it was indeed a moment of sheer humiliation, total embarrassment, and utter shame, added to by the contorted and twisted laughter of Sulia Sulti. They say that hate is a powerful word and perhaps an even stronger emotion; but in that moment, I just hated her even more than I thought possible. However, she was none the wiser; The one thing I had learnt to master really well was the display or rather non- display of my emotions in public. By the end of the third year, I had come to expect low marks in all subjects as standard and had resolved myself into not really giving a damn about it. My heart had turned to stone concerning this and right here right now I just wanted out. My problem was simple, or so they thought.

Due to receiving such low marks for the core subjects such as English and Math's, I would be moved out of each of those classes and sent to the bottom classes. We did not have level classes for science, so those who were expected to be non-achievers were plonked somewhere, thankfully not in a corner, and usually ignored. Sufferers of Post-Traumatic Stress and Dyslexia were completely overlooked and ADH had not even been brought to the table. No-one knew how to identify any of the above or even what the implications would be. However, once I had settled into the bottom class for Math's, I did so well that my marks went straight back up so much that they would be forced to move me right back up to my regular classes again. So, in fact, I began to experience a sort of yo-yo style, type of teaching all throughout my second and third years.

At the end of the third year my marks for English were better than some of those in the GCSE higher exam class so at the start of the fourth year I was frog marched back up to my old GCSE class, by the new English teacher who slightly resembled my dad in looks and build. I had really been looking forward to having him as my English teacher and finding out all about him. I thought I would ask him some questions, like where are you from? and why did you want to be a teacher? Unfortunately, he appeared more concerned about doing what was right for me. Nevertheless, my original English teacher was not at all happy to see me; *need I say more...*

The last event in the academic calendar was always the sports day. We had two female P.E.. teachers at secondary school– the older of the two, Lesley, very slightly resembled Virginia Wade. She had asked me to support the school in the Javelin, Discus, and Shot-Put entries, because they had no one who could throw these items in the school. I am guessing, she took one look at my Biceps and decided that she would elect me for the job. She had no idea that I would refuse the offer. Without a candidate the school could not compete in these categories and therefore could not compete in the district trials. I thought about the way all the teachers had treated me over the past three years and how she had overlooked me for every single captaincy in every single sport that I had played for them in, and had played exceedingly well for them in, even if I do say so myself. I lifted up my head, looked her square in the eye, and answered with a categorical 'No!'

It felt good, so good, or so I thought. But little did I really know. Of course, she tried her dam hardest to persuade me to reconsider and tried even harder to change my mind, she even began smiling at me each time she saw me, but it was to no avail. I refused to give in. I mean for several days, she was still asking me and for several days my answer was still no. Truth be known, she didn't even know how to ask. She didn't know how to get the best out of me. She had no idea how to encourage me.

That year, I ran the 100 meters, the 200 meters and the re-lay, receiving first place in the 100 and 200 meters, and team first in the re-lay. Unfortunately, under her ill advisement, I also attempted to run the 400 meters. That was once around the full circumference of the track. There was just one problem I was not a long- distance runner and she knew it. – I mean 100-meter runners don't run the 400 meters. I was a sprinter not a jogger, and after three years of teaching me she knew that, without a shadow of a doubt she knew that, so what was she playing at? Was this yet another attempt to sabotage me; to make me look stupid: to destroy another layer of me? But she wasn't asking me to run she was ordering me to run; I felt I had no choice, no voice, so I slowly walked over to my position on the track.

At the start of the race, we took our positions, the gun was fired and off we ran. For the first 100 to 150 meters, I was clear in the lead, ahead by about 30 meters. I pushed hard till about 180, which required all the juice in my body with the others now hot on my tale.

It was on this first bend that I began to lose my position. It was like being at the top of a tower made from Jelly; I was sliding down from my position fast. My power and speed had begun to dissipate; breathing was becoming difficult and anxiety was setting in.

At 250 meters, all my competitors had caught up to me and were beginning to overtake me one by one. At 300 meters, there was a gap, at 350 meters the gap began to widen. I searched my body for power, there was none. At 360 meters, I was lagging behind; at 370 meters, I was struggling to keep going, my heart was pounding on the inner cavity of my chest like a stick beating a drum. I wanted to stop, but something would not let me. I was barely jogging now; at 380 meters, I had hit the wall, I felt as though I could not make it. I was one pace away from walking. I wanted to drop onto the floor. I was knocking on every internal door in search of energy... there was none.

At 390 meters, I was in excruciating pain. As I looked ahead to where we were camped on the grass, I could see Sulia mocking me and laughing hysterically ... yes at me. She was jumping up and down and rolling around on the ground, like a monkey out of its cage. But something inside me pushed through. I was so determined to finish.

At 395 meters, I realised that I was the only person on the track; in fact, this had been case since approximately 360 meters; my competitors had all finished. The more she laughed the more my determination was fueled, and it was sheer determination that brought me home.

I came in last but more important was the fact that I had finished. Sulia laughed and laughed and laughed and continued laughing as I came back to our team and even as I collapsed in a heap on the floor, she was still laughing. In that moment, I really wanted to hit her and hit her so hard. She was making me sick. Everyone was laughing. Unfortunately, I just had to grin and bear it. I had the 100, 200 and the relay in the bag, coming first in all three events, so perhaps two fingers for victory was the most appropriate sign to raise at this time.

Once school was finally over, I, for one, was certainly glad. I lived for the holidays; it was the only time I felt really relaxed. This year we were going to holiday in Margate with a day trip to France built in. Wow! I could not wait. Sounds great to me or so I thought.

Last Holiday

Holiday Number 6:

Our next holiday was to Margate. It was the summer of 1980 and counting. I had just turned fifteen, and this was to be my last with the girls, unbeknown to me at the time. We drove up after breakfast and arrived in the late afternoon. We had paired up in twos before we left, and I was sharing with Brandy again. Our room was compact and cosy; it was situated in the basement with a small window above my bed. As soon as we arrived, we just crashed until teatime.

We were on full board, which meant that the hotel provided breakfast as well as an evening meal. Breakfast was always full English and included fruit juices, fresh fruits, toast, an assortment of jams and cereals: they even got real butter in at the girl's request or rather Odette's, but she was backed by all the girls in her request.

Dinner was quite nice, barring one; after which, we received the unwelcome news that all the evening meals were repeated on the second week, which was rather dull to say the least and they weren't very happy at us joining up the dots and pointing this slight fact out to them.

During our stay Sister Coco had very cleverly factored in a day trip to France, which in all honesty although wasn't a bad idea it just didn't fuel you with that expectation of excitement, which it had done earlier.

When the day arrived, the hotel provided a very nice, packed lunch for each of us: one sandwich, a packet of ready salted crisps, and a carton of fruit juice. They also very kindly drove us down to board the ferry, and Sister had arranged with them to collect us later that day at about 21.30 hours, our expected time of arrival.

Door to port, the journey was rather quick. However, unbeknown to us, that year, the French ports were intermittently on strike; quite subtly, our lovely day trip to France would quickly transform from idyllic experiences into a living nightmare.

We arrived in Boulogne within the hour, completely oblivious to all the political problems we had just sailed into. Our arranged meeting place was agreed, and we synchronized our watches. We were all going to meet back at the patisserie at 4:30 pm. *French time.* We had to be back, ready to board the coach that would drive us back to the ferry at 5:30 pm. Believing we had everything in order, we set off for window shopping and fast-food tasting, practicing our French as we went. Some of the shop owners were helpful in trying to make sense of our newly put-together broken French with inserted English snippets; others just totally ignored us, not really wishing to engage with us and therefore didn't really give us the time of day.

As the day came to an end, we filled ourselves up with pain au chocolate, fresh warm croissants, and French fries, all washed down with cups of milky tea and flavored milk. It must have been about 4 pm. when we decided to start making our way back to the meeting point. As the meeting area soon filled with anxious passengers, it was not long before the anxious whispers began to reveal the fearful truth.

We boarded the coach for what we believed was the short journey back to the ferry, only to be dropped off at a disused railway station. We became stuck or rather abandoned there for God only knows how long. The scene had all the trappings of a noir style, third man, cold war film thrown in. Our dilemma reeked of indefinite uncertainty. We never cursed the French so much in all our young lives, each vowing never to return to France ever again. I didn't think things like this actually existed in real life. *You could not have made it up if you had tried.* We were led in like a lamb to the slaughter, and the door was locked tight shut behind us. We all just looked and watched I think we must have been in shock.

It was all so very eerie. My mind was out of all positive scenarios of a good ending from this. I did not know what to think; it was so borderline Auschwitz, with all the trimmings of fear, apprehension and suspense thrown in. We walked around until we were tired of trying to find another way out. Odette was trying to explain; it didn't matter even if there was another way out. *Where were we going to go? Did we know the way back to the port? Even if we did, what did we intend to do... walk?* Clearly not.

I overheard someone say that they were not even letting the passengers on to the boats, and if they did manage to get on, the fishermen and port workers were preventing the ferry's from leaving the ports. They had blocked the mouth of the port with their little fishing boats. We just had to sit tight and wait for the coach. This was the only mode of transport that could take us back to the ferry. We could not even phone the hotel to inform them what had happened. We were stuck without mud.

It must have been about 9:30 pm, when the first coach arrived to take the first load of people back to the ferry. The coach was accompanied by a police car with two officers. One came to open the doors and the other waited by the coach with the driver. Everyone was running around like headless chickens, trying to round up their group members, their bags, their coats, and shoes too.

Had a deal finally been struck with those rebellious fishermen? I thought. Odette told me to wait by the door with as many bags as I could carry, as she attempted to round up our group. There was just one window of opportunity for us to up and leave, and this was it.

Unfortunately, our group had disbursed we had all scattered. The line was getting longer and longer, and the coach was filling up fast; it had exactly fifty-two seats. There were about two hundred passengers waiting. None of us knew where to look for the others; the train station was massive. The coach was almost full. We were the second group waiting to board still with missing members. Odette was counting anxiously, 5, 6, 7. Alas, three of us were still missing; we could not board.

The first group had all their members, and all fifty-two seats were filled on the coach. That was it; off they went, the doors were closed, and we were locked in again. Those who could, cursed, and those who couldn't, just swore under their breath. Of course, it was Ann, Kiara, and Sister Gin who had gone missing. Even Sister Coco looked frantic and fuming.

Odette now ordered that we all remain together and stay as near to the door as possible, because when the next coach returned, we were getting on it and sod everyone else. We were all beginning to feel tired and irritable now. Many people were falling asleep as it was getting late.

By now we had been waiting for five hours and counting. When we had arrived, it was daylight but now, we only had the night and it was dark, pitch-black in fact. It had been a long day, and it wasn't over yet. At 10:15 pm, another coach arrived and again everyone started scuttling around like confused chickens. The coach waited for ten minutes before the doors opened and out came another fifty-two passengers; they too were now being locked in with us. Some people got all hot under the collar and tried to demand answers from the officials; none were forthcoming, no-one was talking, and others cursed them to their faces. Then someone mentioned the nuns as a behavioral control indicator. Silent apologies were whispered out across the floor and heads were nodded indicating acceptance.

Eventually, the people calmed down again, and we waited and waited and waited, then someone mentioned prayer. We turned to look at the nuns. I guess this would have been an appropriate time to pray. I am sure the nuns were already praying under their breath; I think we all must have said something beginning with 'Dear LORD' and ending in 'Amen.'

At approximately 11:30 p.m. another coach pulled up in the distance. Dionne had been keeping a lookout. Suddenly, she started screaming for our group to get ready by the doors, which also alerted those not in our group. It was becoming a free for all. Everyone started rushing, pushing, and shoving; yes, it was indeed a *rat race* and the panic was on to form the first queue for the second time. We rounded everyone up in our group, including the sleepy nuns; they too seemed to be feeling the pinch. I had never seen them in this condition before; *so they are human after all?* I thought. Usually, they always looked so well-groomed and so pristine; not a hair out of place and crinkle-free.

After a brief discussion, outside between the driver and the officer, the officer walked up to the building and unlocked the doors. He had escorted the coach using his own vehicle, which was strange. I think he had been off duty and was asked or perhaps even ordered to come back on duty. Everyone started to frantically gather their belongings together and run to board the coach. This time we were prepared, we were ready, and we had learnt our lessons. We were the first group to board, and it filled up very quickly. Once it was full the doors closed, and we made the short drive back to the port.

I could feel my entire body just wanting to relax, just wanting to go sleep, but I couldn't. We were all absolutely exhausted, all running on borrowed time. I kept telling myself that we were almost there, willing myself to stay awake. Once on the ferry, we immediately hit the café, where we were offered free food; it was little consolation compared with the ordeal we had just experienced, but we were thankful. We made small talk with the crew before going to sit back down with a cup of tea. We were all just so tired; we needed caffeine for the final leg of the journey because all of us so desperately wanted to sleep, albeit we knew we had to stay awake.

It was after 2 a.m. when we finally docked on British soil. Thank God, the hotel manager had not let us down; he was waiting faithfully with the minibus, cross but waiting, annoyed but waiting, mumbling but waiting. He was indeed a welcome sight as was the bus. The engine had been on, so the bus was warm. We made the drive back to the hotel, still trying not to fall into deep sleep. When we arrived, we all fell into our respective beds and slept in way past breakfast, but the hotel manager very kindly made us some midday snacks. *Thank you Sir.*

We continued to frequent all the local clubs for the duration of the holiday, comparing the best features with last year's and trying as hard as possible to place the incident as far behind us as we possibly could. Our day of departure could not have come too soon either.

When we returned, it was just two days before we were off again, packed up for the journey back to London. On this occasion, I did not visit the Featherstone's' – I went directly to Jeanie's with Odette and we stayed at her house for the remainder of our summer holidays. From there we would return once more to visit our Dad. Thankfully, Mordecka was out again when we visited.

This was our second time visiting that year. Again, we just sat there talking but without really speaking, looking without really seeing. Only the muscles in our faces were actually communicating.

Apparently, a person has 45 muscles in the face that are not used for speaking, they are not used for laughing, they are not even used for crying; they are used solely for the act of communication, the muscles in our faces speak their own language.

There was so much we both had wanted to say but felt we couldn't. It was as though the cat really did have our tongues again. Dad asked us about school and if we were getting on all right with everyone, to which the answer was always a resounding *yes*. Bobby just sat there staring at us. Corina ran around the room like a crazy over hyper child that had eaten too much sugar, before running into Odette's arms once she finally remembered who we were, but Andre didn't. He was only a few months old when we had both departed and still in the cot. He just stared at us as though we were imposters.

Soon it was time to go again. Dad asked whether we could come back again. His question really pleased Odette; I guess it was easy to think he had accepted us back into the fold, which felt good.

Our next visit would be at Christmas. We said our goodbyes, me without touching, but Odette hugged our younger siblings, holding them close to her heart. Dad remained reserved and rigid but lifted his hand to wave us goodbye. Just as we reached the bottom landing and were walking across to exit onto Wilson Road, I looked back only to see whom I knew was Mordecka, walking along the top landing again.

Dad and Bobby were still standing at the door waving. I desperately wanted them to go in. I didn't want Mordecka to see us. I knew that if she did something bad would happen; I felt anxious again. Suddenly I had a bad feeling. Then it happened: Mordecka turned to see who they were waving at. She glanced at us briefly and looked away, then they all disappeared inside, and the door was closed once more. We had no idea what the far reaching ramifications would be for having visited them, in fact we had no idea of how well Mordecka would have received this news.

We returned to Jeanie's for the end of the holiday and I tried not to think about it. Jeanie had some visitors staying with her too and we hung out with their children and spent the last leg of our holidays watching films and going swimming with them. Conveniently, the pool was directly across the road. It was quite new in fact, we had witnessed parts of the build and watched it develop over the months of our visits with Jeanie.

It must have been about two days before we were due to depart when the older child of Jeanie's visitors came rushing in with a movie called *Scum*. We all sat around the TV eager to watch it, yet none of us having any idea as to what it was about. I was just fifteen years old at the time, and what unfolded was nothing short of a harrowing living nightmare, yet all throughout the movie, I found I was unable to excuse myself from it. It scared me half to death, scaring deeply the dimensions of my mind, and this would be the case for many, many moons, right up until adulthood. I cried when I found out that it was in fact true.

Once all our holidays came to an end, it was back on the Portsmouth train again. Like clockwork, the nuns would always be there to collect us from Havant Station in the minibus as per usual. They would always be there waiting for us in advance, but this time, they were late. And something felt different, strange even. When they did finally arrive some thirty minutes later, there was no apology and no excuse for their lateness, which felt odd to say the least.

We silently loaded our bags into the back of the minibus and made the short drive back to Waterlooville – a journey that I had always found so relaxing, yet never long enough. I loved to take in the scenery of color, mainly greens and blues. I guess deep down, I was always subconsciously on the lookout for an escape to a better life, where tranquil colors would play a poignant part.

When we returned to Mansion Heights, we never saw Sister P again, which was really quite odd, neither were we given an honest explanation as to her absence. We were only fed some sheepish one liner that she had gone on her holidays; strangely, she never returned even after the usual two weeks that they all took. We knew something was wrong, but it was very much like cloaks-and-daggers with all the suspense of Agatha Christie's Mrs. Marple and Poirot thrown in. *Did they not know that we would be marred by all the lies?*

I mean, this was the woman who had stood up for each and every one of us and who had physically stood in *loco parentus* for us all, continuously, and meant it. This was the woman who had placed her own head on the chopping block, time after time. This was the woman who had stood up to the establishment's red tape of bullshit bureaucracy and deliberately said, 'I care!' out loud, up close, and personal and meant it. And, yes, she had earned the right to wear the title of 'Mum', 'Mummy', 'Mother', and oh so many more. And right here, right now, we were all her children, her girls, who all loved her dearly and we all needed to know what was going on? And how long it was going to go on for? Nevertheless, no one was giving us so much as an inch of information. This is not how she would have wanted it. We knew she would have wanted to give us all an everlasting memorial, a powerful word of encouragement that would stay in our hearts forever. But they didn't understand that.

We all knew who was behind it, the writing was on the wall... the spiteful Sister Hucefen. Well, of course right about now she was in her absolute element. She had for a long time wanted to tear down, in minutes, what Sister P had taken years to build up, and this was her chance. On the contrary, she was not going to waste a single second of it.

Sister P was ill. How ill? We did not know. Ill with what? We were not told. W*ho will defend me at school now, I thought?* If I get Mr. Propretus for my form tutor this year, I'm stuffed, finished even.

Mr. Propretus was an out and out racist and he didn't hide it; he was proud of it. He bathed in it. He made color jokes on a daily basis, and the color of reference elected was always black. He would always 'rinse' his jokes until the class felt they had to laugh just to make him stop. *'A bit like the jury who can't reach a unanimous decision so find the defendant guilty, despite the evidence pointing to a different outcome'*. I wasn't sure how I was going to make it through the year without Sr P, more so if I had him on my case on a daily basis. He gave new meaning to the word *demoralize*. In retaliation, I found myself slipping. I began letting off loud bangers in the corridors and stairwells of the school; I had purchased them on our day trip to France. I would miss out on getting caught every time by mere seconds. Without doubt, that would have been another suspension; it wasn't needed right now, not on top of everything else going on with Sister P.

Upon returning to school we geared up for the autumn, incorporating all the usual religious traditions, such as the harvest, where we would give any tin or packed foods we didn't want or had not used all year, to those in need; usually the elderly, I would later come to learn that they were not the ones in need. 'Giving' had a nice ring to it and it made you feel better about yourself somehow. I would later learn the physical and spiritual laws that walked with it; and that could not be detached from it, and the clock was ticking… tick tock… tick tock...

New Term New Year Another Departure

It must have been some time in October 1980 when I had my desk searched for the bangers, that I had been letting off around the school. It was about this time that I had made up my mind completely; my only option was to throw in the towel and return to London.

I would tell the teachers that I was going away for a while and planned to ask them for books and course work that I could do whilst I was away, so as not to arouse any suspicions.

I finally left Pressing Reed secondary school and all it had on offer in the first term of my fourth year. The fall of 1980. I seemed to be making a bit of a habit of leaving home around this time of year. It would be another 39 years before I would come to learn of the significance.

I left school with no qualifications, no accolades, no certificates, and no prom. I left with absolutely nothing.

I thought I would finish off my education at the secondary school, where I had started just five years earlier at Darlington Bassett Grammar. Given the fact that my crazy head of year had already left, I thought it would be a safe bet to return there and armed with the confidence that I could make it, this decision became part of my plan.

After lunch one Wednesday, I waited by the phone to call my rescuers once more and inform them of my decision that I was leaving home again, this time two weeks on Friday.

When I arrived back at the house after school, I went straight to my room and packed everything I owned into the old broken suitcase that Jeanie had given me when I had left Acorns. Apparently she felt disgusted at the fact that I was always using plastic bags as the mode for transporting my clothes and possessions from place to place; to tell you the truth I hadn't really noticed.

Once packed, I placed the suitcase in my wardrobe and closed the doors and waited. The countdown was on and Friday arrived exactly on time. I was to take a weekend bag with me and take the 5:17 pm to London. I would meet one of my rescuers at the station where I would present my case for yet another departure, from another home, another town, and another people.

'*What was the point of telling her anything,*' I thought? I mean the only voices she ever listened to were those in her own head. I remember my own thoughts being plagued by worry, which prevented me from concentrating on the questions being put to me or finding the strength to answer them in a timely manner, if at all. My thoughts kept being interrupted by the lack of safety that surrounded them. Although all my things had been packed up neatly in the wardrobe, there was no lock for my bedroom door, the wardrobe door or even my case for that matter, and given the fact that Kiara was now a known thief, roaming around freely, my possessions were once again at risk: and the nuns, having built up a reputation for being long overtly laid-back in their detective skills and even more so in their disciplinary methods, I was not really expecting any miracles, such as finding my case still intact with nothing missing from it. As it transpired, I never did return to Mansion Heights in that season, and certainly not as one of the girls in the next.

Back in London Town

After arriving back in London, initially I stayed at Jeanie's for a while. Without me knowing Jeanie drove all the way down to Mansion Heights, just to retrieve my case and surprised me with it, when she returned home one day. I thought how thoughtful of her until I learned that she was being put under pressure by the nuns as they needed the space. Then she dropped another bomb shell of completely unwelcome news - she had now decided that I should go and stay with *another* set of FPs.

Oh, great, I thought. She kept singing the foster mother's praises for the entire journey there, but I wasn't listening, I was too busy looking for any familiar destinations on the front of any buses that were going in the same direction from which we were coming. Then I saw one, the A21 going to Turnpike Lane; that's good I thought to myself I know my way from there. So off I went like a good little doggy.

When I arrived, I didn't like the house at all or the feelings that went with it and that was just from the outside. It was one of those maisonettes two up and two down. There seemed to be too many people for too little space, the furniture was worn out as was the bed linen, but it was clean, the bed linen that is. I had become quite good at sussing people out and somehow, I knew this was never gonna work out, my spirit could not relax here. Each day I began to time her routine for the school run to the minute and after the third day I was on the move again. I couldn't manage the case and the bag together as well as having a bag on my back, so I had to choose between the case or the bag, which was an arduous task to say the least. The bag was brand new; Jeanie had brought it for me whilst my case was still down south. Unfortunately, the case could not fit all my possessions in, and neither could the bag, but the case could hold significantly more than the bag. After a mental tug of war, it was the case that won out in the end. I decided to stuff as much as I could into it and leave Jeanie's brand-new hold-all behind, as much as it pained me to do so.

The day of my departure was a Wednesday. The second the FP left to commence the school run, I counted to twenty and then followed out the door behind her, dragging this big, old, broken case behind me, like some naughty, overweight, disobedient child. It was so heavy I strained as I pulled it. Eventually, after a few buses, I found my way back to Jeanie's again.

Back to Grimshaw Hall

I managed to stay another couple of nights before being packed off again; this time it was back to Grimshaw Hall. *Ooooooh no,* I thought. Jeanie was trying desperately hard to assure me, by saying that they were under new management; she just didn't get it? It felt like punishment, like reliving hell, all over again; it felt like prison. I could not bloody believe it! Sanquingay Park was now located in Grimshaw Hall, on the Chillingham Estate; they had moved location.

However, this time, it was Mr. Don Padwick who was in charge. I remembered his name from Sanquingay Park. Although I never saw his face when I was there, I remembered the rumors. The one who loved children, or lover of children, the male gender and particularly the little ones with blond hair and blue eyes.

Back then, at Sanquingay Park the children called him the 'Batty-man'. I was afraid of him even now despite not ever having ever met the man, until now that is. He seemed to have the word menace written all over him.

You know children have a good sense of people, whether they are good or bad I mean, and whether they are into things that they shouldn't be, such as pornography. I would see him roaming around the place, just like a lion probably seeing whom he could devour next. I can't really recall how long I had been there before making our first acquaintance from under the antique mahogany sideboard, which was stacked back against the wall to the left as you entered through the door into B room. I had noticed that 5 years on and it had not moved so much as an inch from its position.

He bent his face down so that it was almost at the same level as mine. His cologne was sickly, overpowering and mixed in with his really bad body odor, his eyes were bulging from his head as if in competition with each other and his hair was excessively greasy, and in dire need of a good wash. True to the rumor he had in tow a young, blond, blue-eyed boy.

The very sight of this picture caused me to shudder. The boy could not have been much older than six. Mr. Padwick bent down further, stuck his face right into mine, right into my personal air space and said, 'I'm not taking any shit from you, so get the f*%k out from under there, you bloody black bastard.' His breath absolutely stunk. It was a mixture of bad coffee and cigarettes. This was indeed my alien moment… I looked at him and he looked at me, we were eye ball to eye ball, then I glanced over at the door, which was standing just ajar. I wondered whether I could scramble out of there and make it out the door without coming into contact with him as I went. It was every minute of it Deja vu, in action. I had been here before. It was the same moment from Dukesbury house when I was stabbed in the bum with pins by Mrs. Manfred, all those moons ago.

In this moment, as I weighed up my options, with his free hand, he swooped in and dragged me out by the scruff of my clothes. He pulled me up to his face, and then as hard as he could, he slapped me right across my left cheek. It was so hard that even after the smack, that was all I could hear as my head swung around to the right. I was just able to catch a glimpse of the saliva bubbles spraying through the air before falling down on to the floor. I was the boxer who had been knocked down, but this was so not Rocky Balboa. My face red sore, and my ear still ringing. He was still talking, but I couldn't hear a thing. I looked around locking my eyes on to the door, which was still slightly ajar, and then with everything inside me, without even one word, I got up and made a run for it.

I slipped through without my clothes getting caught on the handle or the catch, which was good news. I had had lots of practice from the days of Flannigan gone by. I scarpered up the stairs directly outside B room and barricaded myself in my bedroom with the furniture behind it. I was shaking. I was so scared. I was terrified; No tea for me that night.

I think a piece more of me broke off that day, but I didn't care; a plan was brewing on the inside of me. I packed up my things again and this time I kept them packed and ready to go, waiting in the wardrobe. Now I was becoming the runner.

Once a week there was a trip and the route that they would take took them through Crouch End, exactly where the clock tower was. I realised that I knew this area, Jeanie just lived down the road. I made up my mind that the next time we made the trip I was going to jump out of the bus, hoping it would come to a slow at the lights. The following week we didn't go out in the bus; we were in all week like prisoners. Eventually, I asked one of the staffs when we would make the trip again. I told him that I had really enjoyed it. 'Oh really,' he said, 'perhaps next week then.' I could not wait and began to count down the days.

Ryan was also residing at Grimshaw Hall; he was a young slim boy, he looked under nourished and had overgrown brown hair, he was what is known as a constant runner. But every time he could not run far enough. He never made it anywhere before getting caught. He had nowhere to hide. In the end, they took his shoes away. I watched him squirm and scream from the top of his lungs as they pinned him down to strip him of them. I felt sorry for him. Yet, I had not given up on my own exodus.

Today was Wednesday and we were due to go out in the minibus. We arrived at our destination and I counted down the hours, and minutes and seconds until it was time to leave. On the way back just like before as we came into Crouch End, the bus slowed down to a stop in traffic at the lights. I stared at the door handle, 'Pull the door handle! pull the door handle!', I kept saying to myself all the while my heart beating faster and faster with every breath. I looked over at the lights – they were still red. Then I looked at every member of staff in the bus then I looked back at the lights – they were still red. I looked down at the door handle again. 'Pull the door handle! pull the door handle!', said the same voice in my head. I pictured myself squeezing the handle up to release the catch to open the door. I looked back at the lights – they were still on red and then switched to amber I could feel the gear stick being thrust into first and the clutch slowly being released from its biting point.

'This is it I thought now or never I screamed to myself!'

Immediately, I went over to the door, almost transient like, eyes locked on to the door, my stare not breaking and squeezed the handle upward and opened the door, quickly jumping out of the minibus. I didn't close the door behind me, I didn't turn around, I didn't look back. I just kept on walking right into Coleridge Gardens. I would learn later of its significance to me and the clock was ticking... tick... tock...tick... tock...

I hid behind some bins in a random front porch and waited. I waited for about 15 minutes before coming out and going back to the road to check that they were gone. Thank God, they were nowhere to be seen.

Jeanie lived just a short walk from where I was and so I began to make the short journey over to her house. When I arrived, she wasn't in again; only Zachary was there. We called her on the telephone, and she tried to talk me into returning to Grimshaw Hall, but I had made up my mind: it was an emphatic No! She then asked Zach to get me something to eat and she would reimburse him. We walked around to the kebab shop and for the first time I could see the inconvenience in his face. I was his inconvenience. He had been on his way out when I had turned up just like that out of the blue. Now his evening was on hold, possibly ruined.

In hindsight, looking back, it seemed evident that Jeanie had no interpretation of people at all, especially the young and vulnerable. Absolutely no understanding. According to her, the sun shone out of everyone's rear end, particularly those who worked for the SS. They were the true saints of this world, according to Jeanie; unfortunately, her wake-up call was already on its way, and it was going to hit her and hit her hard, right between the eyes. Her theory was, you look after 'A', and we pay you 'B' and everybody is happy, but were they? Perhaps, in theory, it was supposed to work without a hitch and in everybody's mind it probably did, but in practice, they were building a hidden haven for some of society's sickest deviants, aiding and abetting them to get their kicks through abusing and hurting the young, the weak, and the vulnerable and to be paid for doing so.

Every complaint was covered up, and Jeanie was a part of that cover-up. She heard what was going on, so she knew what was going on, but did nothing. In fact, they all did the same: absolutely nothing. All our complaints fell on deaf ears. Perhaps they had too many. When she questioned me one to one about returning, she received a loud categorical 'No!' 'I shall not be going back there ever again!' I added. Remarkably, she didn't argue, she didn't plead, and she didn't even try to persuade me. She just said she would find me somewhere else to stay, but I reinforced my decision quite firmly that I would not be going to any more of her FPs and neither would I be going into any more children's homes. As for my things, well, they tried to say I took all my possessions with me, but Jeanie wasn't having any of it; she had to become quite angry before they suddenly found them and sent them straight over.

As the days passed, I began to settle back down at Jeanie's and enjoy my time there joking around with Zach, until her untimely announcement came, that she had found me somewhere else to stay, and then my bubble really did burst. I wanted to stay at hers forever; there were no rules and no regulations, and I had Zach to make me laugh every day. What more could a young girl want? Just as it couldn't get any worse, crashing news came of Sister P's untimely death; the funeral was going to be held in exactly two weeks, and I was expected to attend. They wanted me to arrive early so I could rekindle my ties with the girls. Albeit I didn't know if I wanted that. I wasn't sure who I wanted to see. I just knew no more tears. I didn't want to cry about this anymore.

About the same time Jeanie began to go on and on about this new place she had found. 'Really' I thought...

She assured me that this place that she had in mind was great, really great, it was not that far, and I could come down whenever I wanted. In fact, it was at the top of the hill, Muswell hill. In truth, I just felt rejected all over again. 'Gee thanks Jeanie.'

That weekend, surprisingly, I ended up staying at Andy's, for the first time. I met his dad and younger sister. He was really nice to me, but his younger sister wasn't. Andy hadn't had it easy either. His mum had left them for a new life in the sun with an Arab. I was guessing that it must have been hard for his dad. She didn't look back and never stayed in touch; she just left. Just like that.

His dad was trying hard to wash away the pain by drowning it with the help of a liter of a bottle of Malt Scotch Whiskey every night and then numbing it with superior quality cigars. Somehow I recognized his pain and I felt it.

I was only supposed to stay one night, but one became two, and two became three, right up until the night before the funeral, I was still there. But Jeanie just accepted it. She had to, I guess, at least it wasn't her doorstep I was at. She had arranged for me to take the 9:05 a.m. train from Waterloo Station, and the nuns would collect me at Havant. The tickets were already there, waiting to be collected from the station. Well, I got as far as Waterloo and then no further; I just could not board the train.

I called Andy from the station after the train had left the platform, and after the short conversation between us had ended, I just found myself going straight back up to Andy's dad's place again. I told Andy I just could not get on the train; he gave me a hug. This was the first time he had hugged me in fact, in that moment I felt as though he did care, even if it was just for a moment. However, we both knew that I couldn't stay there forever; but there was fun to be had whilst I was.

Every evening after his dad had gone to bed, we would sneak back into the living room, like two thieves in the night and sip at any scotch left in his dad's glass. We would then take turns to puff on his dad's cigar butts and try not to laugh out loud at each other's sputtering from the smoke. Sometimes there was quite a bit of scotch and an even bigger cigar butt.

On one occasion there was hardly any left so Andy opened the bottle to pour some more out, but the bottles knocked together making a clinking sound when he went to put them back. We stopped dead in our tracks, both holding our breath for a response. Then it came, his Dad called out to his son. 'Andy! what's going on Andy?' he called out.

'Err... oh nothing Dad, just tidying up the living room a little.'

At the time I thought it rather odd that his dad didn't mind us sharing a room together. In asking why he was so liberal, Andy explained that they only had three rooms, and he was the only one who was willing to share; I burst into laughter at his response and it felt good, to laugh again, even if it was just for a moment.

In the mornings, after his Dad left for work and his sister left for college, he would introduce me to his musical heroes: Bruce Springsteen, Pink Floyd, and the Eagles. He would educate me on instrumental sounds and what he called 'real music'. He also introduced me to real comedy, Richard Pryor *(probably because of his foul mouth)*, but he was extremely funny, especially on the issues of life; and then there was real action with Mel Gibson; in his youth, yes, he really was *sex on legs*.

He took me to see Mel in '*Mad Max*' and 'Richard Pryor Live', both playing at the cinema on Oxford Street. I really did enjoy both movies. He also introduced me to peanut butter and jam on burnt toast and other things that only adults should do. We seemed to be getting on so well, until it was time for me to leave again.

Jeanie kept calling me, at first, I kept telling her I was coming tomorrow, *well we all know that tomorrow never comes*, then I told Andy to tell her I wasn't in. This appeared to work for a bit as her phone calls lessened. Jeanie was adamant that she wanted me to go to this new place she had found at the top of Muswell hill called the Muswell Hill Motel. I don't know what she said to Andy to cause him to switch camps so suddenly, but now he appeared to be completely on her side. He said he would come with me so we agreed to meet Jeanie at her house in two days, from there we would travel to the 'new place'. When we arrived, I could tell instantly simply from just standing outside the front door that it was in fact a complete hovel, and upon entry my preconception was not wrong. Apparently, I was all out of options, the only choice remaining was to either remain here or go to some even less impressive institution surrounded by eight-meter-high fencing.

This was indeed a grotty hovel, a sad excuse for a hotel, perhaps even the grottiest in the world. It gave new meaning to the word 'hotel' which, in so doing, seemed to do no more than to insult the term. Jeanie began to boast out loud, in the fact that they would be providing bed *and* breakfast, all included in the price; she always did love a bargain. Well, I certainly knew that I would not be having any breakfast here, and I asked for three sets of sheets and a blanket to cover the stained mattress before I forced myself to get into the bed. I think I absolutely despised Jeanie in that moment, more so than I ever felt was possible. *How could she put me here? How could she be so thoughtless, so clueless, and so reckless?*

The hotel was filled to the brim with drunks, drug addicts, and prostitutes, and I was perhaps the only child not at home but all alone, very alone. It was depressing beyond belief. Each night, there was screaming and banging and shouting and running and maybe the odd glass breaking. The scent of stale smoke and empty beer cans filled the hallways and landings. This was one place I never felt like exploring. I kept completely to myself.

Every morning, I was woken by the smell of stale oil frying cheap bacon, battery eggs, and value beans. It was so bad it forged a permanent odor into the front reception area grinding itself into the once royal blue carpet and old-fashioned wallpaper. I did not even want to get up out of bed each day.

I just wanted to close my eyes, never having to open them ever again; it was so bloody awful. When in bed, I would stare so long at the curtains that I would begin to make faces from the patterns. I didn't eat, and I didn't drink. I just lay there.

After a while, Andy came up to see me. I asked him whether Jeanie had sent him. As he seemed to be moving in slowly, his reluctant yes almost began to restore some small beacon of faith in her, but I was still very cross with her. We shared a single bed, which was not really ideal, as it was so uncomfortable. Eventually, the sleeping arrangements became so cramped that it began to feel as though we were on top of each other all the time, which became taxing on our makeshift relationship.

At least one good thing about having Andy around was that he always made sure I ate properly, at least one meal a day even if it was from the Wimpy. After about three weeks or so, Andy got a job far away, so he had to move nearer the job; this placed a further strain on our relationship. I remember trying my best to bring the relationship to a very mature and civilized end. Although, at just fifteen, I'm not sure exactly what if anything I knew about being mature.

In any event, it wasn't long before I found myself alone again; and this time even more depressed than I had ever been before. Every Friday, I would drag myself up to meet with Lottie. I would climb the stairs to meet her in her newly built office which sat behind the common at Turnpike Lane. We would sit and talk *small talk* for fifteen to twenty minutes before making the short walk down the high street to get some lunch.

It was at one of these visits that I learned when the children called to speak to their social workers the social worker would call down to the receptionist and say,

'Tell them I'm not in the office, would you.'

I was shocked; I could not believe it. '*Yes, you are,*' I thought. Instantly I thought back to my time at the Chillingham Estate, which still sent shudders down my spine, even to this day, and I thought about the amount of times we had all called up the SS all crying out for help, screaming out for anyone to help us, yet no one ever came to the phone, not one single social worker ever came to the phone and from all the left messages no one ever responded, from all the pleas for help no one ever called us back neither did they ever come to visit. The message was loud and clear, no one cared.

In that moment in finding out this truth I had no words, I was shocked. We had placed so much faith in these adults to care for us and to protect us. And now, if ever I wondered why no one ever did answer us, why no one ever did come back to us? Here was my answer - loud and clear.

Lottie tried to talk to Graham, who was out-right refusing to speak to his charge. She tried as hard as possible to persuade him, but he wasn't having any of it. He could not be bothered to take the call or to return it and he made it crystal clear that there was nothing she could do to change his mind.

'If I don't want to take a call I don't have to,' he said rather tersely. Lottie continued to press on the point saying

'Yes, Graham but that's not the right way to handle the situation.'

I said absolutely nothing. I just listened to their conversation. I could not make out whether Lottie was for real or just putting on a show for me. Either way it was very convincing. Unfortunately, I was all out of change for BS. I just felt sad and disappointed.

We left the office and began to walk up the high street on Wood Green, which used to be a place of greenery but was now all concrete and glass. I would always select the Wimpy as my choice of eatery. I enjoyed their burgers and grilled frankfurter; *I had no idea that it was actually pigs' nose I was eating;* and I loved their banana shakes too. My order was always the same: one burger with onions and chips, on occasions I would have two burgers, *this usually depended on whether I had had a bar of chocolate for breakfast, in any event it was* always followed by a long, tall, ice-cold banana shake, or sometimes I would have chips, burger, grilled frankfurter, and beans. The shake never changed, always banana, always ice cold.

We would continue talking about nothing. I guess my state of mind was etched across my face; she became worried when our conversation died out altogether, and my answers were reduced to 'yes' and 'no'. After lunch, we would then make the slow walk back to the office.

Once we got back, she would give me some money for food toiletries and travel for the week ahead, which I would sign for, and we would say our goodbyes until the following week, where we would repeat the entire process all over again. Oddly, we never made contact at all during the week.

Of course, the money was never enough to buy proper healthy meals, but who cared? No one. My guess was that the establishment would much rather pay an arm and a leg for a dump in which to dump a child in, just to fulfil its legal obligation and tick the box for the provision of accommodation as opposed to finding a real home where the child could be happy. They were unable to identify with the fact or even begin to understand the truth that a child would also require healthy food and adequate clothing or if they did understand it no one did anything about it. At a stretch, the budget could just about buy two days of proper meals as well as purchase toiletries and travel.

I always made sure I ate properly on Sundays. I would have chicken and chips from the Kentucky and sometimes with beans – not the healthiest meal in the world I know, but it was something I felt could be nutritional and it was the only time during the week that I could afford to eat meat.

The days soon passed into weeks and the weeks became months with my routine remaining much the same. Jeanie tried her hardest to get me back into school, really, she did, but the schools in London were now on a sharp decline, and discipline had gone right out of the window, *with the bath water*, so rebellion was on the rise. *What had changed?* I wondered.

The teachers from my old school felt that if I was living such an 'independent life', then perhaps, I should study 'independently' too. They thought I should skip school altogether and go straight to college or something, but at just fifteen, clearly, I was too young to attend college. When the decision was made, it meant that I would have to wait until the next academic year before continuing my education because now it was November; I had missed almost all the first term. Missing education was fast becoming the story of my life, this was the fourth time I was missing school.

This news sent me into an even deeper spiral of sadness and depression. *What on earth was I going to do for nine months?* I knew no one bar the SS, and I certainly did not want to speak to them every day for nine months. But after a short while, some good news came my way. My rescuers telephoned me at the dumpy motel and left a message for me to call them back straight away, collect. When I called, they told me they had some good news, and that I should come to the office the next day and we would go to lunch. It was then that she dropped it.

'We have been thinking,' she said.

'Yes,' I said, completely unmoved and unfazed in my facial expressions, my facial muscles refusing to communicate on purpose.

'We have been thinking,' she started again, 'and we have agreed that you can go ahead and rent a flat with Andy.'

Well, that was some good news. I could not believe my ears.

'What do you mean?' I asked. 'You sure?' I added waiting for the punch line.

'Yes, you have been together a long time now, and in fact, you would need him to come in with you as he would have to share the rent liability with you. That would be the only way we could make it work because the department would not be able to pick up the entire bill,' she said, trying not to cough. Of course, there had to be a hitch, but it was one I was prepared to bear just to get out of the dumpy motel.

'Well, what do I need to do now?' I asked, revealing my interest. She told me which papers to look in and had brought me a whole load to get me started, which she conveniently pulled out from under her desk and gave me some change for the phone. We called so many and went to visit some too. They were all terrible. I could not believe what was on offer for the budget we had, which was just £80.00 per week.

Christmas came and went, and we still had not found anywhere. I spent that Christmas between Jeanie's and Andy's dads. I didn't like the dinner, I had never liked turkey and Jeanie had burnt the stuffing cakes, which she also offered up at the makeshift table, that she had set up in her tiny kitchen, to accommodate everyone. We forced ourselves to fit around it as each fighting for a piece, upon which to hold an odd piece of crockery or cutlery that did not match. We shared the day and the dinner with Jeanie's friends who enjoyed the food. I realized that I was even fussier when it came to eating.

Missing Family

In the New Year, Odette was excited to return to see Dad and his children again. She had saved up all her money from her Saturday job at the Patisserie, owned by her friends Dad, and brought Dad and the children a load of Christmas presents – two carrier bags full in fact. I could see that she felt extremely proud by the way she walked; she had a certain bounce in her step, one I had never seen before. We met at Jeanie's that day and made the journey over to the farm.

Once we had reached the fourth floor, we walked the short distance along the landing, stopping outside number 58. She was glistening with pride, probably convinced with all the positive feelings of praise that she believed she would be rewarded with once they opened all their presents. I on the other hand - brought nothing.

We knocked on the door and waited. In all honesty, the thought had not even entered my mind. There was no sound or answer, so we knocked again a little harder this time and waited. Again, there was no sound or movement or footsteps. We knocked a third time, and this time we called out through the letter box; there was still no response.

Odette now becoming slightly agitated began to walk back to the lift.

'What are you going to do now?' I asked as I tried to keep up with her. She did not answer. I followed her as she marched in the direction of Kitchener Road... again... Well, we had certainly been here before...

When we arrived, Uncle Matthew was in. It was almost déjà vu. Odette explained the entire story of what had just happened back at the flat. Uncle Matthew immediately got dressed and drove us straight back to the farm. We went up in the lift, walked along the landing; upon arriving at number 58, Uncle Matthew banged on the door rather fiercely. We waited, but there was no answer. He banged again and called out, the door, shaking in its frame, almost coming away at the lock, still there was no answer; we looked through the letter box, pulling back the vertical blinds, which had been blocking our view, to one side and continued to call out.

As the blinds parted, we could see directly down the passage and through into the lounge as the living room door had been left wide open. Whatever had happened, it had been in a hurry. We could see that the furniture was gone, the orange blinds, which once had dressed the incredibly wide, lounge windows, were now hanging down from one side, as if someone had tried to remove them in a hurry but then had given up. Also, on the list of gone was our siblings, Dad and of course Mordecka was also gone, but neither of us was bothered about anything to do with her at this time.

The truth, once apparent was followed by our departure. With it we walked slowly back to our uncle's car, heads bowed low as we went. He asked us where we wanted him to drop us, I looked up in Odette's direction for the answer. 'At the bus stop,' she whispered softly. For the first time in my life, I felt her pain, her disappointment; it was a massive weight, almost unbearable.

On the journey, back to Jeanie's, she never spoke at all, and I knew not to speak to her at this time. Once we arrived back at Jeanie's, she just shut herself away and became quite aloof, not speaking at all about how she felt regarding what had just happened, right up into our adulthood in fact, and

I never asked her what she did with the presents either. I just didn't have the guts. Jeanie promised that she would find out what had happened and get them traced but ended up doing what she always did best... nothing, absolutely nothing. *Thank you Jeanie.*

We finished off the holidays at Jeanie's before Odette returned back to Mansion Heights in Hampshire; and me, up the hill to the dumpy motel. However, everyone already seemed to know what had happened without mentioning a word. Sometimes, Jeanie really did have a big mouth, and not just when eating. *Gee thanks Jeanie.*

Coleridge Gardens

After about three months of looking for my own flat, we eventually found one. It was a super-sized studio on the ground floor with plenty of storage. It had its own bathroom, large kitchen, and rooftop garden. It was perfect. Ironically, it was at the end of the very same road I had walked into after exiting the minibus that day I left Grimshaw Hall for the second time. *Was heaven trying to tell me something?* In any event, it was lovely, even the road was lovely, it was nice and quiet and very clean. Odette came to stay with me, and I learnt to laugh again.

I got a Saturday job at the Wimpy, of all places; well, I had faithfully tithed there long enough for all those years, perhaps that was the least they could have done for me after all my investment. It was just for two weeks though because after that I moved over to the hairdresser's; in truth that's where I had really wanted to be. I don't know what it is about young girls and hair. But I had it.

Several months earlier, when I had made some inquiries, the owner had asked me to come back when I was sixteen, so I did. On my day off I would catch up with some well-earned TV and was introduced to Oprah; she looked very different then, her shows were so gripping, uplifting, and inspiring even then. Once you started watching it was impossible to move away from in front of the TV. She always had you eating out of the palm of her hand. I also began to receive mail from my Dad's mother, Gran Ma May, who still lived in the Caribbean.

Things seemed to be going really great for me and life seemed bearable again, at least until Andy began to mess about with his share of the rent and his attendance as a responsible participant at the flat full stop. He began to spend more and more time at Zach's, going out with just Zach and hanging out with just Zach. I felt completely ignored and neglected. I knew no one. I was all alone, and I began to feel as though I was completely on my own again.

There were times when I would feel so low it was absolutely unbearable; it was in these moments that I would travel all the way down to Harrods in Knightsbridge, to the drinks bar in the basement, and order an ice cream soda. Ironically, it was Andy who had first introduced me to this well-kept secret, and it was a wonderful pick-me up to set you right back on track. I would take my time in drinking it, whilst people watching and taking in the scenery before making the long journey back to the empty flat again. At other times, I would make the long journey, by tube, all the way down to Heathrow Airport.

I would take my seat in the departure lounge. I would sit there for hours, just watching the passengers leave for their various destinations, wishing that someone, anyone, would take me away with them. My deepest thought was that anything must be better than this existence, than this life. I even carried my passport with me, just in case... When it started to get late, I would return once more to the empty flat.

On one occasion, feeling so completely fed up, I tried to confront Andy about his behavior, but he was so dismissive and lacked any kind of understanding or empathy about the pain his actions were causing me. On this night, he was already in bed, and I was standing at the end of it, nearer to the shelves stacked up in the alcove. There was a glass bottle sitting there containing some West Indian Bay Rub; it was familiar amongst Caribbean families who used it when someone had a cold. I had brought it for Andy when he had a cold and what was left had remained on the shelf.

When I looked over at him, he wasn't even looking at me, he wasn't engaging with me in the slightest. Clearly, it was evident that he was not in the least bothered. With one hand, I willfully and deliberately knocked the bottle with some force right off the shelf. It collided with the wall before hitting the ground and smashing into hundreds of pieces upon contact.

We carried on arguing, neither of us prepared to show the other any compassion, neither of us prepared to show any sort of understanding, neither of us prepared to back down, both of us demanding the spotlight, both of us demanding to be the center of attention. I bent down and picked up a piece of the broken glass and allowed it to run the length of my forearm in three places on my left arm. My skin opened and my arm began to bleed out without stopping.

In that moment, the pain of the skin severing as painful as it was, seemed almost to dilute the emotional pain I was simultaneously experiencing. Andy popped his head out from under the covers and saw the blood dripping from my arm; how he saw it I don't know, as my arm was in the downward position. It was as though he intuitively knew something was wrong. He jumped up and took me straight into the bathroom where he attempted to apply his limited knowledge of emergency first aid. He began by first bandaging the wound without having cleaned it. I didn't comment though, I just stared at him and he stared right back at me, neither of us speaking. I wondered what thoughts were going through his mind, I already knew what was in my own mind and my desires hadn't changed. Albeit we never discussed this incident again; in fact, we continued like some old married couple, as if nothing had ever happened at all.

The following morning, I was starting my first day at the Wimpy and it was when I rolled up my sleeves to start the washing up that all the 'How' and 'Why' questions started; of course, it was the imaginary cat that got the blame – I didn't want them to think I was some kind of freak, because to most this would appear a crazy thing to do.

But we were not designed to be in emotional pain.

I worked there for only two consecutive Saturdays and hated every minute of it; don't get me wrong the staff were absolutely lovely, sincerely kind, and very friendly, but for me, the work was excruciatingly brain numbing. Halfway through my second week, I returned to the hairdressers to remind the boss that I would be starting on Saturday because I had just turned sixteen. She looked at me in amazement before answering my question regarding the start time.

'Errrr... 8:30 a.m... and 8:15 a.m., so if you would like to come at about 8:15 am that would be fine,' she said stumbling over her words.

'OK, great, see you then,' I replied as I left her office.

At about the same time, I also signed up with a youth project, who found me a weekly placement at a nursery. Things were really starting to look up, and I began to feel more positive in myself and about the life I was living. I had a new focus now. I really enjoyed working in the nursery with the children, and after some minor challenges, I managed to introduce the staff members to the idea of baking with the children. Of course, they were worried about the children cutting themselves with the cutters. I explained that they were the same cutters they used for cutting plasticine with. Then they were worried about the children burning themselves on the oven. Again, I explained that the chef would be the only person putting the trays in the oven and taking them out. Finally, I got the green light and the session could go ahead.

In our first cooking lesson, I made jam tarts with the children. Positioned in a circle, we passed the mixing bowl from child to child and they each took it in turns to rub the butter into the flour, roll out the pastry and use the plastic ring cutters to cut out the circles of the pastry to fit in to the tins. They spooned on the jam with excitement, each one licking the stickiness from off their fingers. I took the trays to the kitchen where cook placed them in the oven. At the end of the day, we all enjoyed delicious warm jam tarts. It was a success so much so that they wanted to know what we would cook next.

Each day after work, I would walk back down the hill to my bedsit and crash out on the bed completely exhausted. I think the turning point or rather the breaking point, came when out of the blue, the children would run up to me and start hugging me; I couldn't handle it, I would become so overwhelmed, it would always make me cry. I found that any kind of physical contact would cause me real physical pain in my stomach, even if it was from my sister. Albeit I never told anyone.

I would always try and hide my tears from the children and from the staff members. In the end, I decided that I couldn't continue to work with the children as it was just too painful. As a result, I began working full time in the hair salon.

It would always be nice to arrive back at the flat and be greeted by a letter from Grandma May, more so because she could not read and write herself so all her outgoing mail had to be dictated by her and all her incoming mail had to be read to her, usually by the wife of one of her other sons who had remained on the island. Unbeknown to me at the time I would eventually get to meet the scribe of her letters just 35 years later. She and her husband would be a guest at my dinner table; and the clock was ticking… tick tock…, tick tock... tick tock.

Hearing from Gran Ma May was the closest thing to any form of human contact to another family member, it was the only impression of 'family' that I had felt in years; and more so since we had no idea of where Dad was, and it gave me an innate kind of confidence and life was ok again. Gran Ma May had six sons in total – two had come here to the UK, the second of whom was Dad, until his dramatic disappearance, two were in the USA, and two had remained in the Caribbean with her.

Life continued on and then one day, out of the blue, I received a telephone call from one of my uncles in the USA. It was Uncle Kipling. He was a landscaper and had done all right for himself. He must have got my details from Gran Ma May, his mother, with whom he had remained in contact, unlike dad.

'Hello, do you know who this is?' he asked in a very gentle voice; he had a very strong American accent. 'I am your Dad's brother, Uncle Kipling and I'm living in the US,' he said rather proudly. 'Which one am I speaking to?' he asked.

'Hello, I'm Jacqueline.' I said quietly.

'I'm really sorry to hear what has happened to you and your sister,' He paused, then asked. 'Is she there?'

'Err no,' I answered, choking back the tears.

'Well I have a proposition for you,' he said full of enthusiasm. 'I want you and your sister to come out here for a visit and if you like it you can stay,' he said. 'How does that sound to you?' as if expecting the same degree of enthusiasm and excitement in return.

'Err yes,' I said. Trying to take it all in, at the same time trying to remember when it was my turn to speak. *This was my ticket out of here; or so I thought.*

'Odette should come first though because she is the oldest,' he said. Instantly, I could feel this gesture of kindness slipping away from me, like sand through my fingers. No-one knew where Odette was from one day to the next; I for one certainly did not know how to reach her. But for now, I refused to let go of his outstretched hand of kindness; right here right now it was a lifeline out of hell, my hell.

Little did I know that this was to be the first and the last conversation I was ever to have with Uncle Kipling; little did I know that I would never hear his sweet kind voice ever again. I was never to meet him or see him face to face before his body would prematurely go down into the cold unrepentant ground and the dust would cover him over.

He gave me his number before coming off the phone. I felt so elated, I began to imagine his home and in my mind's eye I could see a massive white house with two formidable pillars standing boldly at both sides of the entrance and loads of sunshine everywhere. I could see beautiful colored flowers lining the path up to the door and everyone was smiling with happiness. I could not wait to get there.

I remember I took it everywhere I went, I guess it was the closest I could be to his kindness, but for some silly reason I never wrote it down in my address book. Why I don't know, because normally I always wrote down all the numbers in my book.

Still excited by the news, I felt as though I wanted to share this wonderful news with someone, anyone, so the following Sunday, I went to visit Uncle Matthew at his home in North London.

When I arrived, I was greeted by his wife, Shaniqua, a smallish woman, who probably held the world record on moaning, mumbling, and complaining. If ever there was one to be had, she certainly had it. Uncle Matthew was not in, so she carefully sat me down at the kitchen table to wait for him. I was completely blind and naive as to what I had just walked into. Unbeknown to me, my aunt and uncle were experiencing some matrimonial differences or rather difficulties, and had been doing so for many years, only now they were bubbling over for all and sundry to see and hear. Despite being officially separated; my aunt just couldn't help herself. She would use any excuse to drag the father of her own children through the mud and mire.

However, upon seeing me, I was easy prey and she was determined to drag me through it with him right into the middle of what usually was a blazing row. What started off as a really lovely afternoon ended with Uncle Matthew slapping my face as hard as he possibly could, me trying to stab him in the chest with a long arm three prong cooking fork, *usually used for turning the chicken over in the oven or large pan,* and him breaking my bag, removing uncle Kipling's number, and ripping it into a hundred tiny little pieces, completely illegible to the human eye and me being completely devastated and crashing in to a heap on the floor. I burst into tears as I tried to piece the miniature segments of the tiny textbook paper back together. I never did get his number, neither did I get the opportunity to speak to him ever again. I would only hear of his premature death some thirty years later at the alleged negligent hands of a reckless medical consultant and the absence of loving care from his second wife. And the clock was ticking ...tick tock ...tick tock... tick tock.

My ray of hope had gone forever. Like a butterfly his gestures of kindness just flew away. After the ordeal I left the house; Uncle Matthew stood at the door, unmoved by his own actions or my distress. I told him he was the worst dad ever and the worst uncle on the planet, before departing from the gate. And in passing his car, I broke off the aerial and with one swing allowing it to make contact. The front windscreen smashed into a thousand tiny pieces. I cried all the way home; great sobs of tears fell heavy with emotion. I never visited my uncle again after that; at least, not in that decade anyway. He could have done so much more but always chose not to; at least it always appeared that way.

By the time the lease came up for renewal at the flat, the landlord said she had no intention of renewing it with us, particularly after all the complaints she had received from the silent neighbors. Truth be known, Andy and I had had one too many nights of speaking too loudly in the flat, with the last one leading to me having to call out the emergency services and the emergency GP who visited at 2 a.m. to attend to my wounds after having been kicked in the back. I had ripped from his neck the gold chain that I had purchased for him at Christmas; clearly, that didn't go down too well, and as I walked away he Kung fu'd me in the back from behind.

When the day of our departure arrived, and we were all packed and ready to go, I reluctantly returned to the dumpy Motel, alone, and Andy returned to his Dad's. I think we both knew that it was over. We never lived together again after that. We just dated or just about. Our relationship never really fully recovered.

Upon my return, they moved me into a much larger room; it was double the size this time and was in a rather better part of the motel; it was much quieter on this side. However, the bathroom and the toilet were still the pits. You had to scrub a rub tub before you could use anything in that motel, including the handrails.

In order to use up my time productively during the days and in my desperation to communicate with the outside world and have fellowship with others, I began writing to various companies, giving them feedback on their products, that I had purchased, tried, and tested. They would always write a letter of acknowledgement and thanks back to me which was really nice I thought, and sometimes they would even send me loads of free samples, which was also very nice. It was so nice to read their letters; I would read them over and over and try to imagine what the author looked like and how they would be dressed: writing long hand letters was the closest thing I could get to a conversation with another person; another human being.

That summer, 1981, Lady Diana Spencer and Prince Charles, the Prince of Wales, got engaged. For some reason, I felt so akin to her, I don't know if it had anything to do with being born on the same day and all. I began to track her life in paper cuttings, yet never got to stick them in my scrapbook.

I could not have imagined in my wildest dreams, that just 15 years later I would be knocking on the door of her apartment at Kensington palace to drop off the tapes, for her book that she was writing, 'Diana'. And the clock was ticking tick… tock… tick… tock.

False Imprisonment

Despite my efforts to connect with people, I found that I was still very much alone. One evening, when I was feeling particularly low, I thought I would go for a walk. There was a bench at the end of the road and next to it was a red telephone box. I sat down on the bench and looked up at the night sky and began to think about my future, as I stared up at all the stars lighting up the sky. Just at that point of exiting this world and entering into my safe world of daydream, an odd-looking, middle-aged man wearing a long dark overcoat came over and sat down next to me.

He began to speak to me, but I could not answer him. I could barely hear what he was saying. I was too far gone. I thought I heard him say the word police and then he got up and left. I looked to my right, witnessing him enter the phone box. I thought that was the end of him and so continued gazing up at the stars. There were so many of them right above my head.

Then suddenly, in the blink of an eye, I saw a flashing blue light whiz past right in front of me, and the sound of screeching brakes ringing out from somewhere up the road near the hotel. I jumped up and looked up the road. In my panic, I thought I could make it back to the hotel, get in and shut the door behind me without being intercepted. I was very wrong. They caught me no problem. There were three of them and one of me, they had me completely surrounded. I had nowhere to run. I tried to run out in the road but alas they caught me. They threw me into the back of the van, pressing my face down hard on to the cold, wet, dirty, floor and twisting my arms up behind my back. The older one told the younger one to take his foot from off my back.

'She's just a kid,' he said. I was completely incensed. They carted me off to the police station all puffed up with their catch.

The WPC was the worst; she was bragging about how she knew me, swearing blue bloody murder, and that I was a runaway from the house on the hill… It was true; I had lived there, just not in that decade. I overheard the sergeant telling the WPC if she was wrong, they could get into trouble, big trouble.

'I swear to you Sarge!' She said. *She must have been new.* He confirmed the awkward truth with a brief telephone call to Sandy Lodge. 'There were no runaways that night.' Said the voice at the end of the phone.

If that wasn't enough humiliation for one night, they then wanted someone to confirm who I was. Clearly, this was the Sargent trying to be clever. I had to give him a name. I could not give the motel; the SS were in bed so that only left Zac. I thought they would have just spoken to him on the phone, embarrassingly, they made him come all the way down to the police station to identify me at 2 am. I could not bloody believe it. He identified me… how excruciatingly embarrassing. How was I ever going to look at him again? They did not care that they had got him out of bed, or that he had work the next day. It was not until he revealed that he worked for the police that they found some respect.

It was then they wanted to be all nice to me and offer me tea which was accidently on purpose spilled all over the WPC. She tried to complain to the Sergeant. He said she was lucky that was all she got; It was false imprisonment and assault.

A short while after that they escorted me back to the hotel. It was about 3:00 am when we arrived, but the front door was locked, so they rung the bell. Luckily for me, my embarrassment did not go past Zachary. Once the door was opened, I ran straight in without speaking a word; thank God, the hotel manager thought no more about the situation other than I had been accidently locked out, and this was the reason for me being accompanied by the police, who just went along with it.

In the morning, he kept on apologising to me. Thankfully, the boys in blue had saved me from any further embarrassment by failing to explain what had really happened, which perhaps for them was also an embarrassment as well as a possible law suit. I mean you can't just go around picking people up from off the street you know, granted I was a kid, but I was outside where I lived, and I wasn't doing anything wrong.

The following day, he was trying to explain to me what I should do if ever I got locked out again – something about the key and the big plant pot, but I wasn't really listening. The manager became very kind to me after that incident.

Finally, September came, and I started college at the 'Meredith Adult Education Center'. I picked my subjects – Math, English Language, English Literature, Commerce, Biology, and Law. I was encouraged to pick Law as one of my options, as I had reached the point where after my last ordeal with the boys in blue; I felt I needed to know my rights. But it was after being taught by a retired High Court Judge of the Middle Temple that I decided that's what I wanted to be when I grew up.

Two days later, Odette joined me at the motel. I hadn't seen her for ages, albeit her stay was short-lived as per usual. No sooner had she put down her two carrier bags, no sooner was she gone again. She never came back, not even for her bags, and I was left once more all alone at the dumpy motel. I was completely unaware of what had been happening in her life or what the nuns had done to her after Sr P's untimely death. We had not spoken in months, not even on the phone: The chasm between us really was that wide.

I hardly saw Andy too; then suddenly he would turn up out of the blue after not having been around for weeks like some dribbling bitch on heat. Finally, I was beginning to see the truth of what was really going on and began to feel that I really did not want to be with him anymore, but in the same breath, I couldn't bear to be alone. I was in between a rock and a hard place. I decided to hang on for the last chance for him to change; I kept telling myself: I guess I didn't have the courage to end it myself at that time.

On my first day of enrolment, I met a girl called Penny Pemberton. We had both arrived early for the talk and tour and were heading for the same seat in the same aisle. Upon realizing what was happening, we both offered the other the seat. We laughed simultaneously and began talking to each other and from that moment onwards, our friendship grew. We quickly became best friends.

After classes, Penny would take me home with her like some lost puppy and feed me; she introduced me to her mum, dad, and elder sister, who had just had a baby. She said she had another sister who was from her mom's first marriage, but she was married now and so didn't live at home with the rest of the family. Like me, her middle sister was also interested in law and planned to become a solicitor. However, she was much further along in the process than I was.

I was just starting out on foundational law; she was just starting her articles, right before becoming a solicitor. Penny's parents were from the island of Barbados; remarkably, this was the same place that Mordecka was from, yet they were so kind and so loving and so giving. *How could this be so?* I thought.

They lived at the top of a very steep hill, and every time we climbed it, I would vow to myself that *that* was the last climb, and I would never visit her again, but of course, I did. *Still it was good exercise I suppose.*

Her mum would always cook for me and make me feel very welcome; it was as though she knew it all, without me having to explain a thing, without me having to say a word and she was also an exceedingly good cook at all things Caribbean; it was always absolutely, delicious.

I never told Penny exactly where I lived. I was too embarrassed or rather ashamed to tell anyone, but one day she admitted to me that she knew where I lived. Of course, I did not believe her because I had always been so careful, even walking around the block at least once before going back to the grotty motel. However, she had been very clever as she admitted to having secretly followed me. Of course, I was annoyed and a bit upset, but from then on, she would just walk with me up to the door, if we were not going to hers, and when she did, she never asked me if she could come in; I really respected her for that. At college, they often mocked my accent because even after a year I still spoke as though I had a plum in my mouth.

I remember I would practice every night at speaking how they did, with a good dollop of profanity mixed in.

I was so desperate to fit in.

In our home lives the news came that we were on the move again. The plan was that we were now moving to the Y MCA. It was a newly built establishment, and there was a long waiting list to get in, but somehow Lottie had swung it for us - as per usual. She was good at that. I guess I never actually stopped to think exactly how many rules she broke for us in total. She had secretly some of the same qualities as Sister P, which was a good thing, I guess.

Upon my arrival, I found the rooms to be equally balanced, fully equipped with bed, built-in sink, workstation, and a reading lamp. It was just a stone's throw away from Jeanie's and still easy to get to college. It was just one bus from the clock tower, which was the hub of Crouch End, where all the shops stood, and journey interchanges could be made. It was also closer to Penny's too; now we lived just one road apart, which was a good thing, I guess.

I moved in first, with Odette to follow afterwards. She had asked me to pack her things for her and take them over with me upon my departure from the dumpy motel. As she had never actually unpacked, it was not that difficult. Jeanie had booked a taxi for the short journey over to assist with all our things, which helped.

Odette's possessions consisted of no more than just two white plastic bags, and it was a further two weeks before she followed. Just before her arrival Lottie decided that it was better value for money if we shared a room. We didn't mind so we were relocated to the penthouse on the top floor, our only neighbors being the manager and his wife.

It was great. We had our own showers, extra beds, and a mini kitchen equipped with cupboards and fridge, but no cooker. It was enough though, or so we thought. We also had my rubbish second-hand TV, which I had brought when I moved into Coleridge Gardens for the grand sum of £60.00 from the second-hand shop.

Yes, I'm quite sure he was laughing all the way to the bank after that sale.

I had dragged it to the dumpy motel with me like some unfaithful lover, even though it kept going on the blink every 3 minutes.

It was not long before Odette was off again, and once more, I was on my own in this great spacious room. However, after a good night out with my college chums, I would always invite them to spend the night to save them money on cabs and from them going home alone.

The months continued to tick on by and soon Christmas was upon us. We had a slightly longer academic holiday that year, and so I managed to secure a job with Presto, the supermarket situated at the top of the high street.

My intention was to stay there just for the holiday period which I did. I met a really nice girl on the checkouts. She had shoulder length hair and brown eyes and a huge smile. Her name was Janice Scott and we became friends. She reminded me of Annabel and at times I would call her Annie by mistake. We went out a couple of times for after work drinks and I met her boyfriend who was a lot older than her. On one occasion her boyfriend brought his friend in an attempt to make two sets of couples, but we didn't hit it off.

After the Christmas holiday's I told her that I would be leaving to return to college in January, she said she would be leaving too. When we told the manager, he was incensed beyond reason. He took us into the office one by one and when it was my turn, he asked me for my pay packet, I was shocked and afraid. I did what he said and from it he took out £35.00. I felt so violated, so hurt, so sick to my stomach. We thought we were doing the right thing by letting him know, but he was absolutely infuriated, and we could not understand why, but this, what he had done was theft.

I had become very good at saving and managed to buy a lot of wonderful things for Christmas, as well as feed my savings account. I bought Andy a lovely grey woolen blazer and other bits and pieces totally oblivious to what he was planning for me. Christmas came, and we exchanged our gifts, except he did not have the time to get me anything, or so he said, and promised that he would get me something during the New Year. Odd though I thought, but I did not attach any real weight to it at the time. And I'm guessing it must have been just a few days after the Christmas break when both he and Zach paid me a surprise visit.

Clearly, something was wrong because he had telephoned to see if I was in first, which he never did and then he asked whether Zach could come up with him as well; this was also very strange because Zach had never accompanied Andy to visit me before. I had no objections, so of course I agreed. I knew something was wrong, but I just could not put my finger on it. I ran around the room frantically, like a blue arse fly, picking up clothes and books and papers as I went, shoving everything into the built in wardrobes and cupboards.

Upon their arrival, he began to ask me strange questions like 'Have I got a grey pair of trousers here?' and 'Have I got a pair of jeans?' and 'Is my jean jacket here?'. My answer to each of his questions was an emphatic no! I gazed over at Zach after each question and after each answer. He wasn't looking at me; in fact, he made no gesture.

Andy then began to open the doors to my wardrobes as he continued pottering around the room. 'No,' I replied immediately, jumping up and over the end of the bed to close back the door quickly, tripping over the carpet as I went and feeling a little embarrassed, hoping that neither of them had noticed the mess that lay behind it.

Andy kept walking up and down, picking up things, and looking under them as he went. His behavior was extremely absurd: he was making me very nervous and a little annoyed to say the least. I guess more so because Zach was with him, and I wasn't sure why.

Then as brass as day, from out of nowhere, he asked me for the engagement ring he had given me two years earlier. I had not wanted to get engaged to him, at the time as I felt I was just too young but lacked the courage to say no. Feeling completely surprised and even more embarrassed, I told him that I did not know where it was at that moment, but that I would find it for him. Then even more bizarrely, he announced that he was going to collect something, and he left me alone with Zach, which felt even more strange. Oddly enough, I didn't even question his actions or his bizarre statements. I guess I just wanted his searching and his walking up and down to end.

He left the apartment at 8:20 pm and I just waited...and waited...and waited and waited... It must have been close to an hour that had passed before I turned to Zach and asked him where Andy had gone. Zach answered saying that he did not know. I then asked him how long he was going to be. Surprisingly enough, he did not have the answer to that question either. I then asked him what was going on because it was getting rather late, and I had college in the morning. With that Zachary opened his mouth and began to speak. The room began spinning. His mouth was moving, but after the words

'Andy has… Andy has asked me to....to.... tell you, to tell you that... that...that it's over.' I could hear nothing except airplane engines. They were so loud. My entire body felt as though the base had been turned up and was shaking with the vibrations. I was not sure how to feel.

Once I returned to earth again, I sat there for a moment, staring at the floor; then I looked up and said, 'Right! Take me to your flat.' I think his obedience was probably more out of sheer fear than desire or agreement. I was so cross with Andy and his little charade. I stormed all the way there on foot as if a footman of the fifth battalion, with Zach lagging behind, like some lost child, perhaps wondering what he had allowed himself to be drawn into.

When we arrived, I immediately began to take back everything that I had just given Andy for Christmas and some of his records too, which I knew would really, annoy him; all the while Zach was attempting to verbalize his concerns with phrases like 'oh no' 'not that', and 'oh no, please don't take that'. Then I marched all the way back down to the YMCA with two big black bin liners on my back, *but oh... so not Father Christmas.* Zach was still following, still lagging, still trailing quite some distance behind; What for? I did not know. For what? I did not care. I certainly wish he hadn't bothered. I kept hoping he would just go home. I certainly had no use for him now.

Once we got back it was almost 11 pm, I kept pacing the room fueled with undiluted anger; I continued to pace until the early hours of the morning, mumbling, muttering, and murmuring to myself as though I had lost my mind. Zach wanted to stay with me but ended up falling asleep on my bed, fully dressed, and snoring rather loudly. Yuck! I lay down fully dressed on one of the spare beds. In that moment, as I stared at him, I was so relieved that I had not gone out with him. His snoring was so loud that he could have snored for the entire nation. I could not wait until the morning just so he could leave, and I could try to get some sleep even if it was just for an hour before having to get up and leave for college.

I never told Lottie what happened, I was too ashamed. I just continued to see her as normal every Friday and pretend like everything was OK. I felt so embarrassed, and I certainly did not want to talk about it.

I would have appreciated it more if he had just told me
by himself, I thought; it was the way he did it.

However, one day, Lottie happened to bump into him with his new girlfriend in tow, arm in arm on the high street. She asked him where I was, and needless to say he didn't have an answer. Then Lottie went potty, and really let him have it. I think she called him a 'shit' or something and a 'scum bag', but he knew he deserved it and I thought it strange for her as I had never heard her use language like that before. She must have been really angry. She said she had wanted to hit him very hard with her handbag; she made me smile when she said that.

It felt good to have my honor defended like that I thought.

Andy's behavior had certainly placed a strain on his friendship with Zachary too. I don't think their relationship was ever quite the same again after that. After about two days, Andy showed up at the YMCA. Somehow, he had managed to bypass security and was now trying to intimidate us by banging aggressively on the door and kicking it in an attempt to reclaim his stuff. But he didn't know us; we had been through much worse than this. He was not going to succeed in his futile attempts at intimidation, and there was no way on earth we were going to let him in.

Odette had heard what had happened and was no longer a member of Team Andy. He banged and banged on the door. She repeatedly told him that I was not in. But he continued banging and punching the door. We said nothing. Then he began kicking on the door again for about twenty minutes. I whispered to Odette to tell him we were calling security; I then began to press the buttons on the intercom phone, which made high sounding pitches. We called down for security to send up the police. Now we had moved to the position of intimidation ourselves.

I used a different voice so that he could not be sure who was in the room. Then security could be heard responding over the intercom although it was unclear whether they could hear or understand what we were saying. I then shouted to Andy to go. He was completely unaware of my presence in the room up until that point. Then we called his bluff and told him that the police were outside the building and were coming up now. I had no idea whether he would believe us or not, but we called it anyway. I told him that upon their arrival he would be arrested, and now they were parking up right outside the building as we spoke. '…they have parked on the pavement right in front of the doors.' I said.

I filled him in, every step of the way to add realism and weight to the situation, so that he could begin to get a clear picture that he was going to be in a lot of trouble. I wanted him to begin to visualize that trouble and ask himself whether he could afford it. 'They are talking on their radios,' I said. 'They are coming into the building now,' I added. I then asked him whether he could afford for that to happen.

Then the manager came up and looked at him before going into his own apartment. I guess his wife must have called him up after having listened to all that banging Andy was making. After a short while, Andy went away and never returned again to bother us there. Thank God.

Unfortunately, whilst Andy had been banging and kicking away at the door with full force, he had been heard by the manager's wife who had been in the whole time; the manager had also seen him standing outside the door.

After that episode, the manager then decided that he wanted us to move back downstairs perhaps more at the 'say so' of his wife. They wanted the top floor to be left solely for themselves. But Lottie was in her own battle over this very issue. She was not prepared to pay astronomical prices for two separate rooms when the department could save money if we shared and when we did not mind sharing and they had the facilities for sharing, it seemed silly not to take advantage. Their bitter feud could not be resolved and with neither party prepared to back down it was not long before we were on the move again, this time to the Palmers Green Hotel.

Odette found it in the Yellow Pages. It was much better than the Muswell Hill dumpy motel in that it was a lot cleaner and quieter, and there was no fighting, screaming, or shouting at all hours of the day and night. Our rooms, although single, were situated together in our own small part of the hotel. The bathroom and toilet were shared only by us as the third room remained empty right up until Odette's departure. The good news was that they also kept the bath and toilet lovely and clean and very tidy too. The other good news was that Andy did not know where we were now so that was also a relief too. I felt as though I could relax a bit.

Odette ate the breakfast they provided every morning. She had to, she had to stay healthy, because she was now eating for two. I was not, and so did not. Nevertheless, it was certainly a struggle to continue to eat healthily without access to a cooker or even a fridge. However, one of the perks of the hotel was that I could change my sheets as often as I liked and so I did, sometimes as often as seven times a week. There's nothing like sliding into crispy, clean, 100 % cotton sheets. I loved it. It made me feel cared for, even if it was, only in my mind, even if it was, only for a moment..

I continued to commute to college from Palmers Green, which meant I had to leave much earlier in the mornings. I also started to rave quite heavily, with Penny, every night of the week, in fact, apart from Tuesday – not sure why exactly.

Every Saturday, there was a special dance or a wedding which we would faithfully attend. Odette would always sew me a new dress by hand for the Saturday dance. I would buy the materials, cottons, and needles and describe the style of the dress I envisaged, Odette would sketch it out in her note pad, what it was I was describing, and then she would draw it out on to a large piece of paper, cut it out. Pin the material onto it and cut it out. Then she would tack it and begin to sew it all by hand; she was incredible, amazing in fact, when I think about it; and all the dresses were stunning. I would then buy a hat, bag, and shoes to match. I seemed to be having the time of my life without a single care in the world or for anyone in it, including Odette. I never stopped to think about her, I never stopped to spend time to talk to her, listening to her. I was incredibly selfish and completely oblivious to my own short failings.

They say hindsight is the best teacher and from that day to this I do regret that I could have actually been so selfish. When the day of remembrance hit, I cried like a baby.

I remember, one Saturday, I was so excited about going out. We were going to a Lover's Rock dance. I couldn't wait. I had prepared all my clothes for the dance in advance and polished my shoes to a high shine. When the night in question arrived, I had my shower, did my hair and my make-up, laid out my clothes, and waited for Penny to arrive to pick me up, as she would normally do, with Simon, her boyfriend, who always did the driving, every weekend like clockwork. That night, I waited, and waited, and waited until eventually I fell asleep.

When I woke up, it was exactly 3 am. I believed that I had missed her altogether. I began to ring my hands in bitter disappointment. Tears of frustration filled my eyes and were being lowered slowly, like on an old rusty elevator, descending down my face. I was very cross and annoyed with Penny, but I never told her.

When I met her at college on the Monday, I thought I would wait until she gave her excuses before I said anything, and it was in that moment, and for the first time, I saw her pride which stood between her and a real heartfelt apology like a solid brick wall. For the first time, I saw her in a different light... a selfish light.

But look who was talking...wasn't I really no better? ...

After fumbling with her words, but before giving up completely, I interrupted her and told her it was OK. I had already made up my mind that I would meet her at all future dances, if I felt that I was going to go, that was. She later told me that she was expecting, and this was the reason she did not come to collect me on Saturday night. I guess she could see the disappointment etched across my face, no matter how hard I tried to mask it. Apparently, she had just found out that day and felt she had to speak to her boyfriend to see where they stood as a family: a conversation that clearly took longer than expected.

The following week, the dance was just at the end of the high street, approximately five minutes on the bus from the hotel. I arrived around twelve, expecting to see her there, but again, she did not show up, neither did her boyfriend. It was no big deal though, as I could have easily taken the bus back just from across the road from the venue. It was not that far back to the hotel, but instead, I decided to ask the DJ, who happened to be a member of the sound system in which her boyfriend was the CEO, for a lift. He could not believe he's ears at my question and was almost beside himself with agreement.

I thought it rather sweet that he was a complete gentleman, as he ran to open the car door for me and waited patiently before closing it after me. I felt like royalty just for a moment. After the short drive to the top of the road where the hotel was situated he walked me up to my front door, before asking whether he could give me a lift to the dance the following week? Of course, I was a little taken back to say the least, but nevertheless I agreed.

Independent Living

Odette got her flat in May 1982 with just weeks to spare before she was due to give birth. We all chipped in with time, effort, and labor to help her get her flat up to a livable standard. It was all so filthy, and dirty, and dusty, and stunk to high heaven of pee wee. We did not even want to think about who had lived there before her or how they left or even if they left of their own free will.

We cleaned, we scrubbed, and we peeled off God only knows how many layers of paper. We painted walls and skirting, and we hung curtains, guided in furniture, and oversaw the laying of the carpets; she only had enough for the bedroom, we would find out later why this was.

This was her first real home. It was her own home, at least for now anyway. Every weekend, she would cook me a lovely Sunday dinner and make an apple or rhubarb crumble or cherry pie with custard for dessert and all from scratch – yummy! It was really nice to spend Sunday afternoons with her. But when it was time to go, I didn't like the hugging thing, I just found it all too painful. But I never told her.

She would always tell me she loved me and say, 'Be good'. But I never knew how things were for her. I never knew how utterly lonely she was or how completely sad she felt deep down. I had no idea of what the nuns had put her through after Sr P's death. How could I? All my sockets were blown.

She had no phone so the only way I could contact her without visiting her was to write to her. However, she could always call me or leave a message for me at the hotel if she needed me; but she never did.

When it was time for her to go to the hospital to have the baby, I received a call at the hotel from the midwifery suite. I went straight to the hospital and arrived at the Princess Grace at about 2:40 pm and by 3:30 pm I was completely exhausted. It was all taking so long – I thought. I kept asking her how long she thought it would be. After a while of her rolling around in what I now know to be absolute agony, she sent me away and told me to come back later, but I wasn't sure when later was. Did she mean the same day or the following day? After mulling it over in my mind and arriving at the conclusion that later was, in fact, the following day I went back to her apartment.

The next morning, I found myself at college as normal. I don't know what it was that caused Penny to enquire as to the wellbeing of Odette but when Penny found out that she was in the hospital, she could hardly contain herself. Clearly, the child inside her must have jumped too with excitement. She was so ecstatically elated that she told absolutely everyone including our teacher. Unanimously, they all agreed that I should go back to the hospital at once because she was alone. The father of the child, unable to get work here in the UK, had been sent to the middle east, by his mother, to work in the special forces force; so, he missed out on the birth of his first child.

When I arrived and finally found out where they had moved her to, I could not believe my eyes when I saw that little bundle of joy; she was so tiny, so pale with pink blotches all over her face. She was so very beautiful even despite her funny little hat that they had put on her head, in an attempt to re-shape it after a rather aggressive forceps delivery. It was like a little miracle, yes it was a miracle.

life itself is always a miracle.

Odette had to sit on a rubber ring to cushion her B-U-T tom, which was very sore following her stitches. After her discharge from hospital I thought that I could give Odette some support with her new baby daughter, but it wasn't long before we clashed again, and I had to return to the hotel alone. It was then that I realised how lonely I felt. I really just wanted to move out as well. In fact, I became so desperate to move out, to the point where Lottie and I would take it in turns to call up the housing, on a daily basis.

The Hunt for Housing

It must have been approximately two weeks after my seventeenth birthday when my turn finally came up. First, they offered me a place somewhere in Highgate or rather Lower Gate, it was situated in the basement of one of those large wedding-cake houses with access to a small garden through the long rectangular garden doors, which were all made of glass, set in a thin metal frame. It was well proportioned and very clean, but it was a long way from the bus stop.

When you really want something, there are no deterrents.

Albeit the truth was that I felt I wanted to live near water, I had no idea why, I knew I had to live near water. Strange but true. Somehow, I just knew this would be a positive thing for me. So, I refused the flat on that basis and told them exactly what I was looking for and the officer wrote it down.

Write down the vision make it clear who reads it.

During one of my days off from college, I accompanied a friend over to the Horse Ferry Lane Estate, which overlooked the River Lee. I had never heard of the place before. At one point boats would have actually been a common sight up and down the river. I had never been there before but remember feeling very moved by the water. I decided that it was here that I wanted to live. I now had to find an empty flat by myself because no one was going to do it for me, so the onus was on me and time was tick, tick, ticking on by.

I decided to come back to the estate alone; I walked the length of the flats that overlooked the river. However, after a certain point, it felt that I should proceed no further. The atmosphere was different further down and so was the scenery. There was rubbish everywhere that had just been dumped.

In one place, there was a whole line of it in fact. I felt very uncomfortable, so I came back again towards the end that was nearer the road. In so doing I found three empty flats all overlooking the river. I took down the details and presented them to the local housing office and waited. Two weeks went by but there was no word. I called Lottie to see whether she had heard anything.

'No, I haven't heard a thing.'

'Ok let's start calling again.' I told her about the empty flats that I had found and informed her that I had handed the information in to the housing office.

'Oh, that's great,' she said. 'Well done, let's start calling again,' she added. By the end of the third week I was then sent an offer by post, but upon inspection, it was too deep into the estate, I knew instantly that my safety would be compromised on dark evenings returning late, so I refused it on that basis explaining my reasons why for my refusal. So, the search was on again to find an empty one-bedroom flat nearer to the road this time. Again, I found another three all empty, and again, I took the details into the relevant body and waited.

The answer came just two weeks later. It was number 59. I collected the keys and found that upon inspection that it was clean, it was dry, it was a one bed and it was home: I accepted it.

Back then in the early 1980s all care leavers moving into independent living received an allowance of just £200.00. This was supposed to make all the necessary purchases for them. That being a cooker, fridge, bed, bed linen, wardrobes and so on.

I had already used up £60.00 of mine on a stereo system so now there was only £140.00 remaining. I had to make a choice on whether to purchase a cooker upon which to cook hot meals, a fridge to assist with the preservation of foods, or a bed upon which to sleep at night, I could not afford all three or even two for that matter; I could only afford one. After careful consideration on the matter I decided to select option two and purchased a brand-new Philips fridge with small freezer attached. This meant that I had to sleep on the floor until I could save enough money for a bed and no hot meals, at least not cooked by me anyway. To the remaining £14.00 I added a further £6.00 so I could buy two sleeping bags and two bean bags with a bit of bartering.

I would spread the sleeping bags over some large flat cardboard boxes, in an attempt to soften the blow from the hardness of the cold, concrete floor below me. Armed with the feeling of elation I also asked the carpet shop owner for any unwanted cut-off pieces of carpet. From what they gave me I could make a giant puzzle of mats for the living room. Jeanie got me a wardrobe from a charity and arranged its delivery. It was burnt mahogany. It had some decorative detail on the side panel of the door. It reminded me of the great wardrobe we had had at dad's, only this one was a little darker. It smelt rather musty, but nothing air freshener could not handle, and it did the hanging job rather well too.

In time, with money saved from my Saturday job, now at Tesco where I earned a giant £10.00 per day, I managed to buy a small plug-in slow cooker and took out a Granada TV on HP with the help from my sister. With time, I was eventually able to purchase my very own bed and Odette came down to try it out. It came complete with an orthopedic mattress; it was very comfortable. Unfortunately, her stay was dramatically cut short, due to a terrible row, caused by her failing to replace the tweezers back in exactly the same spot from where she had taken them. *Oh dear.*

I had a makeshift dressing table, set up in my bedroom. It was made from one large piece of wood, which perhaps had spent its former life as an interior door somewhere, I think. I saddled it across two cardboard boxes almost at the same height but not quite, and despite having placed tissues under the smaller one for balance, I still had to be very careful not to knock it off balance when sitting in front of it, at the mirror. Nevertheless, this too soon became the start of argument number two, when Odette bashed her knee into it, whilst attempting to sit in front of it. She bashed it so hard that she completely knocked it over, turning it upside down. Of course, I went potty: and again, her stay was cut short and she went home early, all the *sorry* in the world could not make her stay.

During my stay here, my diet consisted of orange juice from cartons, and lots of it, cereals, mainly Rice Krispies, and every possible vitamin known to man that I could take. It also included the occasional cheese sandwich at lunchtime, always with salad. And I would try to eat one piece of chicken with chips and beans from the KFC on Sundays, if I was not eating with Penny, Odette, or Flavia.

This was my first flat, and for now, it was home. I would stay here for just eleven short months before my premature departure after seeing a mouse. I had no idea what to do, so I left leaving everything behind.

The Long Goodbye

Even after severing all my ties with the SS, I tried to remain in contact with Jeanie, and so one day whilst in her area I thought I would pop in and just surprise her. I had not seen her for a while. Strangely, she took ages to open the door, and when she did, I met her with one of my biggest smiles, as I usually did. But as I stepped forward as if expecting her to gesture me to come in, as she had done so many times before, weirdly she didn't move. She didn't flinch. In fact, she didn't budge an inch. She just stared at me without speaking with such a haunting vacant look. Her eyes unmoving, devoid of all emotion. I repeated my hello, but again she didn't answer. Then without warning, she closed the door quietly and gently, right in my face.

Embarrassment tried to creep upon me, but I just shrugged it off like wet rain. I never visited her again, and oddly I never told anyone of what had happened either; I was a bit abashed to say the least.

In hindsight looking back, I realize that the cases against the SS had already started, and under her barrister's instructions she would have been advised not to speak to anyone who could possibly incriminate her, so on the contrary that included me.

As she stared at me, she was probably wondering whether I still remembered my pleading to her, begging her to help me, and she didn't even bother to return any of my calls… not one. Neither did she ever visit me.

My guess was that the evidence against her was strong. I was also convinced that she probably wished she had acted sooner on the information that I had given her regarding the warped practices of Dukesbury House, and in particular, it's crazy proprietor, Mrs. Manfred. Her response was always, 'Oh, don't be so silly.'

I was shocked to hear that even then at that time Mrs. Manfred had managed to get-a-way with her evil practices for 12 years, that I knew of. In truth I was convinced it was even longer. It took Jennie an entire year to act on the information I had given her. A year too late for those helpless children caught in that window of mental, emotional, psychological, and physical abuse, *I guess*.

I continued to remain in contact with Flavia and her family, avoiding only their confusing church rituals. I would deliberately plan my visits around dinner times on Sundays, when I knew their Sabbath was over and done with and to be sure of a hot meal, whenever they invited me. I never invited myself or turned up unannounced.

I remember after they had moved out of Tottenham, I was looking for their new house in Edmonton. Flavia had invited me up for dinner as she was bursting to show it off to me. It was almost dinner time and in my mind's eye I could see Flavia's mum, who was also a very good cook standing over the hot stove adding her finishing touches to the meal she had just prepared. I began to lick my lips as saliva began to dance on my tongue looking for day light.

I got off the bus and was trying to remember her instructions as to where I was to walk next. I don't think I had taken more than about 5 steps when I heard a kind sounding voice call out to me.

'Jacqueline! Jacqueline!' said the voice. I turned to see who it was behind the voice. I recognized him right away: Oh, my goodness it was John. I mean I could never forget John. How could I?

'It is you?' he said. 'How are you?' I just stared very vaguely, trying to close my mouth, gesturing, using body language only.

'Oh, my good God, it is you isn't it, you have to come with me,' he said, as he hurriedly stuffed his elderly passenger into the rear of his car, using his torso to assist.

John was a driving instructor now. He must have given up teaching, I thought. He ran around to the near side of the car to open the door for me and beckoned me to get in.

'Come on! Quick, get in the car.' It was a bit like *The Professionals*, I thought. I got in the car, and he asked if I remembered him. Strangely, I did.

'How have you been then? Where are you living now? Are you in London?' he asked all at once without coming up for air.

'OK,' I said with a soft voice, slowly overcoming my surprise. John had been in the middle of a lesson with some old man when he saw me, to the total bewilderment of his tutee. We drove all the way to John and Jessie's new house, which ironically was also in Edmonton.

'Don't worry,' he said. 'I will bring you right back to this very spot afterwards; there is someone I want you to meet.'

In a trance- like state I got into his car, not having a clue as to where we were going or why. He weaved in and out of traffic as fast as he could, he cut down back roads, over humps and turned into side streets, if asked no - I couldn't remember them now. Apparently, John was taking me to see Jessie now. *I wasn't really sure how I felt about that - at the time I mean.* Albeit, unbeknown to me then, this was to be the last time I was ever to see Jessie and John in that lifetime. I was just 17.

Where are you now? Please call. Find me again.

We went into the house and stood in the front room, which opened up into a kitchen through diner. The downstairs of the house was sort of open plan. I remember it being very dark or dim and very unorganized as if they had just moved in or something. Jessie just stared at me, and I stared back. She looked the same: she hadn't aged, not one bit, and she hadn't changed either, her hair was still the same, blond, down to her shoulders with an eye lash fringe. Her face was still the same, gentle, and warm; it was as though time had not moved on.

Then suddenly, out of nowhere, she let out the strangest noise I had ever heard, it was like a cry or a call or something and then she started shouting, almost screaming, followed by crying, a sort of deep, deep sobbing out loud wailing even. I wanted to leave, I felt so uncomfortable, but did not know where I was exactly, so I just stayed where I was, standing without speaking, without moving. I was really all out of words. John went quickly over to her, his body language telling.

Clearly, he was not in unfamiliar territory; he had been here before. He attempted, quite hurriedly, to comfort her and calm her down. Oddly, I did not share the same enthusiasm and therefore made no effort to greet her, or to hug her, or even to comfort her; I perhaps appeared stuck. I stood my ground and kept my distance. I guess somehow the thought never even entered my mind. Perhaps I was all out of thoughts.

I guess, I should have done something or said something; after all, this was the person who had saved me time after time. This was my self-elected fairy godmother, but I didn't do a thing to comfort her.

Perhaps this was the first telling sign that something was wrong – with me – and that a little more of me was broken, or missing, or just simply did not fit any more. I did not know it back then, what this was or even what it meant, unbeknown to me then I had no empathy and was unable to feel sympathetic towards anyone or anything, I would learn later the reasons why. And the clock was ticking. Tick, tock… tick, tock...tick, tock…

I think, inside, on that day, I was really freaking out; I mean I just wanted to leave. I couldn't cope. It was all too much. Something was still hurting deep inside. In truth, I never knew how this entire ordeal had equally taken its toll on Jessie and John, neither had I thought about it in the years that had passed. *How could I?* I was just a child. I simply had no idea. *How could I?*

I always thought that it was just Odette and I who had suffered such loss, that hateful day when we had had our last remaining ties completely severed. I thought it was only the two of us who had been wounded, who had been abandoned by goodness and kindness. I never knew or stopped to think how Jessie must have cried herself to sleep night after night for the six long years that followed, never really knowing, and always wondering what had happened to the two beautiful girls that she had once saved from a life of hell: a life less than normal, a life less than ordinary.

I had no idea that Jessie blamed herself for not being able to help us more and that she had probably been even prevented from helping, prevented from staying in contact. I didn't know that.

The truth was that she had been forcibly, intentionally, and quite deliberately locked out. As far as my rescuers were concerned, Jessie was trouble. She would make a noise; therefore, she was a liability and had to be silenced. The only way to do that was to eliminate her from the equation. Truth be known, I would have sold my most precious anything, my everything to have grown up with her and John and Sissy – even as annoying and as selfish as Sissy was back then.

Jessie had stood up for us against Dad, unkind teachers and even the SS and their hit men; there was no way on earth our charge hands were going to get away with beating the crap out of us, not on Jessie's watch, not with Jessie on the scene – no way.

Jessie then began to sob again – uncontrollably this time. It was as though all her emotions of sadness and anger and frustration came flooding up to the surface and now, they had all joined forces together and were now all pouring out of her like a loud, erratic fast-moving river with a strong under - current. As confusing as they were, they appeared to be mixed in with emotions of joy and laughter as temporary as they were. Jessie was our tender fairy godmother, and now she was crying and I, I didn't know what to do.

I was embarrassed because I had never seen an adult cry before. John told her to stop because he feared what it would do to me. Jessie eventually stopped crying and came over to hug me, but I didn't hug her back. I just couldn't; besides, hugging still hurt, I found it all so painful. It was as though I had become bound and could not respond, I could not move. Something was broken, but I had no idea what. She started to cry again.

John comforted her for the last time in front of me, and it wasn't long before his passenger entered the house, the door still ajar after John and I had come in how many minutes ago. He was now displaying signs of complete bewilderment and irritation, scratching his head despite having no hair upon it. John realised he had to get back to his lesson. And I had to get to my lunch. We left the house and he took me back to the road from where he had picked me up just as he had promised; And then before allowing me to leave, John made me promise that I would come back and visit, and despite my telling him that I would, I never did. I could not remember the way for one. I never wrote it down for two, and back then the very thought of it conjured up emotions of real pain.

'John and Jessie where are you now? I just want to say thank you. I want to say I miss you. I just want to say I love you. Find me again.'

By the age of 17 I had been in 27 homes, some on repeat visits, but this *so* wasn't 27 dresses.

I did see Stacy, their daughter, one last time too, she was working in a fast-food eatery on the High Road in Wood Green. I was still 17 at the time. Again, she recognized me immediately and begged me to come home with her to see Jessie and John that very day.

'They never stop talking about you and your sister you know,' she said. But I knew I could not, despite promising faithfully to meet her after work that same day I never did. It was just all too soon for me. The pain was still very raw, and my wounds were still open, wet, and weeping; it was only going to be the passing of time that would distance the sensation of that pain and allow my wounds to close.

I never saw Stacy again after that, despite going back to look for her time after time in the fast food diner. Just like time, she too had moved on. And now twenty-eight years on, I pine for them all, I cry for them all, and I pray for them all. Now it is me who is filled with uncontrollable emotion every time their names pop up or I think about them. Sometimes, I think I see her and go chasing after people just to see their faces.

'Oh, I'm so sorry I thought you were someone else,' I would always end up saying.

I wish I could see them now, even if it's just to tell them 'I love you... and... to say Thank you'. Jessie and John, where are you now

my sweet loves?

A teacher is *not* just someone who teaches a subject in one chapter of your life, sometimes, a teacher is that very person who, in their own way, saves it.

'Jessie, we love you, thank you.
And God Bless you forever.'

Someone once said
The Lord is my stand up and
I choose to be recovered,
I choose to be recovered NOW!
Thank you for revealing yourself to me, thank
you for revealing the truth to me.
Thank you for saving me, to tell this story.

GOD touches people
from the inside with goodness and kindness
and the outside changes.

When we look up
we look in,
when we look in
we look out.

Who can you see who needs you today?

This is my story; this is my song.

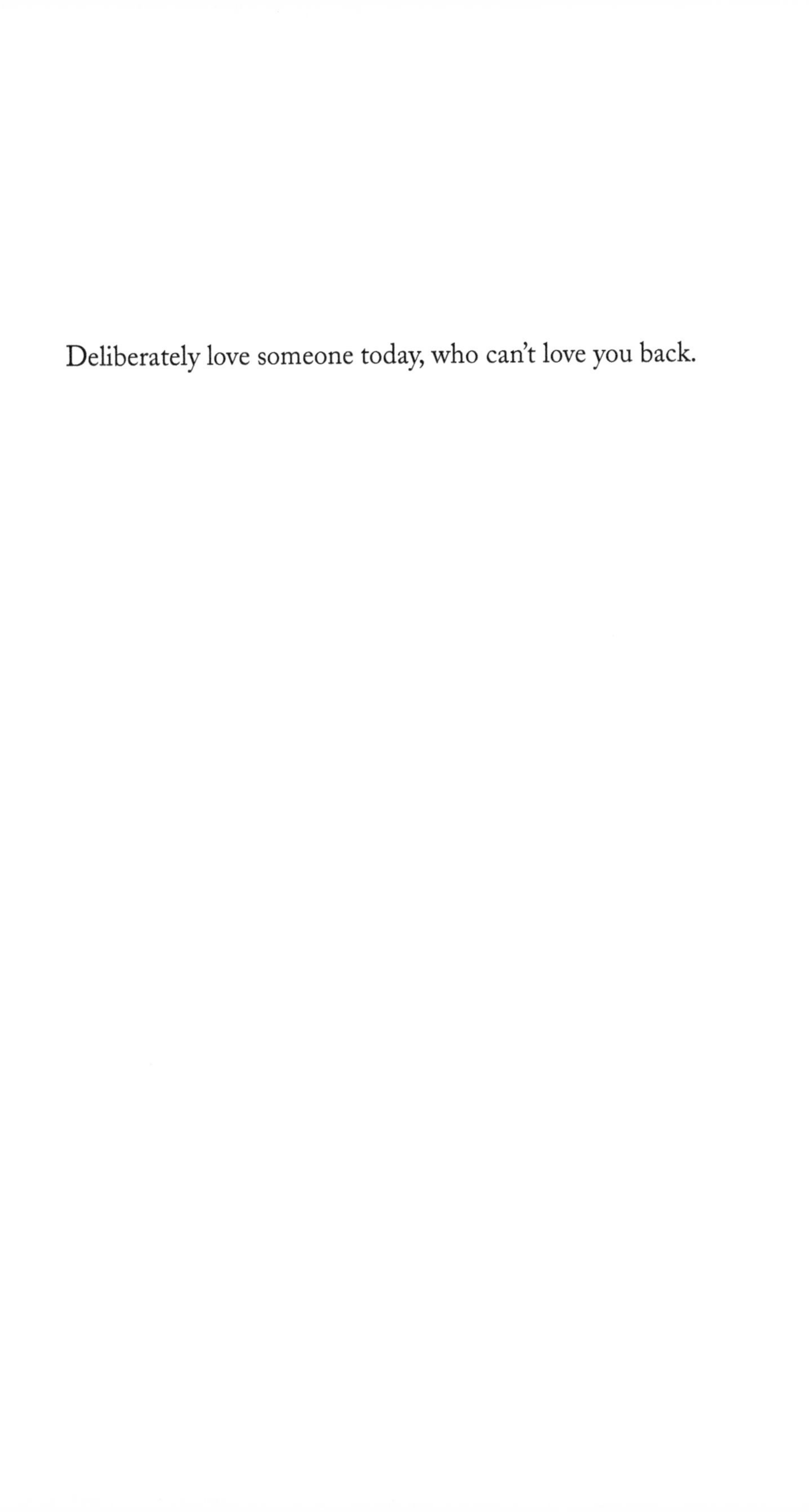

Deliberately love someone today, who can't love you back.

You have a story to tell
so, tell it
You have a song to sing
so, sing it
a song of freedom
A song of redemption

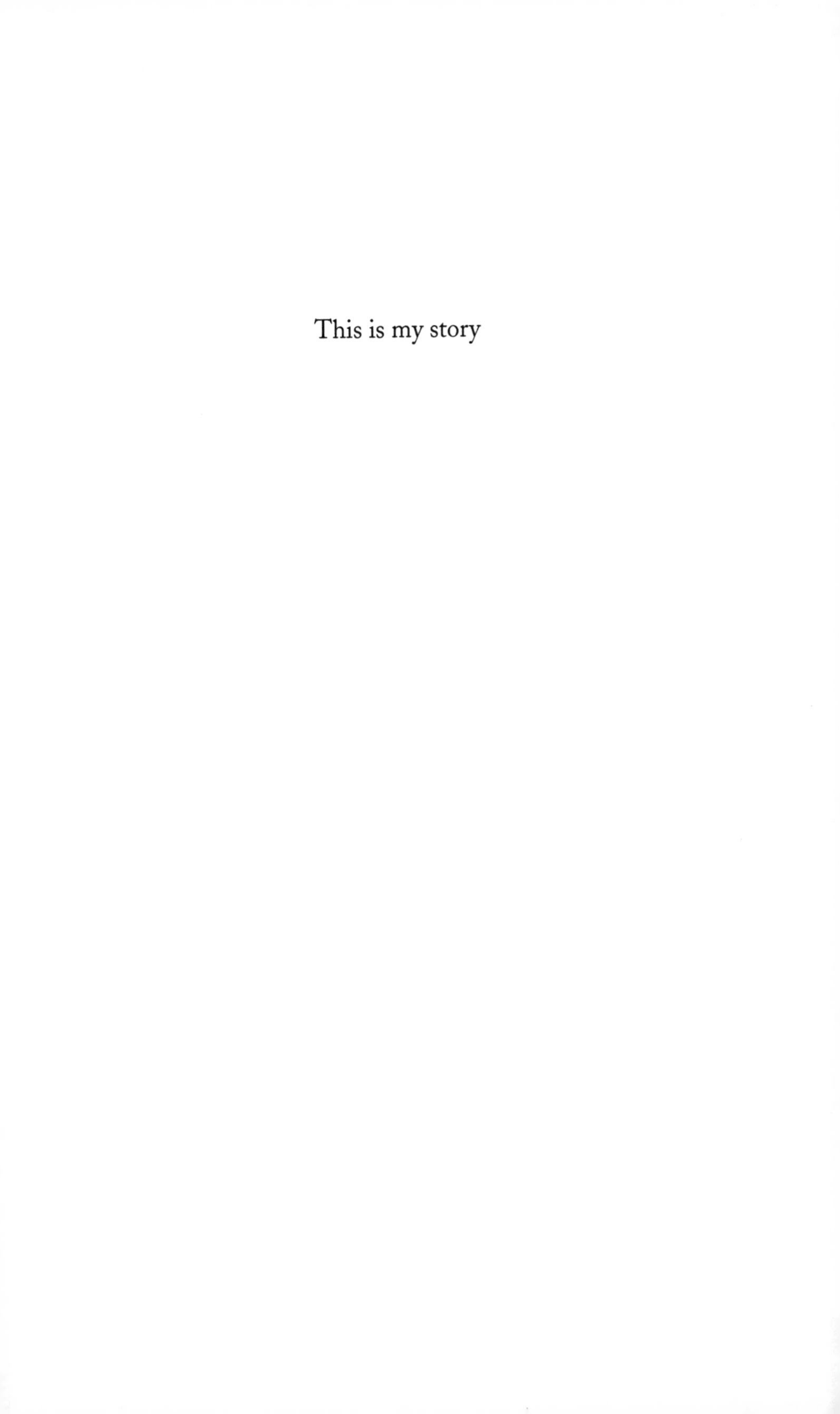

This is my story

When the storms of life rage
there is still hope
and you will rise again
up and out of the valley
you will rise higher
than on Eagles' wings
If you believe.

The End

of

Part One.

Message from the Author

All grammatical errors are on purpose

Lightning Source UK Ltd.
Milton Keynes UK
UKHW040655060522
402599UK00001B/102